The Shadow Knows

Crocken lurched to his feet with a moan—then stood swaying, gripping the rough stones with one hand. The guard snickered.

Suddenly a familiar voice echoed in Crocken's head. *I thought I'd taught you better by now.*

Crocken stood frozen, watching as his shadow crept along the damp wall toward the guard. Shadow fingers slipped around the fellow's scabbard, and his sword came sailing across the room to Crocken—who was just as abruptly hauled forward by the shadow's other arm, stretched thin as rope.

The guard shouted. Crocken fell to his knees, his hand landing flat on the sword hilt. Metal rang against paving stone.

Try to hold onto it, the shadow suggested as the guard drew a knife and jumped forward with a yell.

By Susan Dexter
Published by Ballantine Books:

THE WIZARD'S SHADOW

The Winter King's War
THE RING OF ALLAIRE
THE SWORD OF CALANDRA
THE MOUNTAINS OF CHANNADRAN

THE WIZARD'S SHADOW

Susan Dexter

A Del Rey Book

BALLANTINE BOOKS • NEW YORK

A Del Rey Book
Published by Ballantine Books

Copyright © 1993 by Susan Dexter

Library of Congress Catalog Card Number: 93-90177

ISBN 0-345-38064-9

Printed in Canada

First Edition: August 1993

This book is for:

Judie and Bruce Gall, and the rest of the Richard III Society, worldwide.

Elvira's Uncle John, who lent me a name.

Faye, Denny and Kathy, good friends all.

Cody and Fritz, packmates.

And for Max—truly made without equal.

Author's Note on Names

Most of the given names herein may be taken as the reader finds them and pronounced as the reader likes. However, it is well to know that in the Borderlands, the *sh* sound is represented by the letters *si*. Thus, the steward-protector's name is RISH-art—not nearly the tongue torturer that it appears.

Chapter One

Do not shed the wizard's lifeblood. Spilled, it will rise up from the very ground and curse those who cause his death. Subdue his tongue, bind his hands—and thus make a safe end to him.

THUS THEY DID, when the wizard had traveled far enough out of their land to lose a little of his caution. Overtaking him, they dropped a noose of silken rope over his head and, whilst he choked and struggled, delivered a calculated blow to the back of his head, the club padded sufficiently to forfend the least chance of spilling his blood. Stunned so, he was safe prey while they continued with their ordered task.

Grave disturbances accompany a wizard's violent death—if the wizard has aught to say in the matter. The instructions for dealing with this wizard were precise, thoroughly rehearsed, and not deviated from in the smallest particular. A hot iron for his tongue, to prevent his speaking a curse to work his vengeance after him. That he might not use his sorcerer's hands to cast a spell against them—nor even to drag himself away—they used the club again, and broke his back. He had begun to regain his senses by then, but whatever he felt, he had few means left of expressing.

Per instruction, no tiniest drop of his dangerous wizard's blood was let fall, to cry his tale by magic. Aiming to be well outside the area his death would presently affect, they left him.

The pain was far less than he might have anticipated, of far less moment than the iron fetter clasped about his left wrist. He felt nothing at all below his neck, only a sort of chill, and the jelly of hurt between his jaws seemed irrelevant. The wizard

1

attempted no outcry—so long as he resisted that futility, the pain in his mouth would not wax, and might even seem to wane as he accustomed himself to its fiery touch. A cramp in his neck—which he could not ease—was sufficient to distract his attention.

Had they blinded him also, or had night merely fallen? The wizard's mind drifted, its ties to his broken body steadily loosening. He might have let it go and simply died, but he had ever been a stubborn man. Anger nourished him, hate sustained him, as he lay through the long, dark hours of the night and most of an overcast day.

Planning dark plans, dreaming of vengeance, gradually the wizard became aware that when his eyes were open, he could see the gray and amber of the gravel he lay upon. A few sunbeams broke through the cloud cover, flinging his shadow before him across the stones. The wizard's lips, clotted with sweat and dust, twisted into what might have been meant for a smile. He was scarcely able to draw a breath by then—paralysis was creeping inward toward his lungs—but he felt he had a few moments remaining to his account, and a use for them.

The sun was sinking, somewhere behind him. As it fell, his shadow stretched and stretched away from him, black and solid as a spill of ink, attached to him by only the barest edge. He could see the whole of it, pooled before him.

The earth creaked, turning slowly through its daily round. The wizard's lips shifted faintly. He uttered no slightest sound, but words of sorcery were painstakingly shaped. The sun touched the jagged horizon of mountain peaks. At once the interface between shadow and body thinned, dissolved—and the shadow tore free as if slashed loose. It seemed, by a trick of the fading light, to take refuge under a nearby rock.

The wizard's fond gaze followed it. His last exhalation sped it on its way. Night fell.

Scavengers found him, kites and ravens, and what bones of his they did not carry off were at last scattered by the wind and rain of a summer thunderstorm. Secure beneath its rock, the shadow remained.

Chapter Two

SPRING CAME TARDY to the mountains—and he was premature in expecting it anywhere, Crocken reminded himself. He blew on his chilled fingers, drawing an extra breath to curse the ill fate that sent him staggering along the trading trails so early in the season. He glanced warily at the heavy sky—he'd been anticipating rain for the past hour, though as yet no drops had fallen. Probably they were waiting till they'd crystalized into snowflakes and could thereby compound his abject misery.

All he'd ever desired—since he'd been a barefoot orphan scrounging coppers for errands run in the street mazes of the wizards' city of Kôvelir—was a warm home to return to at each day's end. It was a heaven beyond anything gods could offer. In pursuit of that utterly basic goal, he'd lived more frugally than was the norm for the peddlers who wandered the croplands crying wares of cookpots and pins. Crocken was as fond of good food and good drink as any such, and as to the comforts a woman might offer—he shoved the thought away, irritated. He'd endured years of painstaking thrift, resisting most of the lures of inns and dice games, his self-imposed privations always made to seem worthwhile by the spectacle of his cherished dream drawing ever nearer to reality.

One day he'd be a wandering peddler no longer. He'd have put by coin enough to purchase a little shop, with living space above or behind it, and he'd then be a respectable merchant, with a proper home, however humble. Nor would he be alone in his comfort—by then he'd met a girl, a lass with skin like milk and hair the color of autumn oak leaves. He'd paid her court and had entrusted his savings to his betrothed before embarking upon an extended trading venture that took him all the way to Hamippa, land of fine-blooded horses and bronze-columned temples, where he added measurably to his store of capital.

How was he to know that that year upon the road was to be the last happy one of his life?

Crocken gave his pack-pony a slap upon its rump, encouraging it up a difficult bit of trail while his memories possessed him. When he'd returned to Kôvelir, he'd found his Litsa in the taproom of an inn, her bonny hair shorn to her ears and her soft flesh more than doubled in bulk.

He'd weathered the small shocks. He'd coped when Litsa informed him that she'd bought the inn with those monies he'd left in her keeping. Crocken harbored no wish to become an innkeeper—at least he'd never detected any such—but he'd have thought it over carefully if Litsa had given him the chance instead of coolly informing him that he'd be no partner in the venture beyond receiving a proper share of the profits—she didn't intend to marry him, ever.

Crocken had left the inn, gone blindly to another, and gotten himself falling-down drunk for only the second or third time in his life. He then entered a dice game with a will and a disregard for his losses that was a nine-day's wonder in Kôvelir, a city where not much impresses anyone for long. When Crocken finally staggered away from the game, Litsa—all unwitting—had a new partner in innkeeping, and Crocken owned nothing in the world save a shaggy pack-pony and whatever load he could put on it.

The consequences of his revenge appalled Crocken, when he'd sobered. He couldn't imagine that Litsa was similarly discomfited, though it would have been pleasant to think so. After all, she still had the inn. *He* was the one out in the cold, too far ahead of the trade season, coinless and comfortless.

Crocken tried—now he was neither drunk nor miserably hung over—to be stern with himself. Litsa was far from the only woman in the wide world. There'd be others, and he could begin to build again . . . His argument did not hold firm. Litsa had been only a piece of his dream, but by her actions she had callously killed *all* of it, and his world was ashes around him, scattering in the chill wind.

That wind carried a good bit of grit, picked up higher on the rising trail. Larger pebbles made the footing suddenly treacherous. Crocken stumbled, colliding roughly with the laden pony. The beast complained bitterly about the mishap, then neighed shrilly once more when Crocken slapped its rump to encourage forward progress. It hastened over the next few yards of trail, allowing Crocken to quicken his own pace.

His panting breath plumed out in front of him—the air was colder by the moment. The pony faltered, and Crocken climbed reluctantly past it, taking hold of its halter to assist it over the steep spot by main force. When they reached a more or less level spot, he let the beast halt, filled its nosebag with grain, and leaned his back against a rock while the pony greedily fed. Recovering his wind after a moment's rest, Crocken broke out his own travel rations, chewing at a scrap of jerked beef while he reflected upon memories of toothsome stews and hot breads, readily available in more civilized parts of the world.

At least his drunken choice of the mountain pass had proved shrewd. Cold it was—but it was not snow-choked as were the other, lower routes into Kinark. Gale winds kept the Morien Pass bitter-weathered but scoured bare and easy to traverse. Crocken squinted ahead, concerned. He had hoped such foul weather was done for the season. The cloud cover had been thin that morning, offering no hint of a coming storm, but the day was visibly dimming. If a late blizzard was in the offing, he could hardly arrange to meet it in a less-favored place. The winds would scour his bones, the snow would shroud him.

Best he get moving. If he could cross the pass itself swiftly, the lower slopes should offer him protection from the storm. There were pine forests there, both shelter and fuel for a life-sustaining fire. Crocken roused the pony from its quest after strayed oats in the seams of its feedbag, snugged the girths of the pack saddle, and prodded his reluctant partner-in-commerce onward once more.

Surely a storm was in the offing. The wind had quickened, and the pony was restless. Nervous, even, though ordinarily it was the most placid of beasts, concerned solely with its meals and with avoiding as much work as possible. It began shying at each bend the trail made, first balking and then hurrying forward ere Crocken could urge it. The pony's bushy tail switched rapidly from one side to the other, and the eye it turned back to Crocken was white-rimmed, promising trouble. He held back a trifle, wary of kicks, but that left him unable to reach the beast when it needed prodding. Progress became erratic.

By contrast, the landscape was quiet—indeed, silent. No bird called or flew, no fat marmot whistled alarm at the sight of a pair of intruders. All at once the wind died, abruptly as if a door had been slammed shut against it.

Crocken scanned the sky once more. He beheld no dark snow clouds, only an odd twilight—though the hour was barely past sun-high. He sought the sun, but could not discover it save for a glow just past the zenith, which was where it ought to be. Likely clouds muffled it—or wind-whipped dust.

The weather pattern was unfamiliar, but there didn't seem to be immediate peril in it. Crocken smacked the pony's hind-quarters smartly, gratified as it bounded forward with even greater initiative than he'd hoped to inspire. He hastened after—and cursed the beast roundly when it stopped flat and provoked another collision between them. Wild-eyed and not the least contrite, the pony instantly tried to back over him.

Crocken divided his curses evenhandedly between the pony's treacherousness and his luck. The trail had narrowed till there was scarcely a good place between the rockface to the left and the steep downslope on his right hand. Just in front of the pony's tossing nose, a snag of tree branches and brambles blocked the passage. It didn't look as bad to Crocken as it doubtless did to the pony—with one eye on the footing at the trail's edge, he began to push past. He could clear the brush away, he supposed, then lead the pony through or over.

As he drew alongside its shoulder, the pony plunged, spooking as it perceived his movement without recognizing him. Its right shoulder and the pack saddle's edge slammed hard into Crocken's chest.

The unlooked-for bump shoved him half a pace straight backward, which was quite sufficient to send Crocken stumbling over the edge of the downslope. His boots slid on loose dirt and stones. The struggle for his balance quickly lost, Crocken grabbed frantically at the pony's legs, got stepped on, lost his hold, and resumed his fall.

His bruised fingers snared a projecting rock, arresting his downward slide. Crocken scrabbled desperately for a foothold. Finding a marginal one—it was insufficient to support his weight, but took a measure of the strain from his hands and arms—the peddler drew a deep breath, prepared to sigh his relief. He spat out a mouthful of grit instead.

A nasty surprise, and too close a call. Crocken began the climb back to the trail at once, ere his knees could begin to shake or his hammering heart choke him. Stones cut into his hands, but he ignored the discomfort.

He was almost level with the trail when his chancy luck and the stone he was climbing over gave out simultaneously. The boulder pulled free of the mud. Crocken yelped despairingly as he slid downward once more, with ever-increasing speed and an ever-larger entourage of dirt and pebbles. By the time he reached the bottom he was moving fast enough to be rolled helplessly over twice before his momentum spent itself, and the stones were a stinging cloud.

Crocken lay prone, half stunned, listening to the spatter of debris falling around and over him. The pony's whinny sounded a long way off, which it doubtless was.

Awkwardly achieved, but well within the bounds of the summoning, a smug voice said.

Crocken lifted his head but found no source for the acerbic comment. He rubbed one hand over his eyes, to clear them of dust, but he still found himself to be quite alone. The voice had seemed close—so near he'd surely have seen the speaker had it been full night in place of the weird midday dusk. Sitting up, Crocken apprehensively looked over the rocky ground. He must have cracked his head when he landed, though his hasty examination found no tangible evidence. He poked a finger into his left ear experimentally, and ferreted out a pebble.

And a black sun casts no shadows.

Crocken, one hand yet pressed to his head, looked instinctively skyward. The cloud cover parted just in time to let him observe the eclipse reaching totality. The sun's disc was indeed black, haloed with writhing white flames. He frowned. An eclipse certainly answered for the sun-high darkness—but what of the speakerless voice? Crocken glanced nervously about.

He was sprawling on fairly flat ground some two dozen feet below the trail he and the pony had been following. The spot was barren of the usual scrubby alpine growth, suggesting a landslip sometime in the course of the last winter. Crocken could discover no cave, no tree or dead trunk, not a single rock large enough to conceal a healthy sheep—far less a man. The voice, if it had not come from his own dazed mind, had to have come from the trail above—yet it had not sounded so distant as that.

Crocken assessed the slope between him and the trail. Climbing out should still be feasible. His limbs were whole, though battered, and the slope looked less forbidding a few paces off. Once he had decent light he should be able to manage it handily. From what he'd heard of them, eclipses didn't last all that long, and there'd be plenty of daylight for the adventure. Crocken got carefully to his feet, groaning a bit and planning an elaborate thrashing for the pony, if and when he caught the faithless beast.

I would strike a bargain with you, peddler.

Crocken spun, landing on one knee and both hands as his feet skidded on pebbles and his joints went to water. There was a man's shadow on the slope before him, cast by—Crocken realized that there was no one there to cast it. Nor was the shadow his own. Even if he'd been on his feet, in the gloom he *had* no shadow—nor should anyone else.

A bargain, the shadow continued casually. *You understand the principle, I'm certain. Something for you—and something for me.*

Blood surged furiously through Crocken's ears. He expected to find himself fainting, but the moment and the feeling passed. His heartbeat steadied. The shadow remained, dark as nightfall.

"What *are* you?" Crocken asked, whispering because he was frightened of what the answer might be.

The shadow stirred restively. *You've no need to know that. Do you always query your customers so rudely?*

Crocken gave his head a violent shake, but the shadow stubbornly refused to become the insubstantial product of a rock-cracked skull. All the peddler accomplished was an unwelcome increase in his dizziness.

I'll grant, your clients perhaps generally let you initiate the process. As that would prove a trifle impractical in this matter, let us reverse the roles for a space.

Crocken listened politely, his stare becoming glazed.

I will state my terms. I wish to engage your services for a journey—and for a brief period after its completion. For this you will be paid thirty marks of gold—when I release you. This journey will be somewhat more lengthy than the venture you may be engaged in at present, but it will be no more hazardous and far more profitable to you. I will further undertake to guarantee your safety—if you agree to my proposal.

Crocken felt the hairs lifting on the nape of his neck. He strove to keep his voice steady, but had no success with the effort. "And if I *don't* agree?"

That would be foolish. I am a thing without substance now, but I was not always such. Some power remains to me. In a few moments the sunlight will return—your opportunity to bargain will cease, as will your usefulness to me. The shadow paused. *However, you will then have a shadow of your own once again. And I assure you, what such as I do to a man's shadow is as good as done to the man.*

The shadow-shape dipped forward, came upright once more.

A jagged chunk of rock hovered before it, held in shadow-hands. Crocken blinked at the impossibility of that. Then the shadow let the rock fall, and it struck with a thud that proved its solidity and made Crocken wince. He had never given the briefest thought to his shadow's safety, but he was mightily glad that he possessed none at the moment.

Escape me you may—or you may try to. However, your shadow will trail behind you as you go—there is no way you can prevent that, or my acting upon it. I can split your brain like a melon, peddler.

"What will you gain by that?" Crocken asked, trembling too violently to reason as sharply as he might have preferred to. He couldn't decide if he regretted his inability to stand.

Nothing, the shadow answered. *Nor do I lose aught. Whereas you lose much. I leave you the choice.*

"You want my soul?" Crocken inquired, despairing.

The shade laughed a bitter laugh. *Your soul is of neither use nor interest to me. I merely require your services for a brief span of days. If you agree, it is time we began.*

Or if he didn't agree. Crocken's lips moved by reflex, responding automatically to the anxiety he read in his client, despite the powers it claimed. Bargaining. It was as natural as drawing breath. "*Forty* marks."

He knew he'd been right when the shadow laughed once more. *Done.*

The shadow loomed larger against the black sky, but Crocken wasn't sure whether it had moved closer or had instead drawn him toward itself. His senses spun, reporting to him erratically. He could have been standing upright—he supposed he was—but he might just as easily have been lying on his back again. His eyes reported motion, as if the shadow's hands moved in conjuration. His ears heard words he could make no sense of. Crocken grew warm, then chill—and suddenly felt empty, as if something had abruptly been reft from him, torn out by its roots. As he tried to deal with the unpleasant sensation, the empty place was as suddenly filled, taken once more by some substance nearly—but not quite—the same as had been taken from him. His belly squirmed, as if he'd tasted rotten food. He felt as if he were about to choke.

Done, the shadow repeated, just as the sun's crisp gold edge emerged from the shadow of the eclipse.

* * *

It considered for a space, then made fine adjustments to its shape. The peddler was of less than average height, and slightly built, though he seemed possessed of stamina enough. His travel hood had fallen down around his shoulders, revealing hair in need of barbering. Brown—not that color matters to a shadow, for whom all is one shade of gray or another—but it marked and copied the habitual gesture the peddler used as he shoved it out of his eyes. The peddler's features were in no wise an aristocrat's, though his nose was high-bridged and sharp. The shadow mirrored the features with distaste—the arrangement was too cramped, and the assemblage reminded it of a ferret's, all the features pressed too closely together. It liked better the peddler's hands, whose fingers were nearly as long and fully as supple as those the shadow was accustomed to.

The shade wriggled with delight upon the barren ground. At last, to take a form beyond that of a shapeless blotch, to wield the powers therewith entailed! True, by day it was constrained to take only this man's less than elegant shadow-shape, inexorably bound to return to him at each and every dawning—but at night! When shadows reign, it was now free to move as it wished, in whatever shape it chose or required—man, beast, or even a branch of pine . . . Crocken glanced about stupidly, trying to come awake from his daze. Rocks and pebbles cast faint shadows once more, under the thin spring sun. His own shadow stretched before him, seeming for a bad moment darker and more substantial than it should have been. Crocken lifted a hand. His shadow aped him. He shook his head at his fancy, not troubling to watch his shadow carefully doing the same.

Chapter Three

CROCKEN HAD LITTLE recollection of his climb back to the trail, but his hands assured him he'd made it. He ruefully examined a nail ripped half away and wincingly probed cuts deepengrained with dirt. He cleaned the scrapes with brandy—then administered a tot internally, as well, physick for minor hurts too numerous to be tended individually by the campfire's flickering light. Assuring himself one final time that the sulky pony was securely picketed, Crocken settled himself for badly needed sleep.

Sleep he did, but rest he had little of, being much plagued with disordered dreams.

He couldn't make them out—they all seemed to be shadows against a greater dark. Animal forms mingled with human—deer, and wolves, and something else with wings. All of them struggling, running—he could not turn around, in the dream, to see what he and they fled from. At last the shadows faded into something he was more familiar with, but that was scarcely more pleasant.

Litsa's impassive face, as she informed him she would never wed him. Emptiness, where he had thought to find acceptance, if not love. As baffled sleeping as awake over his betrothed's behavior, Crocken struggled to puzzle out why she'd done it—changed so utterly toward him without the barest warning, tossed his suit back in his face with no anger, only indifference. He found no answers. The only difference between sleeping and waking was that, asleep, he was unguarded, unable to shove unwelcome memory aside or bury it handily under a pile of his own anger. The dream pummeled him. Waking was a relief that was curiously long postponed.

Crocken fried a bit of bacon for his breakfast, wiped out the cooling pan, and struck his camp. He'd made a sloppy job of setting it up—his gear appeared to be scattered wherever he'd been when he'd taken the notion to drop it, and he seemed to have been taken by many notions. His scrapes and bruises pained him continually as he gathered the gear, and the extra steps were a nuisance. Crocken rubbed at his still-aching head, then proceeded to load the pony. The animal shied away from him once, but settled when he showed he wasn't minded to put up with further misbehavior from it. Well, it stood still enough, but its eyes rolled to track him wherever he went. Crocken made a rude gesture at the beast.

He hung a last few bits of gear from the pack saddle's various straps, taking a more than usually careful look round to ensure he was leaving nothing behind. Nothing was visibly laying about. A mental inventory suggested nothing should be. Reassured that he seemed to have his wits in hand once more, Crocken caught up the pony's lead rope and set off toward the trail. Another eight-day should see him well into Kinark—or perchance there'd be sizable settlements at the foot of the pass, in which happy case he wouldn't have to traipse far inland to find trade. He'd be glad to be among people again, Crocken thought with a shiver.

Where do you think you're going?

Crocken reacted as practically as he could manage, allowing for his fright. He whirled toward the voice, dropping the pony's rope, his fingers closing round the dagger he wore at his belt. He held the blade low, mostly out of sight—but quite ready for use. Small wonder the pony had been nervous, if there were brigands lurking about.

Only those putative brigands were awfully well hidden. Crocken frowned at the empty landscape. Nothing save rocks and a few stunted trees not yet budding out. And his shadow, splashed across the hillside, over the dry brown leaves. Crocken fingered his left ear thoughtfully and sheathed the knife.

We need not bear any closer to Kinark. Our best route lies to sun-fall. His shadow lifted a shadow arm to point the appropriate course change.

Crocken twitched his eyes to take in first the pointing shadow, then his own arms—the left at his side, the right yet gripping the knife scabbard—neither of them what one might consider pointing, no matter how the angle of the sun might shift their shadow counterparts. The waking world was not all that preferable to that of dreams, suddenly.

I trust our bargain has not slipped free of your recollection?

Crocken's muscles had slipped free of his control, that was

sure enough. He staggered when his joints betrayed him, and when the startled pony shied, snorting away from his attempt to borrow its support, he fell to his knees in the dust.

His shadow remained upright, though its elongated feet were still connected to his dusty knees.

At this rate, we won't see Armyn till next winter! On your feet, peddler. We've traveling to do.

Crocken couldn't have moved had he desired to. One of his evil dreams was coming back to him—a jumble of shadows and falling. It paralyzed him, while the memories ran back. Snatches of conversation—it *had* been a dream, surely? Crocken stared at the shadow, uneasily recalling something about a bargain, and unusual terms he'd agreed to.

Come, the sun's already high. The tone was impatient.

A shadow would have a keen awareness of the sun's position, Crocken thought sagely, priding himself on his rationality. So wherefore did this shadow not dwindle as the day turned toward sun-high? He began to fear he'd soon recall precisely what he'd promised.

"Bargain?" Crocken asked in a cracked whisper, scarcely audible. But the shade's hearing was acute.

Begins to come back to you, does it? The shadow bent close. Crocken cringed back. *You agreed to escort me to Armyn, peddler. In return for this small service, you shall be paid forty marks of gold. To sweeten the pot, you'll stay alive to collect your fortune.*

"What . . . who are you, lord?" His lips shook, making Crocken stutter.

No lord, the voice corrected softly. *Shadow will do well enough for your purpose.*

"Are you some manner of demon?" Crocken was terrified that it might touch him, beyond their knee-to-foot interface. Lay a dark hand on his face, say. Crocken felt he'd expire on the spot.

No. It gestured at him, eloquently. *Don't be more afraid of me than you need to be, peddler. Do as I say, and you won't come to any harm. I promise you that.*

Crocken thought he remembered other promises the thing had made. They had mostly had to do with hurting him.

"What does a demon swear by?" he wondered aloud.

The shadow hissed. *Peddling breeds a sharp tongue, I see. Be thankful I have need of it—or I'd have it out.*

Crocken got to his feet warily. His legs felt numb, and he

took a step or two, testing them—he realized suddenly that he was trying to put a few yards between himself and the shadow, as he would a human enemy. He stood still. Such attempts were vain. No matter how he moved, the shadow remained attached to his feet, whether it chose to shift with him or not.

"How do you do that?" he asked, unaccountably curious. And unwisely, too, he did not doubt. He had never paid much attention to his own shadow, an oversight he now regretted. How did a demon compare to a sun-flung shadow? Would their characteristics match? Were they governed by the same laws?

This is what I require you for, peddler. I shall be with you thus while the sun crosses the sky. Close as your shadow, you might well say.

Crocken wondered where his own shadow had fled when this one took him over. Then he became amazed that he could stand so, quietly debating philosophy with an impossibility, like two scholars in the temple courts. Perchance he'd simply gone mad, lost his few remaining wits. That would explain much, and comfort him no little. He nodded.

Where you cast a strong shadow, I am bound to you, as you behold me now. Limited, and a trifle weaker than I will be during the hours of darkness. The shadow had come very close again. *But never so weak that you can cast me off, peddler. Never think that.*

Crocken shook his head solemnly, denying any such speculation.

My powers are . . . different from what they once were—but they will suffice for the likes of you. Don't force me to prove that to you.

Crocken shook his head once more. No, he didn't expect he'd venture to try that. It was certain to be unpleasant.

A shadow-arm gestured broadly toward the trail. *Then if you've no objection, it's a long way to Armyn.*

Indeed. Crocken tried to call maps of such a route to mind. He frowned when he succeeded. "I had business in Kinark." The lie sprang readily to his lips, but it sounded thin when he voiced it.

Don't whine and hope to pad your fee, peddler. You'll get gold in plenty—and you can peddle your wares as profitably in Armyn as in Kinark.

"But Armyn's a longer walk." And forty marks of gold—to be paid at that walk's completion—hardly struck him as fair compensation. The habit of bargaining was strong in Crocken's blood. Stronger than sense, even under such strange conditions.

If you walk swiftly, you may turn a greater profit. I'd not fret over that. Concern yourself with the benefits due you if I do not need to enforce the word you pledged to me.

The implication was unmistakable, as the shadow had doubtless intended. Such threats might, of course, be empty—Crocken was needed, and therefore couldn't be damaged all that severely, if this creature had any sense. He could set fear aside. Crocken considered.

As a business dealing, the opportunity set before him looked no worse than anything he had reason to expect in Kinark. It interested him, which was an odd feeling. His life, past and future, had been cold ashes for the best part of a month, and the sudden alteration stirred him.

Crocken's curiosity was piqued. That, not fear, decided him. With all the rest he'd lost or thrown away or left behind, what mattered his own mere shadow? A blotch upon the ground, no more, trailing mindlessly after him when the sun shone. Nothing of import. Crocken caught up the pony's lead rope once more, encouraged the beast with a shove to get it moving, and set off to the shadow's direction.

By sun-fall, the peddler was once more actively doubting his choice. His feet ached, and he kept remembering hopelessly how near he'd been to Kinark—just a few days' more travel would have seen him to civilized parts, where he'd have been able to rest while trading goods for a copper or two, downing a pint of dark ale to rinse the trail dust from his throat. The track the shadow had insisted he follow didn't seem to be much frequented—Crocken had not laid eyes on a soul, and there was sign of neither man nor pack-beast. The only tracks he saw were dainty paired crescents, made by deer. Early season or no, few fared this wild and lonely way. Crocken hadn't walked the Kinark route in close to a dozen years, of course—but he'd *never* been on his present course and was uneasy not knowing what to expect from it. He had no liking for surprises, no yearning for novelties, in trackless wilderness.

As the day waned, he descended into foothills. Gradually the rocky trail was cushioned with the fallen debris of the long-needle pines that flanked it, muffling the pony's hoofbeats and making for chancy footing on the downslope. Branches overhanging the trail cast a deep gloom, and the way was difficult to pick out. Crocken fretted about missing it altogether—then wondered how he'd know if he did. Mapless, he had no means to detect errors. Fortunately the trail followed the easiest way, and his feet could lead him if his eyes did not.

The shadow had not bespoken him in hours. No need, Crocken guessed, so long as he straitly did what it required of him. That probably meant he was still on the trail—else the thing was as lost as he was. As the day darkened in, the sun dipping behind the trees, Crocken wondered uneasily just what he'd bound himself to. It apparently would be loose once night fell, not tethered to him. It had said so, hadn't it? Surely he remembered that.

Might it go off about its own business and let him draw a few private breaths? Crocken felt a sudden desperate need of that, becoming tensely aware of the shadow keeping pace just behind him, visible from the tail of his eye. Could it divine his thoughts, or could it hear him only when he spoke aloud? So much he didn't know, so much one took for granted with a conventional employer. So many queries he feared to make.

The gurgle of water running over stones reached Crocken's ears, and the fading light gleamed on a brook at the bottom of a trailside gully. There were still plentiful drifts of the fallen needles—he could sleep in fair comfort, bedded on those. It seemed a decent place to camp—and soon it would be too dark to entertain hopes of finding a better.

Crocken considered his situation. He'd be best off did he treat it with utmost seriousness every moment. He'd been striving to avoid looking at the shadow, no matter where the sun's position placed it. Now he deliberately turned to face it. *It.* His employer.

"May we stop here? We might not find water up ahead, and the pony's tired. Or do you know of a better place?"

The shadow inclined its head—Crocken thought. Hard to be sure, for it was an indistinct dark against the blurry woodland darkness.

Choice of camp is your privilege, peddler. I have no requirements that you need concern yourself with.

No, Crocken supposed not. He nodded. After all, what did a shadow require by way of food, or rest? "I just wanted to be sure we'd come far enough to suit you."

Tomorrow we will make an earlier start, peddler.

"My *name* is Crocken." Against all sense, he turned his back, stalking away toward the stream, all at once too furious for either caution or manners. This journey promised to be a long one. Being bespoken like a servant the whole while would neither shorten nor sweeten it. Even if he *was* a hired hand—or a bought pair of legs—being so blatantly treated as such galled him.

It proved difficult, however, to outwalk his own shadow.

I thank you for the gift of name, Crocken, the shadow said smoothly. *Names have power. Not many men would share theirs so freely with such a one as I am.*

Crocken stopped to stare at the dark man-shape. He wasn't certain whether the words were meant to reassure—or to frighten him so he'd be more thoroughly subservient. "I don't believe in those superstitions," he said, hoping to sound casual.

Nor take fright at shadows?

Was that the hint of a sardonic laugh? Did it know he was lying?

"It takes getting used to—but this is just business," Crocken replied, putting a bold face on it. "We need to talk."

Indeed?

Likely the thing could read his thoughts only if he voiced them—or if they reached such a peak of agitation that *anyone* could have discerned them at a glance, Crocken thought. He had been lately thinking some very rude thoughts, but there had been nary a response, as there would surely have been had those thoughts been eavesdropped upon. It seemed that he *did* have some privacy—but he'd best be careful of questions, which his new master seemed always to hear, if not to answer to his satisfaction.

Likewise his most recent vocal suggestion—the thing heard, but that was as far as it went. The shadow's response had the air of a raised eyebrow that seeks to end an inappropriate line of conversation.

"I need to know what I've agreed to," Crocken floundered on. "Yesterday—I can't even remember most of it! I—"

You will do well to stifle second thoughts, the shadow whispered direly. The menace in its tone, in the very air, grew stronger.

"Not second thoughts," Crocken protested, hoping to make it true by saying it. "A bargain is a bargain, and I swore. I'll keep my word. Only maybe I can do better service for you if I understand what it is I'm doing."

That is not your concern.

Crocken opened his mouth, angry past sense again—but the shadow had vanished among the trees, under the deeper shadows of the pine boughs.

Chapter Four

A SHADOW—WHAT could be more commonplace, homier? Every man had one, no matter how exalted or humble he might be in all else. Babes had them. Animals owned them. You could tell the hour by them, in any city square. But another's shadow battening itself onto him—Crocken could not shake the suspicion that he'd made an ill bargain indeed, perchance an evil one, as well. What had become of his own dear familiar shadow, the one he'd owned his whole life, when it was thrust from its place? Had he unknowingly condemned it to wander masterless, when it could no longer drag at his heels?

It's not as if I had a choice, Crocken argued dolefully with his guilt. *The job or my life.* What else could he have done? He sat miserably upon the prickly pine needles, arms clasped round knees, trying not to stare at the dark trees, or the empty spot where the firelight should have thrown a shadow-shape of him.

He didn't glimpse his shadow master again ere he slept, but it was back come morning, stretched out alongside him when the sun's rays broke through the interlacing pine branches overhead. Crocken's first impulse was to shrink away from its touch, but he managed in time to remember how pointless and humiliating such behavior was. Instead he arose, to begin the routine of striking his camp, and the shadow rose with him. Crocken avoided gazing at it. The morning air was more chill than the ground, once he was out of his nest of blankets, and he shivered and sneezed. The fire was gray coals. Crocken fed a fresh branch to it and heated a kettle of water.

He didn't much fancy pine-flavored bacon, and there was no wood better for cooking handy, so Crocken had to content himself with cold journeybread and hot tea. Recalling the mention—best name it an order—of an earlier start, he kept

18

himself dutifully on the move, munching his bread and loading the pony while the tea steeped, pouring water on the fire the moment he was finished with it. Not hurrying, precisely, yet moving with an economy that gave his eldritch employer no grounds for any accusation of dawdling.

The tea tasted of resin. Crocken swallowed one cup down anyway, since the warmth was welcome, then hung the kettle from the back of the pack-saddle, stoppering the spout so drips couldn't scald the pony's flanks. The beast shied as he unhobbled it, nearly knocking him down. Crocken wondered what the pony saw when his shadow brushed it. To his eyes its appearance was no different from what it had ever been, save that this shadow sometimes failed or chose not to copy his movements precisely. Surely not something a pony would detect. He wondered whether the difference was symptomatic of carelessness or contempt.

He set himself to observe it as he walked. Ignoring the thing plainly hadn't caused it to vanish, so he ought instead to learn what he could about it—rather than falling back on the childish custom of hiding his eyes from a thing he didn't wish to see. Their partnership was going to last for a fair while, and best he adjust to that unpleasant fact—if he could.

The adjustment proved difficult. Crocken spent miles trying to work out what the full distance to Armyn would be, but he could arrive at no clear notion. It was as if motion addled his thinking, which was not a usual problem. Normally walking cleared his head. If he was remembering the maps aright, he was going to travel the whole way down the long coast of Sheir. That was in itself a considerable journey, and by his recall Armyn lay some way beyond it. This promised to be much farther than he'd previously journeyed, even afloat on a distance-eating galley—a most daunting prospect for him, afoot.

Just after sun-high the trail abruptly dissolved into heavy undergrowth. The dead-looking brush tended toward small trees in places, and Crocken had nasty work finding a way through that wouldn't push the pony into outright rebellion. He *was* still on the trail, such as it was. With none of the plants yet leafed out, he could make out where feet and hooves had long ago worn the way down below the level of the surrounding forest. And the shadow had not rebuked him for straying from the true way, not in some hours. That was always his touchstone.

The young trees were not the dominant conifers of the region, but maples, which was a puzzle. Second growth, Crocken supposed, though plainly that growing had been going on for some while. Most of the saplings were as thick as his arm, and tall as a ship's mast.

Ahead, a wilderness of brambles and sapling groves choked the trail almost totally, the slender gray trunks barely elbow-room apart. Stifling a moan, Crocken led the pony over the rockiest ground he could spy out—bramble thorns still tormented the passage, but thinner soil supported fewer trees. He couldn't imagine how the trees managed to survive, so close-set. The shadow slipped along after him, silent as a dark cloud.

"Not much used, this track," Crocken remarked pointedly, as he unwound a twine of bramble from about his left calf, then struggled cursing to pull it loose from its new grip on his fingers. Thorns stitched his skin.

The shadow stood at his side, when it ought to have been under his boots, to accord with the sun's position. There was no one about save Crocken to note the flouting of nature—he supposed the shadow would not be so careless if matters were otherwise. Could it not see so well as he, lying upon the ground? Did it have such a limitation as a man would have? Surely it did not do him the courtesy of allowing him to address it as another person?

This was the old route, the shadow whispered. *The Sheiran galley fleet has rendered the coast way safer than it once was, so traders go nearer the sea, or better yet upon it, which is swifter. None come this way now.* It paused, and the only sound was the empty keen of the wind. *Sheiran sorcerors stopped an army of Armyn here once. The way was not so choked before those saplings were here.*

Crocken let his gaze rove about, trying to understand. The wood was still. No hint of past sorceries showed—at least not to him. He wasn't sure he wanted to know about it, even if his employer was deigning to converse with him again. Should the way look blasted, scarred?

Each sapling you behold was a footsoldier of Armyn. 'Tis said they sleep soundly—but you'll want to be away from here ere nightfall, peddler.

Crocken, looking at the ranks of the trees, wholeheartedly agreed.

The road cleared just before they forded a small river. Running water negated witchery, Crocken had always heard, and he watched to see how the shadow would react to it. It seemed not at all discomfitted—yet he could not tell how it actually crossed.

The pony unexpectedly commanded his entire attention, frightened of walking into the swift-running water while laden. Crocken waded downstream of it, lending his shoulder when the beast faltered or floundered into a hole in the river's bed, and was thus thoroughly occupied until they were on the far shore. Once he thought he saw a dark salmon-shape sliding through the water, but it could easily have been a real fish.

That shore was less thickly wooded than the one they had left at their backs, and all the trees appeared normal. The dripping pony had regained a shadow. So had Crocken.

"Where do you go when it rains?" he asked—then wondered with a chill of dread whether he'd overstepped himself.

The shadow made him no answer. Crocken took up the pony's soaked lead rope and began questing for the remnants of the road. At length he chanced upon it—ruinous as its other half on the far bank of the river. Crocken looked sidelong at the shadow.

"Ah . . . just how well do you know this route? Myself, all I know about going to Armyn is it's likely to take us awhile. You'd have done better to hire yourself a man with a horse."

Yes. The word was thoughtfully drawn out. *Unhappily, necessity differs from choice.*

Crocken stiffened. "Thanks so *much*." He began to drag the pony rapidly along what passed for the trail, his wet boots squeaking and sloshing in protest.

In a few moments Crocken halted—aware that he was punishing himself a great deal and his shadow not in the least. It slipped along behind him effortlessly, oblivious to rocks or mud, unaware of grades or brambles. The pony fetched him an evil backward look and pulled away to snatch some grass. Crocken took a deep breath. He let it carefully out and drew another.

"You need me," he said as evenly as possible, trying to sound reasonable rather than furious. "That much is obvious even to a want-wit like me! Whatever the reason, whether you *chose* me or not, you need me and you're stuck with me. There's not much you can threaten me with—not if you want me able to walk to Armyn! I'm not asking the earth—I just want to know where I'm going. I haven't asked you *why*, and let me assure you that I don't care! I don't want it to become any of my business." Crocken shook his head for emphasis. "I'd like to conclude this transaction as quickly as I can—as I'm sure you would. We'll both be best off if you let me cooperate with you. This isn't—" He gestured at the nearly invisible trail. "—some secret trade route you have to guard from me. I'm not likely to want to come this way again.''

Crocken paused for breath, but not so long as to seem to be expecting an answer. He hadn't finished. "What I *do* want to know is what to expect *this* time. If you don't know what's ahead, all you need do is say so—there's no cause to treat me like a pat of cow dung you nearly stepped in, just because I ask a legitimate question!''

When his words had finished spilling out, the peddler belatedly recognized that his pretended calm had deserted him somewhere into his second sentence. He closed his lips apprehensively. For an extended moment the wood was silent save for the tearing sound of the pony's grazing.

You are quite right, the shadow whispered, scarcely more audible than the breeze in the branches above. *Your pardon, Crocken. My thoughts are often elsewhere. Being recalled is . . . irksome. What you have asked is nothing I cannot or should not grant. I have been this way only once, and the way was not difficult to find then, but years have passed . . .*

The shadow contracted, stooping beside a patch of bright sunlight athwart the path. Dead leaves flipped away abruptly, baring the packed soil. Shadow-fingers stretched over the spot, taking on a shape that was no longer human. Crocken was briefly baffled—till enough took shape to make the device's intent plain to him. He knelt down to study the developing map more closely.

These are the mountains of Kinark, the shadow voice said. *This, the Great Sea.* It extended the map swiftly. *Here is the stream we lately forded. It and its twin run seaward, and where they reach the sea lie the three cities called the Quatrain: Fithian, Asgeirr, and Talfryn-Norval. Our present road runs nowhere near that coast. It crosses the wilderness through the foothills of these mountains bordering Sheir, until at last it reaches the Arinwater, the river that flows out of Lake Arinna.* Mountains sprouted, and the reverse thread of the river sliced through them. *That will find us in the marshlands of Cordis. Once across the river Bruns, we will be in Armyn proper.*

"Your road's a long way short of crow's flight," Crocken ventured, testing. "Following the coast would be a lot quicker.'' He traced above that route with one finger to demonstrate, careful not to touch the map itself.

I choose to be seen by as few folk as is possible. The extra time required will be a fair exchange.

Crocken shrugged. "The customer's entitled to a choice of route, I suppose. That's another river there?"

The Frostwater, which we will reach by nightfall.

"With time to ford it? I'd rather not chance that in bad light." Or, he thought, have a second soaking on such a cold day.

If conditions are poor, I will permit you to delay the crossing till morning. We may need to risk a night crossing of the Arinwater, however. The Borderlands are sometimes . . . troubled.

Crocken let the ominous remark turn over in his brain, while he studied the map. The Arinwater was a long way off yet, and he wanted to have the map firm in his memory, so he needn't ask to have it repeated later. Such a trek! All the way along the fringe of the Sheiran Empire, when he'd never been farther inside that vast collection of principalities than Asgeirr, where the Great Market was held twice yearly and uncounted tons of goods passed daily by land, sea, and canal. Asgeirr itself was a fair distance to walk from their present location. At the moment the shadow seemed less concerned with haste—but Crocken knew that could alter. Best if he expected it to and did not come to depend upon the respite.

Satisfied at last that he could call most of the map to mind when he chose to, Crocken got to his feet, brushing dust from his breeches.

"Thank you," he addressed the shadow, and thought it cocked its head at him—but just then Crocken realized how far the pony had strayed, and he set off hastily in pursuit of the silly beast.

At least it had wandered onward, and not back toward the river. Seeing Crocken's approach, the pony snatched a final mouthful of fodder, then resigned itself to his direction once more. It did not, however, resist slapping him in the face with its still-river-wet tail when he bent to check the pack saddle's girths.

The Frostwater was reached at dusk and crossed in the morning light. It well deserved its chilly name, and neither Crocken nor the pony liked the crossing much. The shadow had no comment. Again Crocken failed to see just how the thing crossed, though he had intended to pay close attention. Events continually conspired to distract him.

As the day was walked away, the scenery subtly changed. Conifers gave way to lofty cedars as the thin soil deepened enough to support their vast-spreading roots. Crocken reckoned some of them even taller than those so fabled in Kinark. The heavy shade their needled branches cast kept undergrowth in check, and the trail happily became easier to pick out. Once or twice Crocken saw ruins he took for way-stations, ancient Sheiran fortifications to protect what had been the trade route in far-off days.

Toward evening he smelled smoke—merely a tickle to his nose, but Crocken thought he might follow it to a settlement, perchance even one graced by an inn. Then the peddler dashed his own hopes, recalling his client's aversion to company other than his own. No sense seeking permission that would certainly be refused.

Crocken ignored the woodsmoke and kept the pony walking till nearly full dark. Finally a small clearing in the cedars offered a bit of grass—and there was no getting the pony past it. Crocken hobbled the beast, unloaded it, then set up his camp at the edge of the trees. Hopeful because of the grass, he set snares for rabbit—fresh meat would be a welcome change of diet. There should have been other game in the forest, but Crocken knew himself to be no hunter, even if he'd supposed the shadow would allow him time for it. Snares were the best he could manage.

Apparently there were no other hunters in the area—assuming there was anyone else in the area at all. Crocken had hoped at best for success by morning, but an unwary rabbit tripped the snare while he was laying his fire—he found it when he ventured into the meadow to gather a few armloads of soft grass for his bed.

A hot meal, a warm bed—and no more freezing rivers to cross for a long while, unless the shadow had omitted lesser streams from the map as unimportant. There being no way to determine that, Crocken settled himself for the night, well fed and well enough content.

He rested quietly awhile, then began to dream.

A sable deer was walking along a snowy forest trail, limping at a slow pace that spoke of exhaustion relentlessly driven onward by desperation. Even as Crocken watched, it turned its head back to search the way it had come. It found neither scent nor sound of pursuit, but it knew the pursuit was there, as surely as Crocken did. After a moment, it staggered on and was lost among the trees—lost except for the trail of blood it was leaving with every step upon rock and dirt and snow.

Crocken woke at dawn, subdued and perplexed, still wrapped in the dream's enigma. The air was no colder than it had been, but it was quite still. No vagrant breeze disturbed it, nor any sound. Pushing his blankets back, Crocken sat up, holding his own breath back in sympathy.

The world was glowing white. A light, damp snow had fallen, and where the forest had been dark and open, it now was light and closed up. Snow clung luminously to even the least twigs, shutting out a sky only slightly less white. Every surface was thickened by its powdering, even the trunks of the trees. It was almost difficult to breathe—there seemed to be no free air.

Crocken stared as one ensorcelled, fearful a careless motion might loosen the lovely spell. He drew breath at last, but the air still did not stir. In the directionless light, he hadn't the least notion where the trail lay—for all he knew, the world itself ceased beyond the fifty or so paces that he could personally see, and he was alone in it. His gear was all touched by fantasy—packs turned to sugar loaves, the pack saddle a spun-sugar subtlety fit for a great lord's table, his rough blankets as finely broidered as the damask upon that lordly board.

One object only, no snow clung to. Slender and dark as pitch, it drifted out from among the trees. Crocken slipped from under his blankets before the shadow could order him to do so, stirred the fire to life, and answered nature's needs. The fey beauty of his surroundings no longer had his attention—he dared spare it none.

There were, however, fresh reminders of it, every few paces along the trail. Branches slender enough to go unseen in any other weather commanded the eye like borders on a page of manuscript. Lavender canes of blackberry brambles rivaled anything found upon the Street of Jewelers in Kôvelir, and the patterns of the tree trunks were beyond any weaver's skill. There were of course no shadows, not under a smoothly clouded sky the hue of old silver. None save one, sliding along beside Crocken, blithely unaware as it always was. Crocken framed a score of questions to put to it, but deemed them one by one less than advisable, and so held his peace.

Chapter Five

IT SHOULD HAVE been three hours past sun-high, if Crocken could have been sure just when the midmark of the day took place. Morning breezes had shaken most of the precariously settled snow from the branches and needles overhead, sending it sifting down to deepen the thin layer on the forest floor. Though no longer appearing enchanted, the wood remained a world of stark blacks and whites. Simple for a shadow to lose itself in, Crocken realized—as his shadow did precisely that, vanishing like a snowflake fallen into water.

He frowned, then squinted. No sign of it. What now?

Crocken heard bells, and the pony whinnied loudly. In a dozen heartbeats the whole landscape was alive with teeming color, riotous sound, and moving shapes.

Shaggy brown bulks, startling flashes of scarlet and cobalt silk, a continual jangle of brass bells and bronze harness fittings—all Crocken's senses were assailed. White mist puffed from the mouths of the laden camels, and from those of their riders as one called out to another, passing some word back along the line of march.

The rock walls of a defile had hidden them and swallowed the sound of their passage—the caravan thus came into Crocken's sight and into his solitary world abruptly, where the Trapper's Road intersected the trail he was following. He wondered furiously whether the shadow could have given him more timely warning than its disappearance.

The camel lords' occupation was obvious, even had Crocken never heard the tales he had of them. The camels were all well burdened with pelts besides their own—snow leopard, mountain antelope, marten, mink, lynx, and fox. Their riders and guides were clad in fine furs that might have been shelter against the mountains' cold or the recent choicest pickings from the trap-lines, donned at a whim. On the heads of more than a few, golden gryphon feathers jutted up, trophies of perilous hunts few other folk dared attempt.

Crocken had encountered Trappers ere then on his trade travels—though never in such terrifying numbers. He counted twoscore men and twice that number of their two-humped pack-beasts, with more perhaps out of sight in the defile. The trapping season was at its end, and the usually solitary mountain men had banded together for the descent toward the Quatrain, where they'd sell off their winter's takings.

Crocken forced a smile to his chapped lips, feigning pleasure. Given such circumstances, he could expect the Trappers to be in a riotous mood. Rough enough at the best of times—few towns outside the Quatrain welcomed them with any enthusiasm even singly, far less en masse—Trappers were fierce, bold lon-ers, quarrelsome and frequently drunken and destructive. These had been deprived of those few civilized pleasures they deigned to indulge in for an entire winter! Crocken well supposed his health and fortunes would depend in large part upon his adapting himself to whatever their present mood chanced to be. He had seen them too late to take flight, so the peddler hoped that wouldn't prove to have been his best option. The shadow re-mained vanished, or faded to the faint shade it should have been under the sky conditions, and would plainly be of no help to him.

Fortunately, the trail crossing was wide. The lead camels halted before they had Crocken surrounded, and there was am-ple room for those following to gather about without undue or irritating jostling. They gave aside easily, a wooly sea parting before one black riding camel making its stately way to the fore.

The beast's size, quality, and unburdened state—most of the camels bore bales of fur *and* a rider—proclaimed its rider to be of some importance. Crocken was surprised that the unruly Trappers would subjugate themselves to any sort of leader, but he nonetheless bowed respectfully before the thickset, fur-wrapped figure. Peddlers were well versed in the paramount importance of manners—or they didn't survive long at their trade.

The Trapper lord leaned down over the shaggy shoulder of his mount. The black camel tossed its head, setting brass bridle bells ringing merrily.

"Whither bound, little man?"

Crocken, well aware that even such open friendliness could mask dark purposes, smiled and spoke formal greetings suitable to the occasion. He was relieved that every camel he could see appeared well laden. After a good winter's trapping—and with the prospect of sumptuous profits before them—the Trappers were unlikely to bother a lone trader like himself. He was no threat to them, and they were too merry at present to molest him solely for the sport of it—or so he hoped.

Crocken felt it prudent to be vague as to his destination, saying only that he was headed for Talfryn-Norval, sister cities and trade centers along the coast.

"You're foolish to venture so far on yon lonely forest track, with Asgeirr lying at Frostwater's mouth," the Trapper lord boomed. "Come you along with us, little man, we'll see you safely there."

Truly, this Master of Trappers was in a good temper, full of his success. The offer was perchance lightly made, but if made at all 'twas sincere. And under such a leader's public protection, Crocken supposed he would be safe from any of the other Trappers' malice or mirth.

He felt a tug of temptation. The shadow had expressed an aversion to company—what would happen if he joined with so large a group? Some pair of sharp eyes would always be upon him, the stranger, the curiosity. Would that buy him safety, or only the shadow's anger? Could it act upon that anger? If he could reach the Quatrain, there were surely wizards capable of setting him free from his mysterious and dangerous employer. The Trappers could take him there.

He could be safe—or, perchance, unwittingly put himself in greater peril. Crocken had not forgotten the shadow's threats. He did not take them lightly. He knew little about it and its powers—not enough to be certain he wouldn't commit some fatal error. Or worse than fatal, he dared not lose sight of that possibility. There was no telling what it might be able to do to him.

Besides, he nimbly argued, when had he ever gone back on his pledged word? The bargain might not have been of his seeking, might not be quite to his taste—but he *had* agreed to it.

And, in all the while since betrayal and desertion had laid his past and his future waste, the shadow was the sole thing able to engage his interest. It promised to be a diversion beyond the daily search for food and shelter, at least. He didn't trust the shadow—Crocken trusted no one now, and was determined not to. Fate had shown him plainly that he was no better than a hand-to-mouth peddler, had left him unable even to put on airs about it—yet still he found he wanted to discover what the shadow was up to, and it was a curiosity that would not be set aside. In the end, 'twas stronger than temptation, or the hope of freedom.

He declined the Trapper's offer, courteously. "I am afoot, as you see, master. I would not permit myself to slow your journey—the first furs to reach Asgeirr always command the best prices, do they not? I cannot let you risk your profits for my comfort, grateful as I am for your kindness."

"Spoken like a true trader!" the Trapper lord shouted. "Sup with us then, and part we after. There's fresh-killed aurochs for the roasting." He waved, a signal to the company to pitch camp. A frenzy of activity commenced.

Crocken would have preferred to decline the meal as well as the travel company. Aurochs was a better meat if aged a proper while. Fresh, its flavor was strong, though mayhap not to the Trappers, who surely ate worse than charred wild bull while deep in the mountains. But he understood he was being invited to show his wares as well as fill his belly—and a peddler who passed up a chance at a customer would be subject to a great deal of suspicion—and possibly subjected to worse. Better to avoid trouble.

There was yet another thing to consider—Trappers freshly down from the mountains would be carrying no coin. The medium of exchange could only be furs. Fine furs, worth far more than Crocken's goods, and he'd be cheerfully overpaid in every transaction.

The practical trade items Crocken carried were left where he'd packed them. Needles and pins, however fine their steel or sharp their points, were of scant interest to Trappers. Strings of gaudy glass beads and scarves of Kôvelir's second-quality silks were traded briskly, but most highly prized of all were the clay pots full of apricot-laced honey. By the nature of their trade, Trappers had free access to all the fresh meat they could chew, but after months on such a diet they were ripe for an alteration and greedy as children for sweets. Crocken was smugly content. He'd purchased the honey pots at dirt-low prices and had still thought them a risk, possibly not worth their carry-weight. Now his shrewdness was proved and his luck seemed to be turning. It should not have surprised him. Trappers dressed like bears.

Proper they should dine like bears, also, and clever of him to have come across them.

Crocken was up most of that night, strolling among the camp-fires, between the strings of tethered camels, trading and oiling the wheels of commerce with flagons of the mead that the Trapper chief pressed upon all his men. No one would hear of his retiring to his blankets. The burly men waved him on his way when camp was broken at dawn, and Crocken could still hear their enthusiastic if unmelodious singing while he put the first mile of trail behind him.

He proudly stroked the little bale of furs strapped atop his pony's pack saddle. Two fox pelts, one nearly blood red, the other slate blue. A shadow-dark sable, and half a dozen brown marten skins. Finest of all, the spotted pelt of a lynx in its full late-winter magnificence, worth far more alone than all the pots of honey the furs had replaced. Even the pony was cheerful—the furs weighed less than the pots had.

The sun was barely up and still hid its face behind the clouds—but all at once Crocken could see his shadow.

Profitable transactions, it said conversationally.

Crocken conceded that cautiously. "Yes."

You will do well to remember that your time is in hire to me, peddler. I have no use for furs. A shadow-hand passed contemptuously over the bale of pelts.

Crocken eyed his master sidelong and decided to stand his ground.

"How much use do you have for a servant who's been tortured in half the hundred ways Sheiran Trappers are properly famous for? A peddler who isn't eager to trade is probably something else. Something worth remembering and attending to. Trappers are a touch . . . simpleminded about that sort of thing."

The shadow was silent for a space. *I see.*

"I thought about getting away from them sooner," Crocken volunteered helpfully. "But I'd have had to camp for the night anyway, and trouble with Trappers surely takes longer than socializing does. Most of them learn to draw a bow before they can walk, and being pursued by archers in forest like this—" Crocken swept a hand at the thick trees flanking the narrow trail. "You at my back is one thing. I don't want Trappers, too."

Are we likely to encounter more such?

As if the woodland route was *his* choice, in *his* knowledge. Crocken shrugged the old irritation off and thought about the question. "Trappers? Not if we're lucky. The season for the best pelts is over now, the animals are breeding. The Trappers will all be in the lowlands soon, selling off their harvest and drinking up their profits.'' He resisted the urge to finger the lynx pelt again. That one he might just keep for his own use. He'd cut a fine figure. ''I don't know much about the rest of Sheir, but I'd think the same would hold true anywhere.''

Even supposing there are no more Trappers on the move, there will be woodcutters, foresters, and hunters. Perhaps even a few traders like yourself, deeper into Sheir. Bear in mind that I will not brook delays that stem from chance encounters.

''Understood,'' Crocken agreed reluctantly. ''But—I'll have to trade sometimes. Aside from it looking peculiar if I refuse to—I think neither of us wants me taken for a spy—I'm going to need supplies. By your map, we're going three times farther than I'd planned provisions for.''

Live off the country, peddler.

What else *was* trading for supplies locally? Crocken wondered. The odd rabbit was the pinnacle of his trapping skill. He shrugged. ''Living off the country takes time no matter how it's done, but I guarantee you I'll be quicker about it if you let me go at it the way I'm used to—in the villages. If you make me hunt and set snares, we'll be all summer getting to Armyn.''

The trail is easier ahead.

''Fine,'' Crocken said, doubting it. There'd been a wheedling tone to the statement. ''Then probably there'll be more people, to keep the way open and repaired. I need to know—do you expect me to hide whenever we meet other folk? That's going to mean delays, too. Which is fine with me—but if it's a part of your conditions for employment, don't go blaming me for it.'' Best if he kept his position clear, and safe enough to do it while his master was coaxing rather than ordering. Maybe he *could* have escaped by going with the Trappers, and his shadow was aware of that risk.

You won't need to hide, peddler. There are . . . arts I must practice before we go into company, but you may move freely. Proceed as you normally would—bearing always in mind that this journey has a destination and a need for haste.

And best not to line his own pockets too obviously, Crocken took that to mean. A condition he could accept, if not endorse. Certainly he could manage to live with it. Forty marks of promised gold bought a lot of tolerance, he found.

Chapter Six

THE TRAIL KEPT to the forests and the foothills, high above the fertile Sheiran plain. It was little used even through more settled areas, always high and wild even when no longer thickly forested. Crocken had few opportunities to annoy his master by conversing with strangers.

Not a single inn appeared to tempt him or refresh him. Most of the settlements he passed were so small that he feared they'd have no food to spare at winter's end, not even to sell to him. If he saw chickens, he bought eggs. Once there was a mill, and he bought enough meal—though 'twas stale—to make gruel for several days. The shadow didn't begrudge him the time the transactions required—Crocken thought it must be obvious that he was gaining far too little to be slowing their progress deliberately.

The moon passed through her phases once. The sun was moving, also, and the days lengthened into true spring. On the plain, plowing began in the warmed soil. Each day Crocken saw more fallow fields furrowed and readied for planting. The pony began to shed out its winter coat and had to be watched closely due to its consuming desire to scratch itself upon each tree and boulder it passed.

The mountains were ever at his left hand, but Crocken could tell by signs of sun and moon and stars that those mountains were steadily shifting themselves and pushing the foothills and the trail toward his right. He recalled the map easily and knew, days ere it came into his sight, that they neared the Arinwater.

Rain was falling when they reached the river, as it had been for the past two dismal days, turning the trail to brown glue. The distant hills—somewhere among which lay Lake Arinna—drifted mistily, appearing, vanishing, then reappearing like a conjuror's smoke tricks. The Arinwater, unfortunately, did no such convenient thing, but grew ever more substantial and rain-swollen as they approached it. The shadow seemed blissfully unaware of the mud.

Lake-fed, the river should have run clear by Crocken's expectation, but smaller streams fed it, too, and it was brown and frothy as ale, running fast as a blooded horse. It was far out over its banks, drowning the woodland. A white mist rose from the river and coiled about the trunks of the trees, just above the water. The effect was unreal—water and mist twisting through the forest. Crocken halted the pony on high ground under marginally sheltering branches. Too bad the trees hadn't leafed out yet. He turned to his shadow.

"Which way's the ferry?" Not far, he hoped. Unlikely the trail wouldn't lead directly to it.

There is no ferry, peddler.

Crocken, expecting a direction, was dumbfounded. "But— there must be! That current can't be forded. Look at it!" He swept a hand, though he never could tell where the shadow was looking. For all he knew, it could see out the back of its head as easily as the front—if it *had* a back or front.

There is no ferry, the shadow repeated patiently. *These are the Borderlands. There is precious little crossing for trade now, and there is no welcome given. Usually its armies come over the Arinwater, and such manage without the amenities of ferries.*

Crocken swore, brushing dripping hair out of his eyes. "Well, fine for them! They'd have men enough to form a chain, or boats they could anchor upstream to tame the current—and I'd wager a lot of them would *still* drown! What am *I* supposed to do?"

Take me across the Arinwater, into Armyn, the shadow said implacably.

Crocken stared—but a shadow has no expression to its face, for a man to read.

"Is there at least an easier place?" he asked desperately. "What about upstream?"

The access is more difficult. Cliffs on both sides, with the river's channel deep between.

That didn't sound promising, Crocken had to agree. He pulled his hood up, but rain still soaked him. "Downstream? Maybe we've hit too high—I might have missed that last bit of trail. Wouldn't there be a castle, to protect a ford?"

The whole of the Borderlands protects Armyn—her buffer to Sheir. You will see castles aplenty, but there is none at this ford. We have not missed our way. This is the crossing. Be about it.

"I don't want to cross here. I don't like the look of that water. Can't we wait for the flood to drop?" It was a desperate offer, one Crocken had no hope for, even as he made it.

It will rise higher ere it falls—the rain still comes down. And the sooner we are across, the sooner our bargain will be fulfilled, peddler.

Crocken measured the wicked look of the gray river against the promised forty marks of gold. The exchange seemed uneven to him. The floodwaters could prove deadly, and dead men spend no gold. He bit his lip thoughtfully. On the other hand, the shadow was probably right about the water level. Could he spend a week camped beside the Arinwater, with the shadow ever fretting to be across and about its business—and blaming him all the while for the delay? What if it tried to force him across when conditions were worse?

After a little search among the trees, Crocken cut himself a sapling and made a longish pole, a tool with which to scout out the riverbed for hazards invisible under the water. He double-lashed his gear onto the pony and did what he could to water-proof the packs, which was not much, once he'd seen all the fastenings were secure. Mostly the load would be above the water—or so he hoped. If the flood was higher than the pony's back, nothing would avail. With one final sigh at the folly of it, Crocken set off into the Arinwater.

The river looked broader still, as he came close to it. Crocken hoped that meant the Arinwater was shallow, though he could not hope that knee-depth would prevail. It was so far out over its normal banks that he had no idea what to expect—or where to expect it. He felt carefully ahead with his pole before each step, unwilling to be taken unawares by the drop-off into the main channel, which might be extreme. The pony liked the cold water even less than Crocken did and pulled back on its tether, resisting his orders to advance. He shouted a mixture of curses and orders at it, and dragged the beast after him into the rushing water.

The water was chest-high on Crocken, and the pony seemed to be trying to decide about swimming. Rain slapped down at them, soaking from above what the waters below had so far not reached. Crocken kept up a steady pace, reaching ahead always with the pole, feeling the current forcing him half a step down-stream for each step he managed toward the far bank. He held still to let a floating branch go by, and shivered to think what he'd shift to do if a bigger log got too close to dodge. His mind began to insist that he could reach safety if he ran for it at once— one tiny spark of rationality reminded him that it would be like running in a dream, where much motion produces no result. To distract himself from the temptation, he took a long look at the pony's load. So far, all was still abovewater. The current lapped at the bottommost bundles, but those were furs, which would take little harm. Animals got wet all the time . . .

Crocken floundered into a shallow hole the pole had missed, and saved himself only by grabbing at the pony. The mishap soaked him to the nose and scared the pony, which plunged madly ahead of what it took for danger, with Crocken in frantic pursuit. It was faster in the deep water than he was, but he dared not let it escape him. Just what he needed, to have the beast decide that turning back was easier than going onward whilst it was out of his control. That was definitely a risk—even though the far shore was by then the closer bank. The pony would know no better, but would turn instinctively for home, which was Kôvelir.

It was the pony who stumbled into unexpected depths next— probably close to the Arinwater's usual bank on the Armyn side. They were so close to the shore that Crocken had begun to feel they'd make it after all, especially as he'd recaptured the lead rope, when the pony lost its footing and smashed against him. He went right under and felt the cold fingers of the current seize him implacably before he could stand again.

Crocken gave in to his panic and struck out wildly. He was close enough to the shallows, surely he could gain them if he could get his feet under him once more. He slid on treacherous pebbles, bruised himself against larger rocks, fell into other holes, and swallowed buckets of water as he went under again and again. The pony screamed wildly.

Incredulous, Crocken found he still had the pole in his grasp, and he tried to use it to gain purchase to right himself. It seemed to succeed. The pole's tip jammed between two unseen rocks and held firm. Crocken held his head above water long enough to draw in two panicky breaths. He got his boots under him, took one step shoreward—and the pole broke.

The fierce current had him once more, as the bottom dropped out of the Arinwater and the world. Crocken was swept away struggling in the brown flood, and when he finally slammed

against something solid enough to stop him he scarcely marked
the impact.

He drifted among shadows for an endless while. Finally
Crocken opened his eyes, but one shadow was still there,
stretching out toward him.

Take my hand, he heard it say.

Crocken shook his head, not tempted in the least. He still had
the pole, he realized. It was broken, but the length he had left
was jammed against a tangle of driftwood, all that had kept him
from drifting right downriver till he—drowned, of course—
reached the Great Sea. His head ached, and his wits were
disarranged.

Take my hand.

Not so disarranged as to forget that a shadow can touch nothing much and hold nothing at all. Crocken would reach out to a
trick of the light, if he foolishly obeyed the voice, and then drift
away and drown. He chose to cling to the driftwood. Safe as
being in a beloved's arms, it felt, though wet and cold.

It is night now—when shadows reign. I am stronger now, the
shadow insisted. *I can pull you to the bank.*

Crocken wondered if that was true. Why should it be? If the
shadow had already gained the far bank, then it was already in
Armyn, and he was superfluous. Why didn't it leave him to
drown in peace?

Don't be a fool, peddler! Give me your hand!

Maybe the shadow still needed him. Or maybe he was already
dead, and dreaming it all, a shadow himself. Crocken reached
out—and felt nothing. He'd been in the cold water so long by
then, he expected no sensation, no proof of life. Something
grasped him, nonetheless, and dragged him to the muddy shore.

Crocken coughed, his lungs half full of water. The cough set
his head to pounding, but he couldn't stifle it, and he must
already have spewed all he was able to, for his belly only heaved
uselessly till he fainted again.

I never was any good at this, a voice said. *Even alive. You'll
have to assist me, peddler.*

A chill object was thrust into each of Crocken's numb hands.
He grasped weakly for an instant, then let them fall. He wasn't
interested in knowing what they were, or helping anyone with
anything. He was beyond struggling, sinking steadily down once

more into black waters. This time, there would be no painful resurfacing. Crocken was determined.

Hands closed over his, and the objects, and beat them into each other. The first time, one of Crocken's fingers got in the way. His numbness muffled the pain, but it still hurt enough to irritate, so he moved the finger out of pain's path and accidentally got a firmer hold on what he realized were a fire-steel and a chunk of flint. The next time his hands were swung together, they produced a bright shower of sparks—the last thing Crocken beheld before the shadowy waters closed over his aching head once more.

When he bobbed to the surface again, Crocken was lying beside a neatly laid fire, still damp but warm enough to feel a welcome difference. He could smell herbs, quite strongly. At length he discovered that something was bound tight to his still-throbbing head. His fingers explored the poultice curiously, and he smelled the herbs more sharply.

A five-fingered shadow pushed him flat when he made to sit up. There was nothing of gentleness in its touch, but its action had been too prompt to be truly rough. Crocken made no further attempt to rise, and the hand drew back again.

Lie still, and let the herbs do what they're meant to, the shadow ordered crossly. *I'm not patching you up twice tonight.*

"Are you still here?" Crocken was horrified at the weakness in his voice. He wouldn't have allowed himself to show such fear if he'd felt better.

Shut up. Do as you're told.

"Which side of the river are we on?" That was the worst thing that Crocken could imagine—that he'd been swept back to the Sheiran side and would have the crossing to do over. Why else would the shadow tend him?

We're in the Borderlands, peddler.

Crocken had never thought it odd that a thing with no throat could speak—but suddenly, that it could chuckle seemed obscene.

Chapter Seven

CROCKEN SAT BESIDE his fire, mournfully polishing pins. Steel pins, brass pins, one after another, endlessly. He laid the rag scraps he was using for the work close by the fire to dry them when they grew damp, and used pinches of gray river sand to smooth away rough spots that would be rust a-making on the metal.

It was tedious work—even though his fingers could manage it without anything like his complete attention. Much toil, and the reward for it, in hard coin, could only be minuscule unless the land of Armyn improbably chanced to be utterly devoid of all knowledge of pins. He had no reason to hope that would be so, and Crocken's expression grew bleaker. All the pins—*all* of them, dried so they'd not rust—might earn him the cost of a single meal, if he ate frugally. Assuming he could sell the whole packet at once, a good fortune he couldn't count on experiencing.

Crocken kept polishing. The pins—and a packet of glass beads—were all the trade goods that remained for him to peddle. They were all the pony hadn't been carrying.

He'd traipsed a league along the bank of the Arinwater in his soaked boots—that distance was all the shadow would permit, before it insisted the river was deviating too greatly from their course—and found no trace of the gray pony, drowned or otherwise. His goods were on their way to the sea, or at the bottom of the Arinwater—or perchance on the far shore, making pony-haste toward the Quatrain.

Greed and laziness, Crocken accused himself. A pretty pass such a combination had brought him to, and so swiftly. He stuck a finger on a pin, then sucked at it while he examined his guilt and mostly undeserved misfortune.

38

He hadn't laden the pony all *that* heavily—the indolent beast hadn't complained, and it would have been quick to—and he'd carried his own gear, not asked the animal to ferry it through the river, as well. Good job he hadn't—he'd have been left with naught save the clothes on his back. His waterlogged pack had come close to drowning him, but he was grateful to have it by him still. He had a little food, and a few clothes that would be dry if he could huddle by the fire long enough. He'd had steel and flint to kindle the fire in the first place.

His head ached, but the herbs had done a deal of good. The pain was only one of many minor miseries, no worse than the blisters his wet boots had produced, or the chill he couldn't seem to chase out of his bones. That the shadow had doctored him still amazed Crocken. Its motive for doing so wasn't something he was comfortable discussing, or even thinking long upon.

An owl hooted. Crocken jumped and dropped a pin. He bent to search for it, glancing sidelong into the darkness overhead. He saw nothing, and an owl was hardly an oddity in a woodland, but the idea of it watching him was somehow unnerving—like the raven that had followed him for hours, until dusk fell among the trees. He'd heard of ravens following armed men, anticipating a battle and plenty of carrion in its wake—but what about his appearance suggested raven-meat? Were travelers in these Borderlands so few?

Crocken realized that he had a shadow once more—though it did not flicker to and fro as those cast by the firelight did. Crocken gazed silently at it, too cast down to be wary. Anyway, he wanted the thing there—he needed to have speech with it.

"We're in Armyn now."

Yes.

Crocken cleared his throat hesitantly. "There doesn't seem to be any gold about. Not one mark, far less forty of them."

The shadow made no answer, though it stirred restively.

"You didn't intend to let me go once we were across the river, did you? You just said that, to make me cross sooner?" Crocken asked. He sighed, when the shadow still did not answer him.

"Not that it matters." He held up a pin, scrutinizing the rust. "I've lost everything—I'm destitute. You know that. If you still need my service, I've got to be grateful for that, not scheme to be free of you." He wiped the pin. "I suppose I'm better off never knowing if I'd have had a choice."

If I tell you I would have offered you a choice, will you believe me?

Crocken wiped the last few pins and folded the rag. "Trying to answer that just makes my head hurt. So, what's our course to be, master-of-mine?"

Do I understand that you are now willing to accompany me past the end of our earlier bargain?

"The end? Our bargain ends when I get my pay, shadow. We haven't made much of a team—I'll take some of the blame for that." He poked a stick into the fire, making all the shadows jump—save one. "But not all of it. I'm willing to be more co-operative than I have been, but it would be easier if I could know where we're going—and why."

You may be better not knowing, peddler. And certainly better not to ask.

Crocken swallowed, waiting for his courage to return. The shadow's tone had been as chilling as the memory of the Arin-water. He was so cold, despite the fire he was nearly sitting in, that warmth seemed only a dream.

"This journey may not have been my choice, but I'm here now. Coercion got me—and you—this far: to the middle of no-where. Do you intend to just sit here?" Crocken looked about, though the wet landscape had melted into the night. "Or do we deal? Surely this wasn't your destination."

I have need to reach the king's seat at Axe-Edge, the shadow hissed abruptly. *I was betrayed there—and left a task unfin-ished.*

Crocken blinked. He wasn't used to being answered, he de-cided. It startled him, and put his courage to flight. And maybe the thing was right—better he didn't know too much. What mad-ness had he been thinking? Could he call back his words?

Axe-Edge sits atop an escarpment, near the mouth of the river Windrush. The shadow made a map, beside the fire-coals, and showed him. *A long way still, but I would have asked you to take me there in any case. I can arrange your payment when we reach the fortress.*

Crocken wondered precisely how it intended to manage that—a matter that should have occurred to him beforetime. Promises of payment weighted no man's pocket. Gold was going to re-quire another person, somewhere, and the shadow shunned all folk, constraining Crocken to do likewise whenever it could. He might never see his gold. Yet if he turned away now, the loss was a certainty.

"And . . . once we reach Axe-Edge? What will you want to do then?" Suppose it just intended to keep him endlessly journeying? There were curses he'd heard tell of, that ran just that way . . .

That depends on what I find there, peddler. Just now I cannot say—it has been many years.

Maybe longer than it thought, Crocken hoped suddenly. A shadow might be supremely conscious of the *hour* of the day— a thing ruled by the sun would obviously always know the sun's position—but how could it reckon the passing years? What means had it to measure them? If those it planned to repay for its betrayal were long since dead, matters could be simpler—and safer. He nodded, reassured.

"You'll be wanting an early start tomorrow. We might just make better time without the pony," he said hopefully. "I suppose the roads are better from here on?"

Good roads ease a border reiver's way in. Rhisiart's men know the moors and the bogs of the Borderlands as a man knows a lover's face. They have little need of roads.

"Rhisiart?"

The Lord of the Borderlands. The man who betrayed me.

Dreams disturbed Crocken's rest—when his sole desire was to huddle into the faint warmth his damp blanket could provide and forget his misfortunes for a few hours. A supper of sodden journeybread might have been the culprit, or the shadow's dire pronouncements—as if being nearly drowned weren't enough to give a man nightmares. Crocken dreamed that he woke— which was much the same to him as actually waking—every few moments throughout the black night.

Of course he was dreaming. In the waking world, wild deer did not walk straight up to a man, even if he did seem to be sleeping. And should that man stir, a deer would flee quick as thought. Crocken sat up. The deer regarded him calmly out of liquid eyes, casually flicked a delicate ear in his direction. He could have touched it by stretching out his arm.

Well, asleep or awake, he was no threat to the creature, having no means to kill it however great his hunger. Crocken took leisure to inspect the doe—for he saw no sign of antlers—by the starlight shining down in his dream. He realized that the deer was black, an unusual variation from the brown or red he saw most often. Her coat was glossy as a raven's feathers, almost iridescent. A breeze ruffled it, and the doe snorted, turning her long head.

Crocken, looking where the creature did, saw movement far

off and dim. The rest of the herd? It wouldn't be wolves, for the
doe would surely have shown alarm, instead of the curiosity she
continued to divide between him and the distance.

He wanted to watch longer, but his lids grew heavy, weighted
with dream-sand. Crocken dragged them open just once more,
then knew again that he dreamed, for he beheld a dark-haired
woman bending over him, her eyes as wide and dark as the doe's
had been.

The deer must have been in some way real, however. Crocken
found cloven tracks all about in the morning's light, proceeding
right up to the cold ashes of his fire. There was a human print
there, too, but Crocken knew it must have been his own, for all
it seemed too narrow to have been made by his rough boots.
Bemused, he was about to try the fit when the shadow rejoined
him and happened to lie across that very spot, so that he could
no longer see any of the tracks clearly. It began to dun him about
moving on, and as breaking what passed for his camp took no
time at all, Crocken was soon on his way, the footprint forgotten.

Breakfast was a handful of wind-dried apples, withered and
tiny. Crocken alternated chewing them with sucking on the fingers he'd pricked to the bone while gathering the fruit. He'd
have cursed the thorns, but Crocken supposed that without them
the deer would have stripped the tree long since, and he'd have
found nothing, at winter's end. But what sort of country was it,
where apple trees grew defensive spikes?

By sun-high Crocken had walked a fair way downhill into the
Borderlands, taking his shadow with him. The grass was starting
to green, and he saw flocks of sheep, moving like clouds over
the newly green hills. The shadow made him steer well clear of
any shepherds, likewise the stone towers that crowned some of
the hills, and the gray villages that nestled in the valleys.

By nightfall, Crocken was famished enough to insist on begging at the nearest farmstead, but no human habitation was in
view. He settled down in a hollow, out of the wind, gathering a
few sticks of wood for a fire and hoping the shadow wouldn't
forbid him to light it. It had left him at nightfall, without a word.

It reappeared just as his fire kindled more normal shadows.

A wolf has killed a rabbit, just over that rise. A shadow-arm
pointed the way.

Crocken eyed it without much interest. "Nice something eats
well tonight, but what's it to me?"

Get your legs under you and fetch the rabbit.

"Take a rabbit from a wolf? I don't think so." Crocken added wood carefully to the yellow-white flames.

The wolf has gone.

Crocken stood up, as much to get peace and quiet as in the hope of a bit of food. He was light-headed with hunger—maybe he'd be able to stomach whatever the wolf had left of the rabbit. Maybe.

"Which way?"

Look for a twisted tree.

Crocken looked. The trees thereabouts *all* looked wind-twisted, but one was much worse than the rest. He walked toward it, eyes alert for the wolf. There wasn't much cover; something a wolf's size shouldn't be able to take him by surprise. Anyway, would the shadow send him straight into a wolf's belly?

It had sent him into the Arinwater. Crocken hoped the wolf was less hungry than he was.

There was a dead rabbit lying against the tree's roots. It was still slightly warm. Crocken stood with alarm, the rabbit dangling. A wolf wouldn't just abandon its prey, it must still be near . . .

Do you want the wolf to cook it for you, as well?

Maybe he could depend on the shadow to fend the wolf off. Crocken snatched up the rabbit and hastened back to the safety of his fire. He dressed the rabbit, spitted it—and ate half of it nearly raw, caring nothing for his burned fingers.

Chapter Eight

CROCKEN AND HIS shadow approached Axe-Edge along the farther bank of the Windrush, having crossed the river at a ferry well upstream, bent on avoiding the cities of Triniol and Rushgate, which sprawled on the flatter bank opposite the citadel's cliffs.

Easy to understand the stronghold's name—its fortifications crowned a hundred-foot height of cliff so sheer that its edge might have been dressed with an axe—if even a god could wield an axe so huge. The cliffs were white chalk, and the stonework of the walls above had been whitewashed—Axe-Edge could be seen by day and some nights, leagues and days off.

Which Crocken grumblingly was. No sooner did he have Axe-Edge in view than the shadow directed him to move away from it once more, into the wooded foothills that lay beyond the Windrush. He caught an occasional glimpse of white towers above the trees, but he never seemed to draw much nearer to them, no matter how long he walked.

Hardened to travel though he had become, Crocken ached deep down in his bones. He'd footed it all the way across the kingdom of Armyn, after all—out of the Borderlands, across the plains of Cordis, over hills, into and out of various river valleys before finally reaching that of the mighty Windrush. When the shadow was done with him, Crocken thought wistfully, he'd book passage on a ship heading back to Kôvelir, though he was at best an indifferent sailor and had never sought sea journeys, but avoided them like plague-houses. Even a Sheiran galley, which would carry him as far back as the Quatrain . . . the walk then from Asgeirr to Kôvelir seemed trifling.

Where he could start all over once again. Hardly an enthralling prospect to contemplate at day's ebb. Crocken's weariness colored all the world in smoky shades. Nothing seemed worth the effort it required, and Litsa crossed his thoughts more than once, as if to repay him for the many days when she'd been absent from them.

At dusk he set up his camp—warned tersely to light no fire.

We are in a royal forest, and there will be king's foresters about, ensuring the safety of the king's deer.

"If we're not allowed here, then why didn't we just follow the main road to the castle? Or shouldn't I ask?" No use his setting snares for rabbit meat he couldn't cook if he caught it. He had a handful of mushrooms that the shadow had said wouldn't harm him, and had been hoping to make a stew.

I am seeking a way into the castle.

"Out here? What was wrong with just going in the gate?" Crocken recalled the smell of new-baked bread—he'd passed a bakery when he disembarked from the ferry, but he'd had no coin for buying bread. He'd paid his ferry passage with a packet of pins. Crocken sighed.

Axe-Edge is city-sized, but it is a fortress, not a town. There isn't the free passage into it that you imagine. The King's Guards control it straitly.

"And I'm a peddler without goods to offer," Crocken frowned. "If I can get to a town on market day, maybe I could trade for something. I've got more pins, and I could string a necklace or two tonight—"

You won't gain goods worthy of royal attention.

Crocken gave the shadow an aggrieved look. "You didn't say you wanted to talk to the king—and I don't need goods a king would look at. You just said you wanted to get into Axe-Edge. Castles have garrisons, and soldiers have their women with them—at least their officers do. Women can't resist peddlers. I can get in, to trade."

I bow to your confidence.

Crocken shrugged off the sarcasm. "It's my livelihood, that's all. And the last bit of our bargain." No harm reminding the shadow that he expected to be paid—and soon.

Come morning, Crocken was half hoping they'd find no village close enough to force him to prove his boast about his trading skills. A packet of pins and three poorly matched strings of glass beads—what could he hope to turn that into? He'd have felt more sanguine about attempting to spin straw into gold, the way peasant girls did in tales. And he was out of practice.

Anyway, no isolated hamlet offered itself for the task. The land was uniformly forested and seemed to be all either uphill or downhill—Axe-Edge's rear was protected by ridges and ravines that cut the land up so drastically that no serious assault could be mounted from it. Cliffs defended its front, the rough country its rear, the shadow explained admiringly. Crocken supposed it was right, and the location was a marvel, so safe yet so handy to the waterway of the Windrush that linked the whole land for commerce—but all the ups and downs, and the windings around between extremes, left him too weary to properly appreciate military strategies, or trade opportunities.

He and his shadow were following a deer track that looked as if it saw occasional human use, as well, when the brassy blast of a huntsman's horn assaulted Crocken's ears. The call was repeated, then answered distantly. Crocken got off the trail, before he could be ordered to do so, and headed for cover. In moments he heard the belling of hounds and felt a pounding of hoofbeats through the soles of his boots, drawing nearer. He crept deeper into the underbrush, watching warily. Harness jingled, and riders called encouragement to mounts and one another.

Soon the hunt passed his hiding place. The horses were sleek, richly harnessed, and their riders finely clad from the brush-framed glimpses Crocken got. His trader's eye assessed them automatically, figuring costs of cloth and leather. A royal hunting party out of Axe-Edge, he did not doubt. Crocken kept his discreet place, then slipped farther away into the forest once the riders had safely passed him. Sunlight slanted into a small clearing. A rabbit, wary as he'd been, burst from its own cover and disappeared into the deeper undergrowth.

Crocken laughed. "I doubt they're after you, my friend. That lot never dines on lowly coney, and you're too small for sport."

They ride after gray deer, to try their pretty toy bows, the shadow said darkly. *There were ladies with them, so they will not risk a fiercer quarry—such as yon boar, which was also wise enough to take cover.*

Boar? Crocken looked across the open space in alarm. The last thing he desired was to meet one of the unpredictable wild pigs. At first he saw nothing, but finally he detected a stirring of the brush that told him the boar's location—fifty paces away but far too near for his comfort. It hadn't seen him yet, but he was not reassured. Crocken began to slip along the clearing's edge. He'd pick up the trail where he could, later—*much* later, and *much* farther away. Where nothing larger or more perilous than a rabbit rustled the bushes . . .

Hoofbeats followed him. Crocken spun open-mouthed, searching desperately for a hiding place. A golden-coated horse trotted out of the trees just as the boar stepped forth to test the air. The horse's rider had left the gaily colored leather reins loose upon her mount's dappled neck—and toppled from her saddle when the horse caught sight and scent of the boar and shied wildly away from it.

The lady landed—in a bright velvet heap—almost athwart the startled boar. The horse fled through crackling brush. The wild pig squealed, dodged clear, and swung back, already on the attack and furious, a point it punctuated with further squeals. Its tusks flashed like lightning. The girl sat up, stared, squealed more shrilly than the pig, and sank back in a faint.

Crocken dropped his pack to the ground. Yelling, he leaped out into the clearing. If he could get the beast's attention . . .

He succeeded beyond his expectations. Distracted, the boar turned from the silent girl and charged straight at the threatening-looking peddler.

Crocken hadn't taken proper account of the boar's fleetness—certainly he couldn't outrun it. Nor could he dodge back among the trees—not in time. The only weapon he carried was a knife—sharp and handy, but woefully inadequate against a monster that weighed as much as three men and ran faster than some horses.

If he couldn't run, he'd have to stand his ground. His knife, whatever its pitiful worth, was already in his hand. Crocken thrust the blade out at arm's length, dropped to one knee as the boar closed in, and braced himself hopelessly for the impact. His nerve failing, he shut his eyes.

Crocken thought fleetingly that he might have braced *too* well—his right arm nearly snapped under the impact of the boar's rush. His eyes flew open again as he was slammed helplessly backward, lifted to his feet and off of them. A tree trunk stopped him rudely, jarring his breath away. Rough hair scoured his fingers. Reeking foam spattered his face. Crocken pushed with both hands, his only coherent thought to hold the monster away.

He might as well have tried to push the tree away from his back. The knife was buried hilt-deep in the boar's body, and the little blade was evidently too short to reach any vital organ. The creature screamed and plunged, and Crocken could only fend it off, dodging the gleaming tusks lest he be sliced to ribbons. The boar's bloodshot eye, glimpsed at terrifyingly close range, fore-told that future unerringly.

What had he been thinking of? Crocken couldn't answer him-self. He was surprised he could wonder so, in such an extremity.

He was pinned fast against the tree, without hope of escape unless the boar backed away. A tusk slammed into his cheek, half cut, half blow.

Crocken pushed again, with all the force terror could lend him. His instinct was simply to hold the beast away—he used the knife blindly, only because his fingers were already wrapped around it. The boar squealed and pounded him with its cloven hooves, undeterred. He couldn't kill it—the blade could go no deeper than the cross-hilt would let it—but he must hold it away. That was the only strategy he could hold to, insist on to the point of mania.

Instead of being thrust back, the boar lost its footing and crashed down on top of Crocken, driving all his breath from his lungs. The world went dark.

When his sight came back, Crocken's hearing seemed to have deserted him. There wasn't a sound from the boar—which still lay athwart him. It was heavy as a millstone, hot as a furnace, stinking like a midden . . . but silent.

A bird called tentatively, three liquid notes. Crocken swiveled his head toward the sound, mystified. Why didn't he hear the boar panting? Why had it stopped pummeling him? It was a long while before he regained his wits sufficiently to realize that the boar did not move because it was dead.

Crocken released the knife. His hand was bloody, marked with an exact copy in relief of the knife hilt, and trembling uncontrollably. "I don't believe I did that," Crocken said hys-terically, almost laughing. "I can't believe I even *thought* of doing that!" He wasn't dead. It amazed him. He touched his chest, feeling his heart frantically pumping beneath layers of wool and skin. He wasn't dead.

His shadow was stretched an impossible length from him, extending clean across the clearing to the still-swooning girl. It inspected her richly appointed hunting costume, the silver-crusted trappings on her mount's skewed saddle and trailing reins, while the horse sidled and snorted. One device was oft-repeated.

The White Falcon.

"What's that?" Crocken had begun to struggle, trying to free himself. He couldn't budge, but at least he could feel his legs, which heartened him. Being pinned between the tree and the dead boar was uncomfortable, but sensation meant his back wasn't broken.

The shadow, unencumbered by the boar, flowed smoothly back to his side. Crocken eyed it sidelong, but with a certain relief.

"If you could just do that trick with its shadow, shift it a bit, I could crawl out," he suggested. "I'm not hurt. If you just take part of the weight off—"

The shadow's head cocked, hearkening—but not to Crocken. Hoofbeats. Harness bells chiming. Voices called.

"Gloriet! Gloriet!"

Not much time, the shadow said. The girl was stirring slightly, moaning to herself.

"You can do it before they get here!" Crocken insisted. "Just shift it a *bit*. Come on!" He put his palms flat to the ground, pushed, and thought he made some progress, but the tree still interfered.

Too golden an opportunity to let slip away.

"What?" Perhaps he could slip a little to one side and avoid the tree.

A slender shadow-hand dipped to the ground. Crocken, busy squirming, didn't notice. He was still dazed from his violent encounter, scarcely able yet to accept that he'd survived it. He was just starting to glance back at the shadow to plead again for its help when a stone, shadow-swung, slammed into the back of his skull.

Regrettable, but needful.

The shadow inspected the scene critically, as cracklings and shouts from the wood kept him informed of the hunt's progress. All was in good order—the fainting princess, the corpse of the savage boar, the injured rescuer of the royal maiden. The story was laid out plain for the royal party to read—and they could surely be expected to gather up the wounded hero and carry him back with them to their citadel. The scheme would gain the entrance to Axe-Edge that the shadow sought.

Hounds bayed, very near. The shadow slid into its proper place beneath Crocken, becoming the small crumb of his shadow that should have been visible.

Chapter Nine

THE HEALER EXPERTLY cut the stranger's clothing away, swiftly stripping off the bloody jerkin, the equally stained linen shirt beneath. Years spent tending tourney casualties had made for much practice, and cloth was in any case quicker to remove than chain mail or plate armor shattered in the lists and bent till only a smith could remove it. Her hands paused. She called for water and sponged away the clotted blood covering the man's chest. No fresh flow replaced what she removed—unsurprising, for there was no wound, not even a bad bruise.

"Not *his* blood, then," she said, clicking her tongue.

Her apprentice bent closer, slopping water from the basin he held and earning a disgusted look.

"Don't drown him, Jaikie. Likely 'tis the boar's lifeblood that soaked him."

"He's not wounded? Was he crushed, then?"

The healer's fingers had already made a professional inspection of the stranger, pressing and prodding and assuring her that the man's bones were whole—a wonder, for he looked as if a horse had fallen on him, not merely a boar. "The ribs are intact. What ails this fellow is the knock on the head he's had. Feel that?"

She raised the stranger's head just enough to pass fingers between it and the cot he lay upon. Jaikie's fingers followed dutifully, and the apprentice winced with sympathy.

"Alaron did say they thought the boar'd flung him against a tree," he recalled aloud. "He said that was where they found him, pressed between the boar and the tree. Is his skull cracked?"

"If I thought it was, neither of us would be poking at it so." Tourney injuries frequently involved such wounds, so the healer

50

had a fair amount of experience to draw upon. "Bruised, aye, but not broken. Bleeding from the ears or the nose, that's a danger sign. He's showing nothing like that. He's just been stunned. So, you'll poultice him with comfrey and willow leaves. See if he sleeps it off in a reasonable time—early yet to worry about trephining him, and time for it later if he turns out to need it. Brew up some willow-twig tea, lad. Get it down him if he starts to stir, and mind he doesn't choke on it."

Jaikie set to work, swinging the copper kettle over the fire and measuring leaves from dark pottery jars. He cut linen cloth for the poultice, folded the herbs in carefully, and waited for the kettle to boil.

"Put the candle out when you've finished," the healer instructed. "I'm off to see if our Princess Gloriet is between swoons yet—I'll send for you if I need more than wine to tend her."

"Was she hurt so badly?" Jaikie asked, aghast. He had assumed all was well with the princess—they'd said this fellow had saved her.

"She got mud on her new riding gown," the healer answered dryly. "And bruised her bottom. I feel she's capable of recovery from the mischance. She thinks she's dying. If she doesn't settle soon, I'm going to give her poppy. Her mother will put her to bed, and when she's exhausted the novelty of it, she'll be up and around again." The healer lifted the flagon of wine. The remains of the stranger's garb lay on the trestle beside it. "And get those filthy rags out of here, when you have a moment."

The door closed behind her. Jaikie returned grumbling to his tasks—reflecting eventually that he ought to be glad of being a lowly apprentice, overburdened but at least not called upon to attend a frequently hysterical princess. He gathered the bits of the woolen jerkin and the bloodied shirt, preparing for a trip to the rubbish cart. He inspected the clothing first.

No blazon of any sort, but Jaikie was certain beyond doubt that the stranger was a knight, wandering incognito through the land for some doubtless high and proper reason. Who but a knight could slay a full-grown boar with nearly his bare hands? Who but a knight would try?

The shadow had free run of nearly the entire castle—Axe-Edge's windows tended to be small for security and more often than not were shuttered to keep dangerously fresh air at bay. The shadow roamed at its pleasure among perpetual shadows, untroubled by the torch flames, which birthed more shadows than they banished.

Time meant nothing, and the shadow did not tire. A day and a night passed ere it returned to the chamber in the infirmary and hovered by Crocken.

The peddler's face was milk-white, and mostly still. Once or twice his eyelids twitched, but he was not trying to lift them. The shadow thought he might be dreaming. It could not discern whether the man had waked at all, since it had struck him.

That troubled it, unexpectedly. The shadow slipped nearer, recalling the blow it had dealt with some apprehension. It had measured the force as carefully as the situation had permitted, intending to do no more than briefly stun the peddler. This prolonged swoon was unanticipated, and worrisome. Had the blow been severe after all? Had the healer bled the man, perchance too enthusiastically, and overweakened him?

Shadow-fingers stretched out and brushed the peddler's face. Crocken's head turned slightly. The shadow saw no evidence of leeches, though the small wounds they left could have been concealed by the bandages.

The peddler stirred restively, and the shadow swiftly withdrew, to wait once more.

"I sent for you, Mole, because I ween you have inherited some measure of your mother's gifts."

The younger man stiffened, but let the old offense of the nickname pass and lifted his cup of sweet wine. He sipped carefully, for the stuff was too like syrup for his taste—and through the dream Crocken could taste the wine, though he knew the lips and gullet it touched were not his own, but another's. He watched the scene, as if 'twere a street play, but curiously partook of some of its sensations.

"I have need of some of that skill." The speaker was richly dressed, in sumptuous velvets and flashing jewels, and he had a proud, haughty face that went well with such accouterments. "I won't be ungrateful."

"Or untrustworthy, Tierce?" The young man raised a brow. "I'm certain Sarris would agree—if he were alive to do so."

The man's face flushed darkly. "Have a care, Mole. You continue to return to us, which suggests to me that you require this family connection."

"Which you will sever, if I will not help you?"

"Or make unbreakably strong, if you *will* aid me. Think upon it—no need, ever again, for you to slink back into your cursed hills because your welcome's outworn. Be fully one of us.'' The wine goblet caught the light, as he drank.

"You must want something *very* badly, Tierce. This is not the drunken whim I expected when you sent for me."

"I need your help."

"And I am relieved you don't bend so far as to call me brother. That would suggest that this need of yours is very dangerous."

Tierce glared, then quaffed more wine, relishing it. "Not such a danger as all that. I require information about my nephew—yours, as well. The queen likes not my attendance upon him, which is peevish of her—I cannot get near him, but I suspect you will have privy ways of seeking out what I wish to know."

"If I'm not what you think I am, I cannot help you." It was hard to make out his expression, for the light was behind him—an odd way to stage a play scene. Crocken realized he'd never yet seen the younger man's face clear.

"If you're not what I think you, you won't *need* to help me. But you do, bastard, and we both of us know it."

Shadows danced gavottes before Crocken's eyes—though his lids were closed. The room whirled around him—he could tell even without seeing it—and that wasn't fair, for he wasn't moving at all, or even attempting to move. He was lying quite still, yet the world spun and his head threatened to split open like an overripe melon.

The senses he had regained were fully occupied with the injustice of all that—he hadn't the wit yet to wonder where he lay, or what mischance had befallen him. Crocken had slept, wakened, and slept again, repeating the cycle several times, and it hadn't quite grown tedious yet. He could have slept again. The shadows kept disturbing him by flitting about, though, and the peddler resented them more each time he detected them, for the worst of his head pain invariably companioned them.

He reached out finally to shoo one away and discovered the wrapping about his head when his hand fell back upon it. Crocken opened his eyes, shut them tightly at once against the pain that stabbed him, and whimpered softly as he examined the linen bandages with his fingers. He wondered if the wrapping was all that held his aching skull together. He felt as if it might be.

Now you've waked, they'll give you willow tea for the pain.

Or poppy, but that would make you sleep again, and you've slept enough.

Crocken opened his eyes once more, focusing with a mighty effort. Most of the shadows merged back into the bed curtains, but one did not.

"You again?" he asked unsteadily. His mouth felt sticky when he spoke. "Where am I?" he asked, baffled by what he could see of his surroundings. Only the shadow was familiar.

Inside Axe-Edge.

"Inside?" Crocken winced at the racket of his own voice. "I don't remember—what happened? How did we get in?" He cast his mind back as best he could, but all that answered him were nasty fragments which he hoped were dreams, rather than true memories.

Courtesy your feat of heroism, the shadow replied smugly. *You slew a savage beast, a wild boar that was about to slash and trample a royal princess. You saved her life, but were injured yourself in the effort. Her attendants carried you here. Thus you are a great hero, and we are where we wished to be.*

"I killed a boar? What with?" It had to be a lie, not even a shadow of the truth.

Your knife. The shadow darkly mimed a thrust.

"My—" Crocken started to sit up, then fell back dizzily onto his pillows. "I'm not that stupid, am I? I'm still dreaming, and you aren't even here. That must be it."

I admit when I saw you attempt it, I was astonished, the shadow answered. *There wasn't time to stop you. It came out well enough, in the end.*

"Easy for you to say—" Crocken's eyes went wide. "*Now* I remember!" he said, outraged. "You *hit* me. You hit me with a *rock*, you black-hearted, scheming—"

To be precise, with the shadow of a rock. The distinction—

"It *felt* like a rock," Crocken protested. "And don't try to split hairs and switch the subject! You almost killed me—that wasn't part of our bargain."

The chance would not have waited. I had to act. And unless you wish the healer to assume you're raving, pray keep your voice down. There are some very unpleasant herbs specific for treating madness, and they won't hesitate to use them.

The shadow vanished among the bed hangings. A moment later those curtains parted.

A face appeared—doughy white, with round blue eyes and a

short cap of brown curls, topped by an even briefer cap of green wool.

"Thought I heard something," Jaikie said. "Awake, are you, sir? I'll just fetch the healer—she said she wanted to be told directly you stirred." He hesitated, one hand on the curtains. "Can I get you anything first, sir? Not wine, I fear—that's not a good idea—but a sip of water?"

Crocken, lying limp against his pillows once more, nodded slightly. Movement made him almost unbearably dizzy. His outrage didn't ease matters, but exacerbated them. His stomach lurched, and parched as he was, Crocken feared to drink the water that was offered him. He could guess how painful retching might prove to be.

The healer woman stood no nonsense over that—when she'd brewed a tisane, she put a cup of it to his lips and poured the brew down his throat without ceremony, save to support his head so he wouldn't choke. When she released him, Crocken tried miserably to orient himself once more—his eyes knew he was still lying flat, but the rest of his senses contradicted them, and he had a struggle to keep the bitter tea down. It was quite some while before he was sure he'd managed it. By and by he felt less wretched, and sipped more tea willingly, since it seemed to ease his headache.

The healer began to question him—his name, his trade, what he'd been doing in the king's forest, what he recalled about the boar. Crocken mumbled a few responses.

Don't answer! the shadow voice hissed inside his head. Crocken was surprised that it didn't pain him. The sound of his own voice still did. He tried to obey the shadow, but he wasn't sure whether he did. The bed and the questions both seemed to fade away around him, as he drifted into dreams, influenced by the potion.

The moment he laid eyes on the child, he felt a kinship that came not from his father's blood, which they shared—the child at one remove—but from some other source, less distinct. He was mightily puzzled. Long he watched, nothing allaying his suspicions, nothing quite proving them.

But he was not bidden only to watch. He needed to prove what he suspected, and that required skills beyond his own. Skills, haply, that he could obtain, but it would require also a bit of substance . . .

A finger would have been best, or a foreskin, but that was out of the present question. He would have to settle for a lock of the child's golden hair.

"Loose in his wits, mayhap," the healer judged. She had wanted to learn what she could ere the stranger recovered enough to think of guarding himself, but he had frustrated her efforts, being too dazed and confused to divulge much of anything. Her apprentice discounted everything the man had told them—save perhaps his name.

"He can't *be* a peddler—a churl would have run from the mere thought of a boar, not slain one so bravely! But why should he think himself a peddler, of all things?"

"Recall Lord Lambert." The healer cleared away pots and jars of dried herbs, putting her workroom in order. "Unhorsed at the Midyear Tourney, landed on his head so hard I had to have a smith cut the helm off him. *He* woke with the notion he was a hunting dog. Spent the next month barking and searching out scraps among the floor rushes. This Crocken may recall himself when he's been recovered for a longer space."

"What are you doing there?"

The man—his back was all Crocken could see, in the dream— let the silver shears fall out of sight and lied calmly. "The child had a twig caught in his hair."

The queen took a step closer, fear washing over her face as she recognized him—he saw it. Fear well beyond that a mother might know at seeing a stranger with a blade close to her son— a different sort of fear.

"Andrayne, bring him here," she commanded. *"Now."*

He did not wait to be handled by the guards. Turning, he fled for his life. He dared not allow them to see him shift, but the instant he had a corner between himself and his pursuit he was a raven, flying low and fast. There was a door opening onto other gardens, and he swerved wildly through the air, making for it.

Too late he saw the ornamental grille that closed the passage while admitting light and air, a tracery of cold iron thorns. He struck it with great force, and had it been fragile woven wicker he would perhaps still have been hurt. Iron, though—its icy bane flung him out of raven form, hurled him into a deep, dark chasm from which he could not rise, not before Andrayne's men caught up to him.

They dragged him to his feet, dazed, and took him back to

the queen. His ears still rang from his fall, but he heard what she ordered done with him, fainting away again only when the iron chains touched his flesh. . . .

Crocken sat bolt upright, his heart pounding till he feared it would burst asunder. The terror gripped him for endless moments, before he could realize he had been dreaming, before he could be certain that he was still safe in his bed.

Such a dream! Mostly Crocken dreamed the same muddles folk ordinarily do, then swiftly forgot them when day dawned. The only dreams that had ever troubled him were of roads—roads between towns, roads that he walked and walked and walked without ever arriving at his destination. Or he might arrive well enough, but not in the place he'd been making for—he'd find himself in another place entirely and have to set off once more, endlessly, till dawn. His life lately imitated his dreams, Crocken realized bitterly.

Those dreams, however bothersome, were nowhere near so vivid as the one that had just assaulted him. And though as full of impossible fantasies as all dreams are—men turning into birds and back again—it had seemed *real*, almost like a memory. A memory of something that had never happened. How could that be?

Crocken's heartbeat steadied, but his head still pounded to the frantic rhythm. He touched the linen bandage fretfully. Small wonder such dreams plagued him, after a clout like that—the true wonder was that he had any wits left, not that they were disordered when he slept. He couldn't tell whether a particular shadow was among the others in the room, but he cast an ill wish at it anyway, then lay back to try to sleep till daylight.

Chapter Ten

OVER THE COURSE of his recovery, Crocken found to his wonderment that he had become a popular curiosity. The princess' ladies came to inquire after his health and lingered to stare discreetly at him, giggling behind their hands. They were fair of face and prettily dressed, and betimes one or another was permitted to play upon a lute for him, in hope that sweet music would speed his convalescence.

Crocken was an intriguing mystery to them. The healer's apprentice had spoken his mind freely to all he met, and the ladies were easily convinced that the "peddler" was in actual fact an exiled king—or at least a renowned knight who'd been robbed of his memory by his accident. Crocken was most tenderly treated for a very pleasant fortnight.

"Perhaps if he were to do the things a gentleman does, 'twould remind him that he's not a peddler," the ladies suggested when lute-playing palled. "Hawking, hunting, jousting—"

The healer looked aghast. "Nothing so violent, I pray you! He should not risk a further injury. Try the man at minstrelry, if you must—better still, get out of my infirmary and let him be! The man will recall himself in good time, unless you lot fret him into a fever first."

The shadow rejoined him just as a particularly lissome maid was departing—planting a chaste kiss upon Crocken's recently unbound brow as he sat in a chair beside his bed. Crocken tilted his head back against the chair's tall frame and sighed.

I see you have come to appreciate the advantages of my scheme.

Crocken turned on the shadow with narrowed eyes. "I might have—if you'd let *me* in on it before you launched it."

The blow would have been no softer if you'd expected it, peddler, the shadow offered soothingly. *Perhaps the reverse.*

"You wouldn't have needed to hit me! I could have gone along with your scheme."

Not half so convincingly. Could you have shammed well enough to dupe the prince's own healer?

"So you saved me the trouble by cracking my skull?" Crocken asked affrontedly.

I was careful of that, the shadow whispered, a trace of annoyance creeping into the reasonable tone. *And you needn't complain of your treatment here. You're a hero—far better, you're a romantic mystery who has charmingly mislaid his memory. Being better treated than any lapdog in the court ought to be worth a trifling headache.*

"You wouldn't think so if it was *your* head," Crocken muttered. Still . . . he could find no fault with being soothed and cosseted. The more he recovered, the more pleasing such attentions would be. He fingered the smooth worsted of the coverlet and remembered that a featherbed was softer for sleeping than bare ground. Warmer, too.

"I never said I'd lost my memory, though," he pointed out. "For instance, I perfectly recall that you owe me forty marks of gold. What about that?"

I am working on it.

"Working on it? You promised me—"

I have not forgotten you, peddler. I have been . . . occupied.

"I'll bet you have." Crocken shut his eyes, wishing that when he opened them the thing would be gone, permanently, gold or no gold. He suspected there would be no gold for him anyway, somehow. His ill fate would prevent it. His head ached fit to burst, and he could force himself to hold onto his temper only because he suspected anger—however justified—would simply make him feel worse.

I had need to discover how matters stood here—it has been some while since I was within Axe-Edge—or Armyn. Much has changed. You have had many questions. I can answer them now.

Crocken wanted very much to retort that he no longer cared. He parted his lips—but did not speak. Somehow, he couldn't do it. He opened one eye.

I'll tell you of Armyn, the shadow whispered.

The telling took a long while—it proved to be a confusing tangle of conquests and family squabbles, usurpations and minority reigns. The shadow didn't even trouble to put names to most of the early bits—Crocken supposed it wouldn't have helped him anyway. His jaws ached with the yawns he'd held back.

Armyn had been at odds with Sheir for generation upon generation, and often at war, as well. Her kings had intermarried with the Sheiran nobility, sometimes right into the very throne line itself, if the wars had been going well for Armyn at that point. The Kings of Armyn had laid claim to the Sheiran throne more than once, and had arranged marriages to buttress their hopes. Currently there appeared to be peace, and Crocken wondered how that had come to pass, till the shadow went on to describe the decay of Armyn's leadership. He supposed a similar fate must have befallen Sheir—he'd heard rumors of that, in Kôvelir—else they'd have pressed their advantage and gathered Armyn into their empire. Crocken wiggled to ease his aching back, which hurt even though he was lying on pillows and a feather tick, having given up his chair for the bed. The shadow was detailing yet another minority reign, which seemed to be an especial curse visited upon Armyn by fate.

When the king came of age, he proved to be a touch simpleminded. So he was deposed—by his cousin, who came out of the Borderlands saying he only wished to claim his rightful place as throne heir and govern the land while the king could not. That sat poorly with the young king's queen, who was Sheiran nobility and aimed to hold her rights—and those of the little son she bore to her lord. She'd let no Borderlord claim his place. She led troops to battle herself, and used Armyn's gold to buy mercenaries, which she loosed upon the Borderlands. Hate was strong in the whispery voice. As if 'twas something the shadow personally remembered, Crocken thought.

Civil war is ever the curse of this land. No man knew for certain which side had the right—successions and inheritance tend to become confused with the passing of years, and finally even the lawyers could not agree upon it. The Great Council backed whichever side had an army nearest, and Rushgate changed her allegiance a dozen times in as many years.

The witling king was captured, then rescued. He was mad. He was judged sane again, by a miracle. The queen fled to Sheir, then returned with more troops. It dragged on for years. The king's cousin was slain by treachery, and that could have been an end to it, if a bitter one—but he left three sons to carry on the fight: Ruane, Tierce—and Rhisiart.

Rhisiart, who betrayed me. The name echoed in Crocken's memory, as if branded thereupon.

They were called the House of the Falcon, after the device their father bore and bequeathed to them. Ruane was a crafty general for all he was young—and lucky in his brothers, as no other king of Armyn had lately been. Rhisiart led cavalry when he'd scarce seen fifteen Borderlands winters pass, and Tierce was battle-seasoned early on. The White Falcon was victorious over and over. Ruane took the throne, then had the deposed king executed to be sure of keeping it. The mad king's heir had been killed in one rout of a battle, his queen had died in prison, mad by then with grief.

Crocken began to notice shadows shifting over the bed curtains. They flickered like dark flames, gone if he gazed too closely at them, telling him much more if he let them dance at the tail of his sight, barely visible. Shadows of armies moving, banners flying, battlements rearing—illustrations of the shadow's tale.

Ruane had a powerful kinsman—Sarris the Bear, Lord of Castlerigg. Sarris did much for Ruane's father, and for Ruane—so much that some named him kingmaker. Sarris relished the title and the fame of having been the power that put Ruane on his throne. He expected to be a power in Ruane's court, as well. He'd given Ruane the victory, and his influence should have been without equal.

An arrogant shape strode across the bed hangings. The other shades seemed to bow before it.

Matters failed to go as Sarris anticipated. Ruane was strong of will, not easily bidden save when he chose to be thought so. Sarris set himself to the work of arranging a marriage for his king. He found a Sheiran heiress of imperial blood—not in the throne line, but near to it. He labored long at the emperor's court, fixing the bride price, and he was proud of his skill as a negotiator, as he was proud in all things. He made a good match for his king, one that would redound greatly to his credit.

Sarris then returned to Axe-Edge in triumph—only to discover that in his absence Ruane had secretly wed with an impoverished widow, Sulien. The new queen was as fair as the moon and already round-bellied with a royal child when Ruane confessed the marriage to the Great Council. Sarris looked to deliver the good news of the Sheiran match—and instead saw himself humiliated before the Council, the Sheiran emperor, and all the world that mattered.

The curtain shadows were like consuming flames.

Maybe 'twas overmastering love made the match—or spell-craft, as some accused. Perchance Ruane wanted to rein in an overmighty vassal, so there could be no question as to who ruled in Armyn, king or kingmaker. Whatever had chanced, Sarris was wroth past healing. His choler grew as he learned how vast a family Ruane's new queen did have—father, mother, a pair of brothers, a quintet of sisters, cousins past numbering—all of them poor as hedge-pigs and needing lands, gifts, rich marriages, and titles: honors that the kingmaker had thought to claim for himself and his.

Life does confound expectations, Crocken mused.

Disappointment turned Sarris' soul black. He rebelled—and he took the king's brother Tierce with him, and wed him to his own daughter to keep him loyal. Tierce was yet his brother's heir, for the fertile queen bore only daughters. Six, she'd had, like beads on a string, when Sarris rode against Ruane. It was said she'd bear no son.

Yet at last she did so, and Sarris' rebellion faltered as the tidings spread. The kingmaker was slain in a battle he should have known better than to fight, and Tierce was besought to rejoin his brothers—and did, though he had to break faith with Sarris to do it. And there were those blamed him for breaking that faith.

Shadow armies were moving, shoving one another forward and back, striking one another down. Cavalry wheeled, spears thrust, and swords rose and fell.

Rhisiart had been loyal, and fought often and hard for Ruane. For his reward, he claimed Cailin, the kingmaker's younger daughter and co-heiress to her sister. There was trouble over that—Tierce not being eager to share his wife's inheritance. So long as Cailin remained unwed, he could control it all, as her brother-in-law and protector. He opposed Rhisiart's suit bitterly. In light of his perfidy and Rhisiart's conspicuous faithfulness, Tierce's position was less than secure, so the matter was patched over, and Rhisiart took Cailin to wife—but Tierce was a trouble to Ruane from that day onward.

Tierce's name tugged at Crocken's memory. He'd heard it before, surely—heard it on someone's lips, he thought. It remained stubbornly out of his reach, and he let it go, to continue following the shadow's narrative.

Tierce was jealous of his dignity, and far too fond of his wine. Sarris' arguments for rebellion had found fertile soil in his heart.

No reward of land or title was sufficient to content him, and he hated Sulien and all her tribe of relations. Whatever Ruane gave to one of them, Tierce now saw as taken from himself. After his wife died trying to give him an heir, Tierce became . . . rash. He never was one to hold his tongue; now he ceased to try. There were many quarrels and incidents Ruane could not overlook. Tierce was charged with treason and sentenced to die. He escaped, but was drowned trying to flee to Sheir.

"What of Rhisiart?" Crocken asked, caught up in the tale despite himself. He'd forgotten his headache. "And Ruane?"

This I heard, the shadow sneered. *Rhisiart had pleaded for his brother's life most urgently, and when that cause was seen as lost, he retired to Castlerigg, to his wife and his little son. He served his king from afar, not setting foot in Axe-Edge again, or stirring from the Borderlands.*

*As for Ruane, he died all unexpectedly, aged but forty years. The king named Rhisiart steward-protector of his crown and his son, but Rhisiart had to fight for his rights—Queen Sulien would liefer control her son and the government with her own greedy hands, lest a few crumbs of gold or prestige go to another. There was blood shed—the queen's relatives'—*the shadow's tone was gleeful, almost—*but a truce was struck.*

Rhisiart upheld his nephew's rights and governed Armyn in Kieron's name. Now the prince Kieron is nearly of age, ready to ascend to his throne. When he does, Rhisiart loses all the power he has held.

Rhisiart, who betrayed me. The words hung in the very air, like letters of fire. Crocken was uncertain whether he heard with his ears or his memory.

That, peddler, is Armyn. Rest now. The healer is putting you out tomorrow—and the queen has requested a sight of you.

"The queen?" Prior, the shadow's tale had been but a pleasant bedtime fable, a trifle bloody, but with no immediacy and no danger. Crocken was chilled to his bones at the sudden shift, and despite the shadow's admonition, it was long ere he slept. And he could not say whether the shadow remained, silent and invisible against the bed hangings, or left him to brood elsewhere.

A dream came. Voices, heard as through a fog, their speakers invisible to Crocken.

"He has tried to harm the prince, sister. Let the king deal with him."

"No! Andrayne, we cannot trust to that. What if Ruane should prove unwilling to prison a second brother? The king's justice is too perilous. Lock this sorceror away where he cannot harm us."

"Suppose someone looks for him?"

"He was ever solitary," the woman's voice mused. "It is unlikely anyone will inquire. If they should—we shall simply appear baffled. 'Tis not as if he commonly kept company with us."

"You cannot keep him prisoned forever."

"Why not? And we do not need forever, Andrayne. Only a little while, till Tierce is disposed of."

Chapter Eleven

A PAGE BROUGHT a suit of clothes to the sickroom for Crocken—not his own things, which had vanished, but dark trews and a short woolen jacket, Armyn-fashion, both brown as nutshells. The linen shirt, the low boots, and the velvet cap that completed the ensemble presented Crocken with no quandaries, but he puzzled long over a final item. It appeared to be a striped blanket, woven in umbers and mauves. The proportions were not quite right for a cloak, and there were neither clasps nor thongs to fasten it. Crocken turned the cloth about, remaining unenlightened. There were over two running yards of it, enough to drag the ground on a far taller man than he.

Jaikie took the cloth from him, smiling at his consternation.

"The beltran drapes so," he said helpfully, pleating the cloth skillfully and swiftly, tucking one end under Crocken's belt in front, arranging the rest to hang over Crocken's left shoulder, from which point it fell straight to his heels. "Unless you're out in the weather, and want to wear it as a cloak. There ought to be a pin—"

There was, it turned out—a plain circle of silver, which had hidden itself amongst the folds.

"Had you family here, the arrangement and color of the stripes would mark you as one of them," Jaikie said, fussing with the folds and the pin, slipping one through to secure the other. "*These* colors tell folk you're a stranger and a guest here—not to be ill-treated, or expected to be overfamiliar with our customs."

Crocken found that information comforting. Otherwise, the prospect of the remainder of his day daunted him utterly. He sensed the shadow happily altering its shape to accommodate his new clothing.

65

"There." The healer's apprentice gave the striped cloth a final, unnecessary tug. "Quite proper. Here's your knife—you'll want it at table, though mayhap roast piglet will be tame meat for it, after it's dined on boar."

Jaikie was plainly hoping to draw out a few juicy reminiscences, but Crocken was too apprehensive to oblige, beyond a twitch of his dry lips to acknowledge the jest.

"Take care then, sir." Jaikie covered his disappointment with professional dispatch. "Send someone to me if you want more of the willow tea—the headache may still return for a time."

A useful thing to bear in mind, should he require a timely escape, Crocken thought anxiously as he followed a queen's page through a bewildering succession of corridors and galleries. He'd lost his bearings within the first hundred paces they'd traveled, but supposed the shadow knew the way well enough. It had certainly had ample hours to range Axe-Edge at its pleasure, while he'd been lying abed. It ought to know every inch of the citadel.

The shadow was holding its peace just then—perchance so that Crocken would not thoughtlessly address it aloud in the page's hearing. Being a romantic mystery could be useful to them; being considered a madman who spoke to thin air might not be, Crocken reckoned.

The sensation of the beltran covering his left side and bumping at his heels took a bit of getting used to. It felt very different from a cloak. Still, the unfamiliar garment did not actually hamper movement, and the close-woven wool was warm—greater comfort than the other thing that dogged Crocken's steps. He had worried that the cloth might slip about, but it did not, so long as he resisted fussing with it, and the shadow did not annoy him with unanswerable comments, either.

Crocken noted how the shadow danced about him as he followed his guide. Sometimes it trailed behind him. It would gradually shorten, and shift till it was beside him. Of a sudden it would dart ahead, leading him on, its feet tugging almost perceptibly at his boots. Now it was on his right hand—now on his left. Never was it quite still. Never was it in the wrong place, but behaved always as if the wall-mounted torches and the sunspill from narrow windows truly cast it. Watch it as diligently as he might, Crocken never caught it in an error.

They arrived. Crocken's guide announced him formally to a gentleman usher, who departed to pass the information on. Liveried men opened carved and gilded doors before Crocken as he was conveyed through a succession of antechambers. The royal rooms were thronged with chattering folk who glanced his way with keen interest and buzzed even louder at his back when he'd passed them. Crocken felt his ears reddening and kept his eyes fixed upon the back of the man before him, praying that his good luck with the beltran held.

The final room seemed made all of gold, flashing between the dancing shadows and the many warm candleflames. It gleamed from tapestries on the walls, from the candlesticks, from gilt paint embellishments on the fine wood furnishings, from clothing and jewels—and most of all from the hair of the queen and five of her royal daughters who'd ranged themselves on both sides of her. Overawed, Crocken had no difficulty in managing a most reverent bow, though the injudicious movement made his head whirl unpleasantly.

Aveline, Jocilyn, Brandys, Seralen, and Cathlin. Which might be which, Crocken had no notion. He was still dizzy, dazzled, hardly able to focus on the problem, and they fussed about him like a gilded flock of sparrows, the five girls speaking all at once, changing their positions continually. The princesses' heights differed slightly, and their gowns, but their faces were all the same—small copies of their mother's. Her, Crocken had no least difficulty in distinguishing.

Sulien the dowager queen had features fair as ice, save for the carmine bow of her flawlessly painted mouth. Arched brows were drawn high above her heavy-lidded sapphire eyes, and her long neck inevitably recalled swans' to the minstrels who'd long and often celebrated her—and certainly to a peddler tossed far above his station by fate and a shadow's machinations. Small wonder the late king had wanted her more than a high-born Sheiran, Crocken thought—even at risk of his kingdom. She'd have been a rare prize yet more penniless than the shadow said she'd been, even if her greedy family had been thrice the size the shadow reported.

Parting those scarlet lips, the queen inquired politely whether Crocken was recovering his health. Crocken was inspired to reply that he could do no other, having had such excellent care lavished upon him. He asked after the Princess Gloriet—a furtive numbering of the blond heads having assured him that she was likely not in the room with her sisters.

Alas, the queen replied sweetly, the Princess Gloriet's humors were still gravely disturbed by her mishap, and she was expected to remain abed for some while. Crocken thought he heard the shadow offer a derisive snort, but he did not respond to it, expressing proper sympathy instead.

The queen extended a graceful white hand to the gentleman who stood beside her gilt chair. "This is our dear brother—Andrayne, Lord Stiles."

Crocken made another bow—more carefully—while something nagged just outside his memory's short reach. Something about the brother's name. He was certain he'd heard it before—but where?

Lord Stiles' face was quite unfamiliar, save that he resembled his sister a trifle. He was her elder, however, and carried his years less lightly—also he did not paint his face as Sulien did. He was as fair as she, but his blue eyes had a faded look and seemed sunken by reason of the puffy flesh that surrounded them. There were deep lines at the corners of Stiles' mouth, and his plump cheeks were more hectic than rosy. Wine, Crocken suspected, seeing proof in the red blotches of broken blood vessels. His golden hair was more silver-gilt where it showed beneath the velvet cap.

Once a warrior and a poet, Andrayne, the shadow whispered in Crocken's head. *What are you now?*

Crocken strove to keep his expression neutral. He *had* heard the name ere this, and lately. One of his dreams? He wished he could recall those in greater detail—bloody as they tended to be. Could they tell him truths? Or were they only dreams . . . the shadows of waking life?

Lord Stiles wore a jacket of purple velvet, a royal hue that did not quite suit his complexion. His beltran looked to be silk and was of an exquisite drape—Crocken, seeing it, felt as if he had a bundle of unwashed wool bunched clumsily over his own shoulder and shifted unhappily. He noted the colors—magentas and blues, the stripings intricate. Did their pattern really inform the initiated?

The princesses, who still flocked around and chirped becomingly, if inconsequentially, wore no beltrans, but rather high-bodiced gowns with tight sleeves and flowing silken skirts that hid their feet, save for a jeweled shoe toe or two. Some of the other ladies—there were many blondes, which Crocken guessed for aunts and cousins by their features—wore similar gowns, while still others were garbed in close-fitted jackets over full skirts striped in the same manner as the beltrans. So ladies—at least well-born ones—wore their family colors, also, betimes. A thing to set in the memory, in case it later might prove useful.

Crocken noted it carefully. He had no notion what the shadow might choose to tax him with later, but expected anything.

The golden portals unclosed again, and another glittering figure made an entrance—a young man beltraned in dawn-color stripes of purpure, gold, orange, and sanguine. He strode forward, took the queen's hand, and kissed it.

"My son, the Prince Kieron," the queen announced, a radiant smile such as she had not graced her daughters' introductions with lighting her features.

Crocken bowed again, resigned to more dizziness. This was, after all, the King of Armyn, though uncrowned yet, and he must show proper manners. Still, he wondered how many more bows he might withstand, ere the dizziness overwhelmed him, and he fervently hoped he'd be victim to no further introductions.

The prince wore a brooch of diamants at his throat, holding in check the bright drape of his beltran. His eyes were just as colorless as the gems, and likewise hard and glittering was his gaze. His features were tiny, like his mother's, and his hair was rosy golden, curling a trifle.

Crocken heard a hiss, which he realized must have come from his shadow. He wished it would control itself and leave off startling him so. His heart raced enough as 'twas.

"Our sister's rescuer—we must do you all honor, sir."

What that honor was to consist of, no one said, and Kieron honored him with no further conversation. Crocken was in the next few moments presented to several of the queen's sisters— more golden heads, but nowhere near so fair of feature—and then to Kieron's promised bride.

His gaze had overpassed her, on earlier cautious roves about the room, for she sat at the rear of the chamber, stitching busily at some needlework by the light spilling from a many-branched candlestick. Once she was pointed out to him, Crocken couldn't believe he'd missed her—even blind and deaf, he'd surely have been aware of her. Her hair was red-gold, not moonbeam pale like that of Sulien's daughters, and she was exquisite—she might have wept pearls in place of tears, or stepped just as she was out of a tapestry of idealized Beauty. Crocken, gazing on her hair, regretted his fox pelt, lost to the Arinwater. What a perfect gift it would have made!

The princess' eyes were topaz, dark-lashed under honey-colored brows. Her features were those every minstrel sang of, and gifted on the less deserving, while the skin over them was smooth and soft as a ripe peach—the very effect Queen Sulien sought and failed to duplicate.

"Mirell, Princess of Calandra," Kieron observed coolly, and the lady turned a look upon him that should have melted him like a tallow dip in midsummer's heat—Crocken knew *he* would not have been unmoved if such a look had befallen him. He'd have died happily at her feet, without drawing another breath. Even seeing her look so at another, his heart stirred within his breast as it had seldom done in all his life.

The princess smiled, but spoke no word. Not to him, not to Kieron. *What's this?* Crocken wondered. *Maidenly modesty, carried to extremes?*

Another girl took half a step forward, from her place behind the princess' chair.

"Ah, Mistress Ivy," the prince gestured. "Explain matters to our guest." Self-released from any further obligation, Kieron turned away.

The girl he had indicated inclined her dark head graciously to Crocken, and her green eyes sparkled. "My lady has taken a vow," she began. "She will not speak—save to me, in private— until she has finished the bridal shirt she stitches to honor her pledged lord."

The shirt so mentioned lay across the princess' silken lap. Its folds were white as new-fallen snow—proper for a bride-groom, Crocken supposed. It looked perfectly complete to his casual glance, but he saw that the golden needle still flashed to and fro upon it, industriously, while Mirell listened to herself being discussed. All the parts of a proper shirt were there— body, sleeves, collar, and buttons—but now the princess was busily embellishing the icy damask with a tracery of stitched vines—blackberries, Crocken thought. It looked to him as if each and every leaf and berry was to be fully represented, in white thread on the white cloth, intricate as frost on a window-pane. The shadow bent close to the garment, and Crocken was terrified someone would notice, but he knew no way to order it to draw back. He leaned as close as he thought he politely could, to cover for his master.

"My lady will wish for me to convey to you her regards—and her sincere thanks that you saved one of her sisters-to-be from a most dreadful fate," Mistress Ivy said.

Crocken bowed once again, which put him in good position to study the stitchery more closely—as well as masking the shadow's behavior the more. There were *thorns* on the berry vines, impossibly tiny. That, as much as his recent injury, made his senses tend to reel.

Most interesting, the shadow commented.

It looked to be a project that could occupy a single needle-woman for her whole lifetime. And she'd vowed not to speak till it was completed? Surely they'd wed her to the prince when he was crowned—an event not many months away. It seemed she'd still be mute, by her own choice.

Crocken decided that to stare longer might be a breach of protocol, no matter what the shadow thought about it. He made a few empty and polite remarks to Mistress Ivy and her lady, then withdrew to the fringes of the room. He hadn't actually been dismissed, but no one was paying him much attention. Yet unless the shadow suggested something to him, he had no notion how he ought to take his leave. Or, for that matter, where he'd go when he did take it. The nine-days-wonder glow seemed to have deserted him—no one bothered to speak to him, or even ask questions.

Bide here awhile, peddler. I wish to observe.

Well, that took care of the question of leaving, at least for the nonce. Crocken resigned himself to it, accepted a cup of sweet wine from a servant's tray, and listened to snatches of conversation to pass the time.

The narrow windows of the queen's apartments had been closely shuttered and heavily swaddled with dark tapestries, lest the bright sun should add blemishing color to Sulien's moon-pale skin, or some too-fresh breeze bring a chill to that swanlike throat. There were rushlights and candles by the score—royalty could afford such costliness—and perfumes were burned to sweeten the stagnant air. Musicians took the place of songbirds.

Crocken soon forgot that what little he had glimpsed of the day had been fair, its air mild with a promise of summer soon to arrive. Summer, after all, was an outdoor pleasure and far more common than Sulien's rarified beauty. He found himself reluctant to tear his gaze from the dais where she sat in solitary state—though the queen plainly had dismissed him from her thoughts almost instantly upon having received him. A lute was plinking sweetly, and a gaily dressed courtier had begun presenting Sulien with an epic of many verses that he recited in a treble voice that was surely an affectation. Lapdogs ran about, yapping for treats. One of the princesses had a monkey on a leash, which tormented the dogs.

Idling about at the edge of the crowd of sycophants left

Crocken feeling awkward, but the self-conscious pain was surely a small price to exchange for gazing upon Sulien, even from afar. Then there were the princesses, those paler and poorer copies of the incandescent original, but with sometimes a kind glance in Crocken's direction. He tried to fix the faces with names, but 'twas hopeless—he had no frame of reference from which to begin the task. Crocken was not even wholly certain which of the fair flock were princesses, given the large number of cousins and other relations, all garbed with an equal richness. With no friendly guide to inform him, such amusements tended toward uselessness, and the shadow wouldn't have helped even if he'd been able to question it in public.

There came a tentative tugging upon his jacket sleeve. Crocken glanced down, hoping absurdly for a small pointed face, silver-gilt hair. Alas, brown hair and common blue eyes, features nondescript though well scrubbed. And a boy, anyhow. Well, what would he have offered a princess, in conversation? Crocken thought the boy might be the page who'd brought his clothes to him, but could not be certain. Already the morn seemed a lifetime ago. He realized suddenly how weary he was.

"My lord merchant—"

The lute was lustily strummed to counterpoint a verse. There was polite applause. Crocken had to lean close to catch the child's words, and still he missed one in three.

"—the steward-protector. If you'll follow?"

Crocken's heart hammered his ribs. What was this? Had he committed some breach, erred in some protocol?

Then the steward-protector would have sent men-at-arms to fetch you, not a page boy. Follow him, the shadow instructed.

At least he needn't fear the shadow's ordering him to remain while the steward-protector demanded that he go. There was that to be grateful for. Crocken swallowed hard, then indicated to the page that he was ready to depart.

They slipped unremarked through the golden door hangings and began the complex traverse of antechambers, corridors, galleries, and staircases once more. Crocken was just as baffled by the castle's complexities as he had been on the previous trek, and this time he was footsore as well. Surely they were faring the entire length of Axe-Edge—if not circumnavigating it. His beltran and his shadow trailed after him tirelessly, but his feet were stumbling and his breathing was rapid.

Through yet another hall, up a very short flight of stairs, footworn deeply at the centers of the treads. Then the page opened one half of a pair of tall doors and motioned Crocken to pass through.

Crocken found himself a pace inside a well-appointed chamber, as the doors closed softly at his back. An oriole window to one side lit the space tolerably well—after the queen's rooms, the ordinary sunlight seemed almost intense. There was a table set by the window, and a clerk was seated behind it, scribbling away at a parchment, his beltran looped over his arm and out of his way.

Crocken glanced about. No sign of another soul. After Sulien's rooms the bright quiet was a restful contrast, but his heart misgave him. Save for the scratching of the clerk's quill, there wasn't a sound.

Nor did his own soft boots break the near-complete silence, as Crocken diffidently ventured deeper into the room. The floor was tiled, unlittered by any rushes, clean or otherwise. The clerk didn't glance up when Crocken halted beside him, and might have been unaware of a visitor, so engrossed was he in the letters he was rapidly forming.

"I was . . . invited . . . to wait upon the steward-protector," Crocken said finally, feeling foolish.

The clerk at last raised his head. Crocken was expecting to be informed that he'd been abandoned in the wrong part of the castle by his guide, or that Rhisiart had changed his mind and ordered him sent straight to the dungeons.

"I'm Rhisiart," the clerk said.

Rhisiart, who betrayed me, the shadow amended helpfully, as if Crocken might have forgotten how the litany ran.

Chapter Twelve

RHISIART'S ELDER BROTHER Ruane had been reckoned handsome by all accounts—the late king must have shared his son's spectacular coloring, Crocken thought. Perchance any younger brother would have seemed plain in comparison, a sparrow hard by a peacock, and thus disparaged. Rhisiart had a plain face, ordinary and unremarkable, save that all its bones were starkly visible under his pale skin.

No, say not a humble sparrow, but a hawk—a dull-plumaged bird nonetheless deadly at its task. Interest animated Rhisiart's thin face, kindled his dark blue eyes, and Crocken was certain in that moment that the steward-protector could see his very bones if he chose, could apprehend any deceit without the least effort, however closely concealed the lie. He was unnerved, as he had not been by all the queen's pomp and magnificence, as he had not been by her son's easy arrogance.

". . . express my personal gratitude," Rhisiart was saying. Crocken had missed all the rest. "My duty to her as Protector of Armyn aside, Gloriet is my niece—though there are five others besides her, and she's easily the worst horsewoman of the lot." Rhisiart smiled, and Crocken realized that the last part of his remark was meant for a jest, though it was certainly true in substance. He was heartened a trifle, but his stomach was still knotted with tension, and he was keenly aware of the shadow, stretched flat across the tiles behind him but flickering with anger like a licking flame that wanted to escape the safety of the hearth.

"The Princess Gloriet is recovering from her ordeal?" Crocken asked.

"So I am informed," the steward-protector said. "Until the next time—she's in some peril each time she mounts that pony.

The child has no control of it, and feeding the beast sweetmeats and braiding its mane to a fare-thee-well doesn't alter the case," Rhisiart amended seriously. "Armyn is fortunate indeed that you were at hand."

Crocken inclined his head politely. He instantly wished he could remember how painful such motions still were—*before* he'd committed to them.

"I thought it best to receive you . . . less than formally," Rhisiart was saying, gesturing apologetically at the empty chamber. "Our healer advises me your recovery will be hastened if you aren't subjected to undue excitement. Be sure your brave deed merits a full court reception—and blame my own curiosity, that I could not put off speaking with you till you were well enough to be entertained as is proper here." Rhisiart's smile was an unexpected lightening of his serious features. "Will you sit, Master Merchant?"

"My lord." Crocken bowed slightly again, then wondered if he ought to stagger as he straightened, before he took the chair Rhisiart was courteously offering. It would be easy enough— actually it was harder *not* to waver by then, and he might find an advantage in pleading illness, if Rhisiart planned to ask him difficult questions. After all, he *was* lately risen from a sickbed and had taken a nasty injury. Surely no one would question him if he feigned infirmity.

Don't overdo it, the shadow voice ordered sharply into his head. *If he finds you're shamming, he'll ask you harder questions than you'll ever care to answer.*

With a startled blink, Crocken sat.

"So." Rhisiart seemed to be striving to put him at his ease. He began to play with his writing quill, as he looked Crocken over. "I trust you have been well looked after, Master Merchant?"

"Incredibly well, my lord," Crocken responded eagerly. "Nursed, fed, clothed, entertained. Even granted an audience with the queen—"

Rhisiart frowned. Crocken wondered where he'd misstepped, and fell awkwardly silent.

"She would interest herself in you, of course." Rhisiart tapped at the tabletop with the quill. "Your pardon—I'd no idea, when I took the notion to send after you, that you'd already been subjected to Sulien's welcome. If you are fatigued now, we could speak at another time."

"I'd only be weary if I'd insisted on memorizing all of the

princesses' names, my lord. Since I gave that up very early on, I'm well enough now.'' Crocken wasn't certain whether he ought to have seized the chance to escape the room and the interview— and the shadow did not direct him, though he remained keenly aware of it, puddled by his chair. It seemed to be watching Rhisiart, though watching for what, Crocken could not imagine.

''Aye, my brother did have a mort of daughters,'' Rhisiart agreed pleasantly. ''Ornaments to the court, but difficult for a stranger to distinguish between. I used to have trouble myself.''

''They're very much alike,'' Crocken expanded, feeling foolish.

Rhisiart offered him an orange, from a silver basket at the end of the table. Crocken accepted, wondering silently what price oranges brought in Armyn. In Kôvelir the fruit was common, thanks to magic-assisted orangeries, but he doubted such could be the case in Armyn. They might need to bring the fruit in from the far reaches of the Sheiran Empire, which could only boost the cost. Fragrant oils in the peelings mingled with the breeze drifting through the tall windows. Crocken remarked on the pleasantness of the air and the light.

Rhisiart seemed disproportionately delighted at his notice. ''My brother Ruane's craftsmen installed this oriole at his command, and I favor the new style of glazing myself—I have incorporated such into those of my border keeps as can bear them.'' He gestured at the gray walls. ''These ancient stones are laid so thick, the rooms are dank and chill even at Midsummer, and fires must be kept burning day and night. 'Tis unhealthy—and dark! The Borderlands are open country, they've spoiled me with light. Sometimes I can scarce bear to come indoors. I'd open this pile of stone wide to the air and the light if I could.''

''Why not do it?'' Crocken wondered, honestly puzzled. This was the ruler of Armyn before him—at least for the present. What could check his wishes? Why should he not have windows if he wanted them?

''My own Borderlands keeps I may maintain as I see fit,'' Rhisiart explained primly. '' 'Tis not proper to add luxuries here with money that isn't mine, but only entrusted to my keeping.'' He smiled ruefully. ''Truth to tell, I'd hardly dare if the funds were to hand. These lowlanders find my fancy for light a most peculiar affectation, and consider a fresh breeze deadly poison. Your liking for the windows surprised me as much as it pleased me.''

Crocken recalled the queen's purposely dark, glamorous rooms, where a hundred candles burned even at sun-high, and felt he could well believe what the steward-protector claimed.

"I journeyed through the Borderlands on my way here," Crocken recalled. "The sky seemed very . . . wide." Thinking back, he could hardly remember seeing a tree, save in the river valleys.

Rhisiart turned his gaze to the window. "And yet so narrow here," he whispered, almost inaudibly. Recalling himself, he faced Crocken once more. "Master Merchant," he said briskly, "I can undertake to help you learn the names of the princesses. Mayhap such gentle exercise will aid you in recalling your own name."

He should, Crocken thought, have been afraid, or at the least wary. Had the shadow not told him he was in danger? Was this not the man of whom it continually inferred dire things? The man who wielded a king's power until the prince should come of age? But fear was not what Crocken felt.

Nor was the shadow urging him to caution. The hour was close to sun-high, only a little past—maybe the thing was weak, forced to silence. Left with only his own judgment to act upon, Crocken realized he didn't mistrust Rhisiart as the shadow did. He'd simply seen no cause to, whatever the shadow claimed. And so he said, carefully:

"My lord, I've no need to recollect who I am. I've never *not* known."

Rhisiart raised a brow. "That is not what I was told."

You are unwise, the shadow commented. Crocken could only agree, but it was too late. The steward-protector's tone struck his nervous ears as dangerous.

"No one ever really asked me," Crocken faltered. "Or they wouldn't believe me when I answered them. I'm not . . . what they seem to think I am." He knew all too well that such as he were not granted audiences with queens.

"And is there a name for what you *are*?" Rhisiart asked him softly.

Crocken wished desperately to wake from one of his too-vivid nightmares. "I'm . . . a peddler, my lord."

"A peddler," Rhisiart repeated, looking perplexed. "You mean you are a merchant. But—"

"Alas, no," Crocken corrected politely. "Merchants pay the peddlers to make rounds for them, sometimes, selling goods from town to town. Otherwise we have little to do with them.

Merchants are wealthy, and own shops in the cities. I have never attained such high estate.'' His dreams of it, his failures, he would not mention, or even think upon. He was a fool to have dreamed.

Rhisiart chewed thoughtfully at his lower lip. "Yet you, Master Crocken, not a rich merchant or a knight on an errantry or a disguised king from some exotic land, but only a common peddler—you slew a wild boar with naught save the belt knife you use at meat?''

Crocken remembered it had seemed like a bad idea to him, too, when the boar charged. He shrugged. "I don't know that I was thinking of killing it. I might have been able to scare it off, before it hurt the girl. But it came after me, and I couldn't outrun it, so there was nothing else to try but stabbing it. I'd rather have had something bigger than a knife.''

"I suppose,'' Rhisiart mused, "that a knight or a king—or even a rich merchant—might have known no man could hope to slay such a monstrous great boar with only a little knife. None of those folk would have attempted such a feat. You, knowing no better, prevailed. The princess is most fortunate.''

And you, peddler, are a great fool.

Crocken had not needed telling.

"Why did you come here?''

Honesty, once begun, could not be conveniently set aside, whatever the shadow might command. Crocken's head had begun to ache, making the framing of successful lies seem unlikely to him. He'd admitted to his name, to remembering the boar. He doubted Rhisiart would swallow a lapse in other areas.

"Only to trade, my lord.''

"What goods?''

Crocken swallowed. "I lost my goods, crossing what I'm told was the Arinwater.''

"Treacherous, this season,'' Rhisiart agreed, nodding. "You did not think to turn back?''

"It was farther back to Kôvelir than onward to Armyn,'' Crocken answered. He wondered if the truth sounded implausible.

"And empty pockets make a long road endless.''

It's a proverb of the Borderlands.

Crocken ignored the shadow and smiled with relief. "Truly spoken, my lord Steward. I'd never been to Armyn, but I *had* fared through the Sheiran Empire, and with my trade permits gone the way of my goods . . : Armyn seemed a better destination to me, given the choices to hand.''

Rhisiart fiddled with the orange he'd been occasionally peeling. ''Aye. Sheir sits tight on all matters touching trade—tight as a miser in his counting house. That may alter. Our prince is to wed a princess of Calandra. When that happens, we hope to acquire markets outside Sheir's influence, in her homeland.''

Crocken's mercenary interest was roused, despite the persistent headache that was by then making him ever so slightly queasy. ''Markets? I met the princess today—a lovely girl. An ornament to any court, to be sure. She brings trade contacts, as well?''

''It is my intention that the marriage will open a cross-seas trade for us,'' Rhisiart said. ''Armyn lacks land routes, save to Sheir itself. And Sheiran galleys control our coastal waters almost as well as their own.''

Crocken called the shadow's map to mind and easily saw the problem. Of a certainty nothing could go out of Armyn save through the Empire—which could set whatever price it chose for the service. Doubtless a ruinously high price. Or Sheir could refuse all trade concessions, given the enmity between the two lands. One solution came to his mind.

''Deepwater ships?'' he asked.

''You touch closely on my own hopes, Master Crocken,'' Rhisiart said approvingly. ''We have precious few as yet—but given time we'll build an adequate fleet, and it will pay its own way. While Sheir, with her long coast to ply, sees no need to venture farther from shore than a galley may safely fare. We are slow to start, but we will win the game, given time.''

''I wish you success, Lord Steward.''

Rhisiart did not acknowledge the politeness. The steward-protector was deep in thought, absently turning the ring he wore on his right hand. *He's fond of rings*, Crocken thought—there were two on his right hand and four on the left. Mayhap so he'd readily have something to occupy his fingers while he thought upon weighty matters. He'd left off torturing the orange.

His is a restless nature, the shadow agreed.

''Now, what are we to do about you, Master Crocken?''

Crocken felt a cool finger of unease stroke down his spine.

''Armyn owes a debt of gratitude to you beyond a few meals and an entertainment or two,'' Rhisiart went on. ''You shall be welcome to stay with us as long as you wish, but it is apparent

to me that you came here to garner trade profits, not to lodge—
however pleasantly.''

The rings were turned back and forth, one after another.
Crocken strove to breathe normally, or at least less erratically.

"It is my experience that a merchant suffers worse from a
lack of credentials than the lack of funds,'' Rhisiart said. ''Given
proper credentials, even a penniless trader can attract investors
and make his fortune with the help of others' gold. Is't not so?''

Crocken blinked, wondering if he dared trust this sudden flash
of sympathy. He didn't feel equal to playing a game with stakes
he could barely guess at, but he wasn't being given a choice.

"It . . . can be, my lord. Investing—''

Rhisiart eyed him with amusement. ''You are wondering how
I know of this—the bluff and double-bluff men name commerce?'Tis little different from ruling a dukedom—or guiding
this whole land, Master Merchant-Adventurer.''

*Merchant-Adventurer. That certainly sounds respectable—
much more prosperous than hand-to-mouth peddler,* the shadow
commented.

"I, too, have known money troubles,'' Rhisiart said.
"Kings—and dukes—are deemed rich by the common folk, but
it is scarcely so. We may have more, but 'tis all bespoken—I've
had frequent need to ask for others' trust and monies. I have
gone a-begging, to raise the funds and the armies my king commanded of me by royal right. So—'' The steward-protector tasted
a bit of orange at last. ''I will gift you with those vital credentials. I shall formally designate you a merchant-adventurer. It's
not gold—'' The steward-protector smiled. ''—but it's worth far
more than the little gold *I* could bestow upon you.''

Crocken's good cheer was short-lived.

Ask yourself what Rhisiart wants from you in return, peddler,
the shadow whispered, while Crocken was politely thanking the
steward-protector for his kindness. The thing's comments had
chilled him so often that day, Crocken half wondered whether
he was about to fall into a fever. He was weary, suddenly—just
keeping his eyes open was an effort. Keeping his wits about him
as well seemed impossible. And word duels, when one opponent must never be acknowledged in front of the other . . . His
heart misgave him. He knew he'd make some fatal error, any
moment.

A clerk crept in and dropped discreet words into the steward-
protector's ear, rescuing Crocken barely in time. The interview
was at an end—other matters pressed, Rhisiart apologized.

Crocken was surprised to have been allotted such a space of the steward's time, but felt too shaky to be flattered. As he left the chamber, a dozen others were entering it, each with some business to transact, and the antechamber was filled with patient petitioners.

The page, Crocken was thankful to note, was waiting to guide him to his quarters. Even if he'd been to them previously—which he had not, what with two interviews since rising from his sickbed—he'd never have found them again. Crocken doubted he could even locate the healer—particularly if he were ill enough to require her. About all he was certain of, direction-wise, was that the sky was above him and the ground beneath.

A good idea, perhaps, to have the shadow map Axe-Edge for him, if it was willing. Certainly it had been given enough time to learn the lay of the fortress. And best to have a surety, in case he wished to move without its guidance—assuming such was ever possible.

The shadow's thoughts were fastened on other matters.

This is a piece of luck, it said from the shadows inside Crocken's head.

"What? That I don't have to sleep on the floor in some hallway? What do you care?" Crocken touched his bedcover wonderingly. Serviceable cloth, not costly but well woven. The straw it was stuffed with would stay put and not poke him suddenly out of sleep. The chamber was small, set within one of the outer walls, he thought. An arrow-slit gave a view of the Windrush far below, and a very little light. And he was alone—save for his shadow—in the chamber. It was a wonder, for even inns put folk half a dozen to a bed, and charged them for the privilege. Vast Axe-Edge could apparently afford to give its folk more privacy than a man could expect elsewhere, and a guest could expect a bed, not a bench in some drafty, smoky great hall.

Rhisiart has given you leave to remain at court. Having slipped us into Axe-Edge, I was a trifle concerned over whether we could remain, once you'd begun to spill your heart to him.

"I'm sure you'd have thought of something." Crocken rubbed at a still-tender spot on his scalp and nursed a resentment he kept out of his voice. "What do you want me to do now?"

What he *hoped* to do was rest. He'd been on his legs too weary a while, and they wouldn't bear him much longer. The fire, laid by a servant who Crocken earnestly hoped he wouldn't be expected to pay, had warmed the small space rapidly, and he was drowsy despite his varied fears concerning his situation, his employer, and his future.

Move about as you will, the shadow replied tolerantly, as if it knew Crocken wished only to cease moving. *This scheme of Rhisiart's gives you excuse to go virtually wherever you choose. If there is a special place or person I require your help to get a look at, I shall inform you.*

Crocken repressed a shiver. *In deep*, he thought, remembering icy river water closing over his head. Just for a moment, he had trouble breathing. *In very deep indeed, and nothing to be done about it.*

Chapter Thirteen

"FORTY MARKS OF gold you promised me, if I brought you here. You extended my service and pledged me more gold for it. You've promised, and promised—but all you've delivered to me was a crack on the head! Now you expect me to prowl all over this pile of stone tonight, spying for you? What if I refuse?" Crocken was feeling stubborn, annoyed at being shadow-prodded ungently out of a sound sleep.

Peddler, there's greater fortune here than the gold I pledged you, if you have the stomach to seek it.

"Or if I had the *means* to seek it!" Crocken snapped. "I'll grant you there's opportunity here—I can smell it, taste it. But you just tell me how I avail myself of it! Not a copper to my name, much less gold. Even my clothes are charity. Nothing to trade. Shall I try to peddle that pathetic packet of half-rusted pins to the queen? Of course the pins are in my pack, which is lying somewhere out in that boar-infested forest, but I expect I could find it again—in about a year!"

Play the game well, and you can regain all that you lost to the Arinwater—and a great deal more, the shadow wheedled.

"More golden promises!" Crocken sat down on his bed. "I'm cheap to hire—and even if I weren't, it shouldn't matter to you. You obviously have no intention of keeping your end of the bargain you've hog-tied me to, and I have no recourse to force you. I can't very well haul a shadow before a magistrate, complaining of breach of contract."

The shadow sat itself down in its fashion, beside him on the bed. Crocken fought the urge to leap to his feet, and glared at it.

"Suppose I simply left?" he asked again.

You will not. You have sense enough to know you will gain

yourself nothing but trouble if you attempt to desert me. Even supposing I did nothing to stop you, still you are penniless in a land strange to you. Should you fare so far back as Sheir, you would find great difficulty dealing with their border guards. A peddler foolish enough to enter their Empire without leave is one thing—quite another if he comes from Armyn, with which they have no friendship.

Crocken put his head in his hands. "You'll never release me. Or pay me. Will you?"

Do I ask so much of you?

"How do I know what you're asking? By the time I find out, it'll be too late. I'm only sure I won't like it." His head hurt again, waves of discomfort lapping at his nerves. "I don't deserve this! What god have I so offended just by being alive?" Crocken asked plaintively of the world in general and not especially of the shadow.

When he looked up, the shadow stood by the door, flung against the wall.

Your complaints of poverty have touched my heart. If you suppose a little gold will mend your troubles, peddler, you shall have it. Come.

"Where?" Crocken eyed it with suspicion.

Come. A shadow hand indicated the door.

Reluctantly Crocken got to his feet and made to put on his beltran—he had removed it when he lay down to sleep, so as to have it for a blanket. Now he could make little sense of the disordered cloth. He fumbled with it, cursing under his breath as he would have cursed the shadow if he'd dared.

Fold it lengthwise, by the stripes, the shadow instructed.

"Why don't they just wear cloaks?" Crocken fussed. The folding did not seem to help much—he had what felt like an acre of woven wool hanging over him.

Gather it a bit. Put the folded side closest to your neck, so that if you require a cloak you can easily spread the beltran. It serves many functions: garment, blanket, shield, and carryall—no cloak serves so well.

Crocken stuck his finger on the business end of the pin, then glared at his shadow, which had no need of unfamiliar garments, but might shape itself as it liked. Warily he made another attempt to fasten the brooch.

Tuck the short end of the cloth beneath your belt. That, with the weight of what hangs behind, keeps the beltran in its place—don't try to force the pin through all the folds.

The adjustments spared his fingers, improving matters and Crocken's temper. He opened the chamber door and followed his shadow out into the shadows between the pools of light the wall torches shed.

The corridor trek began once more, slower-paced this time, since Crocken had to take silent direction rather than simply following. And by torchlight the shadow was difficult to see, even when it chanced to be in his line of sight. Crocken was guided by its whisperings in his head, and that not always promptly enough to prevent his making false turnings. They were outdoors for a time, crossing courtyards, and Crocken discovered he was glad of the beltran's warmth at his back. Even the halls seemed none too warm, being stone-walled and floored.

Of a sudden there were throngs of people about. The shadow urged Crocken onward, through chambers hot with ranked candles and the press of velvet-clad bodies. Crocken was welcomed, offered tidbits, had wine pressed upon him. Sipping, he made his way across carpets to the innermost chamber and came upon the dice game. He recognized the players, and they him.

"Why, 'tis our hero! Welcome, Sir Merchant, slayer of the boar!" Lord Stiles exclaimed, reaching out to clasp his hand.

There was general mirth, directed at the words, Crocken thought, not himself. He was wondering how he might learn just what the jest was, when the queen's brother bespoke him again.

"Come, sir, you shall join our game. The play is for amusement only, the stakes are very small." There were coins stacked upon the table, which by their golden gleam gave lie to the statement. Not that it mattered.

"I fear I'm no gambler, my lord," Crocken objected.

"What? Not a gambler, when you've dared a savage boar armed with a mere toothpick of steel? There are few here who would hazard such! Besides, I vow all merchant folk are gamblers born," Stiles cajoled. "I'll stake you to a toss."

Lord Stiles negligently flicked a coin onto the table. It winked richly in he candlelight, and Crocken swallowed back a sigh. 'Twas true, he was no gambler and never had been. He'd worked too hard and walked too far for the silver he'd slowly accumulated, and he clung to it too tightly—at least till the fateful moment when he'd love-blindly handed it all over to Litsa. Might she never have an instant's joy of it!

Quite as blindly, Crocken cast the dice that had been put into his fist. He realized he didn't even know the game in play. What number won? What ought he to hope for—supposing he dared to hope?

Shadows danced over the game, as torches flared and candles sputtered. One touched the shadow of a cube just settling flat to the table, and the die rolled over one face farther, bringing a new side uppermost. A trey. The other cube mirrored it.

"You win!" An arm wrapped itself about Crocken's shoulders. "See, Sir Merchant, not so difficult after all. Your throw again." The dice were put back into his hand.

Crocken politely insisted on first repaying the coin he'd been gifted with, with another added for courtesy. And he kept his bet small—he refused to risk losing more of his winnings than was needful. One throw and he'd quit, well ahead of the game.

Coward, the shadow said, making his hand shake.

Notwithstanding, he threw another pair, and won that throw—and the next half-dozen plus one. By then Lord Stiles' merry cronies were laying side bets on him and most of the chamber was taking note. Impressive heaps of coin changed hands. Crocken fingered the ivory cubes again. Could they be loaded? Not and throw pairs, he decided.

That's enough, peddler, the shadow informed him. *You've got your forty marks, and enough over to fulfill our agreement.*

Crocken remembered just in time not to protest aloud. Why not continue? he wondered. It was so easy, and so profitable—

Because they'll soon suspect you're cheating. They just won't know how. Keep the next bet small, I'm going to let you lose it.

Crocken angrily did as ordered—and won the toss once again. The satisfaction was fleeting, for he did indeed lose the following throw, and his turn at the dice. Crocken made one tiny side bet on the next player, then heeded the shadow's instruction to drift away. The dice-play was intense. No one noticed his departure, or tried to delay it. The wonder of his beginner's luck had quickly faded, changing hands with the dice.

He had no purse to easily contain his double handful of coins, but the shadow instructed him to secure his winnings in a fold of his beltran, held safely by his belt. One could use the cloth to carry any object from a single coin to a suckling pig, Crocken supposed.

Now that your peddler's heart is gold-contented, the shadow whispered, *wander a bit. I would observe more of this company.*

As if the shadow could not do that without him, Crocken thought sourly. There were true shadows aplenty for it to lose itself among. He accepted a cup of tawny wine from a servitor and strolled slowly, letting the color and the noise of the rooms lap over him.

There was dancing in the largest chamber, conducted to the sweet piping of recorders and the insistent tapping of drums. Tables of food were set out at a safe distance from the dancers' feet. Various other gambling games were on view, and one prettily dressed lordling was displaying his whippet, which had been trained to leap backward in circles through the air, yapping as it did.

"Why, Master Merchant-Adventurer! How unexpected to see you here."

Crocken turned about. He beheld green eyes nearly on a level with his own, a pointed face exquisitely framed with curling dark hair that a circlet of twisted silver scarcely restrained. He scented lavender, which prodded his tardy memory. The princess' lady. "Mistress Ivy?"

"I am flattered you remember, sir." She smiled. "You were thrown so many names yestermorn, I didn't suppose you'd catch mine."

Crocken made her a careful little bow. "It's only the golden-haired princesses I'm likely to embarrass myself over, when I try to name them singly. Rare coloring like yours is far easier to recall."

She dipped her head, setting its dark curls dancing. "Very prettily spoken, and I thank you for it. Though coloring such as mine is hardly rare—save at a court where everyone is kin to Sulien the Fair."

"Your flame-haired mistress will add diversity, when she's wed to the prince, surely?" Crocken asked innocently.

"Surely!" Mistress Ivy laughed sweetly. "Master Adventurer, I like well your wit. Is that because we're strangers here, both observing what natives of Axe-Edge take for granted?"

Crocken found her manner engaging. She made pretty speeches seem simple to him and allowed him to forget all about his shadow master. And she was better to look at, though her face was far from the perfect oval the court limners preferred—it was heart-shaped, wide at the top and narrow at the chin. Nor did she seem capable of the placidity courtly beauty demanded. Ivy's green eyes danced, her lips were quick to shift shape—usually to smile, it appeared. All that loosened the peddler's tongue.

"I'm very green to the ways of Armyn," he ventured. "I should greatly esteem any guidance you could offer me, out of your experience—"

"With its admitted advantage of being quite fresh?"

"Agreed." They were strolling toward the food tables. Spice scents tickled Crocken's nose. "But is your mistress in need of your services? Robbing Armyn's next queen can hardly be wise." Crocken didn't see a red head anywhere among the yellow ones.

"My lady has retired to her bed, giving me leave first to pleasure myself here awhile," Ivy answered. "I promised to linger only till the music was done, which it is, but I could tarry for a question or two, and no harm done."

"Most kind." And far more patient than the shadow tended to be with regard to his queries. As an added advantage, Crocken realized he would be able to ask his questions as they occurred to him, without need to wait till he was alone or unobserved, and safe to speak to the invisible. The idea was almost unnerving.

"I understand Rhisiart plans to formally announce your appointment as Merchant-Adventurer tomorrow," Mistress Ivy said shyly.

Crocken looked at her, startled as much by her interest as by the knowledge.

"It's quite an honor," Ivy went on. "Rhisiart has granted other merchants various charters, but he's never sponsored anyone to such an extent. Of course he does owe you a debt for saving Gloriet, but you must have impressed him. It will be interesting to see which of the other great merchants strive to curry your favor, now that your star is seen to be rising."

Indeed, Crocken thought. The shadow was not much attending to him—he wasn't even quite sure where it was—so he decided to risk a question while it was preoccupied or even safely absent. After all, *he* had no reason to fear Rhisiart—at least no reason he was aware of.

"What sort of man is the steward-protector?"

"You've met him." Ivy frowned at him, as if not sure she had the question right. "He said he spoke with you."

"I've met a great many people here in Axe-Edge," Crocken said mildly. "The steward-protector and I only conversed for a few moments—about windows. And trade, a little. You've months of advantage on me, remember? Or is he so easy to know, that half an hour's acquaintance suffices?"

"You wouldn't be the only one at court baffled by Rhisiart," Ivy admitted, smiling again. "He's always very direct—he says exactly what he means, while all courtiers discourse in riddles, straightforward as smoke. Rhisiart keeps his word. That makes him a good friend to have—or a terrible enemy." It didn't sound like a warning, as it would had the shadow made the observation.

"You have high regard for him." Ivy seemed to describe a man very different from the one the shadow continually hinted at. Crocken wondered where the truth lay—at either extreme or between them? And how could he determine it?

"I do. 'Twas his negotiations brought my lady here—and me with her. Busy as he always is, Rhisiart never neglects my lady's welfare, and that's a great comfort. I suspect Sulien and her folk do not much favor the marriage, but because of Rhisiart they do not quite dare to be cruel to us."

Perfect, Crocken thought. He'd found what he sought—someone inclined to gossip, and well placed to acquire the information. Such gossip was the lifeblood of trade. The import of Ivy's words reached him, as he finished concerning himself with the free flow of them.

"Why should the queen not favor the match?" If he could trust maid's gossip? Wherever two women were about to become mother-in-law and daughter-in-law, there were bound to be intrigues. He'd seen such before. Royalty only put it on a larger scale.

"Why, for that it's Rhisiart's idea! They're bitterest enemies." Ivy took a tiny iced cake from a tray and ate it with obvious relish. "Sulien chooses her enemies very poorly," she added, also with relish.

Crocken sampled a cake. 'Twas sweet, melting on his tongue. "What of Rhisiart's own family? Where's his base of support?" He couldn't recall what the shadow had said of that.

Mistress Ivy's expression saddened. "The steward-protector *has* no family now, save for his brother's children—who are seven little copies of their mother from all I've seen. There are some elder sisters, but they never come to court. All Rhisiart's brothers are dead now—and his mother, from last winter. I never met her, but he speaks of her often."

"I had heard that Rhisiart was wed, surely? Or was that someone else?" Maybe the shadow's tales had tangled in his memory. Without faces, names had tended to be interchangeable, despite the shadow's harping on Rhisiart's perfidy.

"He was wed." Ivy's eyes lost their focus, as if she gazed upon the dim past and not the gaily dressed dancers forming up for the next tune. "His wife was the lady Cailin, daughter of great kingmaker Sarris, whom men still speak in awe of despite his treachery and base death. It's a pretty tale—"

Crocken indicated that she should tell it, as he took another cake.

"They were children together," Ivy began. "Sarris had the fostering of Rhisiart, his own father being dead then. And they were wed when they weren't much more than children—Rhisiart was barely twenty then, and Cailin was younger. But for all of that she'd been wed once already—her father married her off during his rebellion, using her to further his own ambitions." Ivy sighed. It wasn't an unusual fate for a noblewoman, Crocken knew. "Fate was cruel to Rhisiart, too—he was a playing piece as much as Cailin was, moving for another's will and gain in that bloody chess match they still speak of as if 'twas yesterday. But Rhisiart was a knight, and a man. Poor Cailin was but a pawn, without power to change her fate. The only time chance smiled was when she was left a widow and Rhisiart was left Ruane's only loyal brother at almost the same time. Ruane owed Rhisiart much, but Cailin was all he asked for." The dancers were whirling on the floor, stamping feet, clapping hands.

"Rhisiart loved her so," Ivy said. "And they had only a little while once they were together. Cailin bore one child, Edryd. Not long after Rhisiart became steward-protector, the boy died. Cailin lived just a year after—they say it was grief struck her down."

"Was that after you came here?" It seemed it could not have been, but Crocken wasn't sure he'd reckoned the time properly.

Ivy shook her dark head. "No."

She had related the tragic events as if she'd been a witness to them—Crocken permitted himself a mental shrug. She could be bard-trained, for all he knew. It was a skill useful in a lady's companion, to be able to entertain with tales before the fire of a winter's night. And what great sympathy Rhisiart had inspired in her. Ivy looked as if she wished to weep. Mere thoughts of his presumed pain had brought disquiet to her features. Crocken was a trifle sorry he'd coerced her to the tale, and the sorrow. He strove to make amends.

"A tragedy, truly,' he said sympathetically. "Rhisiart seems to me a decent man, deserving of a gentler fate. May I fetch you a cup of wine?" It might bring the shine back to her eyes.

"Thank you, but no." Ivy tried a smile. "I must leave you now. My lady will be wanting me."

"Surely she's abed by now?" Though if true, she was perhaps the only noble in Axe-Edge who was. "Still, time I sought my own chamber. May I escort you, Mistress Ivy? Some of these revelers may have been more free with the wine than we were, and might forget their manners—''

Ivy accepted with a gracious smile that looked practiced and laid a small-boned hand lightly on the arm Crocken offered. ''You'll have to direct me to your lady's suite—and then instruct me on the most likely route back to my own quarters,'' he pointed out lightly. ''Or indeed any route. I swear it's halfway to the Borderlands, and if I'd had any, I'd have left a trail of dried peas, to follow back the way children do in tales—''

His shadow had rejoined him, Crocken realized, hoping belatedly that it wouldn't take exception to his decision to retire. It seemed that it would not, for all he had not consulted it; it was silent as they crossed a suite of chambers, though torch-flames increased its size, or twisted and attenuated it.

Mistress Ivy halted suddenly, as if she'd stumbled in the hall-way's rushes, or grown faint.

''What is it?'' Was she looking at him strangely, or was he merely overcautious?

''Naught.'' But she still frowned. ''A trick of the light. It seems dark to me here, after those over-bright rooms.''

Yet Crocken thought Ivy watched him still, very closely, when she supposed his attention was elsewhere.

''Are you *sure* no one can see you?'' Crocken was alone in his small chamber, save for the shadow that stretched its long, dark hands to the fire in imitation of his attempts to warm himself.

All can see me. This is as it should be—a man without a shadow would cause remark.

''I mean, see a difference between you and a true shadow?'' Crocken said deliberately.

I am a true shadow.

''Mistress Ivy looked at me so . . . intently.'' No matter how he poked up the fire, Crocken still felt a chill. He decided 'twas not the room, but his fear.

What is there to see? A shadow among many? I think your Mistress Ivy sees many shadows, both of the past and of the present. Have no fear, you will not be discovered.

''Easy for you to—''

The shadow waved a hand, cutting him off.

If you cannot accept my reassurances, then do not request them, peddler.

Chapter Fourteen

RHISIART, STEWARD-PROTECTOR OF Armyn, was as good as his pledged word. Within the week Crocken received his trade permits, a thick sheaf of parchment bits with various bright wax seals a-dangle. He was officially designated a merchant-adventurer—not an official title as such went, but it sufficed when a title was required for him socially. The merchant community of course heard of him, and some members made it a point to seek him out, which he found flattering.

Crocken, once a peddler, now a man of position—so long as no one examined that position too closely—began to study the ways of Armyn, whilst diligently committing the byways of Axe-Edge to his memory.

After two days had passed, Crocken determined that he had learned two things. Firstly, the complexities of Axe-Edge would serve to defeat the most determined cartographer, which he had never been. He could get from place to place, but never with assurance. Doubtless no one within Axe-Edge's walls knew every nook, every cranny.

Secondly, he could not hope to ply his merchant's trade within those walls, despite his official permits and papers.

He had forty marks of gold and a few odd bits of silver with which to work, but nothing to exchange them for, unless he chose to gamble without the shadow's assistance and exchange full pockets for empty. Kieron's fortress contained living quarters for his royal family and his illustrious court, barracks for his guards, stables for his horses, mews for his hawks, kennels for his hounds, a menagerie for his exotic pets. Huge kitchens cooked his meals. A bakehouse supplied his bread, a brewery provided beer for his retainers. There were vaulted wine cellars to serve the nobles' needs. There was a library with a scriptorium, a wardrobe, a treasure house, an armory, half a dozen chapels of sizes varying from small to immense. There were gardens, tennis lawns, and bowling greens. There were cloisters for fine weather, solars for foul. There were towers, turrets, ramparts, bastions, gatehouses, walkways, courtyards, and practice yards. There was a laundry the size of a small village. Crocken suspected there was a mint, though he hadn't actually seen it.

But no market.

Crocken accepted that kings didn't choose to have their realm's commerce directly and inconveniently underfoot. That was what cities existed for, after all. He began to scheme over how he might get to Rushgate, which could be seen from the arrow-slit in his room, sprawling upon the far flat bank of the Windrush, spreading right out of sight around the gentle curve the river made before plunging into the Great Sea.

Barge transport seemed most likely. There might be bridges, Crocken thought, but those were evidently far downstream, and he had no horse to take him thither. Anyway, small barges were thick upon the Windrush as water-striders on a pond, clearly they were popular forms of transport. Some vessels bore blazons of fantastic animals and doubtless were the private conveyances of lords of Kieron's court—but others were unmarked and evidently for hire.

But . . . would the shadow permit him to leave Axe-Edge, even if only for a few hours? What did it care that its indentured servant was bored and restless? It was likely to refuse him without feeling that the least explanation was required. Crocken knew he'd need to be clever.

Shadows dwindled as the sun rose toward its zenith. Perhaps that natural fact applied in some way to his own shadow—so at sun-high Crocken made his careful request, stressing that a merchant, adventurous or not, with no desire to visit Armyn's great commercial center would eventually be viewed with suspicion and closely watched. It was an old argument, one of the first he'd successfully used, but still apt. If the shadow didn't want to risk what had been gained . . .

Perhaps his shadow *was* weak at midday. Certainly its assent was given faintly—but given it was. Crocken set off at once, armed with two of the silver coins he'd won at dicing, fearful that the least delay would let the shadow order him back.

The barge ride downriver was swift, since the current willingly assisted the boatman. Crocken suspected that the trip back would be at double the price or worse, when the bargeman had to resort to oars to make headway. He was warned at the outset to start his trip back well before high tide—the sea invaded the Wind-rush to some extent, he learned, and the waters could be turbulent where river became estuary. Yet more costly, Crocken silently translated. He had no need to worry—nor any doubt that his shadow would insist upon his return *long* ere the tide commenced to turn. It had been silent and nearly nonexistent while they were on the water, but appeared instantly when Crocken disembarked.

He strolled along the waterfront, his shadow quiet and faint about his feet, bumpy where it lay over cobbles. Warehouses lined the quayside. There were many ship moorings, and great cranes for loading those ships set amid vast tangles of arcane equipment and bales of goods. The locality was busy, noisy, and notably odiferous. Crocken, never a seafarer, left the river behind happily and in short order.

Rushgate was, he knew, too vast to be explored in the scant hours of peace his shadow would grant him, but Crocken aimed for a good taste of it, and got his wish. He strolled one street after another, unhurried but making the most of his time, taking good note of what was sold in the shops he passed and what seemed to be absent—he observed that the common pin was indeed known in Armyn—and kept his bearings as best he could. When his shadow had lengthened to half his own height and had begun to plague him about encountering the tide, Crocken made his way handily back to the barge landing and arranged for a trip upriver, well enough content. He'd find a reason to coerce the shadow into allowing return visits. Depend on it.

The boat he'd hired slid steadily through the current, making the Windrush's banks seem to glide past it. The distance not being great, even the slower upstream trip was soon over. Axe-Edge rose above them, atop its cliffs. Farther on, gleams of sunlight indicated Triniol: lesser city and best saved for another day.

The shadow began belaboring Crocken to quicken his steps the moment he'd disembarked at the landing stage, but he paid it little heed—something was nagging at him, and no matter how the shadow threatened him, he was unlikely to give in and run up the road to the fortress. Such unseemly behavior would excite comment.

Crocken glanced back at Rushgate, where sunlight glinted briefly on pale stone, as wind tore the smoky pall that shrouded parts of the city. He was thinking not of anything he'd seen, but rather of what he had *not* seen.

Rushgate bustled, being both a major port and the seat of Armyn's government—indeed it was the greatest city in the realm, bar none, boasting some fifty thousand souls. Crocken had needed neither the shadow nor the boatman to tell him that—just walking through parts of the city had convinced him. All the guilds and crafts he was accustomed to seeing were represented—save for being heavy in wool merchants, Rushgate could have been any city in the Quatrain. There were mercers, and mongers of all types of fish and fowl. There were horsetraders, cattle and sheep-drovers. There were butchers, tanners, tailors, chandlers, bakers, and brewers. All that a city ought to have, Rushgate possessed.

Except wizards.

Not that Crocken had expected them to be thick on the cobbles as he was accustomed to by Kôvelir's example. He knew the city of his birth was unique, being in fact a city of wizards where a few nonmagical folk chanced to dwell and conduct business. But every town he'd ever passed through had a conjuror or two in the market, a card-reader or a dream-sifter plying trade in the town square. Crocken cast his mind's eye back down the river, but he could recall no wizard folk, not even of the lowliest grades, where there was less of magic and more of sleight-of-hand and misdirection.

Perchance the lack was to his good. Surely it lessened the likelihood of anyone's discovering that his shadow was more than it ought to be. Crocken wondered how he might discreetly discover whether magic was proscribed in Armyn, or merely uncommon. Such a distinction might come to matter a great deal to him. By the time he decided to question his shadow, though, he was among the castle folk once more and had no chance to speak without causing the very remark he sought to avoid—so Crocken held his peace and settled for some dinner.

"Your mother tells me you dream true," her father said, in Ivy's dream.

The dream-memory was more vivid than she recalled the reality having been. She could smell the dark earth of the herb garden as her father's spade cut into it, saw plainly the fat earth-worms wriggling away from the sudden sunlight. Her father paused considerably between spade thrusts, allowing the worms time to seek safety. He was troubled, Ivy knew, though neither his words nor his tone betrayed that. Her mother always sent him out to dig more herb space when she saw cares pressing him—in the long summers they lived surrounded by gardens, moated by fields of lavender.

"Sometimes," she answered him at last.

"You get that from your mother—prophecy was never one of my gifts," her father said.

Before the words had faded from Ivy's ears, the dream had shifted. Instead of the broad earth and the broader sky, she was within a chamber scarcely spacious—she felt it, though the guttering candle by the bed did not shed light enough to reveal the walls. A man and a woman, hidden by the bedclothes, she placed by their voices when they spoke.

"Faith, but that babe has the sharpest teeth—he pierced my finger as an adder would have, Tierce."

Bemused, Tierce examined the pricked but otherwise delectable digit, then politely transferred his attentions to its fellows. He moved onward to the palm, the wrist, the tender inner surface of Agnella's arm. That led him to still fairer vistas in due course, and the small wound was forgotten by them both in short order.

It was their final tryst. Agnella was dead within twenty hours, and there was frightened talk of plague. The court shifted to another keep at once, to cheat the supposed pestilence, and much incense was burned in supplication that the little Prince Kieron might be spared the dread fate that had overtaken his nurse.

Tierce was panicked at first that he would be the next stricken, but aside from the chill his fear gave him, he remained hale. If Agnella had indeed died of plague, he ought to have taken it, also. That he had not teased at him, and he eventually remembered the tiny wound on her finger—it was the last conversation they'd had. He took to watching his bright-haired nephew closely as the child toddled about, looking for an answer to the puzzle.

There were those who viewed such attentions with alarm. In hardly more time than it had taken his mistress to die, there were clever charges laid against him. They contained just sufficient truth to make them difficult to disprove, especially for a man with his past and nature. Tierce had few friends, and a past with chequered loyalty paramount. His enemies were highly placed and discreet, his brother the king was out of patience with him, and in less than a month Tierce was under sentence of death for treason. He had refused to take his situation—and his sister-in-law's newfound power now that she had at last produced a male heir—seriously enough until far too late.

Chapter Fifteen

STRANGE, THE SHADOWY twists a man's fate might take. Had anyone in Kôvelir ventured to predict that Crocken would find himself, in less than half a year's time, a member of a royal hunting party on such and such a day, he would have been swift to reply with scornful words. That he would bestride a blooded horse, be attended by a brace of coursing hounds, carry a bird of price upon his gauntleted wrist—even farther beyond belief. How the city maidens would smile on him now, could they but see . . .

There was a wormy center to the bright dream. The blooded horse was far too mettlesome for Crocken's peace—of mind or body. He had not the space to draw one quiet breath, lest his slightest inattention breed instant disaster. The couple of hounds only made matters worse—always running under the horse's nervous hooves, startling it and making it shy alarmingly. The goshawk and Crocken eyed each other with mutual suspicion, when he briefly lifted its hood. He hastily replaced the controlling device, but the hawk still seemed discontented. Crocken was no happier, being forced to keep beak and talons so close.

The hunt had halted at the edge of a broad expanse of green meadow. There was water somewhere yonder—Crocken could see a fringe of rushes that betokened either a pond or a stream. He thought they might be hawking after wild duck, which would be plentiful as the nesting season began.

Following some order of precedence he could no more make out than he could the pond, riders trotted forward and cast hawks to the wind. Others stayed back and watched the working birds, their mounts standing placidly.

Save one. Crocken's dark gray palfrey tossed its head, sending white foam flying from the curb bit. It sidestepped restlessly and

snatched for more rein. Crocken snatched back. The horse retreated two quick paces, ran into a tree, and shifted to see if it
might not manage to pin one of Crocken's legs against the trunk.
He kicked at it frantically, hoping no one saw, and pulled its
head around until he could see one rolling eye. Its white-rimmed
expression was alarming. In fact, it terrified him. His pony had
given him evil looks aplenty on the trail, but never such a mad
glare.

The beast settled marginally, and Crocken cautiously released
a little of the rein, to rest his cramping fingers. Instantly the
horse began to sidle, utterly ignoring his urgent attempts to hold
it in place. The goshawk chose the moment to flap its wings,
striking Crocken about the head, though he ducked as best he
might after the first unexpected blow landed. He bitterly wished
that the hawk's red leather jesses were not knotted to his glove—
he would have preferred to drop the bird, not caring that it
couldn't see to fly or what the falconers would say of him. At
least then he'd have had both his hands free to attempt controlling the horse.

Pinions continued assaulting him. His steed had managed to
turn itself about until the combined shadows of horse and man
stretched upon the turf full in its line of sight. Crocken had been
striving to avoid that very happenchance—he had earlier noticed
that the sight bothered the beast inordinately. All the way to the
meadow, it had shied and started and threatened to bolt with
him—whenever it wasn't trotting fit to jolt his bones free from
one another. He was certain 'twas the shadow frightened it.

"Horses can be very brave—just not selective about what they
choose to fear."

Crocken looked up distractedly over his mount's overbent
neck, straight into silver-green eyes that would have done credit
to any cat. Mistress Ivy wore a smile and a riding gown of green
velvet. The ends of her hair had worked their way free of her
velvet cap in the breeze, and her released tresses curled eagerly
all about, like tendrils of dawn-blooming bindweed. Crocken
sighed with relief. Better Mistress Ivy laughing at his predicament than any of the golden princesses. As much a stranger to
Armyn as he was, she was possibly kinder, and he hoped less
likely to criticize his handling of the goshawk, which had that
moment begun to scream.

His horse began backing again, spurred by the hawk's distress. This time there was no tree handy to run into, so it began
to circle, still backward, evidently in hope of finding something

solid and unseen. A hound got stepped on, and yelped. Its mate barked excitedly. The goshawk screamed again. Crocken wished he dared do likewise. He hauled on his reins with the hand that wasn't hampered by the shrieking, thrashing hawk, but without good result. He wondered with alarm whether a horse could gallop backward, and if his would try.

Mistress Ivy brought her mount alongside with a nasty bump, which at least put a stop to the circling. She reached out, caught one rein in her gloved hand, and jerked it free of Crocken's cramped grip. "He thinks you *want* him to back, since you won't let him move forward," she explained patiently.

"Can't he just stand *still*?" Crocken asked unsteadily. He wanted desperately to grab the rein back, but dared not. If the horse made the slightest move, he decided, he'd throw himself free before it could dash him to the ground.

Mistress Ivy laughed, presumably at his expression. "Does he make you as nervous as you make him?"

Crocken glared at the horse's pinned ears. It rolled an eye back at him. "I'd say the odds are greatly in his favor." A sudden loss of nerve prompted him to grab at his mount's mane and his one remaining rein. The hawk beat its wings in outrage.

"Sit still," Ivy ordered. "I won't let him move."

Crocken thought he must be regarding her as suspiciously as the horse did—and with the same trace of relief faintly breaking through.

"You were using your heels to hold on," Ivy informed him conversationally. "That will make him run. Or rear, if you keep holding the reins so tightly. *Shhh*," she said to the horse, which was trying to move off despite her reassurances.

Crocken desperately tried to hang on—then realized with chagrin that the horse had not moved after all.

"Get down," Mistress Ivy bid him firmly. When Crocken had clumsily complied, she gave him back the reins to hold while she herself dismounted. She dropped her reins to the ground, and her mount stood calmly while she approached the gray stallion.

"You are a great fool," Ivy told it softly, holding the beast's head down close to her own. Crocken could not overhear the rest of what she whispered, though he was close, as he still had nominal charge of the reins. He could see the horse relaxing—obviously attending to her words. It ears were trained on Ivy, but not with the desperate alertness Crocken had observed it

giving to every other sound that day. She stroked its face, and
he saw a single ring of silver shining on her right hand, bright
in the sun as a raindrop.

"There," Mistress Ivy pronounced at last. "He's all right
now. If you don't do anything *very* cruel with the bit or the spur,
he won't fight you and he'll likely forgive your mistakes. If you
can manage just to sit on him, he'll let you stay there." She
patted the horse, which nosed her gently.

"He told you that?" Crocken eyed the stallion skeptically. He
was far from anxious to remount, and wanted to postpone the
adventure. "I think he's planning to be the death of me."

Mistress Ivy giggled, a pretty sound. "He thought you knew
what you were doing, but when your heels told him to go and
your hands bid him stop, he got fractious. Now that he's not so
confused, he won't make you so miserable. Master Crocken, I
shall need your assistance to remount. If I might borrow your
knee—"

Crocken had seen ladies mount before, but the foot Ivy placed
onto his leg was marvelously light; she seemed to float back to
her saddle, rather than relying on his lifting her. She deftly arranged her velvet skirts.

"Now your turn." Ivy turned her mount and held his reins,
smiling encouragement to Crocken and clucking it at the stallion.

The horse was suddenly a marvel of cooperation—even though
Crocken's knees were quivering and he lacked a mounting block
to assist him in regaining his saddle. And the stallion actually
consented to move off at a docile walk, resisting the urge to go
jigging along after Mistress Ivy's horse. The hawk shook itself,
settling its feathers.

"Talk to him," Ivy suggested, glancing back. "He's trained
to the voice. He'll do what you tell him."

"You're very good with horses," Crocken observed gratefully.

"Thank my father for that. And my father's horse." Ivy
chirped another reassurance to the gray, which pricked its ears
at her cheerfully.

"What advice have you on hawks? Since I haven't managed
to drop this one, will I have to fly it? Or should I just let it bite
me now and have the suspense over?"

Mistress Ivy laughed. Crocken seemed to give her frequent
cause. "You won't be troubled by it long! The instant you unhood that poor bird, it's going to fly up to the tallest tree and

sulk. The falconers will be days coaxing it back—if they ever do."

Crocken was stricken. Had he done *so* badly? Damaged the bird? He'd been as careful as the horse had allowed him to be . . .

"That will be why they gave it to you," Ivy elaborated kindly. "In case you aren't much of a falconer, they won't risk losing a good bird."

"Suppose I don't unhood it?"

Mistress Ivy turned her horse a little and looked at him appraisingly. "That would be very wise." Giving him a little wave, she trotted off to rejoin her lady and the princesses, who closed ranks around her and began to ask giggling questions.

Crocken managed to dissuade his steed from following her—he didn't want to risk coming close to other riders so soon, especially royal ones. He spent better than half an hour staying out of everyone's way, until the shadow became restless at his success.

I can see nothing from here, it complained.

"You make my horse nervous. I don't want to—"

What you want is of no consequence, peddler. And the horse cannot see me. Go where I tell you.

It tells me. I tell the horse, Crocken thought sourly. *We ought to get along better, this horse and I—we're both just laden beasts.* Complying with the shadow's orders, he managed to get near enough to Lord Stiles' people to observe a bit of hawking without ever being quite obliged to cast his own bird. So far, so good. The morning was advancing, the sun climbing. The dinner hour was drawing near. Soon the hunt would return to Axe-Edge, where Crocken could set his feet on safe, solid ground and finally dispose of the irritable hawk. He could feel its razorlike talons right through the leather gauntlet he wore to carry the bird, and he suspected the glove would offer him little real protection.

A cry broke Crocken's reverie. Kieron's white falcon was diving out of the sun, taking a fat mallard hen unawares midbeat of her wings. The two birds plummeted, locked together, and the prince rode joyously on a course to intercept them. Crocken supposed one had to get the hawk off its catch swiftly, else there'd be little left for the huntsman, and a sated hawk would refuse to fly, he'd been warned. Still, the boy seemed uncommonly eager. His spurs had drawn blood, but still he raked his mount with them, urging more speed.

Follow him, the shadow ordered curtly.

His horse began to trot before Crocken touched his heel to it, and he cast a baleful look at what he could see of the shadow. Its interference might have sent the beast into headlong flight just as easily as an intermediate gait.

However, they trotted decorously enough, never out of control, and were merely a part of the large congratulatory circle that formed about Armyn's uncrowned king. Not prominent, just close enough for the shadow to observe whatever it wanted to cast an eye on. The merriment was general, as the prince passed the duck to one of his gamekeepers and lifted his bird carefully to his fist again before remounting.

The falcon had bloodied her breast feathers as she fed from her kill. Kieron touched a gloved finger to the still-wet crimson spot. Crocken was about to glance away—but something in the boy's expression held his interest. Kihron seemed transfixed, unaware of his surroundings as one ensorcelled. His tongue passed ever so slowly across his lower lip, and he began to tremble, very slightly.

The motion excited his horse, which sidestepped and flung up its head. The falcon cried and beat her wings, and the spell of eager stillness seemed broken—but Crocken thought that the boy's eyes were slow to regain the normal expression a lad a-hunting might wear. For the longest of seconds his gaze seemed more in keeping with one sated by passion. . . .

He dotes on pain . . . on blood, a dark voice whispered into Crocken's thoughts. *Stay near him, if you can do so without raising undue notice among his companions. I would see more of this.*

Crocken did his best, though the instruction was little to his taste—but the hunt returned to Axe-Edge soon after. If the shadow saw what it desired to in those brief moments, it did not speak of the matter.

The golden prince imperiously demanded the toy, in Ivy's prophecy-fraught dream. She would have known 'twas Kieron by his arrogant manner, even had the fair face been less obviously his in miniature. He was a prince of the blood, his father the king's only son, he would be king himself when he was grown, and no one denied him anything, ever.

Yet the little lordling refused, though with well-schooled courtesy, since the request came from his liege. The carved wooden horse was a gift from his father, and much cherished.

When he was a man grown, *he* would have such a horse, a real one, like his father's renowned Stormraker. . . .

The refusal enraged the older boy. He tried to wrest the toy from his small cousin, and when fingers alone could not accomplish his purpose, he put his teeth into the fray also.

There was blood on the white-painted wooden horse, when Edryd ran sobbing to his nurse. Not much—it was a tiny bite, less than a teased cat would have dealt him. His mother knew of it, but never his father—it was too small a matter to trouble the steward-protector with, when he had other troubles aplenty. The finger was kissed, comforted, forgotten about.

Edryd was dead in three days.

Chapter Sixteen

THE COURT DID not hunt every day, Crocken was relieved to discover. Nearly every one of his muscles had belatedly expressed a separate outrage over his untoward activities on horseback and hearing that Kieron had chosen riding with half a dozen of his intimates over another hawking expedition delighted his ears. The shadow could contrive no pretext to include him in such a small, select company.

Therefore his dark master was sullen and uncommunicative when he asked it about the prospect of another trip downriver to Rushgate, but Crocken blithely resolved to make his request again—just before sun-high. At present, he was bent upon the project of procuring himself a candle or two, and his plans for the remainder of the day could wait.

He had a few scraps of vellum and a goose quill, left behind by a careless scribe upon a bench at dinner one day. Crocken could, assuming he ever had any to make note of, begin to keep accounts. And he wanted candlelight to keep them by. He wrote a fair hand, but the fire that warmed his chamber gave only sufficient light to find his bed by, hardly adequate for the counting of his gold pieces when he took them covertly from their hiding place for the purpose. He could poke and prod the blaze to a brighter flame, but then the room swiftly grew unbearably warm. If he huddled close enough to make best use of the little light it customarily offered, smoke that failed to find the chimney found his eyes and throat readily enough. A candle—even the stub of one—would be a great asset.

He could, he supposed, purchase a candle in Rushgate. But Crocken suspected he could acquire one as cheaply as he had his writing materials, if he happened by the queen's apartments at an opportune moment. Candles shed their flattering light upon

Sulien by night and by day, and she would likely not permit them to be guttering and smoking and flickering and casting irregular shadows—so tapers and tallow dips would be changed often by her servants, and need to be disposed of.

Crocken's surmise was on the mark. Sulien's custom evidently was to lie late abed—one who seldom saw the sun would not order her day by it—but her people were bustling, needing to complete their chores before she arose, or suffer her ire. Crocken strolled past her solar and dodged hastily out of the way of a load of fresh-cut rushes intended for her floors. He watched mounds of laundry being carried out, folded stacks of clean linen being carried in. A waiting woman was walking one of Sulien's pampered greyhounds out into the garden, on a gilded leather leash. Behind the dog—cursing it softly as it romped under his feet and he stumbled—came an usher shouldering a lumpy sack. The sack's contents clattered waxily. Crocken followed, accosted the fellow politely, and began sounding out the possibility of his buying a half-burned taper or two.

Ere he had fairly begun to haggle the price, the transaction was over, the harried usher fled back to some other pressing task, leaving his erstwhile burden in Crocken's startled hands, sack and all.

How thoughtful of you, the shadow said. *Now I shall dance the more clearly.*

Crocken hefted the sack as he hastened away. "I only wanted *one*." No one was about to overhear him. "Or maybe two. There must be twoscore here."

The fellow doubtless has more sacks like that one.

"Every day? But the cost—" He began to reckon it in his head.

Sulien cares naught for that. She is as much a queen through her son as she was through Ruane. The shadow slipped along beside him, distorted by paving stones, looking malevolent as its tone. *Queens do not reckon costs.*

A hundred or so candles—each day—were surely never just tossed into the castle midden. Sulien might be uncaring, but doubtless at least one of her servants waxed fat selling off the stubs to his fellow servants. Crocken passed into the gray shadow of an ancient wall, losing his own shadow in the greater gloom, feeling a chill run deep into his own bones. Someone might not be so pleased, should they learn he'd walked off with goods they were accustomed to sell. The usher had been happy to unload half-burned candles—but who usually dealt with him? There might be danger . . .

All he'd wanted was a bit of light. Crocken shivered, feeling ill-used by the world and his fate—then stiffened his spine. There were perils everywhere. He'd face them as he must. The parapet he walked beside gave a view of the river, and of Rushgate lying beside it, teeming with commerce. He'd simply see that the candles were out of his hands within the hour, and take his chances.

Crocken knew where the chandlers plied their trade and had their shops—but even the most addled peddler knew profits were better if you carried your wares to a street where every shop-keeper was *not* busily engaged in creating those same wares. Crocken chose to visit a few mercers whose shops were far removed from the streets wherein the Chandlers Guild made their home. Save a man a walk that will take his servant half a day—an hour's walk for the errand, plus the time the servant would dawdle while not under his master's eye—and such a man would pay a more than fair price for the goods you brought to his door. Crocken returned to Axe-Edge burdened with a bottle of good ink, half a dozen fragrant oranges he happened to lo-cate, and quite a number of coppers to introduce to the rest of his hoard.

He took a wrong turn on the way to his room—he suspected the shadow allowed it as a punishment for his having enjoyed himself—and, righting it, was led through a stretch of formal garden, walled and iron-gated. Crocken paused to watch a game of bowls and ate one of his oranges, finding it most refreshing. Oranges wouldn't grow in Armyn's climate, but they journeyed well, and Sheir exported many. One had only to find the right market square.

A throat was cleared. Crocken looked up with alarm. Had his near theft of the candles been found out so soon? An excuse leapt to his lips, but to his relief, a young gentleman who could not have had the slightest interest in tapers stood before him. Evidently he had been having a turn at the bowls, for his grass-green and rose beltran was looped back over his arm, and his fair face was slightly flushed from air and exercise.

"Master Merchant-Adventurer?" he saluted Crocken hesi-tantly.

Crocken agreed, hardly more confidently. The shadow snorted.

"We have not met, sir, but I'd heard of you. I'm Baldred, Baron of Helier. I—" He flushed once more. "This is awkward, but have you another of those oranges you were enjoying? My lady—"

Crocken followed his sideways glance. He beheld a lady indeed, velvet-clad from cap to slippers, looking on eagerly. "She has a great fancy for them, you see, and I would keep her favor. The cooks say there are none to be had," Baldred complained helplessly.

Crocken smiled reassuringly and held up the sack of fruit. "At your service, my Lord Baron."

"Sir merchant, I am indebted." The baron pulled a ring from his smallest finger, a slender band of gold stamped at the center with a design that looked to Crocken's quick glance like a pomegranate. "I have none of the prince's coinage to hand, but if you would take this as a token—"

The "token" would have purchased every orange in Rushgate, and Crocken would never have dared to suggest such an exchange. He tried to turn it aside, to offer the fruit as a gift.

You'll only offend him, the shadow counseled.

Crocken reluctantly took the ring. Later, as he examined it by his new candle's light, a thought occurred. Few of Kieron's household seemed to descend to the markets of Rushgate. Servants did the market-going, and brought back what they chose. The most common bauble—witness the oranges—was a treasure to them, and therefore a profit waiting to be reaped by some discreet merchant. The possibilities were not lost on Crocken, who went to his bed very well content.

She was a small woman, frail when in her best health, bowed now under the grief of losing full half of the only things she loved in all the violent, untrusted world. The knowledge that she still retained the other half, that she was not completely bereft, alone gave Cailin the strength to go to her sister-in-law, to inquire after the prince's health. Her own little son had been taken ill with such awful swiftness, had died with even crueler speed. The two boys had played together but two days gone, the unknown sickness that had taken Edryd might strike Kieron, as well. His mother must be warned.

The bitter taste of grief, the unselfish action, made Ivy moan in her sleep, as the dream swirled around her. It grew stronger, and drew her down into its memories.

The queen dowager was still with her tiring woman when

Cailin arrived at her rooms. The steward-protector's lady waited in Sulien's misnamed solar, watching Kieron at play with a kitten. The boy seemed hale, perhaps all would be well, calamity would spare him, and Armyn—

The white kitten, batting at a dangled string, reached over-far and lightly raked Kieron's wrist. Without so much as a cry, without even a change of his expression, the prince batted the kitten back—dashing the small furry body hard against the tapestry-covered stone wall.

The kitten lay motionless. A trickle of blood ran from its mouth. Cailin stared unbelieving. Kieron carefully wound the string into a small coil and pocketed it. He stood and walked out of the room. As he passed his aunt, he glanced at her, empty-eyed, licked once at his scratched wrist—and smiled, pulling his lips back from teeth as sharp as the kitten's.

Cailin stared—first at Kieron, then blankly at the wall after he had gone. Her eyes gazed all unseeing. Her mind was re-calling her small son's finger, pricked with a tiny bite she had soothed and bandaged. *I thought 'twas the kitten nipped him. They teased it, boys will do that.*

There was some other connection, which her mind refused to make. Chilled, trembling, Cailin gathered her skirts and rose to flee back to her own rooms and to her husband, who was as grief-mad as she, and did not deserve to have such sick fancies poured into his ear. She had seen a nasty incident, but surely it had not been anything more than an unthinking cruelty. It meant only that Ruane's son was Sulien's, as well. No more than that. *No more . . .*

Sulien came out of her withdrawing room to see Cailin vanishing out the solar door. Her languid gaze lit next upon the dead kitten and she frowned, marring her ivory perfection. The wretched creature was bleeding onto her carpet. After a moment, she sent for her brother Andrayne.

"Rhisiart's lady was here, and left in distress. You are the prince's governor—see to it that he has no more little pets. And take that poor kitten away."

Andrayne did not remind his sister that *she* had allowed the kitten. He wrapped the little corpse in a napkin, and straightened. The expression on his queen's face startled him.

"Sister?"

"The lady Cailin thinks ill of my son. What else may she think?"

Andrayne shook his head. "She's only seen him harm this kitten. An unpleasantness, but—"

"*Her* son is dead."

"She'd never connect the two—"

"You're right, she won't."

Something in her tone chilled Andrayne to his bones. "*Sister—*"

"Rhisiart and his lady are both overborne with grief. I believe I shall send the lady some wine, to mend her doleful mood."

Andrayne's eyes widened. "My queen—" he warned.

"Only wine, Andrayne," Sulien said, and smiled, looking very much like her son.

Crocken continued to make trade contacts—both his private transactions and others of a more formal nature, as high-placed merchants sought him out at the court to satisfy curiosity and left well disposed to him—but it was not commerce that filled his dreams. He thought he rode to the hunt once more, though in the dream his steed was far more cooperative than it had been in reality. He never saw it. The beast might have been made of smoke rather than flesh. Or perchance the dream began with him close enough to see Kieron lifting his falcon from her prey, the ruby drops of blood glittering as if they were actual gems. Kieron seemed to regard them as something precious. He stared, his eyes eager and wild. His friends' congratulations lapped over him unheard, his expression remained as aloof and cold as the face of the moon. Details overlooked in the brief moment of reality blazed full into Crocken's senses in the dream: the way the pupils of Kieron's eyes contracted till they had well nigh vanished, the way his tongue flicked across his lips—

Crocken sat up, berating himself for dozing. Evil dreams came easily enough in bed, but slumping on a bench only invited them. And this obsession his sleeping mind had with the end of the hunt—what business of his, if Armyn's prince had a liking for blood? He cursed the shadow for drawing his attention to it, so that it filled all his unpoliced thoughts, night and day. How did it differ from the sort of battle lust encouraged in nobles and kings, anyway?

It did differ. Crocken knew that incontrovertably, though without anything resembling proof.

He desperately wished the shadow would return. Seldom had it left him lately that he knew of, even while he slept—though he was aware it was free at night. It seemed wary of dangers it would not specify to him, and so Crocken was frightened, too, though more on his own account than the shadow's. The hour was very late, and the shade had been gone since he'd retired to his room after the evening meal—it had parted from him without explanation or instruction, the instant he stepped over the threshold, leaving him to fret and doze off in uncomfortable places, prey to nightmares.

He ought simply to go to bed. The thing would be back come morning—as it must be. And with any luck, abed he'd sleep too sound for dreams. Crocken reached his fingers slowly toward the candle burning upon the table. The stub of wax had a small puddle of shadow, but he had none. He wiggled his fingers experimentally. Still nothing. The absence bothered him mightily, like an itch just out of his reach.

Without warning, shadow-fingers attached themselves to his fingertips. Crocken leapt back, nearly upsetting both candle and table.

"Don't *do* that!" he requested unsteadily, quietly because his breath had been startled away. "I like it better when you sneak up on me from behind, though I never thought I'd say that—" He was almost choked by the acceleration of his heart's beating.

Come with me, peddler.

"What, now?" Crocken stared, but could not read an expression the shadow did not possess. "It's almost—" He couldn't remember the last watch he'd heard called.

Come with me. I require your services.

Somehow the shadow was tugging him toward the door, brooking no opposition. Near dawn, it was still strong, while Crocken was weary and weak. He'd heard somewhere that more men died at the hour before dawn than at any other time. He could believe it. He felt will-less. He left the room, leaving the door ajar and not noticing.

The shadow guided him rapidly along mazy back ways that only servants would normally tread. Such passages were unguarded, save where they crossed more sensitive areas, and barely lighted. Crocken, afraid of the noise his voice would make in the stillness, did not ask whither they were bound. Useless anyway, no doubt. The shadow wouldn't necessarily choose to answer him. He concentrated on not stumbling, not crashing into walls. The shadow urged haste.

They crossed a wine cellar, climbed a flight of stairs. They were once more on the higher level where the quality folk of Axe-Edge spent their lives. There were boy pages sleeping under the next staircase he came to, and Crocken did not need to be urged to watch his feet and make no slightest sound. He glided like a shadow himself, glad there were finally torches, even though they guttered.

Here, the shadow announced.

Crocken halted, before a cross-bound door. The shadow elongated smartly away from him and slid beneath the panel. Crocken blinked. Shadow-boots were still attached to his own, but the rest of it was inside the chamber—thin and well disguised, he very much hoped. Apparently this was the task he'd been required for—to serve as anchor. Could the shadow pass a closed portal by no other means? He was always interested in his eldritch master's limits, whenever he could spy them out, but was usually unable to satisfy that curiosity. Not the sort of questions he dared ask.

On the instant, Crocken fell to fretting. How long would he be expected to remain at his precarious post? At any moment someone might happen along, and what excuse could he offer for loitering at such an hour—wherever he actually was? Whose chamber was he haunting? It could be very dangerous business, there was no telling. He'd never know till far too late.

Or suppose the shadow was doing some harm in there? *He* was the one who'd be blamed for it, if he were seen—on account of being the one who *could* be seen.

Crocken fidgeted in the dark, distracting himself briefly with the comfort that at least he was in place at the shadow's behest, not stupidly succumbing to a desire of his own to spy on his employer. He'd have been caught at that for certain—how does one distinguish one shadow from another, after all?

Leaning carefully, holding his breath, Crocken put his right ear to the panel that hid the shadow from him. For the first moment he heard nothing save the whisper of his own blood. Ignoring that deception, he succeeded in making out sounds from the inner chamber. Someone was within—the shadow would have had little interest in an empty room. Crocken recognized the rustle of fabric—probably someone stirring in his bed.

Actually two someones. There were further rustlings, and a feminine giggle, muffled but beyond mistake. Other sounds followed, equally plain as to their origins. Crocken felt his face flush. To overhear lovemaking by chance, in a crowded inn, for example, was one thing, and nothing remarkable. Sleeping four to a bed was hardly rare. But to eavesdrop on what a couple did

in their supposedly private chamber, in the deep of the night—
Crocken made to step away, annoyed. Was the shadow merely
a Peeping Tom, blessed with a rare advantage?

His ear was no longer at the door, but passion had raised the
voices within—Crocken could still make them out, at least in
snatches. A muffled "my lord—" and in answer to the girl, a
voice Crocken recognized as Kieron's. Coming on the heels of
his dream, the coincidence was unpleasant—but engrossing. The
girl cried out again, more urgently, and Kieron's answer was
unintelligible, as if his mouth was pressed against something.
Crocken thought he knew how the boy's eyes would look—just
as they'd been at the river meadow, rapt at the sight of fresh
blood—the image disgusted him, abruptly. He felt unclean,
guilty, ill used. A flush of shame lapped at his cheeks.

What business of the shadow's, if the prince pleasured himself
with a maid? What young man didn't, when the chance presented itself? Crocken heartily wished he dared return to his
room. The shadow was still stretched under the door. How many
steps could he take, ere the shadow would be forced to follow
him—wrathfully? At least he ought to be able to get out of ear-
shot . . .

He almost succeeded. Then the cry froze him in his tracks.

It was not the volume of the noise that halted him. A slain
rabbit screamed louder than the unseen girl did—and with the
same finality. Crocken, his flush replaced by a chill, laid his ear
to the door once more. He heard some sounds he could not quite
identify—which nonetheless raised the hair on the nape of his
neck—then gentle snoring. He came to a nasty realization.

He had been able to hear both the boy and the woman panting
earlier. Now he could make out only *one* person's breathing.

At that awful moment, Crocken became aware that one of the
corridor shadows possessed rather more substance than did his
master. His ears strained and caught the faint stirring of some
heavy fabric, off to his right. His twitching nose picked up the
startling clue of a familiar scent—lavender. The fragrance was
simpler than those blends Sulien's ladies affected, out of favor—
but he knew who used it.

Mistress Ivy? Crocken's eyes struggled with little success to
pierce the deep gloom. What did she here, at such an hour?

And indeed, where *was* he? These were not Kieron's own
rooms—surely there would be guards posted and torches burning nightlong. If the prince sought his pleasure instead of having
it brought to him—hunting as his falcon did, perchance—how

was Mistress Ivy involved? Did she spy for her lady—and how did she know where to spy? Crocken quit his post at the door and crept toward the girl, his shadow stretching invisibly after him.

Mistress Ivy—for it was indeed she—did not hear his approach, although she had the aspect of one listening intently to *something*. Faintest light from a casement well down the gallery showed her with cocked head, eyes tightly closed. She knelt among the scattering of rushes on the floorstones, careless of her thick skirts spread about her, heedless of the bold rats that tended to infest even the best-traveled passages of Axe-Edge, rapt as if she had her ear pressed to a door, her attitude an unconscious imitation of Crocken's late posture.

Crocken frowned. He could hear Ivy's shallow rapid breathing, but naught else. Not even rustlings, from where he stood. What did she harken to? This was so great a puzzle, he laid aside from his consideration those baffling things he had himself just heard from the chamber. He circled Ivy silently, since she was unaware of him, but gained no smallest clue.

Just as he completed a circuit of her, Ivy turned her head, as one who follows a conversation, glancing from one speaker to another. Her lids parted slightly—then flew wide as she started at the obviously unexpected sight of Crocken crouched before her.

Crocken started as well, lost his balance, and sat down hard upon the floor. He was a good pace away as the girl swooned and slipped sideways.

"Mistress Ivy!" He scrambled, trying in vain to catch her. Curse it, what had he been playing at? What if he'd frightened her into a fit? What if she'd screamed? Crocken propped Ivy's limp form against his chest and began to chafe her hands, which was all he could think of by way of remedy.

Her fingers were cold. He thought he would catch his own hands on the little silver ring she habitually wore, but he never encountered it. Her slender fingers felt quite bare under his.

The anomaly pricked his curiosity, but just at that moment Ivy stirred against him, and Crocken turned his whole attention to soothing her posthaste, without risking further commotion. If someone happened along, he couldn't imagine what the outcome would be.

Mistress Ivy had not spoken, but Crocken's overwary ears detected a faint, metallic rattle. He glanced nervously toward the sound and beheld a small circle of silver, shining faintly among the rushes. It rocked as he stared at it, like a child's hoop fallen on its side. As if it had just lately been rolling . . .

Crocken recognized the object, once he had it between his fingers—after all, it had been in his thoughts not a moment gone. The silver hoop was a finger ring—Mistress Ivy's very ring. Slipped from her limp hand as she fell into the faint, no doubt.

Only Crocken had an unshakable fancy that the ring had been rolling *toward* Ivy when it fell, not away. And the chime—true, the ring was solid silver, so his peddler's eye and fingers assessed it—but the note had been purer than the finest crystal produced when lightly struck. A bell-like sound, really, like an announcement . . .

A shadow fell across the little he could see, in the faint light. Crocken winced, expecting a scathing rebuke for leaving his post by the door, but his master made no comment—neither on Mistress Ivy nor on the ring Crocken held, possessed by matters of its own.

Worse, worse, the shadow moaned into Crocken's head, writhing back and forth. *The evil has grown as the child has. Yet its proof is more impossible to obtain than it was before*—Its distress was self-evident, if utterly unexpected. Crocken waited for it to elaborate, but of course it did not. It fell silent, and was invisible in the darkness, too—unless it had left him again.

Without thinking, Crocken slid the ring he held onto the smallest finger of Ivy's right hand. He'd chosen well, if blindly, for the fit was perfect—so perfect that he instantly wondered how it had chanced to come off in the first place. He frowned. The puzzle was as great as the shadow's odd behavior. The pair of mysteries bothered him only half an instant, for Mistress Ivy's eyes had opened.

She stared at Crocken for what seemed an hour, drew a breath—and he realized she intended to scream, even before the shadow warned him.

"Mistress Ivy!" Crocken grasped the girl firmly, but suspected she'd be more likely to scream if he tried to cover her mouth and failed. "It's me—" He remembered the darkness. "Crocken, the ped—don't scream! You're safe," he added in a desperate whisper.

"Master Crocken? But what do you here?" Ivy looked about, still wildly, not reassured, and she struggled against his hands. "Where is my lady? Where am I?"

Keep her quiet, the shadow ordered, its unexplained grief forgotten.

"I'm not entirely sure," Crocken admitted, trying to obey by answering her. "I . . . wanted a bit of air, and lost my way, walking."

"Oh, Master Crocken, I've had such awful dreams!" Ivy whispered pathetically. She clung to him, tight as her namesake, and she no longer struggled. "What can be happening, that they've driven me from my bed?"

Fully dressed? the shadow observed wryly. *Is that how they lie abed in Calandra?*

Crocken ignored the sarcasm. "Were you abed?" he asked gently. "You don't remember coming here?"

"I swear, I do not." Ivy shook her dark head desperately. Curls bounced against Crocken's face, not unpleasantly. "Please, sir, take me back to my lady! If she finds me gone, she will be frantic, and her vow will not allow her to ask after me—not to anyone!"

If anyone was frantic, 'twas Ivy herself. "It's almost dawn," Crocken offered soothingly. "She'll be asleep. Perhaps she hasn't missed you."

"But if she should! Please—"

Crocken courteously assisted Mistress Ivy to her feet, let her lean upon his arm when she trembled—and they had gone a fair way before it dawned upon him that *she* was subtly guiding his steps, and not the shadow, which was trailing after them at its customary distance and in less than customary silence.

He sought to discard his inconvenient suspicions. The hour was late, he was worn out, overwrought, and no fit judge of anything—he'd had no sleep at all, and a great deal of nervous tension, not to mention an outright fright or two. He should be grateful that he wasn't lost as well.

The Princess Mirell had a pleasant suite of rooms, set in one of the gatehouses that guarded an inner court. Since an enemy would need to breach three outer circles of fortified walls—besides climbing a sheer cliff—to penetrate Axe-Edge so far, the wall above the gateway's arch had been pierced on both sides with four tall windows, all in a row. The gallery so formed was Mirell's solar, as warm and bright by day as any chamber in Axe-Edge could be. At this hour of the night, all was in deep darkness.

At each end of the gallery were the towers that flanked the gateway. A guard was posted on the ground floor. Asleep by the coals of his fire, he'd been easy to slip past. Mirell's servants and goods would share the higher rooms in the tower—while the princess herself would be in the topmost chamber, where little glazed windows looked down on the courtyard and the solar's slate roof. No light burned, not even the faint flame of a night-candle. Mistress Ivy crept to the doorway and stood still to listen, though what one listened for when one's mistress was vowed not to speak, Crocken could not guess. Would the princess be allowed to weep? Sneeze? Yawn?

"Praise be, she's surely still asleep," Ivy said, returning to his side.

"As you should be," Crocken observed. "Are you quite well, mistress? I could fetch the healer—"

"No!" She put her hand on his arm, to forestall him. Crocken felt the cool silver of the little ring against his wrist. "Please, 'twould only alarm my lady! I recall now, when I was but a child, full often a dream would trouble me so that I fled it—and my bed! I must have lost my way in the dark, then fallen asleep again and been confused between dreams and waking. I'm well now, and have come to no harm, thanks to your kindness."

Crocken persisted, concerned. "If you have wine here, you might drink a cup. It would settle you." He wished vainly for a cup of some such spirit himself.

"I'll try that, sir. And my thanks for your kind assistance."

The advice and the courtesies were all whispered, lest any of the waiting women sleeping in the outer chamber be wakened and a scandal raised. When Crocken took his leave—or had it gently given to him—he saw that dawn was lightening the sky outside Axe-Edge. Its halls were still deeply shadowed within, and he bespoke one of those shadows.

"Why do you suppose she was there tonight?"

The same reason we were, the shadow answered maddeningly.

Whyever *that* was. Crocken got no further reply, though he asked thrice before he finally fell into his bed.

Chapter Seventeen

CROCKEN WAS PERMITTED to lie late abed as recompense for his lost night's rest, and the shadow commanded nothing of him until the following evening. Then it bid him undertake a trek to the wing where the Prince Kieron had his rooms, some little way along from his mother's, and hard by Lord Stiles' suite. The richly appointed rooms were thronged with folk, making merry in varied ways. Whether the celebration was a particular one, or merely general frolicking, Crocken could not learn by casual observation. He was uncertain if the prince meant to entertain and issued particular invitations, or if his adherents simply began the dancing and the singing and let Kieron join them if and when he would. Food and drink were set out in costly profusion.

The expense of the candles, too, must have been considerable. Crocken wondered anew where they were obtained and what the going price was for new tapers. He had friends among Kôvelir's chandlers, and if Rhisiart's trade schemes worked out, perhaps he could grasp a share of the market for himself—

His train of merchantly thought was broken whilst he struggled politely to avoid being drawn into a circle dance by one of the queen's nieces. Crocken could justly claim ignorance of the steps involved, but refusing a lesson in them proved more difficult, as the fair-haired girl was adamant. The dance looked to be mostly composed of leaping, so Crocken added for good measure that his barely healed head might pain him if he indulged in such strenuous pleasures. Fortunately, the lie sufficed, and the girl sought a more willing partner after pouting only the barest instant for form's sake.

The entertainments and pleasures were diverse and engaging: dining, drinking, dancing, and games of all sorts, all refined on account of their location. Crocken steered wide of any dicing he saw. He was now accounted formidable with the cubes, but he could never live up to his reputation without the shadow's aid, and if it chose to withhold it he'd be left penniless in short order—to the shadow's delight, he was certain. Best he not be tempted, or tempt his master into lessoning him.

The shadow was content that he should wander through the merrymaking at will, observing and lingering as he chose, conversing or moving on at his own discretion. Such unaccustomed freedom made Crocken uneasy—he was always in readiness, but commands to alter his actions did not come. Crocken had yet to spot the prince and thought Kieron might not yet have joined the throng of his guests. He was certain the shadow would order him close, if Kieron appeared. Just then it was slithering across the patterned carpets dotting the floor, weaving between skirts and booted feet, uncaring whether it was trampled.

The events of the previous night were a dim confusion, so muddled that he might have dreamed them—save that his dreams were generally *less* obscure. Crocken had asked the shadow no more about it, since it had refused him so often, and was schooling himself to discard the memories, though without great success.

Mistress Ivy appeared, at the side of her incomparable and silent lady. The Princess Mirell seemed able to enjoy the festivities well even without speech. Crocken thought her vow was a rather clever scheme that more brides ought to adopt—it allowed her to observe her new homeland and people at her leisure, while making no false steps till she should be sure of herself with them, revealing nothing of herself beyond the surface.

That surface was especially lovely this night—Mirell's chestnut hair was caught up slightly in a net of fine silver, well set off by the pale green of her gown. The embroidery upon it gave Crocken pause to wonder about the state of the prince's promised shirt—he inquired of Mistress Ivy when he paid his respects—but he asked rather softly, not at all boldly, lest the mention be a breach of etiquette.

"All matters in Armyn proceed in their ordered time, Master Crocken," Mistress Ivy answered imperturbably, glancing aside at Mirell. "My lady's gift, the plans for the crowning—there's much to do, though there are months yet for the doing of it." She seemed quite unaffected by her midnight perambulation—perchance only a little weary as the day drew to its close, perhaps anxious that she might not rest well when she sought sleep.

"When is the coronation set?" Crocken was certain the stately preparations would be many, but he had seen no sign of them—or not recognized them as such. He'd have expected to find Rushgate in a ferment of commerce. Was what he'd taken for normal trade actually the brisk activity great events produce? That was a thought to chill a merchant's blood.

"Kieron will reach his majority in four months' time." Ivy formally tasted a cup of wine, then passed it to her lady. "They have chosen his natal day for the crowning."

"And will it be his wedding day, as well?" Crocken glanced at the Princess Mirell, who cast her eyes down demurely, as a maiden ought, and smiled a secret smile. Crocken had not directly addressed her—it was easy to fall into the habit of simply speaking to Ivy as if her mistress were absent—but Mirell had surely heard.

"That's not settled yet," Ivy said brightly. "Nor is the question of the tournament. Kieron is wild to have one. Lord Stiles is far-famed for his jousting skills and would be pleased to display them. He wanted to sponsor a tourney to honor the betrothal, but the steward-protector said war was bad enough without playing at it, and refused to allow it. Remember, my lady? Kieron sulked like a mewed hawk the whole first week we were here?"

Mirell answered with a smile.

"Well, he'll likely get his battle game now—Rhisiart will have a hard time refusing to include one in the coronation festivities, since Kieron will be king then and can order it done!"

Likely his first command will be for battle, not wedding.

Crocken resented the literal shadowing of a pleasant moment, but there was nothing to be done about it. He strove to pretend he hadn't heard.

He and Ivy chatted inconsequentially. Folk were pointed out to him. Other folk came, presented themselves or were introduced, and went. Mirell was drawn off by a flock of her sisters-to-be, to view a new tapestry Lord Stiles had lately acquired.

"Are you your lady's only retainer?" Crocken asked. For Mirell seemed always to be surrounded by her husband-to-be's kin, or alone with Ivy, never attended as he'd seen Sulien was. "How did her father send her here with so little state?" It seemed at odds with what little he knew of court doings. He had learned, for example, that Lord Stiles had a retainer whose sole task was the lighting of his lord's way to the privy, though he did not pass that information on to Ivy.

Mistress Ivy laughed, as if she'd read his thought anyway. "You are lamenting that if only my lady did not require me so much, you might have more leisure to flatter me and turn my simple head with tales of the far-off lands you have traded in." She mockingly waved off Crocken's protests. "Being a diligent courtier is so wearisome! Had my lady brought a huge train of attendants with her into this court—as Sulien did—it might have been ill thought of. Especially as she is not from any part of Armyn, but a stranger naturally rousing suspicions. Bring in a pack of foreigners, and 'twould look· as if my lady wished to associate only with them, not with her husband's people. There would be jealousies, hatreds. And if her folk were expected to remain here with her, they'd need to be fed, clothed, suitably married—provided for. What troubles! My lady very bravely—and most wisely—chose to avoid all difficulties save those I cause." Mistress Ivy cast her eyes down modestly, but her lips twitched.

"Do you cause her so many troubles?" Crocken bantered.

Instead of jauntily replying, Ivy turned the ring she wore, the little silver twist of ribbon and beads. Whatever she was about to answer—whether she *would* have mentioned the previous night—went unspoken, for just then the Princess Jocilyn swept her off to be consulted as to Mirell's preferences in sweetmeats, and Crocken saw little more of her, having no invitation to partake of sweetmeats with the princesses, nor a decent excuse to shadow her through the festivities.

He wandered idly on his own, tasting a bit of cold spiced fowl. He wished he'd thought to ask Ivy where Kieron was. There was no obvious sign of him, nor of his governor. Why did his court, making merry, not lure the young man out? Or was he occupied elsewhere? And occupied with what? Common sense told him that young maids tended to preoccupy young men—even those soon to wed—but that the shadow should care about that made little sense. There was, he suspected, more afoot than dalliance.

A trio of well-dressed older men stood commenting upon one of the new tapestries. Crocken recognized them as wool merchants and made his way to them, happy to give himself something to think upon that had naught to do with Kieron or the puzzles of the past midnight. He instantly became enmeshed in a speculatory discussion of wool prices, coming out of it the pledged owner of a share in a venture that might prove immeasurably popular. The capital involved was beyond his means, but as the proposed venture was also likely years from fruition, Crocken felt safe enough about speculating with coin he had yet to accumulate. Safer than the tasks the shadow set him to, anyway.

The prince's rooms were all in a line, opening into one another, with the private chambers arranged at the sides. Lord Stiles' were linked to Kieron's, and as richly appointed, so Crocken could not tell if the boy and his tutor arrived at the festivities together. He had a straight line of sight through the doorways, but though the chambers were brightly lit, he was still three rooms away, able to make out only generalities. He saw Kieron's colors, the beltran flung over garb of scarlet wool. But then the line of dancers in the second room came together at the end of the measure and blocked his view entirely.

A consort of musicians struck up a simple air, almost counterpoint to the one played for the dancers. One of Lord Stiles' favorite hangers-on—Crocken had met him often—began to sing multitudinous verses to it. The words were subtle and witty at first, then became frankly ribald. The crowd's laughter almost covered—at first—how swiftly their lewdness increased. Crocken smiled, happy to comprehend the jests for once. As yet he had no notion why his boar-slaying reputation birthed puns. He had the impression, from the surprised outbursts of the wool merchants, that the lyrics now offered were not the usual words married to the tune. The title and the subject—"The Cleft Heart"—took on a double meaning, which was elaborated upon endlessly at the end of each verse.

Chance led him to glance aside just as Rhisiart left the room. Crocken had noticed the steward-protector circulating for quite some while—most unusual, apparently, for 'twas much remarked upon behind his back. Crocken conceded that Rhisiart seemed the sort to prefer work to merrymaking, an unlikely guest at one of Kieron's impromptu and continual frolics. Now he exited hurriedly.

After him!

Rhisiart's headlong manner would have sent Crocken after him even without the shadow's prodding, the whole matter struck him as so curious. He was conveniently near to the doorway and so slipped out as silently and nigh as swiftly as had the steward-protector. No one followed him. He managed not to snag his beltran on the stone.

The portal, closely hung to muffle stray drafts, gave onto a high walkway atop the curtain wall. More walls rose above them, then the star-spangled sky. Rhisiart stood alone at the parapet, his fingers tight-clenched upon the ancient stonework, his head bowed. He was breathing in great, desperate gasps—as if he could not draw in sufficient of the cool air for his needs, like a man near drowned and rescued scarce in time.

Crocken had seen men quaff wine so, and evil events had always surely followed. His alarm was such that he instantly judged the height of the parapet. Better than waist-high—if Rhisiart intended to jump, at least there'd be time to stop him, Crocken thought wryly. He shook his head at such folly. Rulers of kingdoms did *not* simply leave a merry entertainment and fling themselves to their deaths. But what *was* going on? The shadow made no comment, gave no further orders. He could see it lying on the stones, very faint, very alert. He was learning to tell where its attention was, though by what signs he could not have explained.

The steward-protector remained where he was, and his breathing slowly calmed, becoming less audible. Crocken shifted uncertainly, wondering belatedly whether he ought to intrude, afraid he could not withdraw without calling attention to himself. He'd acted without thinking and now regretted the spontaneity. How could he explain his pursuit? Odd though such action might seem to him, it was none of *his* business if Rhisiart chose to desert his nephew's party for the cold and lonely dark. He had no excuse for presumptuously shadowing the man—or none he could give.

His boot scraped faintly against stone. Rhisiart turned, his ragged breath stilled at once—easily the most deadly sound Crocken had ever *not* heard. There were tears on the man's face—the starlight showed them plain. Above, his eyes were two black, dangerous holes.

"Your pardon," the steward-protector said, his voice unexpectedly steady. Some of the tension went out of his stance, and Crocken realized he had somehow been recognized. Rhisiart gestured toward the doorway—the gay music could still be faintly heard, and the louder laughter punctuating the verses. "The gaiety wearies me betimes. That tune . . . my lady loved it well."

Under other words, I'll be bound, Crocken thought. He recalled that Rhisiart's lady was dead, and that Ivy had called the union a love match. A reminder of her was evidently painful.

Metal gleamed on Rhisiart's left shoulder, pinning his beltran. Silver, an animal of some sort—a hundred jests came home to

Crocken all at once, as he recognized the beast. *A boar*. The prince's folk, the queen's, Lord Stiles—all had made so pointedly merry over his slaying of a boar, and now he understood the jokes at last, which had never been at *his* expense. How had he never seen how the court hated Rhisiart? Ivy had even told him, flat out. Crocken realized that the mockery of the ballad had been no accident, none at all.

And he asks my pardon? Crocken thought, swallowing down a painful lump, new-lodged in his throat. *If I had his authority, I'd have that minstrel's head on a spike—or better yet, his master's*. Suddenly his recollections of the better part of the evening were less than pleasing—drunken courtiers rioting in rooms too hot, too loud, too crowded with colors and bodies. There had been rich food and drink—and vomit among the floor rushes. The sudden freshness of the outside air only made the memory more distasteful. It set his own stomach churning. Small wonder Rhisiart had fled.

"I miss the air, most of all things," the steward-protector was saying softly, almost to himself. "The sky of the Borderlands is so vast—even when the mists settle in, a man can breathe free. Sometimes it seems only a dream—and I wake here, smothering." He shook his head to chase away the fancy and looked sharply at Crocken. "Was there something?"

Crocken shook his own head, then recalled the darkness and spoke politely. "My lord Steward, no. I was by the door and saw you go out. You looked . . . unwell, so I followed—"

Rhisiart frowned and turned half away, back toward the parapet. His hand dropped to his belt, playing with the dagger he carried there.

"No one else saw," Crocken added hastily. "They're past noticing, most of them."

"Truly," Rhisiart agreed, putting aside the irritation. He took his hand away from his belt. "Otherwise, how have you found our court, Master Merchant-Adventurer? I regret not speaking with you sooner. It was not my intention to abandon you, but matters touching Kieron's coronation have lately occupied me more than I had anticipated. Has our bustle of commerce admitted you?"

"Most willingly, my lord. I think I bought some sheep, just this evening."

"Sheep?" Rhisiart sounded startled, probably at the thought of flocks inside Kieron's rooms.

"The wool to be sheared from their backs, actually, and voyaged to Calandra,'' Crocken explained. "I anticipate a tidy profit. Your wool here rivals anything I've seen in Kôvelir.''

"Then you also expect our prince's marriage will bear the trade fruit I hope for?'' Rhisiart put his back to the parapet and leaned on it companionably.

"I never doubt it for a moment, my lord. If others do . . .'' Crocken shrugged. "So much the better for me. I can buy very cheaply, then sell at an even fairer profit.''

"Buy cheap, sell dear—the peddler's maxim.''

"Truly spoken,'' Crocken agreed.

"You might have claimed anything, when you came here,'' Rhisiart mused. "Knighthood, royalty even. Anything you told us would have been believed, encouraged. Wild tales a-plenty were spun around you. Yet *you* never lied about what you were. Why not? Why be a peddler when you could have been a knight? To gain my respect? That's no great matter, and not one you could have expected. Whyfore such risky honesty?''

Crocken wondered that Rhisiart should think a man *could* lie to him, but sought more polite words for his answer and took a moment framing it.

"My lord, one's called to prove one's claims, sometimes. Merchantry, I can demonstrate, though you honor me in lifting me up from common peddler. I know the game. If I'd tried to prove knighthood—'' He considered taking up arms against a skilled opponent and shuddered. He had no skill with sharp weapons beyond his knife, whereas knightly boys grew up with swords in their beds, cutting teeth upon axe-hafts. "I'd likely be dead,'' he finished. "I'm a practical man, and surely the truth is always simplest. That's not a peddler's maxim, of course.''

Rhisiart's teeth flashed against the darkness, as he quietly laughed. "How few here would agree with that principle! Master Crocken, come to the Hall tomorrow—anyone can tell you the way. We hear petitions and grievances there in the foremorn. Some of what chances may well interest you, and I shall value your practical observations of our justice.''

Rhisiart spent an overlong moment fussing with his beltran, and Crocken realized that the man was still laughing and evidently striving to hide the fact lest he offend. The shared jest set Crocken's own lips twitching—and he was cheered as well that he'd lightened Rhisiart's fell mood, however inadvertently. It was inescapable—he liked the man, despite the shadow's dire comments.

The steward-protector then took his leave, with a repetition of his invitation that seemed quite sincere. Crocken noticed that Rhisiart did not reenter Kieron's rooms, but went along the battlement walkway. Now that he listened for it, he could hear the tramp of sentries, challenge and answer as Rhisiart reached their post, all faint with distance but carrying on the night air.

Good sense, checking one's guards oneself. Crocken recalled that Rhisiart was accounted a formidable commander, with an obvious eye for such disciplines. He could not imagine Kieron noticing that men-at-arms were about, save as decor, far less noticing whether they were attentive at their posts. Rhisiart was wiser—but then he was also older, seasoned by many troubles and by the hard school of warfare. He'd led an army at Kieron's age, if what the shadow related was true.

Crocken sensed that shadow stretching itself restively—now there was no witness, it need not conform to him so straitly.

"Do you want me to go back inside?" Crocken thought of the scene he'd left and suddenly dreaded returning, but it was better to ask than to be ordered. Strange the shadow had made no earlier complaint, seeing how it loathed Rhisiart. It might not care to be near him long. Perchance it had only been hoping to see him jump from the battlements and was now disappointed.

No. You may rest. I did not see Lord Stiles. Kieron has at last joined the frolic and will be safely there all evening.

So, *that* was the event they'd been awaiting. But why?

The business in the Hall will begin early, if I am any judge of Rhisiart's custom.

"You *want* me to go?" Crocken was startled.

I insist upon it.

That was a surprise. He'd been wondering how to ask for permission. "I thought you didn't trust Rhisiart?"

I said he betrayed me. It is of no matter—you may attend him if he requests it. Your compassion may afford me . . . opportunities.

After that exchange, Crocken wondered whether he might best serve his liking for Rhisiart by leaving Axe-Edge at once—but he was not such a fool as to think such behavior would be tolerated. He buried the shadow's remark deep in his memory, promising himself that he would not allow it to force him to commit unjustifiable harm. Or allow it to do such harm itself—assuming there was any way he could see of stopping it. At the first, he had been fearful of what it intended to do to *him*, now he realized it might intend far worse to others—particularly Rhisiart—and he was loath to be party to any such action. Spying was bad enough.

There was room a-plenty in the Hall, which alone of Axe-Edge's many halls needed no distinguishing name. Located at the heart of what looked to be the most ancient part of the citadel, it dwarfed even the proudest guildhalls Crocken had on occasion visited in Kôvelir. He would not have been much surprised to see clouds a-forming among its lofty rafters.

Assuming, of course, that he could have seen those rafters. No windows broke the long walls, and the torchlight faltered and was swallowed long ere it reached the roof. The Hall's vastness made itself known by stages, as Crocken's senses slowly adjusted to it.

There was not, as would have been usual, a second-storey walkway about the edges of the great room. One entered from the ground and remained there, humbled. Daylight admitted by doors at each end revealed bare hints of carven beams spanning an impossible width. Not a single pillar broke the floor space at the center of the room, where a whole forest of columns should have been required. Great building-craft had been plied, and Crocken shook his head in wonderment, recalling the apparent dearth of wizardly folk in Armyn. In Kôvelir, such a hall's stones and beams would have been mage-bolstered, and the place would have been magic-lit to show it off. Yet in Armyn the great wonder was wrought without sorcery and left mostly unseen.

A broad dais crossed one end. Stairs led down onto it for the Protector's Council and his justiciars to enter by; other stairs rose up from the floor where the clumps of petitioners waited their turns. Voices carried well, since there was little in the room to deflect them. Crocken did not need to elbow his way into the crowd, but could stand comfortably beside his shadow on the fringes, close by a tapestry depicting an ancient battle scene in murky colors.

Betimes, that faded weaving was the most entertaining thing in the Hall. Infringements of fishing rights and inheritance squabbles could hold Crocken's interest only up to a point, and he marveled that Rhisiart could follow the ramblings with even apparent efficiency. Experience was in play, of course, but there must be some liking in it as well, for the job to be done and done justly. On the whole, the petitioners seemed pleased with the verdicts dispensed, even when they were referred for further discussion.

After a good two hours, the Prince Kieron entered, resplendent as usual in his beltran of gold, purple, and sanguine over a suit of dark blue, companioned by his governor Lord Stiles and a gay flourish of attendants. Rhisiart yielded the central chair to his nephew at once, taking a place at the prince's right hand. Matters turned more esoteric as laws and writs earlier proposed were discussed, their ramifications examined. The petitioners had all been dealt with and had departed, so the crowd had thinned.

Crocken was surprised to find that the new matters engaged his interest more surely than the grievance-hearing had. It wasn't only that he had always found it good sense and sound policy to be cognizant of the laws of any realm where he traded; those policies Rhisiart laid out for the formality of Kieron's inspection were most enlightened. In fact, he'd never heard their like.

Peers asked to judge their fellows in legal matters were to be straitly protected from threats as well as bribes—Crocken knew the abuse was a problem, but few lords took serious steps to resolve it.

A man standing accused of wrongdoing should, in prescribed circumstances, be allowed to post security monies and be let go free to conduct his defense while waiting for the matter to come to trial—most novel.

Too novel, haply, to sit well with Armyn's next ruler.

"Uncle, what madness is this? When I imprison a man, I want him jailed, not enjoying his liberty!" Kieron's mouth set petulantly, and his eyes narrowed.

The shadow came to attention, though keeping to its proper place. Crocken was interested, too—this was the first public meeting he'd witnessed between the prince and the steward-protector, and the tales of friction seemed true.

"My lord, once a man stands *convicted* of wrongdoing, such should indeed be so," Rhisiart answered patiently. "We speak here of men only *accused* of crimes. Should a man languish in jail because a slanderous neighbor has a malice against him? Suppose the charge be false? It is wrong. It punishes the innocent."

"If the man is innocent, what does he before my courts, Uncle? I will not accept this." The prince's voice rose with his obstinacy. The steward-protector looked weary.

The shadow made a derisive noise. *He argues like his uncle on the other side*, it said.

"Rhisiart shouldn't explain the new laws to Kieron. The prince never challenges the ones he doesn't understand, and he can't figure them out on his own."

Crocken started, realizing the wicked comment had not come from his shadow.

Mistress Ivy stood by the tapestry, her hands folded demurely before her as she played with her silver ring, turn and turn about on her white fingers. Her green eyes danced with mischief.

"This is a strange choice for a lady's entertainment, is it not, Mistress Ivy?" Crocken asked softly, trying to swallow his heart back down. His fright had it jumping like a hooked trout.

"And should the king's coffers be expected to feed and house every man accused of wrongdoing?" Ivy continued. "Wiser to allow them to purchase their freedom till they're tried, and let them feed themselves. No, Master Crocken, my lady is here, also, and not for sport but for knowledge. She wishes to learn how the land is governed, as queens must know such things."

Crocken bowed slightly. He saw Mirell, now that he looked, seated a little way off, in a graceful chair. "It was rankest ingratitude for me to question an occasion for seeing you again," he said. "If I hold myself rebuked, will you pardon me?"

"Since you plead your case so prettily. Otherwise I suppose you'll insist I must feed you!" Ivy laughed merrily at her jest. "My lady should invite you to sup with us some even. Doubtless you have many diverting tales to share with us. Ah, look! Kieron's leaving."

If there had been a full-blown quarrel, it had been brief and softly spoken. Crocken hadn't heard a thing, nor had the shadow warned him to attend anything beyond Mistress Ivy. But the prince was indeed quitting the Hall, and his attendants were scrambling to follow him, so the departure was unexpected. The steward-protector watched them go, his face without expression. Rhisiart did not speak till the Hall had finally quieted even of echoes.

"Gentlemen. Let us continue. We have much work before us still. Lord Chamberlain, have you a report to make on the preparations for the prince's coronation?"

"He takes it calmly," Crocken declared, astounded.

"He's used to it," Ivy corrected, compressing her lips. "Kieron always finds a pretext to take offense once he's bored. Last week he left because Rhisiart decided an inheritance dispute in a manner the queen's family found objectionable. That happens from time to time,'' Ivy added wisely. ''Appease them as he may, Rhisiart cannot match the riches Ruane accustomed Sulien's relations to. The steward-protector tries to be politic and says the false grants are mistakes Ruane must not have been aware of, but still Sulien is full of spleen.''

''Why not let the prince deal with it?'' Crocken wondered. That would have been *his* choice. Why did Rhisiart step into a fray with every hand against him?

'' 'Tis the protector's duty to govern till his liege is of age,'' Ivy explained. ''Rhisiart takes that most seriously. The prince is here—or was here—to observe, to learn.''

Fine job he makes of it. The shadow had taken up a place among the stitched figures of the tapestry. Crocken resisted the urge to shoo it away and forced his eyes to look elsewhere.

''King in all but name—so Sulien's people slander Rhisiart,'' Ivy said bitterly. ''They put about false tidings, insist that he will never crown Kieron. Yet when he's been urged to take the crown for himself, Rhisiart has sent the urgers away, and not overgently.''

Crocken found himself staring at the girl with appalled respect. This was no feather-headed maiden, as he was belatedly discovering. Had a princess need of a tiring maid so well versed in politics? Perhaps not. It might be entirely an accident—or useful for her to seem only such. Mistress Ivy, still passionately gazing at the steward-protector, took no note of Crocken's startled scrutiny.

''There was a man,'' she said companionably, ''a bosom friend of Ruane's, and a friend of Rhisiart's, too, for long years. This man had little liking for the queen and none for her folk, so he began a rising, hoping to force Rhisiart to set aside the stewardship and take the throne in his own right. This was when Kieron was a child in years as well as manners, and most folk feared the mishaps of a child's reign.''

''What happened?'' Though the outcome of the rising was plain. It had to have failed, for Rhisiart was not king.

''Rhisiart had him beheaded, on charge of treason,'' Ivy answered calmly.

Rhisiart, who betrayed me, the shadow reminded him.

Crocken felt as if the Hall had begun to gently sway, a giddiness much akin to that which he'd felt while still recovering from his head-knock. He shut his eyes, waiting for the weakness to pass. ''He cut off a friend's head?'' he asked, very softly.

The penalty for treason, the shadow assured him.

The Council's business went on, and on, and at length was concluded.

"Gentlemen, a week hence. I wish you good progress in all endeavors."

The crowd had thinned and ebbed away. Crocken opened his eyes and found that with the intervening folk gone, he was closer to the dais than he'd supposed, closer than he liked to be. He was about to slip away when Rhisiart headed in his direction, having descended from the dais. Crocken's legs went weak with dread. His heart recommenced the troutlike leaping.

Let him pass me by, he wished desperately, unready to assay conversation with a man who cut off a friend's head and had shown him such great friendliness.

As if his wishes were possessed of wizardly powers, Rhisiart halted a dozen paces off, while a man clad in his livery spoke softly into his ear.

The steward-protector's grave face was transformed. *He looks his age when he smiles*, Crocken thought, startled into recalling Rhisiart's relative youth. Thus transfixed, he neglected to slip away when the chance was before him, and then Rhisiart was passing close to him, passing and turning aside to speak to him.

"Master Merchant-Adventurer, this may interest you! Have you a moment?"

Chapter Eighteen

CROCKEN, FORCING HIMSELF to be optimistic, knowing Rhisiart could not read his thoughts, was anticipating trade goods of some sort, but it was the stables they finally fetched up at, bypassing the storerooms along their route. He followed the steward-protector warily between long rows of horse rumps in tie stalls, till they arrived at a spacious loose box. Rhisiart entered at once, but nothing could have induced Crocken to continue following him.

Even Rhisiart halted once he was inside, carefully latching the door. The white horse that turned to face him looked half the size of a mountain, and it laid back its ears the instant it perceived its visitors, presenting a most unwelcoming aspect. Rhisiart laughed, with apparently genuine amusement.

"Were you sorry to leave the Borderlands, my Stormraker? There are fair mares here, as well, I do assure you."

The stallion snorted, then advanced, nostrils fluttering. Rhisiart stood still, waiting. The stallion nickered very softly and stretched out its head. When the horse had done sniffing at him, the steward-protector began to rub the crest of its mighty neck, his fingers greeting it as another horse would have, while he spoke over his shoulder to Crocken.

"This is Stormraker, my war-stallion. Having done service to most of the mares in the Borderlands—and a fair number upon his journey here—he has been brought to Axe-Edge to continue his work. His is a bloodline I wish very much to increase."

Stormraker's arrival seemed to have *decreased* the number of royal grooms. Crocken didn't fault them for making themselves scarce. Any stallion could turn nasty, but war-stallions were *trained* to kill men in battle, and 'twas a short step from that to simply squashing any human that annoyed them. Stormraker

131

rested his gray nose against Rhisiart's chest, but the eye he turned upon Crocken was white-rimmed and restless. Aware of the bad effect his shadow seemed to have on horses, Crocken went no closer, though the stable was fairly dim and he could only sense the shadow, not see it.

"Ah, beautiful! See, my lady, the size of him, yet such grace!" And there was Mistress Ivy, at his elbow again, with her lady on her other side. "My lord, we overheard the news that he had at last arrived and, having heard such fair report of him, could not resist seeing Stormraker for ourselves."

Crocken stepped back a pace to let the ladies have a better view of the horse, and was more comfortable for the added distance—though he held ready to yank either of them back to safety should the stallion make a sudden move. Stormraker pawed at his bedding with a hoof the size of a porringer and arched his neck to handsome effect. His mane was a silken fringe, white as a waterfall.

"Surely a monarch of horses," Ivy said, laughing at the proud display the stallion put on for his audience. "How old is he, my lord Steward?"

"The same age as the prince, Mistress Ivy. They were born the same month." The stallion stamped close by his right boot, but Rhisiart forbore to flinch. "When he was rising three and still black as an inkpot, my brother Miall commended him to me. I bought him on the spot—once I'd made certain there was an iron bit in his mouth." Rhisiart's fingers had worked their way to the stallion's withers, and Stormraker reached around with a flash of teeth, offering to repay the grooming in kind.

"That sounds like the start of a good Borderlands tale," Mistress Ivy observed, as Rhisiart nimbly dodged the horse's attentions. "My lord Steward, pray don't just toss it in front of us and then leave it lying untold! My lady will never forgive me if I allow you."

Mirell nodded enthusiastic agreement, while Crocken looked on with bemusement. What tale could there be, other than it being good sense to want a bit in a horse's mouth? Especially such an unruly mountain of a horse? *He'd* have wanted it hobbled, as well—or caged, by choice.

Rhisiart was smiling. "I suspect someone has already been telling you tales, Mistress. 'Tis only a foolish superstition—we have an ample supply of those."

Ivy looked encouraging. "We hear many tales, but seldom from one who's dwelt in the Borderlands. Please, my lord?"

Rhisiart shook his head, seemingly in wonderment. "I'm no minstrel. I fear I shall disappoint you—but if you insist—"

"I'm sure my lady would instruct me to."

Mirell bobbed her head once more. Crocken discovered he was not unwilling, either.

The steward-protector turned his attention back to Stormraker, as if embarrassed to tell the tale while looking any of them in the face. "It's said that the hill folk have the power of shape-shifting—many things are claimed of them, and some are true. They are a very old people, and though we took their land from them, we never conquered them—they only drew back farther into their hills. Any mischief they can work upon us, they esteem as an obligation. Sometimes, 'tis said, they will band together to thieve from decent folk, and this is the manner of it: One will shape himself into an animal, a fine black horse or perchance a wolfhound, and let his friends sell him at some town's market day. The friends fetch the gold home, and come nightfall the thief shifts back to human form, lifts off collar or bridle, and vanishes away."

Very neat, Crocken thought. He could not tell, from Rhisiart's careful tone, whether the steward-protector believed the superstition or not. He had stopped very carefully short of endorsing it.

"So, if you buy a horse or a dog in the border country, you do well to see that it wears an iron bit or an iron-spiked collar—the hill folk cannot abide the touch of cold iron, and if it comes near them, they cannot deceive you." Rhisiart shrugged. "Of course, no one admits to believing such idle fancies. And if the hill folk were such puissant sorcerers, how was it not they, but we, that conquered? But you'll find no man in the Borderlands who'd buy a horse—especially a black one—without seeing it bitted. As soon not clasp hands to seal a bargain." He stroked Stormraker's white neck again. "I will admit, I was something relieved when he began to gray."

Ivy presented one tiny hand, which the stallion first sniffed, then politely licked. Making much of him, she coaxed her lady closer, also. Crocken shivered, wondering how well the princess could stitch her betrothed's shirt with only eight or nine fingers.

"Your brother Miall? Which one was that, sir? I had not heard that name before."

"No. I suppose you would not." Rhisiart was busy with a thorough inspection of his horse, clucking over the state of his steel-shod hooves, his tangled tail. "It's been a long time—look at this beast. He's ten stone over his proper weight, even after the exercise of the journey here! Stud life's too soft—you need work, boyo!'' Stormraker tossed his head, but Rhisiart easily avoided it. ''You've grown indolent, and it does your temper little good.''

''Will you ride him to hunt, my lord?'' Ivy asked. ''The Prince Kieron has promised to take us hawking again on the morrow.''

Rhisiart laughed sharply. ''I think not. We'd both be well advised to avoid the royal pack. No, I'll try him alone, when he's had a day to settle from his journey.''

''Is that wise, my lord? Alone?'' Crocken instantly wished he'd bitten his tongue, for the look Rhisiart turned on him. Presently the steward-protector's gaze softened, as he considered the question's intent.

''I was thinking of the hounds' safety, not my own, but there's sense in what you ask,'' he replied reasonably. ''I'll send someone to collect you in the foremorn. Stormraker and I will introduce you to the country hereabouts. There's more to Armyn than Axe-Edge and Rushgate.''

The morning was overcast and mostly shadowless. Crocken had been desperately devout in his hope for rain—surely Rhisiart would not insist on exercising his horse in a chill downpour? But Crocken was early summoned and conducted to the stables, there helped into the saddle of a tall bay horse that he assumed was a gelding—who'd send two stallions out together, unless to war? And still no rain fell, or seriously offered to. He cursed his luck—and his tongue, to have landed him in the predicament.

He also longed for the gray he'd ridden to the hunt. Crocken felt he'd been close to an understanding with that beast, at least toward the end of their previous outing. Now he had to begin afresh, with another strange, skittish beast that seemed to see shadows invisible to him, and which lacked the benefit of Mistress Ivy's half-magical gentling. And he had to cope alone, for the steward-protector was nowhere in sight, having gone on ahead. The groom told him that and gave brief directions as he led Crocken's horse to the stable gate. Crocken's heart misgave him—how could he hope to control his mount and accurately recall directions, as well?

If this horse somehow does not know the way, I shall guide you, his nearly invisible shadow offered derisively. *You're only going down to the river meadow.*

Crocken cautiously touched a heel to his horse's side, and let it trot off down the road, remembering with difficulty not to drag on the reins. He was tempted to simply keep following the beast's nose—but as the shadow still occasionally pointed out to him, he had nowhere to go if he ran off. Besides, his tiny hoard of gold pieces was tucked under a carefully loosened stone by the hearth in his room, and he wasn't so fond of being penniless as to desert it.

Axe-Edge's builders had forestalled sieges by enclosing nearly all the flat ground at the cliff top within the fortress's outer walls. All of the roads could be easily cut from above. Deep ravines slashed much of the ground, and if one wanted to move in a direction that was neither uphill nor down, then one had first to wind down one of the ravines to reach the bottomland of the Windrush. The way was easy enough for a horse, and the main road was passable for cargo, but taking an army up to the citadel would have been impossible by any of the routes.

As he reached the flat, Crocken saw the white stallion a long way off, circling beside the bright thread of the river. It made a pretty show, as it bent this way and that, the horse obeying its rider's will without apparent dissent. Crocken, impressed, drew rein and halted to watch the performance, which he suspected might end with his arrival.

At last Rhisiart reined in and leaned forward to pat his stallion's neck, looking pleased. Seeing Crocken, he cantered closer. "Master Crocken! You are timely come—no trouble finding the way, I trust?" Stormraker pranced in place when he halted, most prettily or terrifyingly, depending on one's point of view.

"None, my lord," Crocken lied. "It promises to be a fine morning." So long as his mount made no sudden moves, to be sure. The gelding seemed properly apprehensive of Stormraker, who was snorting a challenge.

"We needed a little time to ourselves, Stormraker and I, to be sure of our tempers, so we came ahead," Rhisiart explained. "It's as well we did—I had to let him run the nonsense out of himself before he'd settle. We've been halfway to Rushgate. Generally we agree right well, but we have been some months apart. Most of the grooms walk in deadly fear of him, and a horse learns to take advantage of that."

"I can see the grooms' point," Crocken said soberly. Stormraker was using pinned ears and bared teeth to intimidate the bay gelding, which was only too willing to keep a respectful distance.

Rhisiart chuckled. ''True. They are unused to war-stallions here—wars are fought at the borders in these quiet days, not in the heart of the land. At least 'tis true since my brother Ruane won his throne.'' He swiftly forestalled Stormraker's attempt to reach the gelding with his teeth. ''Let us move off. He hates to stand still.''

''I'm told he was a mighty warrior, Ruane.'' Such a line of conversation could do no harm—Crocken had been told often enough that Rhisiart had worshipped his brother. And he needed a safe topic—riding near to a dangerous horse did not incline him to dangerous conversation.

''That's so,'' the steward-protector agreed. ''Though he seemed mightier yet to me. Ruane was a man grown, while I was still a child—and a sickly one at that,'' he explained. ''He was truly formidable in battle—not many cared to stand against Ruane's sword. When the wars were done, he proved to be an equally mighty king. My duty now is to see that his son becomes the same.''

''Kieron is fortunate, to have so devoted a councillor.''

Rhisiart flashed him a startled look—probably he was unused to the sentiment being expressed with anything approaching sincerity.

''I would Kieron's mother could allow him to think so. The prince could in fact have many such councillors.''

They urged the horses forward and trotted along beside the river. A gray heron flapped up from among the reeds and rushes, beating slowly up the Windrush, legs a-dangle just above the rippling water. Stormraker snorted a challenge to it.

''Armyn is governed now by the Protectorate Council,'' Rhisiart went on. ''A Great Council cannot meet until there is a crowned king to call it into being. When Kieron is crowned, my council in his name will be dissolved, and Kieron will choose his own councillors. Armyn is best served if that transition is orderly. I have drawn up a list of names, worthy men from among whose number the prince might choose his advisors. The Council has seen it, also, and approves. Working alongside the Protectorate Council, those men could study the policies already in effect—and so better serve their king after he is crowned.''

Crocken nodded, seeing the sense of Rhisiart's plan. His horse seemed well trained. Once Stormraker allowed it to, it moved calmly and let him attend to the conversation.

''I intend to present the list to the prince at the next meeting of the Council—six days hence,'' Rhisiart offered. ''If you enjoyed yesterday's spectacle . . ." He shrugged. "Come early. It may not last long."

"The prince will oppose the idea?" Crocken guessed. "Why?" He was uncertain whether he should be prying, but Rhisiart answered him willingly.

"His mother will have told him that I am attempting to keep a measure of control over his first Council. And so I am—but only so that Kieron will have reliable men to advise him after I return to the Borderlands."

"Why not stay, to advise him? He's used to you—"

Rhisiart looked off to the horizon. "I have a fancy to die at home," he said.

"Why did he say that?" The rest of their ride had been fairly uneventful—Rhisiart had blandly pointed out various places of interest, they had galloped the horses a little and then had returned to the stables, whereupon they parted company. Crocken allowed himself to realize that he had neither fallen off his horse nor been rent by the war-stallion's teeth, and thought back to other matters. "That bit about dying?"

Have you been asleep, or deaf? The shadow wondered. *Rhisiart's power ceases when his protectorate does—when Kieron is crowned—and what happens to him then? You won't get odds on his living out the year.*

"I haven't your knack for eavesdropping," Crocken protested, disbelieving.

Think on what you have witnessed—Rhisiart has kept the queen's party from seizing the power they crave, but he has not gathered that power into his own hands. He thinks—naïvely— to govern wisely and show his nephew how the process works. The prince has little interest in enlightened government, and Rhisiart's scruples permit the queen's people to block him at every turn. They hate him, and when they may safely do so, they will kill him—as he well knows.

A life of constant work, with little result and vast frustration, Crocken saw, remembering the scene between Kieron and his uncle, the insult of the ballad. Rhisiart was in effect alone in an enemy stronghold, his only power one he'd chosen not to wield. But if true, why? It seemed a mad course.

The shadow wondered, as well.

I have seen none of his retainers here, and few other Border-lords. Rhisiart could not hope to bring his own administrators

*here in numbers—folk this side of Cordis mistrust Borderlanders
in the extreme—but not even the grooms are his own people.*

"Rhisiart could have support here, if he hadn't sent his friends
home? Why can't he call some of them back?"

Apparently it keeps the peace. To Rhisiart, that matters.

The shadow's implied sympathy seemed at odds with its pronounced attitude toward the steward-protector. Crocken questioned it.

"I thought you hated him."

*I have said that he betrayed me. It is not the same thing. This
land is in Rhisiart's trust, put there by his brother Ruane, whom
he loved more than any other, and swore to serve in all things.
He will sacrifice himself for Armyn. Noble and foolish, but not
cause for hatred.*

"We've got to warn him!"

Of what? Rhisiart can see his fate. It sounded almost amused.

"He's throwing his life away," Crocken insisted. "The prince
doesn't listen to him—"

*What do you care, peddler? There's profit to be made no
matter who rules here.*

Perhaps so—though Crocken suspected trade might prosper
more surely under Rhisiart's management than Kieron's. He
could think of no means to broach such a loaded subject anyway,
though he and Rhisiart rode together twice more ere the Council
sat again, and thus he had opportunity if never the nerve to make
use of it.

Crocken had made his case about the necessity of visible trading so often that the shadow no longer contested him upon that
score. So long as he did not wish to permanently remove himself
to Rushgate, he could venture to the city whenever he liked—
provided he best liked the early morning, when his shadow was
either weary or engrossed in pondering whatever arcane information it had gleaned the night before.

Artisans were bustling already with matters touching Kieron's
coronation. The prince would, Crocken had learned, be crowned
within Rushgate itself. At the center of the oldest part of the city
there was a venerable hall, not so vast as the great one in Axe-
Edge, or even some of the smaller ones in the citadel, but more
significant. All the kings of Armyn had been crowned there,
and many had been buried there, also, though Ruane was not.
For many folk it would be a first opportunity to gaze upon their
king—Kieron had been reared in Cordis by his uncle Lord Stiles,

in accordance with the queen's wishes and Ruane's consent. When he was brought back to Axe-Edge after Ruane's death, his mother still sought to keep him close, safe from the perils of the city. It was widely said he had never set foot inside it.

Just within great windows, shutters thrown wide to let in the light, tailors were at work on robes of all descriptions. The grand affair of a coronation required new, sumptuous clothes, and every denizen of Axe-Edge as well as the well-to-do citizens of Rushgate had some garment on order. The furriers and skinners were busy, too, the Embroiderer's Guild no less so, to judge by the activity in their namesake streets. The goldsmiths and jewelers throve.

The city itself would be as finely decked as its merchants. Crocken paused by a roofed but wall-less stall, watching a limner painting upon a great banner of gilded canvas. A holy warrior was lavishly depicted vanquishing a scaly dragon. His fair young face was made to Kieron's general pattern, and the depiction was plainly meant to symbolize the new king in his role as protector of the land.

No banners for Armyn's true protector, Crocken supposed. Rhisiart took no ostentatious part in anything touching his nephew's coronation. He oversaw every least detail of it painstakingly, but as self-effacingly as might be. And none of the queen's folk would pay him credit.

No, no banner for Rhisiart, not even a little boar painted into the background of one dedicated to Kieron. Crocken pondered the injustice of that while he watched the painter work. The pliant brush curved gracefully under the pressure of the stroke, mimicking the bold curve of the artist's nose. The painter's fingers were wide-tipped, yet they produced the sure, flawless strokes without apparent effort. The dragon seemed on the point of expelling its final steamy breath as the warrior's spear entered its breast. The delicate mane of the white horse the warrior bestrode blew upon a breeze that could almost be felt.

The painter looked up inquiringly, needing a moment to shift focus to his visitor, smiling when Crocken complimented him on the banner.

"Ten more like it ordered, sir, to hang along Fishmongers Way." He stroked his short beard, which was dark peppered with white, then indicated the dragon. "They like the scales done especially well, you see, on account of their trade. But there's ample time for other work—the days wax longer now, and the light holds good for a decent while. Were you wanting to order something? For your shop, to honor the prince?''

"Maybe," Crocken answered idly. "Perhaps one of a boar?" he added perversely, and watched for a reaction.

Only a day before, chance mention of boar's meat at dinner had moved one of Lord Stiles' men to spit and offer a bold curse. It was the same most anywhere in Axe-Edge. But the painter only nodded matter-of-factly. "To honor the Lord of the Borderlands, aye. Most appropriate."

Crocken was so startled, he forgot to wonder whether such a project's cost was within his means—much less what he'd do with such an inflammatory banner. The painter's brown eyes were fixed hopefully upon him.

"I'll let you know next week," Crocken prevaricated, trying not to sound ungracious. The painter nodded equably and turned away to oversee some lesser work his apprentice was hunched over.

Deep in thought, Crocken strolled the streets, his shadow beside him except when the street itself was shadowed by overhanging second storeys. Where two ways crossed to make a miniature square, he began to take better note of his surroundings—mostly because several barrows blocked his way, forcing him to squeeze past. He was forced to watch his feet, too—the barrows were full of piled fruit that threatened to cascade at a touch, and vegetables of all sorts were heaped and piled and spilled upon the cobbles.

Crocken sought oranges, but saw nothing of that color save some wintered-over carrots and a few rather wrinkled pumpkins. Too early for crops from the present year, he supposed. This market was too small to deal in goods brought from warmer Sheir. He settled upon some red-brown apples that were tiny but firm. The one he tested was a pleasing mix of tart and sweet, not overly burdened with seeds.

He folded the apples carefully into his beltran for carrying and walked back to the ferry. It was still early afternoon, and the Windrush sparkled fiercely in the sun. Shadows were blobby puddles underfoot, and Crocken did not bespeak his when he decided upon impulse to take the apples as a gift to the Princess Mirell.

He found the lady in her little garden behind the gatehouse, her needle throwing brief sparks in the sunlight as she worked upon the white linen of Kieron's shirt. Mistress Ivy was seated beside her, reading aloud from a slim volume of historical verse. She greeted Crocken warmly, as did Mirell's golden-brown eyes, and Ivy further expressed her mistress' obvious delight over the tiny apples. A waiting woman was sent for a bowl, the shirt was packed safely away in the little woven hamper where it lived when it was not in Mirell's hands, and they passed the afternoon in the warm sun and the dappled shade of a quince tree, eating apples and some bits of cheese the waiting woman had brought.

Crocken was just relating the beauty of the banner he had seen a-making—after all, the subject of it was Mirell's betrothed—when he sensed his shadow coming alert where it lay beside him, all prickled with green grass blades. Looking up, he saw Rhisiart coming under the arch of the gatehouse. Mistress Ivy greeted the steward-protector cheerfully.

"My lady, Mistress Ivy, Master Crocken. I shan't disturb you more than need be. I only came to request the princess' attendance in the Hall tomorrow morn—there will be cloth merchants there to meet with the Master of the Wardrobe, and if you could make your needs known to him, 'twould be most helpful."

Mirell nodded, glancing at Ivy.

"My lady will be there, my lord Steward." She looked to Mirell for permission, then went on. "Can you not tarry awhile with us, my lord? Master Crocken has brought us some fine apples from the city markets, and I fear if you do not aid us we shall eat every last one of them, and be ill all night from our foolish gluttony." She smiled.

Rhisiart smiled back uncertainly. "Well," he said finally, "I would not force such a dire fate upon you."

The colic or the company? the shadow wondered coldly. Crocken ignored the silent outburst with difficulty.

Rhisiart sat himself down atop the low wall that bordered a raised bed of pink and yellow lilies and reached into the bowl when Ivy held it out to him. There were only two apples left, Crocken noted with amusement. They *had* been gluttons, for he'd bought three dozens of the fruit.

"They're very good," he said, seeing how Rhisiart merely gazed at his apple. "For fruit wintered over."

"No," Rhisiart corrected softly. "The first of the season, these. You were fortunate to find them, Master Crocken—not many thorn apples find their way far from the Borderlands, and still fewer are carried so far as Rushgate."

"These apples are from the Borderlands, my lord?" Ivy asked

in surprise. Mirell took up the remaining fruit and examined it more closely.

"Yes." Rhisiart polished his apple lightly against his beltran and admired the chestnut sheen of it. "Thorn apples grow wild in the hedges and thickets, wherever the land has not been plowed and planted with red barley. The fruit sets in the fall, but it does not ripen until the spring—it needs the cold of the snow to sweeten it. By spring it's worth the scars you get gathering it—the thorns are an inch long or better, and very numerous," he explained. Crocken winced, and wondered how he'd forgotten the fruit he'd collected in those first hungry days after he'd crossed the Arinwater. For certain this was the same fruit, come to full flavor. "Winters are hard in the Borderlands," the steward-protector went on. "Many's the holding saved from starvation when the thorn apples and the dandelions arrived with the spring. It's light fare, an incomprehensible choice to the beef-fed folk of Axe-Edge—but when the pig salted down in the fall has been eaten, all but the squeal, folk feast right gladly on whatever's to hand."

He bit into the apple. Juice ran over his lip—and something glittered at the corner of his eye.

Chapter Nineteen

RHISIART PRESENTED KIERON with the list of prospective councillors matter-of-factly, much as one might handle a young horse one expected to be fractious upon its first acquaintance with saddle and bit. The steward-protector could, alas, but offer. And Kieron's mood was far from compliant.

"Why does my uncle Andrayne's name not appear upon your list?" he asked angrily, squinting at the parchment. "My lord father found him worthy to educate me—is he not fit to be at my side now that my schooling is done?"

Andrayne has instructed his pupil well in rhetoric, the shadow observed.

Lord Stiles sat at his royal nephew's left hand, not visibly discommoded at being the subject of discussion. He examined the condition of his nails unconcernedly.

Rhisiart touched the parchment he had offered Kieron with one finger and spoke calmly. "My Prince, you know better than any your uncle's good qualities—therefore I need not list them out for you. This roll of names is intended to make you aware of other worthy men who may be of use to you. Some already serve, though their names may be unfamiliar to you. Others have wisdom and experience that could prove valuable."

Well played.

Crocken wanted to applaud the diplomacy of Rhisiart's answer. It should have rendered Kieron speechless, struck him mute with awe.

"Must I choose now?" Kieron whined. "The Sheiran emperor has sent me a brace of gyrfalcons, royal birds, white as diamonds. I would try their mettle, as the day is so fine."

"If they were my hawks, I would let them bide a few days, to settle ere I flew them—a bird that goes out in an ill temper is like to find freedom more tempting than the falconer's lure,'' Rhisiart advised seriously.

Kieron stuck his lip out. ''Must I decide this matter *today*?''

Translation: Do you think you can order me so? the shadow supplied. *True fruit of his mother—and what more besides?*

Rhisiart allowed the fractious colt more rein, so that it could not effectively fight him. ''The Council sits again in a week. If there are those on the list—or others—you would like to have attend it, you need only give the men sufficient time to gather.''

''Men should attend their king on the instant, at his least pleasure,'' Kieron said quickly. Even Stiles winced a trifle.

Indeed Andrayne has taught him royal ways.

Rhisiart's smile was without humor. ''My lord, you are choosing councillors, not jailing felons. There is a small matter of distinction, and certain courtesies apply.''

Kieron frowned, but the retort he framed was forestalled by whatever Lord Stiles hastily whispered into the princely ear, when he leaned close for a long moment.

Kieron tried his new hawks that day. In an ill omen for the House of the Falcon, both the white falcon and her snowy tiercel refused to return to either fist or lure and were eventually given up for lost, though a falconer tried to keep them in view all that night. Kieron angrily denounced the emperor for sending him unfit birds by way of a gift and loudly claimed insult from Sheir to any willing ear.

At the next meeting of the Council, the Prince Kieron was accompanied by Lord Stiles and by the husbands of two of his young blond aunts, both men noted primarily for their boundless capacity for wine and land grants. Crocken winced when he saw them seated by Kieron, knowing he saw also the failure of Rhisiart's forlorn hope for an enlightened King's Council succeeding his Protectorate Council.

Sulien and her brother had advised her son all too well.

The steward-protector shrugged the insult off and went on doggedly with the governing and the detail work needful for the forthcoming coronation.

A solemn observance of the anniversary of Ruane's death distracted everyone for too brief a time. The rites and pageantry occupied an entire week and a vast number of priests and acolytes. Kieron had a part to play and did so dutifully, as befit his station, but seemed otherwise unmoved. His father had been dead a long while, and he had seen him seldom in life. The shadow nonetheless watched him intently, but Crocken found more of interest when he watched Kieron's uncles.

Andrayne, brother to Ruane's queen, tutor to Ruane's son, moved through the ceremonies with grace both of person and of tongue, reciting his speeches flawlessly. He had been a bosom friend of Ruane's, 'twas said, but it had been long years since his loss, and no grief marred Andrayne's fair face beyond what was seemly.

Not so the steward-protector's countenance. Emotion gripped Rhisiart, plain for any to see. Crocken might easily have believed that Ruane had died bare days before, rather than years, by his brother's grieving. Rhisiart fasted, keeping vigil each night. By the week's end he looked drained, as if fallen victim to some wasting fever.

There was a banquet held, to mark the culmination of the ceremonies. The courtiers all put off their somber mourning garb, but Rhisiart's beltran, striped dark green and a still-darker blue, made it seem he still wore funeral colors, and he did not seem equal to the gaiety of the occasion. Crocken watched from his place at one of the trestles and noticed Mistress Ivy long in conversation with the steward-protector, her expression nigh as dour as Rhisiart's. He craved to ask the shadow to eavesdrop for him, but dared not, lest his fellow diners overhear.

And best not—it would likely refuse him, and relish that refusal. Its actions and motives still baffled him.

The next item upon the steward-protector's agenda was the royal marriage. Rhisiart wished it celebrated before the coronation. The queen dowager wished the ceremony delayed—so, she elegantly said, Ruane's son need not share the glory of the day with any other. She proposed that the nuptials take place after Kieron's crowning, at a date she did not specify.

There, Rhisiart held firm at last. Wisely, Crocken thought, as if his opinion counted for anything. If Sulien truly opposed the marriage, then she would somehow see that it never took place—which would disgrace Mirell. The queen dowager dragged her feet as to plans for it, although she was amenable enough in all matters touching the crowning, from all he witnessed or overheard. That surely boded no good.

Rhisiart worked resignedly on, and the Princess Mirell kept much to her chamber and out of the storm's path, ostensibly working at her betrothed's shirt, which she intended him to be wed in.

"Ah, but, Uncle, I cannot be wed yet! Surely my bride has not fulfilled her vow and completed my wedding costume?" Kieron lifted a bit of salted fish from the salver of dainties before him and licked it once, delicately. "Not a vow of my choosing, certes—but I'd not ask her to set it aside. Surely its making speaks well for her character."

"The Princess Mirell's vow involves speech, not marriage, my liege," Rhisiart replied patiently. "In any case, I have good report that she has all but completed her stitchery."

Crocken blinked. Such was not what *he'd* heard, from Mistress Ivy the very evening before, when he'd chanced to inquire.

"My lord, my lords of the Council, I am fixing the date for the ceremony. A month hence will allow us ample time to complete preparations, and when you are crowned, Kieron, Mirell may be crowned just after."

"It's *my* kingdom." The prince fixed his pale eyes upon the steward-protector. And his red mouth was not nearly so winsome when he poked his bottom lip out, giving him the look of the sulky boy he was rather than the king he claimed the rights of.

"True," Rhisiart conceded, unperturbed. "Yet Calandra is a strong kingdom whose friendship will benefit Armyn. To delay this marriage, when the princess has already been with us nigh on a year, would give offense where none can be afforded."

"Perhaps the taking of a mute wife offends *me*, Uncle."

Crocken blinked. Public councils and family quarrels were a very volatile mixture. It was not the place for such discussion, but Kieron seemed determined that it should be.

Rhisiart sighed. "My liege, as your guardian, your marriage falls within my rights of bestowal. I will not quarrel with you over it, for it is my duty and our law, by your own father's wish." He was thoughtful a moment, and then sought to soften his words, if not his position. "It is natural to be wary of what is unknown, unfamiliar. Do not fear that being free to speak will render the Princess Mirell ungracious, Kieron. She is a gentle maiden, well bred. Treat her well, and she will make a fine wife for you and a good queen for Armyn. And harbor no apprehension that she is truly mute. Our envoys spoke with her, in Calandra, and called her well spoken. It is simply as you have said, a vow that does her credit."

"I mislike this, Uncle." Something in the way Kieron said it led Crocken to think he was at a loss—as if someone had instructed him in the protests he was to make, but had not gone far enough, and now the prince was floundering along on his own while the protests still failed to sway Rhisiart.

"Kieron, you are young, and thus uneasy. This humor will pass—if not before you are wed, then afterward." A hand on the boy's shoulder, a comfort from a man who had been wed and found it not so terrible a fate, seemed natural there, but Kieron's hateful glare forestalled it.

Rhisiart would discuss the matter no more, no matter how pressed or provoked. He never raised his voice, but he was implacable. He had seldom shown Kieron so firm a hand—particularly not in public. The quarrel was the talk of Axe-Edge for days.

The queen's opinion was not heard, which was either odd or polite depending upon the speaker's charity. Sulien, the dowager queen, had walked long in the place Kieron's wife would have. If he was wed before he was crowned, Sulien was queen no longer and must yield up her glittering place to Mirell. Was she eager to yield it? No one who knew her expected her to relish her loss of position.

Chapter Twenty

THREE STEALTHY MEN entered the lower chamber, treading with care between the wool-stuffed pallets and wooden trestles whereupon half a dozen noble maidens slumbered, ostensibly ladies of Mirell's bedchamber. One man remained by the door, posted on guard in case any of the girls had omitted drinking the customary cup of wine before retiring—wine that tonight had been drugged. The other two intruders passed up the stair to the upper chamber, silent as shadows.

The bulk of a great bed with rich hangings confronted them, shadowy against the faint glow from the banked hearth beyond it. One girl should lie within its curtained darkness. Another should sleep upon a pallet hard by the bed—between it and the door. They were cautious about their footing in the gloom, lest they tread on her.

There was poppy juice ready, and soft cords for binding, but the leader signed his henchman to hold back. He watched the sleeping face, peering intently by the aid of a close-shuttered lantern. The first sips of poppy-laced wine had done the work intended. The girl seemed to slumber deeply—it was unlikely she would wake within the next few quiet minutes, and they had been instructed to leave no sign behind of their work.

The man slipped to the far side of the bed and parted the hangings with one hand, whilst the other reached out for rag and bottle. The flame-haired princess never stirred as he swiftly completed his work, and then the drug she breathed made sure she could not.

They carried Mirell—awkwardly limp, but at least light enough—like a child down the stair and through the room of sleeping women. Not a one was disturbed, and when the men had vanished, they might never have existed save as a dream.

* * *

Upon her pallet, Mistress Ivy lay in the throes of a true-dream. She embraced it, though 'twas fearful—she knew the difference, mostly, between her dreams of fancy and those of foretelling. Had she not possessed that skill, she never could have won her mother's consent for the journey to Armyn—and certainly not her father's.

It was the dark of the moon, as she dreamed. The hour was midnight, and Sulien the Queen had been delivered of her seventh girl-child. There was only one trusted woman to tend her, busy disposing of the herbs she had helped the queen use to bring the child when Sulien, not nature, chose.

The midwife lifted up the unwanted girl-child and laid it aside upon the sheets. At her queen's bidding, she lifted the cover from the alder basket that waited beside the royal couch. Sulien, her pale eyes aglow, reached in with her white hands and eagerly drew out the hatchling ice adder.

The breast she held the young serpent to was swollen with the first milk her new daughter should have sucked. More herbs had been required, to freshen the supply ahead of its time. As the snake's forked tongue began to lap clumsily at the milk, the midwife was putting the child into the alder basket, tightly replacing the lid. The scarce-born princess gave no cry, at least none strong enough to pierce the basket's reeds as the woman carried her—and a bright bodkin of silver—away into the dark.

The queen—who had thus far bravely borne her labor pangs—commenced to make a great outcry. Her women rushed from the outer chamber to aid her. There was much bustle, and many accusations thrown between them when they saw that she had birthed her child alone and untended, but much was forgiven as the women realized their queen was safe-delivered of a lusty son.

His infant fuzz of hair was fair as a puff of thistledown, his seldom-opened eyes almost of a hue to match—proof sure of his pedigree, many said in jest when his golden father returned from war's adventures to greet his long-awaited heir. Ruane's joy was echoed by all Armyn. It was made into songs. Six daughters needed to smooth Kieron's way out of the womb and into the world, six sisters to guide his first steps and fetch back his golden rattle when he flung it. It seemed only fitting, especially to the minstrels.

Of the seventh sister, no slightest rumor, far less remembrance. By the dictates of the spell used to gain her a brother,

the unnamed one never knew her mother's touch before she
went back into the shadows once more. Ere long, the midwife
had joined her, followed swiftly by the old henwife who had
taught her queen a sorcerous means of gaining a son at all
costs.

Ivy, sweat-soaked, sat bolt upright with an alarmed cry—and
looked at once toward the bed, fearful she'd wakened Mirell.
Best if she had not; she needed a private moment to absorb the
dream, before repeating it to Mirell for her comment. All her
muscles ached from tension. She breathed deep, mastering
herself in the ways her mother had taught her. Her heartbeat
steadied.

Rising to kneel upon her pallet, Ivy parted the bed curtains
and peered between them.

The bed was empty, save for Mirell's down-stuffed pillows,
tumbled about.

The shadow had left Crocken at the third hour past sun-fall,
imparting strict instructions that he should for no reason quit his
chamber. Crocken had not bothered to protest. He'd had a good
dinner. Frequently up early at Rhisiart's request and kept out
late at the shadow's, he welcomed the opportunity to seek his
bed at an early hour for once. Before doing so, he took a reassuring audit of his finances, safe in their hidden nest. His tangible
assets soothed and composed him, as always.

Crocken had gratefully laid aside the heavy length of his beltran, though not yet stripped for sleep, when the hammering
began upon his door.

A firm tapping it was, actually. Someone wanted to rouse him
if he slept, but not disturb his near neighbors. That reassured
Crocken, who found it alarming to be summoned at all—he kept
somehow still expecting to be arrested as a rank imposter. Rhisiart knew his secret and was evidently amused by it, but the old
unease refused to leave him, reappearing whenever he was startled. Crocken opened his door a crack and peeped out.

Only a donzel—one of the older pages—in Kieron's livery like
all the others in Axe-Edge. No men-at-arms in sight, Crocken
thought, so he was likely safe. He opened the door a bit wider.

"Sir, Mistress Ivy has sent me," the donzel said, politely not
noticing the game with the door. "Most urgently, she desires to
see you—"

"Tonight?" Crocken interrupted, puzzled. Not that the hour

was so *very* late, but what could Mistress Ivy want of him, that could not bide till day?

"At once, sir," the donzel answered impatiently. "I'm to conduct you to her."

Then Ivy must not be in Mirell's suite, to which he knew his way well enough to require no guide. Crocken was mindful of the shadow's order—but if Ivy sent so, it must indeed be an important matter. Urgent, the donzel had said. Crocken picked up his beltran and followed the boy, struggling to arrange the still-uncooperative cloth as he walked. One had to be born to it, Crocken guessed, for the garment to become second nature.

They reached a corridor's end just as he was attempting to fasten the round brooch. Crocken strode incautiously, looking at the pin, trod on an edge he'd arranged to trail too much, and pitched forward, his hands going out in vain hope of catching his balance.

Instead, he caught a sharp buffet to the left side of his head, while something else simultaneously slammed into his ribs from the opposite direction. Crocken gasped, then choked as a rag was shoved into his mouth and halfway down his throat.

"*Careful*, you fool! We'll need him awake again before the night's out. Not so much!"

Crocken felt hands on him, prisoning his arms, and automatically tried to struggle free of them. That proved fruitless, but he did manage to pull free of the rag for an instant. The cloth had a sweet smell, not pleasant—Crocken realized there must be a drug on it and held his breath when unseen hands pressed it back against his face.

For that, he was rewarded with another blow to his ribs, sharp enough to knock one breath out of him so that he was forced to draw in another, helpless to halt the reaction. The voices hissed something more, but Crocken could make the words out only faintly, as he faded away from them into shadows.

His ribs hurt.

Crocken curled about the pain, tight as a wood louse, and dimly wondered where he might be. He hoped desperately to be suffering from merely another weird nightmare—there'd been enough of those. He felt cold stone under his right cheek. By the sensation, he oriented himself—he must be lying on his right side.

But lying where? In the dank underdungeons, or along some deserted corridor? On the battlements? *Please let it be a dream,*

Crocken wished—so many of them involved imprisonment, this predicament was not so very different. A dream he could hope to wake from. He squeezed his eyelids tighter, not wanting to risk what he might see if he opened them.

He heard soft boots scratching upon the floor, rapidly shuffling, and smelled disturbed dust. No dream, then. He'd never smelled anything in a dream. There was another sound, like that of a bundle being set down. Crocken cautiously opened his eyelids, the barest crack.

What light there was came from a hand-held torch, which flared and wavered. Crocken counted two sets of legs, all dark-hosed, besides the torch-holder's, which were particolored yellow and red. The oblong bundle was white, or some other very light color—with a tumble of chestnut hair poking out of one end.

Crocken blinked, which finished clearing his vision. The bundle became the Princess Mirell, or else he had lost his wits altogether. Her lovely eyes were closed, her soft lips were slack and parted—the lady was either in a swoon or drugged as he had but lately been. His confusion could hardly have been increased, but Crocken's terror grew, boundlessly.

The torch-holder spoke cheerfully.

"This, now, is what comes of allowing filthy merchants from who-knows-where the run of our court. Only Rhisiart could have been such a fool! Look—this creature of his has abducted the Princess Mirell, and who'd choose to wed her now? She's been despoiled, and Kieron is forced to find another bride."

Upon saying that, the man tore at the bodice of Mirell's linen nightrobe till stitches pulled free and threads snapped. She did not respond greatly, only rolling her head to one side, averting her face from the deed.

"Or perchance *she's* a wanton, trysting with this stranger while her royal betrothed innocently slumbers. Who's to know, about these foreign women? Rhisiart did ill, to bind our prince to such a one!"

Now which is it to be? Crocken wondered. *They need to get their story straight, before they try to tell it. Can't they decide?* He felt oddly detached from the question. There was a sickly sweet taste in his mouth, which he feared to swallow, and had no other means of ridding himself of.

"When she begins to wake, you may proceed with attracting a few of the palace guards," the torchbearer said coolly to one of his fellows. "Once they arrive, our work is done—save for one thing." He poked a toe into Crocken's side. "Once he's been caught in the act, we don't require this peddler fellow, so there's no need to be overgentle in capturing him. Let the guards think he put up a fight and made you kill him. You regretted it, of course." He poked harder, and Crocken struggled not to gasp, or give other satisfaction to his tormentor.

"We don't need to try him before the Council?" asked the taller man.

The torchbearer answered him sharply. "Are you daft? The scandal is quite sufficient to our purpose—we don't want anyone looking too closely. So make quite sure of him. I'm away now— I must be in attendance upon the prince when the tragic news comes to him."

There were only two of them left, to Crocken's one. And one man would be sent to execute the next stage of the plan— fetching the guards. That would be a perfect opportunity for Crocken—if he could move. He tried, desperately, but his limbs were heavy as if they'd been stuffed with sawdust. It crossed his mind that his captors might have to hold him on his feet while he "resisted."

If only he'd followed the shadow's orders . . .

Mistress Ivy rapped upon the merchant's door. The splintery panel swung open under her hand, startling her, and she flinched back. It took her only an instant—after she'd stepped forward again—to determine that Crocken was nowhere inside the tiny chamber. The only furnishings were the bed, a plain bench, and a clothes chest. There weren't even hangings about the bed to conceal him from her search. Ivy turned half away, frantic— then whirled and rushed all the way into the room. Kneeling by the bed, she drew a silver circlet from her finger and closed her eyes tightly.

When the tall man departed, Crocken felt he had no choice but to act, even if the attempt was likely foredoomed. He lurched to his feet—then stood swaying, gripping the rough stones of the wall with one hand, while his remaining abductor snickered at his comical aspect.

I know you, Crocken thought, recalling having heard the same high-pitched laughter applauding a jest Lord Stiles had made during a dice game. His eyes struggled to pull the face into focus, and it was the very one he anticipated—broad and pale, sandy brows and hair, blue eyes red at the corners—as if the man might have been dragged from his bed and called to this task. The recognition robbed Crocken of his last feeble hope for any sort of survival—if they'd intended to let him live, he never would have seen a one of their faces, and this man was not troubling to conceal his square features.

Crocken tried a step, and his knees threatened at once to give way. As he struggled to stay upright, the stocky man swaggered out of his way, still chuckling.

Suddenly a familiar voice echoed in his head. *I thought I'd taught you the virtues of obedience by now.*

His shadow graced the damp wall, closer to the stocky man than Crocken was. In fact, in the exact opposite direction from the spot where Crocken's true shadow should have been torch-flung, but the man took no notice. The shadow stooped toward him, and the fellow simply stood frowning at Crocken, wondering why he kept supposing his drug-mazed prisoner was moving when he patently was incapable of taking an unsupported step.

Shadow-fingers slipped around the scabbard hanging at his hip. The sword sheath left the man's belt, sailing across the room to meet Crocken, who was just as abruptly being hauled toward it by a shadow arm stretched thin as rope. They met in midroom, even as the guard was exclaiming his amazement. Crocken, falling to his knees and trying to keep himself from going facedown, put his hand right down on the sword hilt. Metal rang against paving stone.

Try to hold onto it, the shadow suggested.

Crocken dazedly did as he was bidden. He closed his fingers and heaved himself back to his feet. His every move was dreamlike—a combination of the lingering drug and muscles being moved involuntarily by the shadow's power rather than by his own will. He saw a knife being drawn and was almost ready when the shadow swung his sword arm to counter the threat, except that the message from his eyes had not quite traveled to his feet.

Steel countered steel—and upon the rough masonry, shadow met shadow. The contact was brief, as the man slipped away from his failed stroke and Crocken was unable to follow swiftly enough to counterattack. He tried—but he'd never known a fencer's footwork. Assaying to learn, he stumbled and made contact accidentally. His foe's shoulder slammed solidly into his bruised ribs.

Crocken staggered back, gasping. Unexpectedly the shadow

swung his arm—and the rest of him with it—back into the fight.
The sword seemed to chime as it slipped down the knife's blade.
The sound got lost in the ringing in his ears.

*Don't let loose of the blade, you idiot! I can't handle cold
iron—*

Crocken dazedly tightened his grip on the sword, which he
had nearly let fall. His whole body was following his right arm,
which the shadow held in a grip stronger than the steel it said it
could not touch. His rubbery legs could not quite keep up with
the rest of his body, and he stumbled with every step, always
narrowly avoiding a fall.

The room spun dizzily past Crocken, fitfully illuminated by
the flaring, smoking torch. By the wall, the Princess Mirell sat—
and her eyes were wide open. Her lips parted, but if she spoke
Crocken could not hear over the pounding of his own heart,
which nearly choked him. She crammed her fingers into her
mouth, and silver gleamed on one of them. Crocken swung
about once more, seeing only dank, mossy stone, next the doorway arch, then Mirell once more. It wasn't a large room, but in
his condition he didn't find that an advantage.

The silver circle grew large in Ivy's mind, spinning and ex-
panding until it was the size of a crown, or at the least a coronet.
She held her eyes tightly closed, that no distraction from phys-
ical sight should disrupt the inner vision she was shaping.

She saw the ring whole, a round of silver beads lightly twined
with a slender ribbon of metal that shone like moonlight in the
dark of her mind. She unfastened one end of the seamless ribbon
and let it curl away from her, out of even her mind's sight. When
it ceased to ripple and move, she knew she had achieved her
goal, and opened her eyes. On her little finger, as at the end of
her shaping, she wore only the round of silver beads.

She drew the ring from her finger with care and set it on its
edge upon the floor flags. It balanced so, rocking a little. Leaning close, Ivy blew her breath upon the tiny hoop, setting it
rolling across the floor. She swiftly arose and followed it, on
legs that felt full of pins from her long moments on her knees.

The ring went through the doorway. So did Ivy. Down a corridor it rolled, and she pursued it on silent feet.

Abruptly the ring right-angled into a turn and began to bounce
down a flight of stone stairs, each drop causing it to leap higher
and higher, gleaming faintly. The final bounce was so great that
the ring should have toppled onto its side, but it landed safely

and raced onward so rapidly that Ivy's slipper-shod feet had to greatly quicken their pace. She was so intent on keeping the ring in sight, only the fresh air on her face told her that she and the ring were outdoors—she did not remember opening a portal that the ring had found a quicker way through, rolling through a vertical space left between two time-shrunken oak boards.

Now the course was more difficult, as cobbles and puddles forced the ring to detour, sometimes widely. And once Ivy had to duck out of sight, while a dark-clad man walked purposefully past her hastily chosen hiding place. For a bad moment after he had passed, she could not locate her ring, and feared the man had trodden on it—then a faint chime reached her ears, and she saw a gleam ahead. Ivy crossed courtyards by the shadows at the edges of them after that, whatever route the ring chose to take, and sometimes it seemed to pause for her, to allow her to catch up when she had to take a longer way for sake of secrecy.

The ring hopped over a patch of dew-moist shepherd's purse growing between the untended pavers, rolled an ell farther, and bounced against a closed door.

Ivy had seen such doors often and ignored them mostly. They led to cellars, either on the ground floor or a level or two below it, and she had never been inside because ladies did not venture into the cellars of Axe-Edge, whatever they might casually do in Calandra. No one dwelt on the lowest floor because 'twas coldest there in the winter, and short stairs led up to the ways of entering the upper levels from outdoors.

This door was closed, and the ring could lead her no farther, even did its other half—and Mirell—lie just inside the portal. And if 'twas barred, Ivy could not enter either.

She resolutely put her shoulder to it. The panel groaned inward slightly and stuck a bit—weather made it hang crookedly on its rusty hinges. Ivy listened tensely in case the small noise had been heard, then slithered through—reaching down first to scoop up her ring.

Once the silver was fitted upon her finger, Ivy whispered softly unto it. The metal commenced to glow gently, and by its light she descended the dank stair that confronted her. Spiraling carefully down, she all at once heard the ringing of metal—like a fencing practice. Save that no one schooled his sword arm in a cellar, in the mid of night . . .

Ivy let the werelight of her ring go out and crept onward. Her right hand stole softly into a slit in the side-seam of her skirt.

Beneath, she had a pair of pockets tied about her waist, and her fingers found one of those, and finally the object she sought.

How long, how *long*, before his foe was reinforced by the anticipated royal guards? Was his shadow aware they'd been summoned? If they happened upon this scene, they were unlikely to be of any help—Crocken would be convicted as surely as his abductors could ever have wished, on the evidence of their eyes. Maybe his opponent thought the same. Contact was harder to make—the man avoided it, staying just out of reach. He led Crocken in a clever martial dance, drawing him on—and drawing out the fight.

Crocken thrust his sword out desperately—but not in the line the shadow had chosen, and the blade wavered, the stroke going very wide.

Stop that! the shadow snapped. The command sounded weak, as if its power was ebbing.

Confusion made Crocken stumble worse than usual. He lurched forward in quest of balance, tripped again on his beltran, and fell to the floor. He lost his hold on the sword at last. He sprawled helplessly on the moldy stone, panting, unwilling to turn that he might see his death on its way to him. The shadow might continue to briefly blind his assailant, but it could not hide him long, and he could not rise in time. He was done for.

If the man stabbed him in the back, it might spoil the story, Crocken hoped bitterly. His shoulder blades quivered, awaiting the blow.

It did not fall. Not a footfall sounded. Crocken heard a gasp, then another. He pushed himself up and looked for the source of the breathing.

Mirell, wide-eyed, huddled still at the wall's base. The man lay upon the floor, almost at her feet, in a spreading dark puddle. He twitched once, then was still. The torchlight gleamed silver upon the dirk that stood upright in his back.

And in the doorway behind him stood Mistress Ivy, her hand still raised from the knife-cast.

Chapter Twenty-one

"DRINK THIS."

"What is it?" Crocken stared numbly at the silver cup Mistress Ivy had put into his hand. The liquid within was dark, and warm, by the feel of the cup. He couldn't recall seeing her brew anything.

"Cailon flower." Ivy frowned at his blank expression. "You might know it as All's-Well. It will settle you."

Crocken shivered and did not try to hide it. He felt wider awake. "It will take more than dried flowers to settle *this* night. Have you some brandy? Or wine?"

"The night wine," Mirell offered, whispering, and moved to fetch it.

"*No!*"

The princess halted in midreach, staring back over her shoulder. Mistress Ivy managed to compose herself before she spoke again.

"It will be drugged," she eventually explained. "Those girls downstairs would never sleep so sound if it wasn't." They had, even in their distracted state, noticed that none of the waiting women were disturbed by their disheveled entrance.

Mirell nodded and sat down on the bed all at once, as if her legs were not to be too long relied upon, having reached a limit. Crocken knew well the feeling—he was far from over it himself.

"How did you find us?" he asked Ivy, ignoring the tea except to use the cup for warming his cold hands.

"I—" Ivy gave her head a shake. "I woke and found my lady gone, and went to seek her. I could not think whose aid to seek at such an hour. Was my lady ill, sleep-wandering as you found me doing? That thought must be what led me to your door."

"I wasn't there," Crocken said dully, forgetting to tell Ivy that her name had been used to lure him from safety.

"No. So I wandered—"

"You wandered all the way across Axe-Edge, and into one of those two-score cellars, where you just happened to find us?" He'd been ready for her to claim sleepwalking again, but not impossible coincidence. The rather blatant insult to his intellect angered Crocken. "Well, of course *this* time you were awake. That would help."

Ivy looked at him sharply.

"I'm not stupid," Crocken pointed out as mildly as he could manage. He felt very much abused. "And your lady has broken her vow twice since you found us. If vow it truly is. Let's try the truth now. Either one of you."

Mistress Ivy took thought, chewing at the nail on her left forefinger, while the princess looked desperately from one of them to the other and said no word. Ivy reached a decision.

"Very well. It was no accident that I found you. My ring . . ." She held up her right hand. "A cunning friend of my father's made it. Its two halves can be separated, one from the other, but still they are one and will call to each other. My lady wears a piece at night, against such a chance as this."

Mirell lifted her hand, which bore a ribbon of silver about one slim pale finger. Ivy took it from her and twined it around the ring of argent beads on her own hand. Crocken blinked— she had made the ring sound like a mechanical toy, a puzzle ring, and it was not such, unless his eyes were still drug-deceived and his senses unreliable. The silver ribbon freely twisted about the other ring, as if 'twere pliant silk, not hard metal. When she had done, Mistress Ivy's ring was its familiar self once more. Crocken realized, too, how closely it resembled the circlet Ivy betimes used to bind her dark hair, and thought the resemblance hardly accidental. He remembered, suddenly, how the ring had come rolling down a dark hallway toward Ivy, when he had merely thought it had slipped from her hand as she swooned. Now he wondered afresh.

"Quite a craftsman, your father's friend," Crocken said. "Adept at witchcraft."

"Cease to talk of witchery, and I will not ask *you* what's amiss with your shadow," Mistress Ivy snapped.

Crocken's blood went to ice. He had to force himself to keep his eyes away from his shadow. How much of the fight could Ivy have seen? Enough to damn him? It had all been so confused, and in a dim cellar . . . the shadow itself was no help to him. It hadn't let out so much as a peep since the end of the battle. Crocken suspected it was overextended, perchance exhausted from heaving him about. He couldn't specifically remember having seen it since they reached Mirell's rooms, but he doubted it had the strength to misbehave.

Still, Crocken lacked sufficient nerve to brazen it out and deny the shadow to Ivy's face. She might have seen something after all, then or earlier, and they were both safer if they each held a secret—like a dagger to the other's throat. Crocken took a casual sip of his tea, which had cooled.

"That's better," Ivy said, accepting the stalemate. "You will perhaps want to know why I ran to you, rather than calling for the guards. I did not know then that you were involved—"

"Being 'involved' wasn't any of my idea," Crocken protested hotly.

Ivy put a restraining hand on his arm. "Of course not. You were caught in it, is all. You are a stranger in the court, a stranger Rhisiart has openly befriended. That put you at risk, a risk I would have done better to have warned you of. They will do whatever they must, use whomever they must, to bring Rhisiart down." Plain whom Ivy meant, but carefully did not name.

"Just let them try again!"

"Well spoken. I am angered, also. The queen's party had no business to involve *any* of us in their deadly game. They have misstepped, and I suspect thereby that we are safe now for a bit; no one will dare confront us about this night's work, when it has gone so far wrong for them. It will . . . ." She half closed her green eyes, calculating. "It will be interesting to see who watches us."

Crocken shuddered. If her tea was intended to calm him, Ivy's words were at odds with the purpose.

"I am going back to Kôvelir," he said resolutely. Then he hesitated, awaiting a retort from the shadow. Nothing. Only silence. Had the shade expired? Was he his own agent once more? "Now," he added, lest there be any question.

"Master Crocken, we need your help!" Ivy's grip tightened, till 'twas painful. "Kieron must *not* be allowed to take Armyn's throne."

Crocken pulled his arm away from her, gently, more bemused than angry. What use one powerless person begging the aid of another such?

"I could hazard a guess that your lady may have cooled a trifle on the marriage—but there's no proof Kieron was personally involved tonight, is there? Probably much the reverse. If

he loves her, surely he'll protect her from his mother."
Crocken could not compass the thought of any man being resistant to Mirell's abundant charms. Of a certainty Kieron would love her . . .

"*Kieron loves nothing*. He cannot, perhaps," Ivy added, a dark codicil to her pronouncement.

Mirell nodded vigorously.

"He makes my bones crawl, too," Crocken admitted. "You might as well speak, my lady. 'Twould do you good. Even if the vow was genuine, it's long broken now." A nasty fate had nearly befallen the girl; talk might lessen the nightmares it could breed. He wanted, suddenly, to hear her voice.

Ivy forestalled him. "I would rather she kept in practice, Master Crocken. There is reason for it, which I would explain if I could. Hark now. I have had a true-dream of Kieron this night. One of many, but clearest of all—"

"True-dream?" Crocken frowned, vexed at the number of puzzles his life kept blithely presenting to him. Kieron was blessed with the sort of looks a maiden might dream of, but that surely was not what Ivy spoke of, not by her tone. And fair Mirell had gone quite pale at her words, to a shade almost the match of her linen bedrobe. Her eyes seemed to grow wider each instant.

"It is a gift I have, Master Crocken," Ivy said. "Some of my dreams come true," she added solemnly.

"And some are only dreams?" His own dreams, however vivid, were but fancies of a sleeping brain, and he recognized them as such.

"I know the difference!"

Crocken sensed that he was only catching spillage from an argument Ivy had certainly had with someone else on the same matter. The vehemence wasn't personal. No harm to let her tell the dream, though, if the telling calmed her. He gave Ivy a courteous nod of his head, by way of concession.

They settled upon Mirell's bed, drawing its curtains around them. Ivy cast a charm around the bed itself, she said to shield them from discovery should any of Mirell's ladies chance to awaken untimely from her drugged sleep and ascend the stair. Crocken didn't know whether to put faith in such a charm or not, but Mirell accepted it without question, so he did likewise.

Ivy carefully recounted her dream. The telling brought a shiver to Crocken's spine, as all good ghost stories ought. Mirell's topaz eyes grew wider and wider still—as she evidently recalled the many hours she had perforce spent in Kieron's tainted company. Ivy laid a reassuring hand on her arm. The tale was not all that long in the telling, fortunately, else the princess might have swooned in fright, or forgotten herself and cried aloud.

"They said Sulien would bear only daughters, but she outstayed the prophecy-spouters. 'Six girls, then at last a princeling,' " Ivy concluded, sounding as if she quoted a comment overheard, some final fragment of dream.

Crocken sighed. His head still ached. His ribs hurt. He was too weary for honesty, but even less able to coddle female fantasies. "Mistress Ivy, you have had an evil dream. Mayhap those men who abducted your lady gave you a whiff of their dark herb, also, and it colored your sleep—"

"There were no men," Ivy said severely, "no dark herbs when last I dreamed of Kieron, Master Crocken. I believe what I saw in that last dream—Kieron killing Rhisiart's little son, his own cousin."

"Killed him?" He discounted her charge. Surely such a scandal could never have been suppressed. "How?"

"He *bit* him. Rhisiart's son died."

"Mistress Ivy, a child doesn't die because another child nips him." Crocken's headache was turning fierce, aggravated by illogic.

"Kieron's no human child. As my dream tonight proves," Ivy insisted.

"Mistress, a dream *proves* nothing." Crocken rubbed his eyes, which burned. "I have dreams myself, but I don't seek to alter the world to fit them."

"You don't believe me!"

"I—" Crocken looked desperately into her incredulous eyes. How had he thought he could avoid a scene? What if she called out, brought guards? He'd be in a worse case than with his abductors. "I fear for you, mistress. This is treason that you talk, if you call it other than dream. You should not speak of it, not even here, not even to me, not even as a dream."

"It's the truth!" Her eyes blazed with outrage.

Crocken was terrified she'd insist on the point, with someone else, perhaps someone dangerous. Distressed, he put a hand on her arm as he implored her to see reason.

"Please, Mistress Ivy, never say such things to anyone! I'll forget your words. I'll forget the rest of this night! Don't you know what they could do to you—"

Particularly as she's right.

Crocken's eyes widened with shock. The shadow chuckled, inside his ears.

The sun is rising. Shadows begin to stretch now, and that refreshes me. Or had you hoped you were free?

Crocken steeled himself against answering the voice and addressed Ivy instead.

"Mistress Ivy, I beg you to put this folly aside."

Ivy gave Crocken a disgusted look, as if she had expected better of him—and the smile she donned was plainly forced. He recalled of a sudden that she had killed a man that night and shed not a single tear over the act, but only went at once to comfort Mirell. Was she mad, or had the deed made her so? His own nerves were none too steady.

"After all, it wasn't *your* dream," Ivy observed coolly. "Think about what I've said, walk about Axe-Edge with your eyes open. And sup with us tonight, so that we may talk again?"

Mirell nodded furiously. Crocken was unsure whether she desired him there to be talked into Ivy's scheme, or to protect them all from it. The unreality of the night was all of a piece— and far too much for his wits. Suddenly he was eager to escape, even if it meant abandoning Ivy and risking the indiscretions she might commit.

"I'll sup with you. That I can promise."

But he'd agree to no more. Of that, he was fiercely determined. The room whirled when he got to his feet. Crocken was happy he'd forestalled more discussion. He needed to gather his scattered wits, if he could contrive such a miracle.

Any hope he harbored of doing that once he was alone in the safety of his chamber was vain, for such hope did not take his shadow into account.

You must believe her, it insisted, even as he closed the chamber door behind them.

"Why?" Crocken asked, irritated. "Because you choose to think Kieron shouldn't be king? I thought it was Rhisiart you mistrusted?"

What did you suppose you were hearing, that midnight in the corridor? Kieron killed the girl he was with.

Crocken was so weary, he refused to be shocked, and disavowed the revelation as he had Ivy's. "He can't have done," he said dully. "Someone would have noticed—"

And accused him, peddler? Your naïveté will be your undoing yet. I assure you, it is quite a simple matter to make someone vanish without trace from Axe-Edge—I have seen it done. The girl was a serving maid, of little account to any save herself. None would search for her. The bloody deed needed little to conceal it, though I think its commission has moved the queen to make this desperate attempt to prevent Kieron's marriage.

"It's not just to cross Rhisiart?" Crocken asked nastily.

Sulien did not oppose her son's betrothal—yet she is plainly fearful of seeing him wed. There must be a reason for that fear.

"How do you know it's the queen? Ivy's dream isn't proof—"

I can give you the proof you require. Sleep now, and we will look for Kieron after the sun-high meal.

"Proof?" Crocken scoffed. "Illusions. Shadows."

What else shall I deal in? You should pay heed—you are in no wise safe because one scheme has miscarried.

"Maybe I should move down to Rushgate."

Perhaps. The shadow seemed to consider the issue seriously. That it should do so argued that it had its own interests at heart, not only his. It cared little enough for his wishes, Crocken knew.

What happens to the shadow if I'm killed? Crocken wondered. Some dire fate, surely. It had probably not protected him out of goodwill, not when he'd gotten into the predicament by disobeying its orders.

No. As well go to Triniol, or Sheir. I will retreat no more. Be on your guard—even Sulien is not such a fool as to repeat a failed move, when she does not know why it failed.

Crocken was little comforted. He gave over trying to settle himself for sleep, having just discovered a spot of blood on his sleeve. Not his blood, but real nonetheless. Not a shadow or an illusion. Not to be explained away. The nightmarish fight kept coming back to him, in snatches. His legs trembled, and he went cold all over.

"I was just convenient for them to use, wasn't I?" If someone *personally* wanted him dead, matters were worse, and he was uncertain he wanted a true answer to his question.

As you wish, the shadow obliged him. *Sleep well.* The irony of the instruction was thick enough to taste.

If Crocken managed to more than doze over the next several hours, 'twas only because he told himself no enemy, however determined, would try anything else so *soon.* And of course the shadow was on guard, unable to leave him by day. No need for Crocken to start at every noise, each footfall along the passageway. No enemy would drag him from his bed . . .

* * *

He dreamed he held a sword in his hand.

He looked across the width of the practice yard and read the challenge on each of their so-alike faces. His father. His three tall elder brothers. He'd reached the age when wooden weapons had taught him all they might, and he had learned their lessons well indeed. Now he graduated to edged weapons of cold iron, weapons that could cut and kill—if he was man enough.

Take up the sword, his father's falcon-eyes ordered. *You claim our blood,* his brothers' gazes echoed. *Prove yourself worthy of it.*

Or else henceforth have neither father nor brothers. And go back into the hills, to folk who did not want half-blood boys either.

The iron blade was heavier than the stoutest oak. That difference, he could have accustomed himself to, given time. But his hand burned already from contact with the fell metal, and his whole arm ached, as if it had taken blows. He knew what that meant. He was his father's son—but his mother's, too. The pain rose, to lodge in his shoulder and shoot down his back. His fingers felt ready to burst into flame.

He refused to cry out, or shed even one tear, refused to be shamed before his father—even as he laid the sword in the dirt and turned his straight back on all his hopes.

The pain of the loss made Crocken toss and mutter in his sleep, though even in the dream he knew the distress was not his own.

Come sun-high, Crocken willingly fled the torture of his hard bed and allowed the shadow to lead his aching body where it chose. The two of them encountered Kieron at sword practice in the lesser armory yard, surrounded by hangers-on. The prince was clad in fancy gilt armor and wielding a sword whose blunted blade rang as if 'twere cast of purest silver. His more simply garbed opponent bore a wooden weapon, that he risk no accidental harm to his liege.

The measures fenced were precise as court dances, and Crocken thought there was surely little risk of shedding anyone's blood, so long as both players kept to their parts. Thrust, parry, counterthrust. Parry—riposte. The combinations varied slightly, but not greatly. Kieron was being given an opportunity to show off his skill, rather than a lesson, Crocken surmised.

The audience of courtiers made a ripple of applause whenever the prince executed a move especially well. It seemed to Crocken that the man with the wooden blade deserved the praise more, since he played the more difficult rôle—losing deliberately without being insultingly obvious about it.

Watch his shadow. The command broke his reverie.

The shadow in question looked most ordinary to Crocken's eyes—a puddle of darkness the prince trod upon as he advanced and lightly retreated. A man might be of exalted rank, but his shadow remained humble. Kieron's behaved as a shadow ought—it dogged him tirelessly—and Crocken was certain that it did not offer the prince unsolicited advice or comment, or any conversation at all.

But I am a better fencer, his shadow said smugly.

Crocken felt the hairs lift on the nape of his neck. He didn't *want* to be reminded of the night past—especially not in public, where he must keep his expression appropriate to the moment. He wished his shadow would respect his difficulties, and he firmly turned his attention back to the fencing bout.

The prince's opponent was a competent swordsman, probably chosen for his even temper, as well, which would allow him to give Kieron a contest only slightly taxing and end it with a victory that appeared legitimate for the prince. He parried nimbly with his wooden stave, making precious few attacks of his own, and those never dangerous ones, but careful feints.

Now!

The prince's silver blade flicked out like a snake's tongue, catching the bright sunlight and then the swordsman's cheek. The attack was poorly conceived—even Crocken could see that in making it Kieron left himself open for a counterthrust, had the soldier been mad enough to essay one. The blood the slash drew was superficial, not a disabling injury by any measure, but Kieron preened himself as if it had been a mortal wound, flourishing his toy blade as he received his friends' shouted accolades.

Heed his shadow, Crocken's shadow reminded him sharply.

Crocken did as bidden, then smothered a cry of alarm. How could a serpent of such a size slither unseen onto the practice field? Surely the creature was deadly dangerous! He opened his lips, but no sound would come. Of all his senses, only sight seemed to function.

The great snake was dark, dark as night, or soot, or pitch, and it wove and coiled about the prince's heels, sliding over the dust. How did Kieron not feel its touch?

You do not feel my touch, unless I choose.

His shadow? That writhing thing was his shadow?

Even as Crocken stared in disbelief, the dark serpent vanished, melting back into a normal pool of shade. Kieron accepted the courtiers' congratulations upon his sword skill, while the soldier quietly staunched his torn cheek with a bit of linen. No one congratulated him for a hard job done well.

The bout ended with first blood. Kieron and his friends went away toward Kieron's rooms and their wine cups, shadows following after them like trains on ladies' court gowns.

Crocken stumbled along amid the throng, blaming his pallor upon the midday heat and the sight of flowing blood, to which his trade had not accustomed him. Dazedly he wondered if the man who asked after his health or any of the others around him had been party to the plot to disgrace and murder him the night previous. The speculation further unsettled him—not that his nerves required the nudge.

He managed to drift free before reaching Kieron's suite, dropping back unnoticed and allowing himself to be left behind. That Crocken was glad of, but all too soon he and his shadow were alone, a prospect he did not relish.

Master your fear, it ordered sternly. *Now that you have seen it once, you may do so at other times. And you must not reveal what you see.*

"He really . . . Ivy was right?" All very well to be told to master his fear—it took all his will just to keep the crust of bread he'd broken his fast with from deserting him . . .

Yes.

"How long have you known?" Crocken wondered bitterly how many such shocks he was expected to weather. The shadow's complacency irked him.

I have been certain only since last night. What Mistress Ivy dreamed confirmed what I had discovered and gave me the last answers I sought.

Crocken leaned against the cool stone wall and tried to steady his breathing. Remembering what he'd seen spoiled the effort. It refused to let him escape Ivy's fantasies.

"This . . . is this why we came to Axe-Edge?"

The shadow leaned against the wall beside him. *I was set this riddle long ago.*

"Set? Set by whom?"

By Tierce, prince of the House of the Falcon. The title was spoken with scorn.

The name was familiar, Crocken thought. He did not recall that the mention of it had been favorable.

"The one they killed for treason?"

Tierce died because he strove to rid Armyn of Sulien without losing his brother's regard in the process. An impossibility, given his own character. How could it look, but that he was jealous of the love Ruane bore for his queen? Tierce made it easy for Sulien to rid herself of him. She might have been content to ruin him— but when his suspicions fell upon her son, Tierce had to die. Now we know the reason.

"What are you going to . . . do . . . now?" Crocken hardly needed to ask—like a fish on a line, he could feel himself being drawn. Only it was toward those deep shadowed waters, not the calm shore. He began to walk again, aimlessly, down a seemingly endless gallery.

We will aid Mistress Ivy, the shadow said as they passed a window and it shifted place beside him.

Chapter Twenty-two

"I DIDN'T KNOW whether you'd come," Ivy said, taking Crocken's hand with a clasp that conveyed her gratitude that he had. Crocken felt the warm metal of her silver ring, snug on her finger at that moment. He wondered whether she'd have sent it rolling after him, to spy, had he refused to keep their meeting. Would he have detected it? Would his shadow? And what had it been witness to, that night when he'd surprised Mistress Ivy in the dark corridor? What had it reported to her?

If Ivy had seen a girl killed, as the shadow claimed had happened, and made no fuss over it, then perhaps it should not surprise him that she could also knife a man in the back and regard it without distress. Ivy might be gently reared, but she seemed equal to whatever task she attempted. Crocken hoped so, given that he was ordered to fall in with her dangerous plans.

Supper was light fare—sun-high being the hour when the day's main meal was taken in Armyn. There was poached chicken, new bread still steaming, a glass bowl piled high with apples and tiny purple grapes. With Mistress Ivy to chaperone Mirell, the three of them were able to dine without the other waiting women, who were in turn glad to be dismissed with a permission to attend the presentation of a new ballad composed by Lord Stiles' pet minstrel. Kieron was not expected to attend the event, so there was no need for his betrothed to do so, either. The princess had, after all, her vow to be fulfilling. The shirt was spread over a velvet pillow atop a chest, ready for work.

The three of them pretended to be interested solely in Crocken's tales of Kôvelir, until the chicken had been picked to its bones, the bread was crumbs, and the apples were reduced to nibbled cores. Ivy picked at a bunch of the miniature grapes—ideal employment for nervous fingers. One needed to unstem a dozen to make a mouthful, and Crocken had given up on them as not worth the effort or the exercise.

"You came," Ivy observed abruptly, fixing Crocken with a peridot gaze. "Does that mean you'll help us?"

Crocken hesitated, wanting desperately to say that none of it was any of his business.

This isn't something you need to debate, peddler, the shadow commanded.

Crocken swallowed down a hot wave of anger. There was no use directing it at Ivy—and no way to explain that it *wasn't* directed at her. Nor any way at all that he might safely retaliate against the shadow's present tyranny.

"What do you intend to do?" he asked politely, all caution.

"Do?" Ivy mimicked, arching her brow high. "Have you forgotten what was nearly done to Mirell, and to you?" She shook her head. "We must unmask him—that's what I intend to *do*! And that doing must begin at once; we cannot waste time and allow Kieron to be crowned." She held up one finger. "In the first place, it's *wrong*. Kieron fouls what a kingship should be, and his rule would blight this land worse than the queen's party could *ever* manage, for all their greed."

I concur, the shadow said, as if it leaned over Crocken's shoulder.

Ivy extended a second finger. "Secondly, coronation grants power, too much power for us to counter. We could never topple Kieron once he has mounted Armyn's throne and taken the crown."

"It's happened before," Crocken protested, knowing more of the wide world, he thought, than any sheltered highborn maiden could. He recalled the shadow's tales of Armyn's tangled past. The overthrow of kings had been mentioned rather frequently. It was nearly the norm, for Armyn, the usual form of succession.

"It happens to *men*," Ivy corrected. "Kieron's no man, nor ever will be. There's no guessing what he'll grow into. Why should we help him to it?" Her green eyes clouded. She held up a third finger. "And when he takes the throne, Kieron's first act will certainly be to order Rhisiart killed."

A thing the shadow might not dislike, Crocken thought. But it held its peace.

"He'd need grounds," Crocken protested. "Rhisiart could get away ere that—"

Ivy shook her head again, dark curls flying, then settling. "I don't say openly. But Rhisiart will die. Even if Kieron was not—what he is—the queen has had it in mind a long while. She will not forgo her revenge."

And Rhisiart expects it, you may recall, the shadow pointed out chillingly. Crocken realized it was true.

"If we warned him, he could leave Axe-Edge—"

He will not.

"He won't do that," Ivy unwittingly agreed. "And if you require other reasons than the land's life or Rhisiart's, think of poor Mirell. How safe is she as Kieron's wife? Would you condemn her to that fate?"

Crocken gave the princess a startled glance. Mirell returned his gaze with such calm as she could manage, but Crocken saw her trembling hands, and how she strove to hide them beneath her needlework.

Your appreciative looks at the princess have deceived Mistress Ivy, peddler, the shadow said archly. *She supposes you value her lady highly. If I may remind you—your own life and fortunes are woven into this web, as well.*

"All right!" Crocken wished there was some way to strike the thing, to swat it away. His inability to do even so much as to touch it was a torment. "If you want to stop the coronation, why not just tell Rhisiart what you know?"

That hardly seems likely to succeed, the shadow remarked.

Ivy frowned, considering. "Would 'twere so simple," she answered quietly. "Rhisiart is stalwart in loyalty to his king-to-be. He was ever faithful to his brother Ruane—now to Ruane's son. It is his pride. Any word that is spoken against Kieron, Rhisiart hears as treason."

"*I* really wouldn't relish trying to convince the steward-protector that his nephew is a transformed snake," Crocken agreed pleasantly. "Or telling him that you know it's true because you dreamed it."

Ivy flushed, then shook the criticism off. "I would risk that, if I thought he'd even listen, but there's no hope of it. There have been councillors banished, for that they told the steward-protector to watch out for himself. 'Twas only sense—anyone but Rhisiart could see it. He called it treason, and sent them out of his sight."

"Rhisiart knows how the queen and her family hate him." How could he not? Crocken wondered. "He probably gets weary of having people tell him the obvious. And I think he knows he's a dead man once Kieron's crowned—he said as much to me once. Yet he works steadily toward the crowning. Explain why he does that.'' He didn't know why he expected Ivy to explain what the shadow could not.

Ivy sighed, attempting the puzzle. ''I wish I knew. Rhisiart tries so hard with Kieron, and never sees that there are no good results. Mayhap he seeks to bring back his own son—but Kieron is not Edryd, and never can be.''

That is not enough to answer, the shadow observed. Crocken could only agree.

''It makes no sense,'' he persisted. ''You know him better than I do. We may need the answer, to save him. To save Mirell.''

''It's a blind spot,'' Ivy amended. ''Rhisiart has less such than most men, but it makes it impossible to go to him with any of this.''

''He'd take it that amiss if you just told him your dream?'' Crocken jibed. He didn't expect success, but he knew that Rhisiart was more than tolerant of Ivy. ''Would he banish you?''

''Master Crocken, Rhisiart would never even hear us out, once he knew where it was heading! We need to discover a way to prove my dream—a way even Rhisiart can't stop.''

Crocken decided he liked her ''we'' very little—consisting as it did of only the two maidens and himself. Not to forget his resourceful shadow.

''Then someone else—someone who could help us.''

''It's no use trying that,'' Ivy protested. ''Understand, it isn't that Rhisiart wouldn't hear *us*—he'll hear *no one* on this.''

''But if you can show him proof—'' Could she?

Perhaps. Proof is difficult, the shadow said.

''There were others, with other reasons, and perchance other proofs, to set before the steward-protector,'' Ivy told him. ''It didn't matter. There's not one of them still at court, or with any influence in Axe-Edge. Lord Tairry actually tried to force a rising. I told you of it once. He'd been Rhisiart's friend since childhood, a boon companion of Ruane's, as well. Rhisiart had Tairry beheaded—that's the punishment, when treason's taken solid form,'' she said when Crocken paled. ''Mere talk only gets you banished. They say Rhisiart wept when he signed the death warrant—and after, he was ill for weeks. But he signed it.''

Crocken could hardly accept the account. ''It had to be something else. How could *anyone*—still less a man like Rhisiart—be so loyal to the likes of Kieron? Even if he wasn't what he is?'' Crocken could conceive of no such unswerving, inopportune devotion—not to an unproven, rude boy, however pretty. Was that because he was himself no courtier? Was it different for the princes of the blood?

''Not to Kieron,'' Ivy answered thoughtfully, her green eyes gone smoky and looking inward. ''To Kieron's *father*. To betray the prince is to betray Ruane. Rhisiart will never do that.''

''Loyalty to the grave—and beyond.'' Crocken whispered incredulously.

''Far beyond.'' Ivy knit her thin brows. ''I don't understand it myself—I never knew Ruane, of course, but still there's a piece missing, somewhere. 'Tis not a *choice* of Rhisiart's. It's as if a fever drives him, consumes him. As if he does not *care* whether Kieron kills him. As if it's the only way he can see to be free.'' Ivy's expression was tortured, Mirell's no less, and the princess' eyes spoke what her lips did not. They had few friends in Armyn, but Rhisiart had been steadfast in his kindness to them.

Crocken called the steward-protector's high-boned face to mind, recalling without difficulty the haunted eyes, the wry and melancholy smile. He decided he could accept Ivy's conjecture, at least for the present moment. He had nothing to offer in its place. He cleared his throat cautiously.

''All right, that leaves what? We need to reveal Kieron *to* Rhisiart. How can we hit him with it before he can stop us? What way won't get us executed?''

Always a consideration, the shadow said. Part of it was on the table, by his elbow.

''You *do* know how dangerous this is?'' Ivy asked, appalled. ''I won't let you, if you take it lightly—I'll find some other way—''

Crocken dared not tell her about the shadow—even though he sometimes thought she suspected it. It pressed darkly at him even then, threatening worse fates than even Rhisiart's anger could hope to deliver. Instead Crocken said, ''Calm yourself. Rhisiart has been a friend to me. That alone guarantees I won't last long with him gone. Loyalty has nothing to do with it. My interest lies in helping him.''

''Your life might lie in getting out of here now,'' Ivy observed shrewdly.

''With what?'' Crocken raised an eyebrow, and lied with dispatch. ''The clothes on my back? Assuming I could ride the horse if I managed to steal one, I still probably wouldn't see the border. And do you think I feel nothing for Rhisiart, after the friendship he's shown me? Or that I could go, knowing the two of you would try something alone?''

Mirell, on the bed, looked solemnly grateful.

"So. How do we help Rhisiart in spite of himself?" Crocken asked, leaning close. His shadow did the same, squashed against the chamber wall though it was.

Crocken awoke with a nagging suspicion that the past evening had ended with him agreeing to something far worse than his ill-considered bargain with the shadow. The fine details of it eluded him—he had at some point swallowed a fair amount of strong cider—but the unease lingered with rare persistence.

And his shadow arose when he did, whispering in his ear.

Kieron must become what he was—and still is, beneath. Leave the method to me.

That should have reassured him. Yet Crocken was bidden to meet Mistress Ivy, at sun-high, in the pleasure garths of Axe-Edge, and his shadow only followed him as all shadows do, without invitation.

The garths were a series of formal gardens, walled, hedged, and quite extensive in scope and acreage. Open-air gossiping space for the nobles of Axe-Edge, when the weather was fair, taking the place of the indoor galleries. Crocken saw no food plants, and supposed such were grown elsewhere, where noble eyes would not be offended by the commonplace. He was to meet Ivy at the bowling green, which had sounded easy to locate.

Crocken was feeling furtive—the light sound of voices carrying over the hedges he passed alarmed him. Almost he turned back, certain that witnesses could be no part of Ivy's plans. The shadow prodded him on mercilessly, though it was at its weakest at sun-high and could deliver only verbal inducements to his good behavior. Sometimes he could scarcely hear it.

The princesses were having a game of bowls on the greensward—or mostly it was princesses. It was hard to take a certain count, when Crocken was somewhat unsure which were Ruane's royal daughters and which might be their cousins and aunts. Carrilet, Sulien's youngest sister, could have passed for the queen's daughter effortlessly, even in merciless daylight. The shadow pointed out Carrilet's husband, viewing the game's progress from beneath a silken canopy emblazoned with his family's heraldry. He was elderly, litter-bound—and of course, wealthy.

"Master Crocken!" cried the Princess Brandys, cupping her wooden ball in both slender hands. "Is it true, that in Kôvelir-city they bowl with hedge-pigs for balls?" She loosed her ball, which rolled wide of the pins and into a planting of privet.

Crocken took the hand she offered and brushed his lips past just shy of the royal fingers, as courtly etiquette demanded. The princess awaited his reply.

"I fear, my lady, some knave has been telling you tales. I have never seen other than wood or ivory used, even by the wizards of Kôvelir."

Brandys pouted her lips, looking disappointed. Mayhap she'd wagered upon his answer.

"But then, bowls was never my game," Crocken amended. "Too tediously heavy to carry with me when I travel."

"Then we won't wager upon you!" exclaimed Jocilyn, who wore sky-blue silk that day. "Thanks for the warning, sir." She and her sister flitted off, to plague the courtier then preparing to hurl his ball. When he eventually managed a cast, his ball went farther afield than had Brandys'. The girls cheered.

"Hedge-pigs?" Ivy repeated in disgusted tones. "And what for pins—geese?"

"Well, they *do* go round if you startle them." Crocken took her hand, to kiss, but Ivy pulled at his fingers instead and led him around the end of a tall boxwood hedge. "I swear they never got that tale from me."

"You could tell that dim lot anything, they'd swallow it whole—and happily."

"Even—for example—that Mirell has vowed silence till she's produced a suitable gift for her bridegroom?"

Ivy glared at him and put a finger to her lips. "Pray, sir, jest about something else! All men have ears, you know!"

Crocken accepted the tongue-lashing gracefully—though he'd been careful to determine that no one was close enough to overhear. Such petty little jabs were the only return he dared make for the uncomfortable tasks she set him to, and he found them therefore hard to resist. He might have been coerced into Ivy's scheme, but his heart wasn't always firmly in it. Had his shadow permitted it, there were times when he'd have gladly walked away. The present was one such.

Side by side, they skirted the edge of a privet maze and found another garth, this one empty of any creature larger than the lumpy brown toad that hopped hastily out of their path.

"Keep your eyes open," Ivy advised.

Crocken glanced about sharply. "What for?"

It's always advisable, his shadow recommended, slipping coolly over the hedge sides.

"Lady's mantle."

Crocken fell out of step with her, confused. Perhaps he'd misheard?

"It's a plant," Ivy said more helpfully.

"Oh." He was no more enlightened. The garth was full of plants, many of them less than familiar to him. Else he'd seen them often, but never learned names to distinguish them from one another.

"The leaves are fanned like a mantle, seen from behind. Covered with silver hairs, very fine. The flowers are like yellow-green stars, but it may not be flowering yet."

Crocken still looked blank. Maybe the shadow would recognize the plant—but it would not necessarily enlighten him.

"Never mind. Just walk with me." Ivy's green eyes flicked busily about, taking in both sides of the graveled path. "Make pretty conversation."

"I know some herbs," Crocken protested. "I've lived off the country often enough. Maybe I know it by another name."

You wouldn't eat lady's mantle, the shadow said. *Unless you suffer from what the leeches term "female complaints."*

"You probably call it a weed." Ivy peered beneath a hedge. "It will have dew upon it."

Crocken glanced at the sun, hanging above at the height of its daily circle, surrounded by sky of the brightest blue. "The deuce it will," he said. "The dew's hours gone."

"That's why we seek lady's mantle."

Dew where there should be none, the shadow pointed out helpfully, and perchance approvingly.

Like a shadow that existed when it should not? Crocken cast a furtive glance at his boots, relieved to see the shadow properly puddled beneath them. He'd been afraid he'd discover it reaching under the hedges, too, in defiance of the sun.

"Here!" Ivy knelt down—with a practiced swirl of skirts—on the pale gravel of the footpath and bent over a low-spreading plant. There were indeed silver drops atop the furry leaves. Those drops shone diamant-bright, while all around was dry as ashes.

From a pocket in her skirts, Ivy drew a silver vial, and bent closer to the plant. Crocken cast a wary glance around, making sure no wandering courtier observed her strange behavior. It was the only purpose he could find for being there.

Ivy was not plucking the leaves, as Crocken had assumed she would, when she located the plant. Instead, she carefully gathered the dewdrops from the leaves, teasing each into the vial without letting her fingers touch the liquid. The process was slow and painstaking, but it hardly appeared to be dangerous. Crocken began to feel superfluous, as pointless as a shadow—normally—was.

"What did you need *me* for, anyway?" he asked, after he'd watched for an uneventful while.

"Had I gone off alone, 'twould have been remarked upon. None of those giddy girls back there would do so strange a thing as spend half an hour alone in a garden. But to steal off with a man—none will think great harm of it, so long as we do not steal too many moments, or stay out of sight too long."

"So just anyone would do?" Crocken's feelings were hurt, his nerves rubbed raw, and now that the danger he'd been miserably anticipating seemed unlikely to rear its head, he felt moved to complain.

"No, Master Crocken, just anyone would *not* do. Just anyone could not be relied upon to be so discreet—or to stand beside us when my lady presents her shirt to Prince Kieron."

There was no teasing in the white face Ivy lifted up to him, nor in the green eyes that burned desperately there. Her hands trembled, and a silver drop slid down the side of the vial instead of into it.

"Is it to be so soon, then?" Crocken asked, ashamed that he still vacillated once he'd agreed to help her with her plan. He had to accept that he was in the adventure, and comport himself accordingly—even though it had been forced upon him. Otherwise, he might endanger them all.

"Ere the crowning. And ere the wedding. It *must* be. In only a few days, perhaps. First I must make sure of the use I'll put this to." Ivy bent back over the vial, coaxing more bright drops to join their fellows. Her hair hid her face, but not her voice. "Be ready."

Crocken nodded, his mouth gone dry as the dust under his boots.

"If you look into the drops, you can see other folk, other places," Ivy said, in a voice that tried to be cheerful.

If you have the way of looking, the shadow amended.

It occurred to Crocken—as he dismissed the fable—that Ivy must surely be missing her home, if only for its safety. So young, she'd perchance never been away from it, ere she came to Armyn and peril.

"As far away as Calandra?" he asked gently.

Ivy sat back and capped the vial with a crystal stopper. "Many places. Calandra I can recognize." She smiled. "You might know some of the others better than I."

Crocken acknowledged that he was well traveled, then added—he knew not why, "I've lived in many places, none of them for very long."

"It keeps one from being homesick, having no home?"

Crocken was too startled at her perception to answer. He didn't know how she could have guessed the truth so surely from the little his statement had offered her.

"When I told my father I wanted to come here, he was working in my mother's herb garden." Ivy dusted off her skirts and wandered a few steps along the greensward. She stooped to pluck a fragrant sprig of lavender from a raised bed. "Whenever she saw he was troubled, my mother sent him out to dig. It got to be quite a large garden."

Crocken fell into step beside her. His shadow, beginning to grow, trailed along. "It's surely an honor to be chosen to wait upon the princess. Didn't your father want you to come?"

"I had dreamed I would come here. My mother believed that I dreamed true; my father wasn't sure. He fretted about that. And he didn't want me to leave Calandra."

Crocken, looking down into her pointed face, found himself in sympathy. *He* would not like to think of parting with Ivy. The depth of the feeling startled him, and he pushed it away—feelings of that sort only led him to pain, and he wasn't planning to remain in Armyn, once the shadow was done with him. They were fated to part.

"I thought it was because I reminded him of my mother, when they were both young. I look very like her," Ivy said. "But my mother said it was because I was like *him*, that we were so close. If I had been the eldest, or the youngest, or the only girl, I'd have had a harder time convincing him—but I am none of those, and in the end he let me go."

Crocken thought of the father he hadn't had a chance to know, the mother who'd let him go—permanently—when he was eight. The older sister he hadn't laid eyes on since she was wed. He wished there'd been someone—anyone—who'd wanted him to stay anywhere. He'd nearly had that in his grasp. Litsa—the old pain was surprisingly fresh, and he counted it a weakness.

"So, you dreamed you came here," he said, to distract himself before misery took firm hold. "At least one of your dreams is proved true, then."

"Almost," Ivy said absently. She might have been dreaming then, with her green eyes open and a fey look in them. "Come. We should take a turn at the bowls before we go, for form's sake."

Gravel crunched, a pattern of footsteps approaching.

Crocken turned, and alert changed to alarm, as he saw the steward-protector walking toward them along the path, the sunlight revealing deep blues and green in the generally dark sweep of his beltran.

All seemed not to be lost, however—Rhisiart had likely not seen them, abstracted as he appeared to be. The man walked slowly, evidently deep in thought and in no hurry, which would give them time to slip away. Crocken reached a hand out, ready to take Ivy's arm and shepherd her swiftly out of sight, back along the path to the green. With luck, Rhisiart would never notice them, far less wonder at their clandestine activity.

Crocken's fingers closed on empty air. Mistress Ivy, her fingers sliding the vial casually into the pocket hidden in the side-seam of her skirt, was moving to intercept the steward-protector.

What a brave, foolish thing, Crocken marveled, as he made the escape she'd arranged for him at her own expense. There was no calling her back from it. He watched from behind the concealment of a mulberry tree as Rhisiart greeted Ivy, his surprise and his pleasure evident. Ivy seemed to enjoy their meeting, also, as if her pocket did not hold the makings of a magical treason that could cost her very life if discovered. Crocken could only sometimes make out a word or two, but Ivy's expression was natural, carefree. And Rhisiart seemed to smile.

To his horror, Crocken saw his shadow creeping away toward Rhisiart—taking advantage of the hedge—trying to overhear what his ears could not. Crocken was furious at the risk it took after Ivy's sacrifice to rescue him, but there was no way he could call it back without losing the precarious safety he had. What if it gave him away?

What crime, to loiter in a garden on a fair day? the shadow asked sarcastically. *Even Rhisiart succumbs to such an innocent pleasure, though rarely. You are in no danger.*

But what of Ivy? Crocken wanted to ask.

She does not appear to think herself in peril.

Ivy was, in fact, walking away down the graveled path, still deep in conversation. Her laughter reached Crocken faintly, as if the harebells along the path had begun to chime in the breeze, and then she and the steward-protector were gone out of sight and sound, unless the shadow could stretch its senses like its form.

Chapter Twenty-three

"No, no, my good lords! We cannot arrange the procession so!" Lord Stiles gestured languidly at the parchment lying before Rhisiart, which his Council had under discussion. "It would seem to some that Jollan is shown precedence over Linnell, and that would make bad blood between them. And what of Maidoc, who is also owed a prominent place? Perhaps if we—"

"Two days past, he sweetly agreed to the entire order of march without a single challenge," Ivy murmured, so faintly that her speech reached only Crocken's ear. "One would think Andrayne was not eager for his nephew's crowning, he does such service toward delaying it."

Crocken softly echoed the thought. "Surely matters would go smoother if they could be agreed upon beforetime?"

Ivy's hand flew to her lips, stifling ill-timed mirth. "As indeed they *are*. I am often called to attend the Council, to speak for my lady while the plans that so concern her are drawn up. These public readings are but formalities—and chances for Lord Stiles to discomfit Rhisiart by going back on his word where none can challenge."

If the steward-protector was indeed discomfitted, Rhisiart kept the fact well hidden. Crocken said so.

"I suppose it comes with practice—dealing with the turbulent Borderlords for so many years. I have heard Rhisiart say so— and say also that he enjoyed the process far more than this overpolite wrangling."

The dispute went on, with false smiles all round, for better than a quarter hour. Crocken lost the thread of the quarrel and had no notion how it was eventually resolved. He was uneasy, waiting and watching Ivy as she waited to make her announcement.

Lord Stiles pled pressing affairs and departed. There was more business done. Crocken thought momentarily that Ivy would make her move, but she was still by his elbow as a small delegation took the fore. Preoccupied, he had missed the preamble of their petition.

"What's this?" he whispered to Ivy.

"These mercers have come to petition the steward-protector for his help in collecting monies owed them." Ivy was only half attending to her answer, as the petitioning was still going on. There was a thin furrow between her fine-drawn brows.

"Who owes them?" Crocken asked. Merchants had guilds to deal with such matters and seldom invited governments to interfere with affairs of commerce. Yet Rhisiart *was* renowned as a judge . . . perchance the matter was too tangled for the guilds.

Ivy did not answer, but the voices from the dais did, reading a roll of the debtors. Andrayne, Lord Stiles, the Prince Kieron, numerous others whom Crocken knew to be Kieron's adherents. He turned a wide-eyed stare on Ivy.

"The merchants can hardly refuse to extend them credit," she said, in the manner of a shrug.

"But then they just don't pay? Did Rhisiart know of this?" *By the look on his face, I should guess not.*

The related tally was immense. Food, cloth, wine, furs, candles, gold and silver table plate. Rhisiart's face went a degree whiter with each mercer who stepped forward and pled his case. By the time the last had finished, his aspect was terrifying, the more so because he held his peace and sat with the stillness of a crossbow bolt loaded and ready to let fly at a touch.

Finally he spoke.

"Gentlemen, your grievances are heard. I thank you for bringing this matter to my attention, and marvel at the patience you have shown. I can only ask for more of that indulgence, while pledging to you that I will attend to this matter with all speed."

The mercers looked uncertainly from one to the other, unsure whether they ought to trust another high-bred promise. Crocken couldn't blame them.

"As a faith token," Rhisiart went on, plainly feeling something more was needed, "I will order you each paid a token sum from my own accounts. Master Haun, conduct these gentlemen, please."

"Kieron owes, Rhisiart pays?" Crocken asked incredulously.

"He'll never see *that* money back, will he?" It didn't require
an answer, and got none, from Ivy or the shadow.

The Council concluded its day's work, ere else could go
wrong, and separated. And Crocken saw with some consternation that Mistress Ivy was no longer in the Hall. He had no idea
when she had departed, or why she had altered her plan, and
the shadow was no help to him.

Crocken was in the Hall again next day, advising the Council—at the steward-protector's personal request—on the quality
of some costly Kôveliran silks being offered by the Mercer's
Guild for coronation apparel.

The Council battle of the moment was over a tournament
proposed to celebrate the crowning. Kieron desperately wanted
one; Rhisiart utterly opposed it as dangerous and wasteful of
life and limb. There were safer parodies of war, he suggested,
and ample processions taking place, enough to satisfy anyone's
love of splendor.

Kieron sulked. His uncle Stiles leaned close and proposed
something into the princely ear. Kieron brightened at once,
rather slyly.

"What did he say?" Crocken whispered to his shadow.

For once, it obliged him with an answer.

Andrayne reminded him that a tourney can easily be arranged
after the crowning—when no man can gainsay him.

Surely Stiles had not expected Kieron to keep the scheme
secret—the boy's tact was nowhere near equal to it. The prince
voiced the plan to his other uncle at once, gloatingly.

Rhisiart made no comment, but he looked full weary, Crocken
thought, as well he might be.

He cannot stop it, but he will never agree to it, either, the
shadow whispered. *Thus, bitterly, is honor satisfied.*

What else does he have? Crocken thought to ask—but did not,
on account of the public circumstances.

Kieron withdrew, and more mundane business was dealt with
for an hour. The Council was nearly ready for adjournment
when Mistress Ivy presented herself before Rhisiart and begged
leave to deliver her lady's message.

She looked so innocent, kneeling with downcast eyes before
the dais, that Crocken would have been taken in, as well, had
his anxiety—or his shadow—permitted him that relief. Unhappily, he knew only too well why she was there.

"Sir, my lady bids me inform you that she has fulfilled her

noble vow—the shirt for her royal bridegroom is completed at last, and she craves to offer it to Prince Kieron before their nuptuals.''

"Most timely," Rhisiart agreed pleasantly. "There should be some ceremony, perhaps?" He was smiling. And why not? After Kieron's theatrics, Mistress Ivy was a rare treat.

"Yes, my lord. Before whatever witnesses you deem proper. My lady is anxious that her customs do not war with yours.''

Or surely anxious on some count? the shadow archly inquired.

Rhisiart came forward and raised Ivy to her little slippered feet. "Your lady need have no fear of that—or of aught else, Mistress Ivy. Her vow is a proper one, nothing at odds with Armyn's ways—though our own maidens do not often practice such vows. Would she prefer to present her gift before the assembled court?''

Ivy's green eyes went wide. It was a larger ceremony than she'd anticipated, or was likely to relish. "My lord knows how modest my lady is! It is so little a time till the wedding itself, I am sure she wishes only a few witnesses, the prince's family and such nobles close to him as you would best know.''

"Then I shall ask those persons—and the Prince Kieron—to assemble in Kieron's rooms tomorrow evening. Will that suit?''

"My lord is most kind." Ivy gracefully took her leave.

So soon, was all Crocken could think as word was formally conveyed to Lord Stiles. The day went chill around him, while he gave his judgment of the Kôveliran silks as if naught was amiss.

Something will be made to happen, before this night ends. We must listen sharply, and learn just what.

"Listen where?" Crocken asked warily. Dreading the next evening was trouble enough for him. And it irritated him to see the shadow in the wrong place—by the door rather than on the far wall where his candle threw the room's other shadows.

A difficult choice. My best guess is the gardens.

"The gardens? It's night," Crocken pointed out. All he desired was sleep—if he could woo it.

I will direct you. Make haste. Unless I am mistaken, matters shall go ill indeed.

The shadow would say no more, save to guide Crocken's steps as it had promised. The pleasure garths were deserted, for which Crocken was glad enough. His worst dread was the mischance of being forced to explain his presence to anyone who might come upon him. He was relieved to be allowed to halt ere any such disaster befell him.

"Now what?" he whispered, but not softly enough to suit his master.

Be silent. Open your ears. Hear as a shadow does—when none suspect it.

If there was anything to listen *to*, then there were ears to overhear *him* as well. Crocken willingly fell silent. He noticed he'd been halted beneath a window, its casement partly opened to the cool night air. Whose chamber did it refresh? He heard a faint voice and strove to listen more intently, crouching in the dark.

"Andrayne, I tell you again, this marriage *must* be stopped. This step toward it cannot take place." A woman's voice, sharp with authority.

Lord Stiles' voice then, an unmistakable whine. "My queen, there's no time to prevent the presentation. We dare not attempt it. How there was no outcry, when the other scheme miscarried—I am still at a loss. Two men dead, and by whose hand? Two men dead, and this silence. I like it not—"

Crocken didn't like it, either. He only knew of one dead man, dead at Ivy's hand. If there was a second, then the shadow had slain him—probably that was the man sent to fetch the guards. So it *could* kill, when it chose to. He had begun to doubt it was as deadly as it claimed; now he must revise that estimation.

Do not forget Mistress Ivy's handy knife.

Was it disavowing the killing? Or was it only trying to mislead him?

"Perhaps you were lied to." Sulien's voice came shrilly, though faint. Crocken strained his ears. "Perchance the men you hired quarreled before the task was begun and slew one another. It is of no matter! We are fortunate only that there was no outcry, not that the plan failed. Mirell is yet a maiden, and my son *cannot* wed her. He dares not. You *know* the risk."

"My queen—" Crocken wondered if Stiles was kneeling at his sister's feet, penitent. "But—to strike at the princess once more—how shall we—"

"I liked well the former plan, it served many a purpose. But, as we know not why it miscarried, it must be discarded. Its time is past. Leave Mirell and find another way."

Crocken heard pacing footfalls. He couldn't see what the shadow was doing. Was it trying to gain better vantage by slipping through the casement, or was that too dangerous even for it?

The queen spoke again, her voice deadly firm. "If there was no steward-protector, matters would stand easier. It is Rhisiart who pushes for this wedding. Without him, we could delay the match, or discard it."

"Strike at Rhisiart? *Now?*"

"I am informed that it has become his custom to fare forth a little before dawn—you know he sleeps ill, Andrayne—to ride alone for an hour before he sets to work governing *my* kingdom. Either Rhisiart is careless of his life, or he feels the span of his days no longer matters much. Either way, an accident should be simple to arrange."

"There is only *this* dawn to work with, my queen. We dare not wait longer, yet there is little time to arrange—"

"You will not fail me, Andrayne."

"My queen." The voice was almost choking.

"I would suggest archers," Sulien said sweetly. "And be certain they are able to complete their task—not cry the tale back upon us if they should fail."

We must flee, the shadow suggested. Crocken hastened to obey, but he stumbled when he arose, his legs badly cramped. The gravel of the path went pattering into the herb beds.

At once a furious yapping began, just within the nearby casement. Perchance the queen, like many another high-born lady, kept lapdogs. The beasts had sharp ears and ready tongues.

"Why do the dogs bark?" the queen asked, with an alarm note in her voice that sent Crocken diving headlong behind a hedge of lavender without the shadow's urging. The plants were too low to offer him much concealment, and when he heard Andrayne's voice at the window, Crocken was certain he'd be discovered momentarily. He flattened himself despairingly, pushing his face into the cropped chamomile of the lawn so the moonlight—if there was any, he could not recall—would not reveal it, while the dog's noise resounded and redoubled.

" 'Tis only a cat, sister. Calm yourself—" The voices faded. The dog was ordered to cease barking, and the casement was closed, the latch clicking as 'twas thrown.

Crocken's wide eyes stared over the lavender at the garden's far wall, where a cat's shadow crept along, coolly contemptuous of the dog's fury. Where there was the shadow of a cat, there must perforce *be* a cat—so Andrayne had reasoned. Only Crocken could see that the feline shadow was as solitary as the moon whose light did not cast it, as it left the wall and rejoined him on the pathway.

Chapter Twenty-four

"ARCHERS?" CROCKEN ASKED with a sick feeling in his belly. "Where did he find archers this time of night?"

Andrayne is more resourceful than I had suspected. I did not think he could arrange so fell a matter so swiftly.

"We should have warned Rhisiart as soon as we heard," Crocken said miserably. Instead, the shadow had forced him to wander all over Axe-Edge to no evident purpose, continually abandoning him in what it assured him were "safe" places for agonizingly long moments while it scouted about and reported back to him at increasingly infrequent intervals.

And how did you intend to explain—to Rhisiart—how you came to learn of his danger?

Crocken shook his head in the darkness. He had no idea whether the shadow actually wanted to warn Rhisiart at all. What if it was really minded to exact its revenge for the betrayal it blamed on the steward-protector? What would that mean to Ivy's plan, which it championed? Or to Ivy's safety?

We will warn him now. And we will need to make haste, if we are to reach Rhisiart ahead of his assassins.

"Why don't we just keep him from leaving the stables?"

The shadow said nothing, which communicated a great deal.

"He's already gone?" Crocken had no idea what the hour was, but it seemed no time—to him—to choose for a pleasure ride.

Rhisiart sleeps ill and rises early. The archers crept out just after. Come. The stables are this way.

The shadow moved off, and Crocken's haste to follow was pathetic. Too easy to lose such a guide at night, when *all* was shadow.

And there were assassins about, and perhaps queen's men.

187

And a prince more serpent than human . . . Crocken was not sure when the change had begun, but his extraordinary master had come to seem the sanest, safest creature in Axe-Edge. Why else did he cling to it so?

Crocken actually recognized the gray stallion he'd ridden to the hunt, but the shadow did not allow him to choose the familiar mount, even when it put its head out and sniffed as if it remembered him kindly.

Too visible, in the night. You need a dark horse. And it led him on, away from safety.

Another white head loomed. Ears went back.

"Stormraker's still here," Crocken whispered angrily, keeping a safe distance. "Are you sure—"

Rhisiart rides other horses betimes, the shadow answered impatiently. *Particularly when he desires a quiet ride. Take this one here. It seems swift.*

Probably true. Long-legged, the beast certainly was. So tall, 'twas all Crocken could do to get a saddle on its back; and had it fought him over having a bit shoved unexpectedly into its mouth, he'd have given the matter up on the spot. Fortunately, the horse had plainly had manners trained into it, and it allowed him to do what the shadow bid him without compounding his errors.

Tighten those buckles, the shadow ordered sternly. *You won't ride far if you and that saddle are swinging under the horse's belly.*

Crocken worked feverishly, feeling that the task was taking him thrice as long as it should have. A riding saddle was none so different from a pack-saddle, and the darkness shouldn't have troubled him so at a familiar task. 'Twas fear of discovery made him thumb-fingered. The stable lads would be asleep in the loft above, and the grooms, too. The horses were wakeful and restive, watching him from their stalls. If just one of them whinnied, thinking he was there to deliver the morning feeding, he was trapped. At long last, with relief, he led the saddled horse out into the relative safety of the cobbled yard.

The horse's manners took an instant shift for the worse, and all cooperation ceased. It shied away as Crocken tried to put a boot into the near stirrup. After that fright, it refused to stand still for him, flinging its head wildly, heedless of his tight hold on the reins, so that he had to leap after it. Its shod hooves rang on the cobbles, loud as alarm bells.

"I tell you, horses can *see* you!" Crocken hissed at his shadow, as they all warily held their new positions. "No one's supposed to have a shadow at night."

And a horse knows this? the shadow rejoined coldly. It stood between Crocken and the horse, safe from its hooves.

"It knows *something*." The animal's nearest eye rolled, and the rest of its body backed away, staying at the end of its reins no matter how Crocken tried to creep closer. Since the shadow was between them, Crocken was not surprised. Rather, he felt vindicated. The horse danced nervously.

Be ready.

"Why? What are you—"

The shadow leapt high and flung itself over the horse's head. Blinded, the animal froze in its place, while Crocken scrambled up into its saddle. All too soon the beast was moving again, but a rider on its back—even a poor one—seemed to comfort the horse. At least it did not bolt out of the stableyard, rousing everyone in the vicinity, but allowed Crocken to walk it quietly to the gate.

The postern was unguarded. No doubt that explained the archers having been able to slip out unchallenged. Was such always the case, or was the apparent desertion part of Andrayne's plot? Were the guards lying dead, somewhere out of sight? Crocken tried to ask the shadow.

No time for that. After the archers.

"How do we get to Rhisiart ahead of them?" Crocken whispered.

They will not seek to hunt Rhisiart down—he could escape them if he runs, or simply slip past them in the dark. He knows the country well. The assassins will take up a position and wait for him to pass it, unaware, returning. Therefore we must ensure Rhisiart does not do so.

Therefore they must also pass by the position themselves, undetected, to learn its location. Crocken did not need to be warned of the danger therein. He fell silent willingly, his heart pounding, racing.

He discovered he could not worry about hidden archers and the horse at the selfsame time. Each concern distracted from its fellow fear. Instead Crocken alternated frequently from one to the other—afraid he would be ambushed in Rhisiart's place, terrified the horse would stumble in the dark and unseat him. An arrow in the back, collision with an unseen tree. He'd be too slow, too late. The horse could run away with him. The night was all terror, with death at its heart, either for him or for Rhisiart.

All trails leading out of Axe-Edge, even the main cartway, did much the same thing—entered woodland and dropped swiftly downhill, following one of the ravines. In the night, the track the shadow chose seemed simply to vanish into nothingness. Crocken managed to halt the horse with a panicked tightening of the reins, just before it walked off what he was certain was a precipice.

"Rhisiart went down *there*? In the dark?" Crocken trembled just thinking of it. The horse reacted by sidling under him. The ravine yawned before him like a pit. He couldn't see the trail, not at all.

Rhisiart has ridden through far worse, in battle and at a gallop. You yourself have ridden this track beforetime, the shadow said impatiently, brushing away his fears. *It winds and does not plunge. You will be safe.*

Assuming that contemptuous reassurance was true, Crocken did not recognize the path. He'd never been out of Axe-Edge by night. Or the shadow could be lying, to coerce him. There was no way to know. He made the horse inch down the trail on a maddeningly tight rein, till he proved to his own satisfaction that he was not riding over the edge of a cliff.

Stop.

Crocken was delighted to do so—though he could not see the cause and doubted it was for his own comfort.

There are the archers. Behind the trees, on the slope. Ahead and below us.

Crocken peered, but could see nothing. He knew better than to question the shadow aloud.

They chose well. The trail is a little washed away, just where it winds closest to them. Rhisiart will have to ride slowly, and uphill. An easy target even in the dark, and by the time he returns they will have the dawnlight.

Crocken's fingers tightened on the reins. "How do we—" He winced at forgetting what he could not see. But how was he to get past the bowmen, to warn Rhisiart?

Softly! Turn the horse about. We're going back to the top.

In moments they had retraced their descent. The shadow directed Crocken's course, through thickset trees along the lip of the ravine. Above the archers they climbed, and well past them, to their rear. There was no real trail, only the trees and thin undergrowth that pressed them close to the downslope. Crocken strove not to think of the disaster waiting should the earth he rode upon prove to be unstable. He could hear small stones falling into the ravine as the horse dislodged them, rattling through the fallen leaves for a long, long way. He hoped the archers couldn't likewise detect them. The shadow said the men were afoot, which it said was a blessing—horses have sharper ears than men and would have given him away for certain.

This should do. Go back down to the trail, and we shall intercept Rhisiart.

Crocken stared. The ground simply fell away, where the shadow indicated. His eyes were adjusted to the night now, but there was no path for them to see.

"I can't get this horse down *that*," he protested. "It's a cliff, not a trail—"

Tie the horse, the shadow instructed. *The way is not easy, but it can be managed.*

He could not, Crocken thought as he went, have done such madness on his own, because he wouldn't have attempted it. He tried to descend the slope quietly, letting his boots sink into the soft earth and the deep bed of leaves blanketing it, leaning back toward the slope for balance. Branches thwarted him, snagged at him, both from the ground and above it. Those buried in the leaves were the worst—if he caught a foot solidly in one, he thought he might break his leg before he could get free. The near misses were nasty enough. He was not so much climbing downward as sliding unsteadily, his legs more or less controlling his speed, and very vulnerable.

Stones were bad, too. Crocken trod upon one, which was roundish and rolled. He pitched sideways, then forward as his center of balance shifted—and suddenly was out of control, tumbling head over heels down the steep hillside. He rolled. He bounced. He discovered more rocks, and narrowly missed trees. Once or twice he almost came back to his feet, but his awful momentum promptly threw him forward again, keeping him rolling. Crocken was dizzy and bruised when he finally reached the relatively level ground of the trail and slid to a painful stop, uncertain for a moment whether or not he might still be falling. His breath and his stomach seemed not to have caught up with the rest of him.

We will wait here, and halt Rhisiart when he comes, the shadow proposed calmly. Crocken, panting, could only stare in its direction, disbelieving. He got his legs under him, somewhat surprised that he could still do so, that neither was broken nor torn away.

A sound made him forget his pain.

"I hear a horse."

Yes. He couldn't see the shadow, but its listening attitude was plain.

Now, if only the rider *was* Rhisiart.

The horseman hove into sight, around the wind of the trail. It was light enough by then for Crocken to make out his general build—the man was either the steward-protector or someone much like him. And who else would be out riding at such an hour?

Crocken took a wobbly step forward, still not quite master of his breath. "My lord! Wait—"

No! The shadow tried to snatch him back, to silence him with a shadowy hand, but it was already too late, the harm was done. Rhisiart heard him, saw only unknown danger on the dark trail, and spurred his horse hard, sending it galloping past Crocken, who had no hope of stopping it even if he'd chosen to jump in front of it instead of away.

You fool! He'll be into the ambush before we can catch him—

The realization of disaster hit Crocken like a sword-thrust. "Do something," he begged, as he had never more desperately begged for any favor.

I can get him off the horse, the shadow replied grimly.

The shadow flowed out from Crocken, smooth as a river flooding—then rose up swiftly where Rhisiart's horse would best catch the motion. It timed the startling move well. The animal shied mightily, swerving three yards to its left, and bolted for home ere its hooves were fairly touching the path once more.

Far better riders than Crocken would have been undone at the outset and left afoot, but Rhisiart kept his seat, startled as he must have been. Crocken watched astonished as the shadow's arms lengthened. It caught hold of the dark length of Rhisiart's beltran, where the cloth streamed out behind him, then yanked hard so that beltran and man came off the horse together and sailed earthward.

The steward-protector hit the ground first on his right shoulder, somersaulting so that he finished lying half on his face, his boots pointing at the fleeing horse. Crocken was running toward him, even as the shadow came flowing back to his side. He dropped to his knees on ground that felt as if 'twere all stones, sized to handily crack a skull. The steward-protector hadn't made a sound—not a groan, not a curse, not even a deep breath. Crocken couldn't hear *any* breathing beyond his own. The more he strained his ears, the less they seemed to report to him.

"What were you trying to do—kill him yourself?" he asked the shadow furiously. He laid a hand on Rhisiart's back. "My lord? My lord, can you hear me?" No response.

Crocken carefully rolled the steward-protector onto his back and felt at his throat, desperately seeking the blood-beat there. His fingers shook so terribly that he learned nothing.

Crocken was too agitated to notice his shadow's copying his examination more effectively. Its dark fingers roved swiftly over the steward-protector from his toes to the crown of his head, lingering awhile over his right arm. Nor did Crocken pay heed to the soft hiss it let loose with—being intent on his own fright.

"My lord?" *What if he's dead?* Crocken wondered. Rhisiart's eyes were closed, his face still. There was no sign of life.

He breathes, the shadow assured him.

Crocken refused the comfort. "Are you sure? You could have broken his neck with that trick." The fall replayed itself in his memory, with awful clarity.

I did not. He lives.

"Or cracked his skull," Crocken said darkly, remembering another stunt of the shadow's. "You nearly did mine."

I will crack it for you again, if you do not hold your peace! the shadow whispered. *Rhisiart has had the breath jarred out of him, but he is barely stunned. Don't assume he cannot hear you because he has not answered.*

As if to prove that, Rhisiart suddenly moaned, stirring as if he would push himself up from the ground. His eyes were open, though he did not seem to be looking at anything in particular. Crocken nearly swooned with relief. He realized that he could still hear the steward-protector's horse, pounding on toward the ambush. He put his arm around Rhisiart's shoulders, his lips close to the steward-protector's ear.

"My lord," he said, as Rhisiart began to struggle. "My lord, it's all right." The man probably had no idea where he was or what had befallen him, and an urge to escape would be only natural.

"What—" Rhisiart bit off the query as Crocken helped him to sit up. His nose was bleeding—Crocken could see the dark smear running down to his chin. His cap was gone, there were twigs in his hair. Crocken tried to brush them away.

"My lord, you've had a fall from your horse." He hoped

Rhisiart could understand the explanation—and that he'd ask for no more of it. His wits were unprepared for subterfuge, and it seemed unlikely he'd collect them soon. His only hope was that Rhisiart's wits were likely even more scattered at the moment.

"Who's there? The merchant?" Rhisiart sounded surprised, as well he might. Crocken was surely the last person he expected to encounter in such a situation.

"Yes, my lord." Crocken glanced at the shadow, which seemed to be keeping a watch on the trail.

"What are you—" Rhisiart put a hand to his head, then swore and took it away. "What are *you* doing out here?"

That horse is going to trip the ambush. We have to get away from here, the shadow said. *Get him on his feet.*

Crocken drew a breath. "My lord, there are bowmen ahead, waiting to kill you. I came to warn you." *And wound up almost getting you killed.* He swallowed, and began to lie effortlessly. "I heard your horse, so I came this way." Bird calls announced the pending dawn. Light would make escape more difficult, would it not?

Rhisiart wiped at his face, then blinked uncertainly at his bloodied fingers. "You said I fell—"

"I didn't actually see, my lord. When I got here, you were lying in the road, and the horse was running like a demon was after it. I thought I was too late, that you'd been attacked. Are you much hurt?"

You may have to carry him. Make haste.

Rhisiart shifted, moving experimentally away from Crocken's support. He groaned again. "I don't . . . think so. Not to last, anyway. My head buzzes like a bee skep, but my breath's come back. Lend me your arm again, let's see if my legs will bear me—"

Rhisiart just managed to get to his feet, though he staggered and nearly pitched over. Crocken kept a hand near him, ready. At least he seemed not to have broken a leg.

Hurry, the shadow urged.

"I must have been no more than ten, the last time I came off a horse like that! It's been too long—" Rhisiart said ruefully, trying to straighten his beltran without toppling over. "I am certainly too old for it now! We'd best be away from here."

"My lord?" Crocken asked stupidly, as the steward-protector unknowingly echoed the shadow. He couldn't have heard it, could he?

"If someone's waiting for me, and I do not presently ride by, then they will come seeking," Rhisiart explained. He took a step, swore, and tried another. "You must have had a horse—you can't have walked this far?" He sounded rather hopeful—walking was likely painful.

Crocken murmured a heartfelt prayer to any god that might have a free ear and a sympathy for poor peddlers out of their element, that his horse wouldn't have broken free and run off for its stable. He helped Rhisiart limp toward the side of the ravine, and they began to climb.

They had scrambled perchance a third of the way to the top when Rhisiart collapsed onto his face—no great distance given the severe angle of the slope at that point. He simply fell forward into the leaves and lay, panting, while Crocken fought to keep his own footing, sliding to his knees when he failed. Crocken assumed the steward-protector had fainted, and he wondered bitterly what further ill that boded.

Up should be easier than down, the shadow insisted cruelly, and lifted Rhisiart a trifle, dragging him onward through the fallen leaves.

Crocken had found tumbling down that very slope to be all *too* easy to accomplish. He didn't want to indulge in it again. He knelt carefully beside Rhisiart, grasped an arm, and began to lift. The steward-protector gasped.

"Not that arm, I pray you—" Rhisiart was getting his legs under him again, though staying low so as not to risk falling over backward, sensibly letting the hillside help him as much as it could. Crocken climbed around and took his left arm.

"Lost my balance," Rhisiart said in apology. "These leaves—" He caught hold of a sapling and gingerly pulled himself up onto firmer ground.

"I fell all the way down," Crocken admitted, reckoning how that accident had led directly to their present trouble. He began seeking out trees to grasp, following the steward-protector's lead, else they might both tumble again, should Rhisiart slip once more. Several times he anticipated precisely that, but something held them in place—the shadow, Crocken thought gratefully. He was out of breath, nearly at the end of the strength that peril had lent him. That strength might fade at any moment, and his own knees were weak. What if the horse was gone?

Then somehow, they were at the top of the slope. One moment there was hillside before Crocken—the next 'twas the equally lofty side of a very nervous horse, tethered to a tree.

Crocken untied the horse, assessing his lack of success in

forcing it to stand still for mounting. He turned to the steward-protector and held out the reins.

"My lord, you'd better take him." Rhisiart looked puzzled at the offer. "I don't doubt you ride better than I do even now! I can walk back—no one's hunting *me*."

"Nonsense." The steward-protector had caught his breath and commenced a rapid inspection of the horse. "He's a sturdy beast. He can carry two—for a while."

Crocken's heart sank. The horse continued to circle him, rolling an eye at his growing shadow. Dawn was breaking. "If you say so. But you steer."

He gave Rhisiart a boost into the saddle—with difficulty, as the saddle was moving. The horse stood still at once, and Crocken gave it a pained look. He accepted the hand extended to help him scramble up behind the saddle, and Rhisiart let the horse move off at once.

"Tell me," the steward-protector said over his muddy shoulder, "when we near this ambush."

Assuming that the ambush was still in place. What if the bowmen had filled Rhisiart's horse with arrows and then gone seeking after its rider? They might meet them anywhere. Crocken's shoulders twitched, anticipating arrows.

They will be unlikely to look for us up here. And you protect Rhisiart's back.

Crocken bit off a furious retort.

In case you cannot recall the spot, the bowmen are in those trees ahead, to the left and below.

Crocken dutifully relayed the information to Rhisiart.

"An excellent spot for an ambush," the steward-protector whispered, almost approvingly. "I wonder if they know of this trail above them?"

They don't expect us to be on it.

Trail? What did Rhisiart mean? To Crocken, their location seemed woodland, just as it had when he'd passed through it earlier—and he saw no sign now of that passage. The fact that a horse could pass between the trees—just—did not make a trail to his way of thinking. Trails were bare, from constant, common passage. This was no trail—but he seemed to be outvoted in the matter.

"Are you ready?" Rhisiart asked. The horse was bunching under them.

"Ready?"

It proved to be more warning than question. Rhisiart kicked the horse into a gallop, and double-burdened or not, the beast obeyed him smartly. Crocken ducked his head, then shut his eyes when the sight of tree trunks dimly whipping past proved too much for his peace of mind. Best he not see near disasters. He thought he heard a shout and imagined the twang of a bow-string loosed.

A branch cracked his right knee, others scraped across his hunched shoulders, gone swiftly as they'd come. He hoped the steward-protector was recovered sufficiently to sit a horse at such speed—riding behind as he was, Crocken had no means of control—and neither stirrup nor saddle, just a bit of saddle-cloth betwixt him and the horse's lurching hindquarters. All he could hold firmly onto was Rhisiart's belt. A new fear plagued him—what if he pulled the man off *this* horse? Rhisiart didn't need another such fall.

Yet, when Rhisiart *did* rein in, Crocken was still frantic enough to urge him on despite all sense, even while the horse was trying to obey and halt.

"Don't slow down!" He nearly lost his precarious perch and had to scramble to maintain it.

"Master Crocken, we cannot expect this horse to carry a double load farther uphill at such a breakneck pace," Rhisiart answered impatiently. "We've leagues to go. He won't reach the stables, and he does not deserve to founder himself attempting it. Those archers will be hard put to come into bowshot now without us hearing their approach. Let the horse breathe."

Remember, you're not the military commander, the shadow admonished.

Crocken reluctantly agreed with both of them. He was breathing harder than the horse was, and sweat dripped into his eyes, though the air was cool.

"How came you to hear of this plot?"

Crocken's heart misgave him. He was too long-terrified to invent a plausible lie. His wits were fear-shriveled and unequal to the task.

A voice whispered into his ear, the third rider the horse carried. *Tell him—*

Unexpectedly, the horse whinnied. Rhisiart cursed and jerked at the reins to silence it, his question forgotten.

"What is it?" Crocken whispered, over the steward-protector's shoulder. He felt his skin rising into goosebumps.

As if to answer, a horse came walking out of the rising mist. Crocken didn't recognize it, but Rhisiart plainly did. In any case, the empty saddle it bore suggested whose horse it might be.

"Didn't get back to your stable after all, eh, Darkling?" Rhisiart swung out of the saddle, after he'd lowered Crocken safely down the horse's side. He handed the reins over, then approached the loose horse slowly. It backed away a step or two, watching him intently, ears pricked. Its neck and flanks were lathered with sweat, and it trembled.

"Shh, you've had fright, and no mistake." Rhisiart got closer, steadily. The horse stood still. "And then I left you, too." He smoothly took hold of the trailing reins. One was broken—the horse would have trodden upon it, Crocken thought. Rhisiart gently stroked the animal's neck, then began to inspect its legs painstakingly in the growing light, running his hands down them one by one.

"Well, you've come to no harm, whatever sent you off like that," the steward-protector said with relief. The horse was still snorting, and Crocken was careful to stand well clear of it, keeping his shadow out of its sight. Rhisiart turned to him. "I'll have to walk him cool—'twill cause too much commotion if I bring him back in such a lather. Best maybe if we don't go in together."

Crocken was appalled. "I'm not leaving you out here."

Rhisiart frowned and set his mouth. Crocken ignored the displeasure.

"My lord, I will *not*. As for causing commotion—aren't you going to send guards out after those assassins?"

"To what purpose?" Rhisiart asked, maddeningly. "Those bowmen will be gone long since, unless they are utter fools. They know by now they have failed. Thanks to your warning, they are guilty of no worse than sitting in the king's forest—they might easily claim to have been hunting, and I am not minded to give Sulien cause to say I ill treat her friends."

"You'd rather they killed you?"

Rhisiart sighed and took hold of the nearside stirrup. He tried to put his foot into it, and bit back a curse. "Master Crocken, I fear I am going to require your help again in getting onto this horse. And you may ride with me as far as the gatehouse, if that will satisfy you. But I beg you then to tarry there a space, before you go in yourself. My sponsorship has tainted you more than sufficiently, I fear."

If you only knew, Crocken thought—but all he said to Rhisiart were a few polite words about cleaning the blood from his face.

Chapter Twenty-five

RELIEVED NOT TO be questioned further as to his fortuitous appearance, Crocken did as Rhisiart bade him, giving his borrowed mount over to the grooms a good half hour after he'd parted company with the steward-protector. He held his breath as he handed over the reins, lest someone take notice of his coming in when he'd never officially gone out. And just whose steed had he appropriated, in the dark stable? Trust the shadow to have purloined Lord Stiles' own favored palfrey.

The grooms were busy, and uninterested. There was a great deal of coming and going, and their services were in constant demand. Crocken's horse was known, even if he wasn't. Crocken himself was unremarked, and desperately grateful for that. Musing on his good fortune, he went through an archway into a dim passage and nearly ran into the steward-protector.

"My lord!" Crocken's heart battered his ribs. "My lord, you didn't need to wait for me—"

Rhisiart pushed himself carefully away from the wall he'd been propped against. "Your pardon," he said vaguely. "I did not intend to loiter here, once I was safely in, but each step brings some new bruise to my attention, and I was dizzy a moment hence. I feared—I had rather not be thought in my cups at this hour."

Crocken observed the difficulty Rhisiart was having in remaining upright without the wall's aid. He looked like to have fallen, had Crocken not been there to take the stonework's place. Reaction, Crocken guessed, else the fall had hurt him worse than had been evident at first.

The shadow was close, in the safe dark. *He's going to faint,* it warned.

How any of the grooms could have seen the man and not

raised alarm, Crocken could not fathom. Rhisiart was grayish pale and sweating fit to soak them both. Crocken recalled the position of the gate—perchance between the light of the rising sun and the white of the lifting fog, no one had gotten a good look, and the steward-protector might have managed a few steps without limping, till he was safely out of public view. The cost of success had been high. Rhisiart looked incapable of taking another such step.

"I'll take you to the healer," Crocken offered hastily.

"No!" Rhisiart's voice was stronger than his grip, which was painful enough. His fingers burned Crocken's forearm like flame. "Just . . . help me to some quiet spot."

"The healer's rooms are quiet," Crocken said stubbornly.

"*No.* I am well enough." The steward-protector didn't sound it, despite the authority he strove to put into his tone.

"Your own rooms, then?" Where exactly would those be? Did the shadow know? Likely it did, and might direct him without being asked.

"No." Rhisiart sounded less firm about it, as he passed a hand over his damp face. "I would liefer not explain—"

Well, Crocken thought he'd rather not explain, either, and he'd likely be the one forced to do just that. He took Rhisiart's arm. He thought Rhisiart might pull away, but the steward-protector did not—perhaps *could* not. He let Crocken lead him and did not even ask whither they were bound till they stopped moving. He hadn't fainted yet, but Crocken did not think the man was far from it, held up only by force of will.

"Since you won't go to your rooms—well, no one will look for you here," Crocken said as he shouldered the door open. He steered Rhisiart to the single bench his room boasted. "Now, if you'll agree to wait here, I'll fetch the healer."

"I don't need the healer," Rhisiart said angrily. "Nor want her, with her prying and her potions."

Crocken thought the foolish insistence stemmed from the steward-protector's desperate hope that if he could act well he'd *be* well. Rhisiart's pallor suggested such a plan was mainly unworkable. He made one attempt to get to his feet, but swiftly gave it up and glared at Crocken.

"I'll get her to give me something to bring back—she told me to seek her if my head pained me again," Crocken said, stirring the coals of the fire to fitful life while keeping a careful eye on Rhisiart, who was slumping on the bench.

That having been weeks ago, won't she wonder why you're asking now? the shadow inquired solicitously.

Crocken shrugged. He couldn't tell whether Rhisiart had protested, too. "Just bide here awhile. I won't be long."

He thought Rhisiart would likely obey him—if he could be quick enough about his fetching. The steward-protector seemed too shaken to go beyond argument to action, he might be content to sit by the fire awhile. At least Rhisiart was out of the sight of any queen's man who might seize the chance to slide a knife between his ribs while he was helpless.

Should he indeed fetch the healer? Risk the steward-protector's wrath? Should he chance that Rhisiart was right about not being so much hurt, or should he get help? What was safe? What was prudent?

Mistress Ivy is skilled with herbs. And safer to fetch.

It was a new straw to grasp. But still—

"Stay with him," Crocken implored.

I?

"He won't notice. He could barely see me. The shutter's closed, it's dark enough in there—"

But not so dark where you go. Are you not concerned for discovery?

"No one has his eyes open this early," Crocken answered, hoping desperately that it would prove true. He bent his steps—swiftly—toward the Princess of Calandra's rooms, and never once missed his unguided way, such was his distraction. The passageways and galleries were dim, his lack of a shadow unremarkable.

He was uncertain whether Mirell's ladies would be astir so early—but Crocken had not reckoned upon the hours it took to prepare a great lady for a great ceremony. He had in any case quite forgotten that the presentation of the vowed shirt was to take place that very evening. Therefore the royal ladies were at work with the dawn. There was the bath, the washing of the princess' hair, which must be spread in the sun to dry before 'twas rubbed to a sheen with silken cloths—Crocken woke no one with his cautious rap on the outer portal, got no maid from her bed to have a message carried to Mistress Ivy. The rooms were full of women, all bustling.

The sleeves of her simple gown, pushed back, were damp, and Ivy looked impatient, even after she'd recognized him. As Mirell's chief lady, Ivy had much to attend to that day. Crocken gave her no time to speak first, but bespoke her in urgent whispers. She, of all folk, might just detect that he was shadowless, and he did not want to prolong the risk.

"Mistress, can your lady spare you for a nonce? And have you simples or salves such as might be helpful to someone who's fallen from a horse?"

"Were you out so early, Master Crocken?" Ivy smiled and took in the mud and leaves still adhering to his clothes, plainly drawing a false conclusion.

"Not for me!' he said, dodging. "It's for Rhisiart."

Ivy raised both fine brows and widened her green eyes. "The *steward-protector* fell off his horse? Master Crocken, if you choose to lie to me, for whatever reason, pray select a tale I could believe. And choose a day when I'll have time to spare for games." She turned to go, hand on the door to close it behind her.

"His horse took fright in the dark," Crocken said obscurely. "And just as well it did—Rhisiart would be dead if he'd ridden a quarter of a league farther. There was an ambush laid."

Ivy's face darkened. "I'll come," she said, and vanished back into the chamber for an impossibly brief span of time, reappearing with a nondescript bundle clasped in one hand, as she drew the portal closed with the other.

They rapidly set off. As they reached the first turn in the corridor, Ivy turned her head to Crocken, but did not stay her quick steps.

"Master Crocken, I pray you, tell me truly—is he much hurt?" She plainly thought he was holding back dire news. Crocken hastened to reassure her.

"Shaken, little more. He rode back to Axe-Edge," Crocken said by way of illustrating Rhisiart's well-being. "He's refused to go to the healer—I suspect he's embarrassed—but I didn't like to just leave him, after a hard fall like that."

Ivy seemed to have trouble accepting that for truth—she frowned and parted her lips. Crocken hoped she wasn't looking for his shadow.

"Mistress, credit me with a little sense!" Crocken forestalled. "If Rhisiart was badly hurt, I'd have gotten the healer to him at once, whatever he said. He's bruised and he doesn't want any bother, no questions. Liniment and willow tea will put him right in short order."

"Where have you left him?" Ivy asked, walking faster.

"On the bench by my fireside. He didn't want to have his

people fussing about, and I couldn't argue him out of that, so I stopped trying."

Ivy forced a smile, though her lips were pale. "That sounds as if he'll live. The ambush failed? He *wasn't* wounded? You're certain of that?"

"He fell off his horse before he rode into the trap. I got to him, warned him, and we rode back another way," Crocken said, exasperated. So put, it made the whole adventure trivial, nothing like what he remembered. "Can't this wait?"

"Shhh—"

There were footsteps approaching. A servant, who paid them no heed, but the risk was evident. They did not essay speech again the rest of the way, for which mercy Crocken was glad.

He glanced past Mistress Ivy with some trepidation, as he held the door open for her. If Rhisiart had left, if the shadow had been unable to restrain him—

The steward-protector looked weary rather than ill—as if he might have passed a very wakeful night. Rhisiart had not left the bench, though he had put back his leaf-festooned beltran a trifle, in the room's warmth. He looked up alertly—vexedly, in truth—as they entered.

Rhisiart made to rise, then must have been mindful of stiffening bruises and stayed where he was—that choice promising him the least by way of painful indignities. Crocken looked quickly about for his shadow and found it at his heels, opposite the sullen glow from the hearth. He felt relief.

Ivy stepped closer to her unwilling patient. "My lord? Master Crocken said my herb lore might do you some discreet service."

Rhisiart's dagger-glance shifted to Crocken—plainly, he was wondering just what wild tale had been blabbered to Ivy. "Your kindness is welcome, mistress, if most likely unnecessary," he said, all courtesy.

Ivy set her bundle down, as Rhisiart made to shift again and bit his lip against discomfort. She saw the gesture and looked sympathetic. "Perhaps not *entirely* unnecessary, my lord? Did your horse fall?"

Rhisiart began his denial with a headshake, but hastily ceased that folly. Crocken thought he could guess why. "I am not certain what the mischance was, mistress. Master Crocken said he did not see, either, but I do not suppose Darkling fell. He came in quite sound—we caught up to him on our way back, and I rode him in. He seemed unharmed."

"A better fate than Darkling deserves, after he gave you such a fall." Ivy unpacked a profusion of jars and cloths, and held up one covered clay pot. "I have a very good ointment here. My mother taught me the recipe, and she is accounted most skilled in herbcraft, by all our folk. I am sure it will bring you some ease, and its scent is most pleasing."

Rhisiart nodded and winced once more. Ivy stepped closer, looking intent. "My lord, may I? I promise you, I shall be very gentle. Can you put your head forward, just a bit?"

"Mistress, it's nothing."

Ivy set her lips. "Then 'twill do you no harm to indulge me." Crocken could see she'd brook no dissent.

Rhisiart sighed resignedly and leaned a little forward. Ivy ran her nimble fingers over the back of his head, parting his hair carefully. They both flinched at the same instant, but Ivy seemed the more stricken. Rhisiart merely hissed with pain, but Ivy's eyes brimmed with tears, as if the hurt she discovered had been her own.

"You have a lump the size of a duck's egg here, my lord," she said, trying to steady her voice.

"I suspected as much," Rhisiart answered with weak humor. "The ground is very hard, this time of year."

Ivy clucked over the injury and ignored the jest. "Well, the skin's whole, but it's a fearful bruise. Were you dizzy at all?"

"I was, but it has passed. My head aches, but not unbearably. Truly, my shoulder took the worst of the fall, as it often reminds me."

"I had best see to that, as well. No, let me—" Ivy said, to forestall Rhisiart's obviously painful attempt to slide his beltran back. She unbuttoned his shirt next, with careful speed. Rhisiart bit his lip as she made her examination, while Crocken shifted uncomfortably from one foot to the other, wishing to be sent on some errand so that he need not watch.

At last Ivy smiled with what Crocken took for relief. "Nothing broken—unless you have felt it catch when you moved it?"

"No. I've broken bones beforetime," Rhisiart said with a soldier's stoicism. "This doesn't feel so."

"Willow tea will ease it, and the headache—I shall brew some for you. You and Master Crocken can apply the ointment later. You will know best where you need it."

Rhisiart looked grateful, for the tea promised, or that his treatment wasn't to include bloodletting—or likely that Mistress Ivy was not minded to strip him on the instant and apply the salve with her own hands. Crocken took Ivy's calm for permission to relax. He felt a desire to sit down, but there was only the bed left for him to choose, so he stayed on his feet.

Ivy drew a small kettle from her useful bundle and poured water from the crockery ewer that stood upon the table. It was not many moments before her work was well advanced. While the willow bark steeped in the kettle, she gave Crocken the jar of salve and filled his ears with instructions as to its best use. She was far more self-possessed than she had been on the way from the princess' chambers—apparently it reassured her mightily to have Rhisiart alive, fairly whole, and safely under her eye.

She poured tea for him, into a plain cup with no handle, and watched while the steward-protector drank it down. "My lord, this brew may make you drowsy, particularly as the headache eases. May I advise you?"

Rhisiart looked amused, which tolerance Ivy accepted as leave to continue. "If I were you, I should bide here awhile. Master Crocken won't put you out, you could rest for a while. Even sleep. 'Twould do you much good."

"Certainly no one will disturb you," Crocken agreed. "Who'd think to look for you here?"

"You convince me," Rhisiart said. "But then, I am loath to hobble across this room, far less all of Axe-Edge." He looked sharply at Ivy. "I'll fall in with your plan if Master Crocken will undertake to see you safe back to your lady first."

Ivy efficiently gathered her things back into their bundle, then turned to Rhisiart once again. "My lord, I am sure my lady would postpone tonight's ceremony, were I to ask her privately."

Rhisiart refused the gesture with a rueful smile. "Mistress Ivy, I daresay I shall not be so halt by this evening that I cannot stand for a few moments' pageantry! If your ointment is as efficacious as you say, there's no need to inconvenience your lady. I am already in her debt for lending you to me. Let the ceremony stand as planned."

Mistress Ivy was fretful. "I wish he would allow me to put off the ceremony."

"That's a trouble with people who aren't in on your plans," Crocken pointed out. "I thought you were in haste?"

"I am. We must be, there's little time left. But I would have Rhisiart there with all his wits about him—it's not fair to expect him to cope with it after what's happened. That knock on the head worries me especially.'' Ivy frowned. ''Watch him closely and send for me again if he seems ill. He'll try to hide it.''

''I thought—isn't he all right?'' For she'd left Rhisiart without insisting on fetching the healer.

''As right as he's going to be for the next few days. That must have been a very nasty fall—he's lucky he wasn't killed.''

Crocken resisted the urge to turn a black look upon his shadow. It was sheltered behind him, and to pay obvious attention to it would have been odd, to Ivy's eyes.

''I won't ask how you came to be there,'' Ivy said, as if she'd read his thoughts.

Crocken felt his tongue stiffening—reduced to the same state as his wits, ill prepared for deceits. ''I . . . overheard something,'' he finally stammered. ''I didn't like the sound of it, that he'd gone out alone, so I got a horse and went out after him.''

''Very fortunate for all of us,'' Ivy said inscrutably. ''We should have considered that Mirell was not the only one in danger.''

A retort that *his* life had been in peril too seemed churlish, so Crocken held his peace—wondering at once why he held himself bound by the standards of his betters. Something else nagged at him as well.

''They'll miss him, when he doesn't turn up,'' Crocken observed uneasily. ''Rhisiart's people, that is.'' That army of servitors and office holders that the nobility took for granted.

''Yes,'' Ivy agreed. ''That's why you're going to see the steward-protector's secretary right now.''

''I am?'' He'd seen the man but once or twice—a barrel on legs, small and solid with thick short hands that were marvelously quick with a pen. But Rhisiart had sent him no message.

Ivy brushed a bit of leaf from Crocken's beltran and surveyed the rest of him critically. She twitched at the beltran, frowning. ''Tell Master Haun that the Mercer's Guild will have the cloth Rhisiart asked to see at the Guildhall when the steward-protector arrives to meet with them.''

''He's meeting with the Mercer's Guild?'' Crocken asked stupidly. Had they not troubles in plenty? Now he had to get Rhisiart on his feet and into Rushgate?

''No. But Master Haun won't know that. He does know Rhisiart asked your advice about the cloth, so if you tell him properly, he'll assume Rhisiart has already gone to Rushgate. Do him a kindness to seal it—ask if there are any messages he'd like you to give his master when you meet him.''

The shadow flickered into being as they walked by a casement. *Very neat. And most devious.*

Crocken could only agree and hope he was equal to the deception. Ivy sent him off to it at once, refusing to let him see her to Mirell's door, or to divulge her plans for the fateful evening.

Having been thus abandoned, Crocken had leisure to address his shadow freely.

"Did you have to be so rough? You said we'd help Ivy, but you almost spoiled her plan, doing that to Rhisiart."

Do you forget it was to save his life?

"Much good avoiding that ambush would have done Rhisiart, if he'd hit his head on a rock instead of dirt." Crocken retorted. "You used the same care with him that you did with me—which is hardly a good recipe for keeping the man alive."

So, do you complain of Rhisiart's hurts—or your own?

"You could have killed him!" Crocken protested furiously.

You could not keep him from entering the ambush. Had I not acted, Rhisiart would be dead. That is the plain truth. Task me no more with this.

Crocken subsided, but refused to accept the guilt the shadow was trying to force him to shoulder. There had to have been another way, he was certain. What revenge was the thing plotting, for the betrayal it so often mentioned? What did Rhisiart's safety mean to it? Ivy's lot—and his own—was close entwined with the steward-protector's fate now, subject to the same perils. That gave the question great importance—so great that Crocken carried off his mission of misrepresentation to Master Haun with scarcely a moment's fretting.

Chapter Twenty-six

CROCKEN PASSED THE long day keeping watch over Rhisiart, while the steward-protector slept. The occupation was at once tedious and nerve-wrenching. Rhisiart gave no sign of stirring, but Crocken dared not turn to any of his usual time-passers—such as tallying his growing store of coins—for fear Rhisiart would wake and observe him at it. And as the hours passed, the man's deep sleep was itself cause for Crocken's concern—was the steward-protector sinking into a fever? Was his sleep too deep? Was he in fact insensible, and in dire need of more than Mistress Ivy's potions? Crocken tried to ask the shadow for advice, but it would not answer his whispers, and he had to be careful how loudly he addressed it, lest Rhisiart somehow overhear. He seethed, knowing the thing could hear him perfectly well, but chose to pretend otherwise.

Ivy's salve was a powerful one. Rhisiart had begun to apply it ere Crocken returned from his double tasks—save to his battered right shoulder, which he could in no wise reach. He was seated on the bed, stoically attempting the awkward task when Crocken came in, but relinquished it with relief and an apology.

Crocken's own face had gone pale as he saw the extent of the bruising. The steward-protector's entire shoulder was empurpled, and Rhisiart could not keep himself from flinching when the cool liniment touched it. Crocken, horrified, had drawn his hand back.

"Go ahead," Rhisiart said through his teeth. "I have taken worse hurts in battle—and soldiers of the Borderlands are not such gentle nurses." He leaned forward as a signal for Crocken to continue—the movement hid his face, which was sweat-beaded.

And the slower you go, the worse it hurts. If you intend him mercy, just get on with it, the shadow suggested.

Crocken had done as he was doubly bid, biting his own lip in sympathy, till he tasted blood. After a moment he had felt Rhisiart relax, and heard him sigh as if the breath were the last one going out of him. He helped the steward-protector to lie down. The man's breathing had deepened at once—Crocken realized he was asleep, that quickly, as if the salve had been some merciful drug. He'd drawn the coverlet up, turned away to wipe the salve from his hands, nervously wondering just what Ivy had concocted it from. He didn't want to be sent to sleep himself—he was supposed to keep watch—

"Cailin," Rhisiart had said faintly, into his pillow. Crocken, heart-stricken, had wondered if Rhisiart called out his dead wife's name every night in his sleep, denying cruel reality. But the steward-protector had been quiet after that and slept calmly, if for a worrisome while.

The hours drifted into one another. Crocken, bored, dozed on the bench, while the fire burned itself out unheeded. His dreams were choked with shadows, unrelenting, and he kept imagining he was falling from his horse into the ravine, and jerking himself out of sleep as he tried to save himself, only to discover that his mount was the wooden bench, in his own room.

"Tierce is dead. Drowned in water as his wits were drowned by the sweet wine he was so fond of. Sister—"

"I want the bastard dead, as well. See to it, Andrayne." The woman's voice was like honey gone bad. Sweet. Deadly.

"Surely he's well enough where he is? No one inquired after him—not even Rhisiart. Now that Rhisiart has gone back to the Borderlands, surely no one will ask."

"He is dangerous to us, Andrayne. Bad enough before, but the task Tierce set him to has distilled his poison till its bane will infect the very air we breathe. I know this." There was a reflective pause. "Yet . . . we dare not risk killing him within Axe-Edge. There might be complications. Better if we set him free."

"Free?"

"Let him think he escaped. He'll run—and the deer that runs is the one the hounds pull down," she finished with satisfaction, as the plan shaped itself. "See to it. Give your huntsmen proper instruction, for this game is difficult to track and will be perilous to slay, but it *must* be done, else we are undone.

"Do not shed a wizard's lifeblood . . ."

* * *

Crocken came awake with the dream voices ringing so plainly in his ears that he glanced at once toward the bed, fearing his dream had been shaded by overheard fever ravings. But all was quiet—Rhisiart slept on, evidently more dreamlessly than Crocken had. The steady whisper of his breathing was lulling, but Crocken feared to allow himself to drift off again. His already strained muscles were stiff after the night's abuses, and sleeping on the bench did little to soothe them.

After a moment's hesitation, he made use of Mistress Ivy's liniment. There was plenty in the jar to serve both of them, and he assumed Ivy needed him at his best that night, as much as she did Rhisiart. It surely favored the success of her plan, if he could manage to move with relative ease when the occasion required it.

Of course, that selfsame salve had sent Rhisiart straight to sleep—but Crocken did not truly fear a similar fate. The salve might not be to blame. He was, for example, nowhere near so much hurt as the steward-protector, and so had less to recover from, unless one counted yet another bad dream—and he was well used to those. The knee he'd battered tumbling down the side of the ravine began to feel much improved as the liniment eased it, and Crocken fervently hoped something similar was true of Rhisiart's shoulder.

Crocken ventured out finally to fetch food and returned to discover Rhisiart on his feet, carefully adjusting his beltran. The man looked if not well, as if he at least might be expected to live some while longer. Crocken offered the fresh bread he'd snatched from an unattended tray outside the bakehouse, but Rhisiart refused politely.

"I'd best take my leave." Rhisiart yawned, a reflex that seemed to catch him by surprise. "Sleep has done well by me, but Master Haun will be something close to frantic by now—if only over the work left undone this morning. I'm off now to placate him for a few hours. May I ask one favor more of you, Master Crocken?"

Crocken assumed the steward-protector would be anxious to head off gossip. "My lord, I had no intention of mentioning this morning's . . . excitement to anyone."

Rhisiart waved that off. "I did not suppose you would, and I am grateful for that. No. Master Crocken, I wanted to request your attendance this evening in Kieron's rooms. I would have this ceremony of vow-fulfilling seen as something more official than the queen may intend. Outside witnesses can only render the event more legitimate."

"If I can help, I shall be honored." *As well as in over my head,* Crocken amended silently.

You would have been there in any case, the shadow whispered. *This way, you needn't skulk at the back.*

Another matter occurred to Crocken, just as Rhisiart was at the door. "My lord?" he asked, concern in his voice. "You won't ride out alone like that again, will you?"

Too late he remembered that Rhisiart had never inquired as to how he'd learned of the ambush, and that he had no lie prepared if the steward-protector, with all his wits about him, should ask him now. The shadow hissed at his stupidity.

Rhisiart, however, began to laugh, till his bruises must have hurt him. He subsided, and leaned on the door frame. "Master Merchant-Adventurer, you may rest easy. I shall be fortunate if I can bestride a *chair* with any comfort this next sennight! You need have no fear of my riding out—alone or otherwise."

They both laughed over that, and Rhisiart went on his way, gifting Crocken with a friendly grip on his shoulder as he passed.

The evening's assembly took place deep within Kieron's suite of interconnected rooms, in his exquisitely appointed reception hall, where the ceiling was painted lapis blue, a golden sunburst centered upon it. The paneling upon the windowless walls was gilt with both gold and silver, in graceful patterns. There was a golden cloth of estate over his chair, all-over embroidered with Kieron's heraldic devices, but the prince did not sit there— enthroned, as 'twere—to receive Mirell. She was as royal as he was, though foreign, 'twould have been a grave insult to protocol. Kieron did, however, stand upon a little dais, on display to his court.

The prince was worthy of such display, resplendent in velvet jacket and trews under a beltran of silken threads, the sunrise colors of it therefore brighter than common woolen cloth would allow. His azure thigh boots were so polished, it might be that they had never been outdoors at all, never exposed to dirt or brambles or even horse sweat. Crocken left off his automatic peddler's appraisal, overmastered by richness piled upon richness.

Rhisiart also wore his best, though 'twas more difficult to take note of, as most of the steward-protector's ensemble was black, and the greens and blues in his beltran were so deep that they

might as well have been sable, also. The boar pinning the beltran at his shoulder gave and took the light, a mass of silver
barely a shade paler than the steward-protector's face. Crocken
wondered if Rhisiart was feeling so unwell as he looked, but
there was no overt sign of that, as the steward-protector conversed with a Council lord in low tones. More likely it was the
contrast between his dark garb and the room's brightness that
gave him a look of ill health. Crocken had, he thought, heard
that remarked upon beforetime. Only his knowledge of the
morning's misadventure made it more than that.

The prince's chambers were generous in size, but they had
rapidly filled to their ample capacity. Most of the Protectorate
Council had assembled, and all of Kieron's sisters flitted about,
flanked by attendants. It was a family occasion, as was proper,
as well as an event of state.

Sulien had pride of place next to her son, and she was keeping
her brother Andrayne close at her other side. Nothing odd about
that—Lord Stiles had been the prince's tutor since his infancy,
Crocken had learned—but did the magnificent Sulien clutch her
brother's brocaded arm with special urgency? Well she might,
with a brace of her schemes gone unaccountably wrong and this
step toward her son's bridal night proceeding unpostponed, in
defiance of her will and her plotting.

Crocken found it hard to look long at the queen, or at Lord
Stiles—fearful his face might give away either his dread or his
knowledge. He tried not to gaze long at his shadow, either, as
it mixed easily among the ordinary shades of councillors and
nobles. Was it up to something, or merely biding its time as he
was? It surely could not be fearful, but its restlessness dovetailed
with his own raw nerves.

The Princess Mirell was formally announced by the gentlemen ushers. She entered, the crowd parting easily for her, and
approached Kieron with tiny, formal steps. Mistress Ivy trailed
her, carrying a velvet pillow upon which the finely embroidered
shirt lay folded. Both maidens wore gowns of green silk, Mirell's embroidered all over with golden threads to set off her topaz
eyes. Her hair was a cascade of sunset colors, hanging free down
her slender back.

"Kieron, my betrothéd and my lord."

Crocken was the only spectator present who recognized the
gentle voice—being the only person in Armyn save Ivy who had
ever heard it—but by its very unfamiliarity, it could have be-
longed to no other than Mirell. The princess spoke clearly,

though softly as was proper for a modest maiden, and kept her eyes cast down.

"My lord, when I came to your land, I vowed I would not permit myself to speak a word until I had made with my own hands this token for you—the shirt that will clothe you at our wedding. I offer it to you now and hope it may find favor with your noble grace."

Kieron answered her formally, stating that she in herself was gift enough, and none other was necessary. It went back and forth like a performance of two street players, Crocken thought, witnessing dutifully and wondering what came next. Rhisiart was looking on approvingly. The queen looked enraged, and Lord Stiles kept very close to her. All the shadows danced to the flicker of the scores of tapers that lit the chamber. Crocken imagined his was shifting from foot to foot in impatience.

Mirell's white hands gracefully took the shirt from Mistress Ivy's care, unfolded it with a modest flourish, and held it out for the prince's inspection. Kieron accepted the garment, remarking politely upon the fineness of the stitching, the artistic quality of the decorative broidery.

"If my lord would deign to test the garment, to be sure I have fitted it truly—"

Did the queen's pale eyes kindle at that? As if, were the shirt somehow ill-fitting, her son might be freed of the marriage? For sure, Lord Stiles was quick to step forward, taking the beltran and other garments that Kieron shed so that he might don the shirt, and his royal sister did not try to hold him back.

Stripped to the waist, the prince was as fairly made, particularly about the shoulders, as any youth Crocken had ever laid eyes upon. His sword partners might cheat themselves to ensure Kieron always had the victory, but they gave him exercise betimes. Crocken's nerve began to fail him, as his doubts blossomed freely. Suppose Ivy was wrong? How could Kieron be what she said he was, and look so? Suppose the shadow had deceived him for some purpose of its own—some purpose he could never begin to guess? If Kieron was only an ordinary youth, arrogant as the noble-born often were . . .

The shirt fitted like a second skin, perchance one even finer and softer than Kieron's own. The linen cloth gleamed in the light of the candles, white as the moon, and every carven pearl button fastened perfectly, roses amid a trellis of stitched vines. Kieron examined the ruffles upon the sleeve ends, where gryphons sported, and the witnesses made admiring noises. A few stepped closer, to better admire Mirell's sumptuous work. On the back of the shirt, dragonflies hovered above a tangle of berry canes.

"My lord, may I hold a glass for you, that you may judge the fit, as well?" Ivy stepped forward past Mirell, her hands wrapped gracefully about the bright silver stem of a hand mirror. Crocken's heart missed a beat—then snatched an extra one to make up the timing. The moment was surely come—and he had no idea what mischief to expect.

The mirror gave back the candles' light—more brightly, Crocken thought, than it should have done. It shone as the dew-drops upon the lady's mantle had. Or was the observation guilt-triggered? Ivy had never revealed how she planned to use the drops he had helped her collect. How had she—

She silvered the mirror with them, the shadow supplied him helpfully. He sensed it leaning as much in advance of him as it dared, anticipating.

But what effect would that silvering have? Water that had sat on a leaf—it shouldn't even function as a mirror, once the drops had dried. What did Ivy intend? The shadow answered no more of his unvoiced questions, but lay incognito among other candle-birthed shadows.

Ivy held the mirror before Kieron, while the prince smiled coldly upon his reflection and said something else formal, empty and polite as his diamond gaze. Ivy's lips moved, silently, and her right hand, mostly hidden in her skirts, stirred subtly. Crocken's eyes widened. She was spell-casting—he had seen that done often enough in Kôvelir to know it, however secretly 'twas executed. Could no one else see? How could she take so fearful a risk, to witch Kieron before all the court. Were she caught . . .

Kieron continued to examine his reflection, fussing with the drape of a sleeve, unsure whether he was to publicly approve shirt and bride. Crocken tried to see what was happening. Shadows got in his way, like cobwebs across his face. Ivy had vowed she would reveal Kieron for what he was. Surely her spell intended to alter either the prince or his reflection—perchance alter him by *means* of that reflection. Why else the mirror? One did not grow up in Kôvelir without some idea of the principles of magic, and the mirror made sense to Crocken, but that was not the same as being privy to Ivy's plan. And Kieron was unchanged, except for being more elegantly clothed than normal.

This isn't working, the shadow observed casually, and it stretched a dark long-fingered hand out past the prince, toward the mirror Ivy clasped in her left hand. Crocken was terror-stricken, then furious. Surely this was a worse risk than Ivy's magic, taken without a word to him! If anyone saw . . .

The looking glass shattered when the black finger met it. There were various squeals of alarm, as shards flew among the courtiers. Kieron, striking fast as the ice adder Ivy had dreamed him, caught Ivy's hand by the wrist as she let the ruined mirror fall.

"Mistress, you have cut yourself."

True, red blood ran in ribbons about her fingers. Kieron, his tongue flicking swiftly about his lips, drew her poisoned hand to him and pressed Ivy's wounded palm to his eager mouth.

There followed two despairing shrieks.

The first was the queen's. Heads turned in her direction.

The second cry came from Kieron, almost an echo. Heads swung back toward him, while Ivy, released, staggered back, then stood transfixed, staring. The prince himself had doubled over as if in agony, but made no further sound while his body jerked and twitched.

The violence of the spasm nearly cast him from his feet, but when he came erect again, Kieron began to stumble toward his mother. Crocken saw Sulien reach her hands out toward him, her fair face a mask of pain. The princesses were screaming, recoiling in all directions, as were the courtiers. Those closest to Kieron floundered back hastily into those pressed behind them, creating confusion and uproar. A woman was knocked from her high-soled shoes. Another swooned. A man made choking sounds.

The commotion grew, as more and more folk saw—or partly saw—what had happened. And through it all, Crocken could hear his shadow laughing.

The prince had his back to Crocken, so he had no clear idea precisely what had befallen the boy. He could still see the queen, her face contorted, reaching out for her son even as she backed slowly away from him. He saw horror and hysteria shining in the eyes of Sulien's daughters and nieces. The cause became at last apparent, when one of Kieron's staggering steps put him in plainer view.

The prince did not speak—the tongue flicking about his lips was now white, narrow, and forked at its tip, utterly unsuited to human speech. Kieron cradled his right hand in his left. The vowed shirt was torn, and the rent revealed scales were there should have been skin, their color a grayish green. Kieron's pale eyes now had only the tiniest of pupils, as if he stared into the sun instead of their faces, effectively blind to their terror. He hissed once, loudly, the tongue flicking wildly.

"Is this what you name a true-born prince in this land?" Mirell whispered, her hand at her throat as if for protection from the monster. She had not fled. She was brave, thanks to Ivy's preparing her for what she now saw before her—but nothing could have prepared Mirell entirely, and her dismay was not in the least feigned.

Kieron lurched about in a panic, unable to reach his mother—Crocken saw a swirl of purple velvet out the tail of his eye, as the queen abruptly fled the room. The prince croaked unintelligibly, clutching at courtiers who frightened him further with their horrified reactions, tumbling over one another in haste to avoid him. Rhisiart, who had stepped forward to staunch Ivy's wound when Kieron released her, stared at his nephew with an expression that suggested the steward-protector might suspect himself of hallucinating.

One of Kieron's guards—a brave man, surely—laid hold of his master's arm, restraining him gently. Kieron spun toward him, cleft tongue darting toward his eyes. The guard shrieked and fell back moaning with a hand clapped to his bleeding face. Some few folk had managed to flee the prince's chambers, while others blundered into the tapestried walls and into each other, noisily. Two women fell in a shrieking tangle of costly fabric, upending a chess table and the game in progress upon it.

Andrayne, the queen's brother, had not joined the stampede, or aided his sister's flight. A space suddenly cleared between him and Mistress Ivy, who stood white-faced and empty-eyed, swaying gently, her blood dripping from her fingers to the floor.

"*What have you done to him, witch?*" Andrayne screamed, lunging at her. Ivy lifted her face blindly, as if the threat were a league off and but dimly perceived. Lord Stiles bore a ceremonial sword at his side, as all the men present save Crocken did—fanciful weapons mostly meant for show, yet deadly enough to harm an unarmored woman. The thin blade flashed in the candlelight, red as if it had already drawn Ivy's blood.

The steward-protector's sword answered it, instincts bred through years of warfare overcoming the shocking sight of his nephew's transformation. Rhisiart fell into a swordsman's stance instantly, giving Andrayne only the narrow edge of his body for a target, behind the flashing protection of his own drawn blade. One difference to the combat—Rhisiart's left arm encircled Mistress Ivy, drawing her close that the slender blade might shelter her, as well.

"Put up your sword, Andrayne," he commanded.

"Do you defend her sorcery?" Andrayne jabbed, but short, a testing blow. Rhisiart ignored the attack, refusing to be drawn after it, and held his ground.

"I will not allow you to do murder and call it justice," the steward-protector said. "What else passed here, what part you had, my Council will discover. For now—" Rhisiart shifted his gaze toward a new commotion, perhaps seeking Kieron. The instant's inattention was all the invitation Andrayne required. His blade flashed in, his whole weight behind the attack.

"*Watch out—*" Crocken shouted, seeing Rhisiart would have no time to avoid the strike. His shadow was more effectual. It launched itself at Andrayne, blinding him, and his thrusting blade went wide of the steward-protector, though only just, skimming Rhisiart's beltran, stirring the fabric like a breeze and narrowly missing Ivy.

Rhisiart sidestepped, catching the other blade with his own sword. He mastered it, then shoved his opponent back a pace. The crossed swords threw sparks right over the shadow, and Crocken heard it hiss as if with pain. It writhed hastily back to his side.

Crocken both heard and saw guards arriving, but the men were of no use—their great halberds were too unwieldy in the confined space and the noble crowd—and they could have little idea in any case of what they were expected to do. There was no one to take charge and direct them. Lord Stiles still pressed his furious attack, screaming his charges of witchery at Ivy, other dire threats at Rhisiart, and none of the guards had a hope of doing anything about *that*. The steward-protector might have given them an order—if he'd seen them or thought of them.

Rhisiart made to parry the oncoming blade—and from his startled expression, his arm refused to answer his command with its accustomed speed. He missed making the firm blade contact he sought, and the swords slid along each other with a ringing sound. Crocken, remembering sickly the steward-protector's fall, and how his sword arm had taken the worst of it, made a despairing noise that echoed Rhisiart's hopeless expression. He could feel his shadow stirring again, trying to spot a useful opening in the fight.

His parry failing, Rhisiart retreated hastily—not much in advance of Andrayne's oncoming point, hampered by Ivy as he was—but sufficiently to let him catch the blade at last, and turn it. Andrayne tried to evade him, but stumbled when the shadow caught at the legs of his own stalking shadow. Metal screamed, as Rhisiart gritted his teeth and shoved Andrayne's blade out of line, keeping the man at a distance and off balance.

Unhurt, the steward-protector would certainly have followed that purely defensive move with a swift counterattack. Plainly Rhisiart realized he dared not now attempt any such action. He quickly sidestepped again, pushing Ivy back against Crocken.

"Take her," he gasped, and was under attack again before he had time for more than a second step.

Crocken hastily grabbed at Ivy, who had nearly fallen when Rhisiart let loose of her, and tried to get them both out of reach of sword-steel. The blades rang together just past his head— Andrayne was still struggling to get at Ivy, and Rhisiart was not having great success at holding him back. Crocken heard the steward-protector grunt as a hard blow shoved him back almost on top of them.

"Give it up, Andrayne," Rhisiart ordered hoarsely.

"Never." Andrayne's eyes were empty of sense. "She dies— you, too, if you persist."

Rhisiart smiled grimly at the notion of surrender and met the next attack.

The contest could not go on much longer, Crocken thought. Neither man wore armor, the first sound thrust must surely end it for one of them. He'd have been far happier if he could have gotten Ivy and himself surely out of Andrayne's reach—but in a small room a long-legged man with a yard of steel blade has all the reach he requires. Ivy was sobbing, twisting to see what was happening, while Crocken strove to cover her body with his own—not that Andrayne couldn't simply spit the two of them together, like a brace of fowl. He wanted to shove her right out of the chamber, but without Ivy's cooperation in that, the distance was too great.

Rhisiart had managed to push Andrayne back to the dais, perhaps hoping he'd trip on its edge. In this he was frustrated— Stiles only mounted it and gained the advantage of the little height. Both men were breathing like foundering horses, but the deadly game of thrust and parry continued relentlessly, the pace scarcely slackening. The guards pressed closer, impotent and in each other's way, confused and without direction.

A parried attack sliced one of the canopy's supports, and Kieron's golden cloth of estate came fluttering down like a wounded bird, beating its painted falcon's wings helplessly. Rhisiart leapt back more nimbly than Crocken dared believe, safe from the entangling folds with which Andrayne had hoped to snare him.

The rippling cloth threw deep shadows. One of them reared up behind Andrayne and shoved him straight onto the steward-protector's blade.

Rhisiart stood looking down at Andrayne's body, the blood draining from his own face nigh as rapidly as it drained from his enemy's corpse, till Crocken feared he would swoon away— then the steward-protector took command of himself and the situation once more. Straightening, he tersely ordered a brace of guards to take the body away. His hand dropped to his side, and he let his sword fall, with what could only have been relief. His fingers twitched like spider's legs.

One of the Council lords stepped hesitantly forward.

"My lord, what evil has chanced here? The prince—what has her blood done to him?" The man looked full at Mistress Ivy, still standing dazedly in Crocken's arms.

"Not her blood," Crocken disagreed strongly. "It's all over *me*, and I'm not changed."

He wondered if he'd have held his peace, had he realized beforetime that every eye in the room would fix upon him so instantly. He'd surely have been tempted, whatever the cost to Ivy. There was no calm, reasonable face anywhere in the chamber—not with the horror they'd just witnessed, not with a brutal fight and a bloody death hard on its heels. Crocken cursed his tongue, which could not seem to stay still and leave him safe. He should have fled the room, should have taken Ivy with him. They could have been safely out of Axe-Edge before anyone thought to look for them. Now they'd escaped one peril only to step straight into another.

Rhisiart stared at Ivy, also, but sense was breaking through the confusion in his eyes. He slowly held up his own hands. There was blood on them—not Andrayne's, which was on the floor, soaking the carpet, and on the blade Rhisiart had cast down.

"Her blood is on me, as well," he said. "And I am not harmed. If we two are not changed, then her blood cannot be poisoned." He worked through the logic methodically, aloud. "But how—" Plainly he was recalling his last sight of his nephew.

"What manner of creature is transformed by a drop of maiden's blood?" Ivy asked, raising her head and looking full at Rhisiart. He knew her well—or thought he did, and she was counting on that. Crocken shivered at her courage.

Now we know why the queen so feared the marriage, the shadow said, for no ears but Crocken's.

Crocken understood. If Kieron's bane was maiden's blood, his bridal night would have been as fraught with danger as *this* night. The queen could stop at nothing, not even murder, to spare her son the peril of bedding a royal maiden. Crocken wished, though, that his shadow had let him in on the secret. It must have realized that Ivy's plan would fail—yet still used that plan for its own ends. And used all the rest of them, as well, all of them unwitting.

Rhisiart rapped out an order. Candlesticks were righted, their tapers hastily relit. The shadows of the room receded—most of them.

"Sulien," Rhisiart asked in a voice of iron, "is this my brother's son?"

He was not answered, until another Council lord came forward. "My lord, the queen has fled. None knows where she has gone. Likewise the . . . prince . . ."

Ivy spoke again. "My lord Steward—"

Rhisiart looked at her, still half supported, her hand yet bleeding. "Send for the healer," he ordered, not ungently.

"Perchance the prince went to her, and we will find him there," someone suggested eagerly.

"I doubt that," Rhisiart snapped. "I would have him found, but it will likely not be so simple. Tell the healer there is a wound to be seen to. Mistress Ivy—" He turned to her.

Ivy straightened, lifted her head, and pulled away from the support Crocken would still have given her. "My lord, I can answer your question, if you will allow me. Kieron is *not* your brother's son."

Chapter Twenty-seven

THE SHADOW RETURNED, sliding back to Crocken's side as silently as ever. He had not bothered to poke up the fire when he returned to his room, so he waited beside the hearth in the chilly dark—but Crocken usually knew when the shadow was not there and when it was again. He was good at such distinctions now.

"Well?"

I lost his trail, the shadow admitted regretfully. *The queen I found barricaded in the chapel, but her son is not with her, though much of her treasure is. Sulien is in great distress.*

"I'll bet." One could, with a good ear, hear that distress over the rest of the turmoil in Axe-Edge. Sulien had screamed her rage until her throat must have bled.

Andrayne her brother is dead. Who else could have spirited Kieron away? Which one of her folk has wit to shield him?

"Maybe he kept on changing and finally slid down a drain-pipe!" Crocken offered nastily.

Perhaps, the shadow said, appearing to consider the possibility.

"You mean he *could* have?" Crocken was horrified. Even if he accepted that such was Kieron's true form, the boy's fate seemed harsh to one who'd witnessed it. A lot of nobles were arrogant. They didn't get shape-shifted into serpents, or deserve to be.

"What did we do to him?" He was overcome with remorse, nearly undone, and hardly able to remember how small his own part in the deed had been.

He was not human.

But the boy had seemed it. Mostly. Crocken shuddered. "Still—"

He was Sulien's victim, not ours.

"Did you know that would happen, when you staged your little stunt?" Crocken asked.

Not precisely. I suspected that blood would reveal his nature—when there is a bane, often the danger attracts the creature it imperils. I did not know how far the revelation would proceed.

"Then you knew Ivy's trick with the mirror wouldn't work?" Crocken tried, without reason, to determine just where the shadow was. He disliked the notion that it might be within a finger's breadth of his face, and he'd not know. Or hovering just behind him, looming unobserved, to touch him unexpectedly.

I suspected the spell would fail. Sulien shielded her son carefully from most sorcerous perils. Yet she feared his marriage and went to great lengths to prevent it. The prince could bed an unchaste serving maid, work his will on her, and his guardians only . . . cleaned up after him . . . yet he dared not wed a royal maiden.

"You let Ivy try it, though. You used her—"

It was necessary.

"You almost got her killed! For all we know, she's being tried as a witch *now*. They could burn her—"

Mistress Ivy is safe. The shadow snorted. *She is this moment back with her lady, her business with Rhisiart being concluded. She has been in his protection all this night.*

Crocken tried again to see his shadow, as if it possessed a face he might read, even in the dawnlight. The attempt was, of course, futile. "You were there? What happened? What did Ivy tell him?"

She told Rhisiart of her dream.

Crocken felt as if he'd been kicked in the belly. "That's all she gave him for proof?" he asked sickly. "Just the dream?"

She could hardly show him the proofs I showed to you. But Rhisiart believed her—remember, he was here in those days. The details of her dream match events that occurred long before Ivy came here—perhaps before she was born. There are things she could not know, unless her dreams were true. So she is believed, and safe.

"Wonderful." Crocken ran a hand across his eyes, which burned with weariness. "If I tell the steward-protector about the dreams *I've* had since I came here, will I be safe, too?"

What dreams, peddler? There was a sharp interest in the shadow's tone.

Crocken was about to answer, but he heard just then the tramp of boots in the passage outside. He opened the door to the summons he had been expecting and let the royal guards conduct him to the Steward-Protector of Armyn.

"The queen has heard that her brother Andrayne is dead at your hand, my lord. She says that she will not commit herself to your care, nor her tender daughters, not even if you tear the chapel down about their heads."

"Which she well knows I will not do," Rhisiart said coldly, his voice carrying plainly down the passage through the open door. "Remind Sulien that sanctuary laws are not intended to shield the guilty, but rather to protect innocents. Her daughters may remain if they choose, but I will have her out, to answer before the law for her crime."

The messenger, looking none too pleased with his charge, exited the chamber.

"My lord, if you will permit me—" came another voice.

"No." Rhisiart said flatly. "No physicks. Go back to the princess."

"As my lord commands." The healer came into the hallway, lips set in a tight line as she held back advice that surely would not be well received. Crocken wanted to ask how Ivy fared, but the guard at his back and the healer's abstracted expression gave him no chance. The woman's soft-shod footfalls faded, as did she, gone down the passage to safety.

Crocken was shoved into the room, with more haste than courtesy, and left there. None of his guards accompanied him, to his amazement. He heard the door close behind his back, but kept his gaze on the room before him, and the man who rose from behind the long Council table.

Rhisiart looked as if he had suffered the loss of more than one night's sleep. The past day's strains were written on his white face, emphasized by his hollow eyes, making plain the healer's wish to have him under her care. He held up his hands, and Crocken could see brown stains on his shirt sleeves.

"It seems I was in error, when I claimed that Mistress Ivy's blood had not changed me," Rhisiart said hoarsely. "It has made me King of Armyn."

Nothing in Rhisiart's tone suggested he expected congratulations, so Crocken held his peace. Indeed, his throat was dry as sand, and he could not manage to swallow in hopes of easing it. Speech would have been impossible. Dawn was lightening the window behind Rhisiart, but there was no other light in the chamber save a single candle left of a dozen in a branched holder. Crocken fixed his gaze on the half-burned taper, unable to meet Rhisiart's haunted eyes.

"The Council has met all this night, deliberating upon its events. They have within this hour pressed the crown upon me, as the only trueborn male heir remaining of the House of the Falcon."

Crocken knelt down—not quite so much from respect for the news as from a troublesome weakness of his legs, now that this dreaded confrontation had come. Rhisiart's thin mouth twitched, not with apparent humor.

"Certainly it is an office for which I am well trained—a king is after all the ultimate steward of the land. What I protected for my nephew, I now hold in trust for all Armyn's folk. So much land, so many folk . . ." Rhisiart shut his eyes, as if the thought worried him immeasurably and his new power did not in the least please him. "And you. The stranger among us. What hand had you in this?"

Crocken hesitated, his lips slightly parted. He wanted to essay a sincere denial—Rhisiart's look froze his tongue and all but stopped his heart. The lie died a-borning.

"On your feet, Master Merchant-Adventurer!" the king ordered. "Events this night distressed you—but did not *surprise* you. That was plain to me. You have spent much time with the Princess Mirell and more with Mistress Ivy—who likewise expected what . . . befell Kieron. What did you know—and how came you to know it?"

Crocken made no answer and was loath to rise up from his knees, to be seen trembling. His explanation seemed impossible to attempt, though he had been miserably anticipating the need for it the latter half of the night. Perhaps *because* he had been rehearsing it so long, his throat now sealed.

"I have spoken with Mistress Ivy," Rhisiart informed him sternly. "She gave me a wearisome long tale, brimful of dreams and foreshadowings. Am I to think that she laid some such before you, also?"

Dared he lay it all at the feet of a woman's fancy?

"My lord." Crocken swallowed hard, then got words out. "I had proof that what she said was true."

As indeed has Rhisiart, unless he doubts his eyes, the shadow interjected helpfully.

"Proof? Why did you not lay what you knew before me, if this is true?" Rhisiart asked, his frown deepening.

"Would my lord have heard me out?' Crocken asked plaintively, wondering if Ivy could have been wrong about that, which had been his first instinct. "Believed me? Forgive me, but I had heard too many tales of the extremity of your loyalty to the prince—tales of nobles no longer at court because they advised you to guard yourself from the queen's plots." Rhisiart was scowling now, and Crocken went on quickly. "It's none of my business. But I myself saw you allow assassins to escape, men who would have taken your life. The proof I had . . . wasn't the sort I could offer before your Council. The only way I could stop the queen's plot was to help Ivy show the court what Kieron truly was."

One dream is nothing. The eyes of many witnesses carry much weight, the shadow agreed happily.

"It's a poor truth, that dares not be known!" Rhisiart rejoined heatedly. "You know they will call *this* sorcery, this night that brought me to this damned high stewardship? I mislike this gift you have helped load upon me, Master Peddler. You will not find me as grateful for your kingmaking aid as you may have anticipated."

Crocken shook his head, wondering how he had not seen that angle before. Had he lost his merchant's instinct for the main chance? "Not kingmaking. My lord, I can't say I'm saddened to see you come to an honor that's yours by right—but I had no part in that." *I wasn't even there,* he thought, but did not offer that defense. Rhisiart would know it for mere dissembling. Who else could the Council have chosen? The matter had been decided the moment Ivy acted.

"They thrust the crown upon me, I could not stop them. Ruane himself could not have stopped them—" Rhisiart groaned. "And now I must spend the rest of my days asking whether I *wanted* to stop them. Could not, or would not?" Rhisiart accused himself, pitilessly.

Indeed, the shadow said, in a tone Crocken almost took for laughter. *Who is to know?*

"There will be none to say I did not seek the crown," Rhisiart complained bitterly. "I kept faith with my brother—and yet now I will stand accused of sorcery, of usurping. I *did* keep faith this time." Rhisiart shut his lips firmly. He sat so a long moment, then looked at Crocken and forlornly smiled. "I had come to trust you. That fault is mine. It appalls me that I needed to rely upon any man—let alone a stranger—so much. If I had shown more self-restraint—you will be well advised not to expect a reward.''

Crocken was still busy trying to fathom a point he'd missed, a moment and some words back. Something about keeping faith. As if Rhisiart could ever *not* keep his word. Could the sun rise in the west?

He betrayed me, the shadow pointed out, ever eager with that accusation.

"My lord, there wasn't time to plan any of this," Crocken said, doggedly ignoring his shadow. "And this I swear to you, we *did* not. Who else to take the crown, but you? Mistress Ivy and I were not thinking of crowns. We sought to prevent a great evil being done in this land, and looked no farther ahead than that.''

"What loyalty have *you* to Armyn?" Rhisiart cracked out.

What indeed, when he came to examine it? The truth was, he was likely raving mad, to think that a shadow spoke to him and ordered his actions. Only the notion that Ivy sometimes saw the shadow kept Crocken in doubt, and he knew he might have been mistaken about that. How did one know if one went mad? What evidence could he trust?

He remembered something else and seized it. "I have a dislike for folk who try to kill me, or harm an innocent girl, plotting in the night to stop a marriage everyone seems to have pleasantly agreed to in the light of day.''

"What's this?" He had Rhisiart's whole attention once more, and wasn't sure such was welcome.

Evidently Mistress Ivy did not choose to mention the matter during her tale.

And he had been fool enough to stumble into it, with no notion as to *why* Ivy had left such dire charges out of her explanation. Nothing for it but to go on, as best he could. Crocken's stomach began to ache.

Crocken briefly related the tale of his abduction, and Mirell's, and the plot he'd heard discussed. He glossed over the manner of their escape.

"Perhaps I shouldn't have listened to Mistress Ivy, in spite of what had happened. But there *was* proof, and she was not wrong in her dream.''

Doubt flicked across Rhisiart's face—or maybe pain. Did his head still ache? There was cause enough.

"Why did you not come to me?" he asked again.

Crocken shrugged. This, from a man who'd lately allowed

his own would-be assassins to go free? He couldn't even remember with certainty whether he'd *wanted* to tell Rhisiart. "I might have. But from what I overheard of their plans, causing a scandal was the main part of the scheme. It would have served them very well if the tale had come out, even failed. Once rumors begin, folk believe what they choose."

All too true.

Rhisiart stood and began to pace about the room. Crocken noticed that he did it badly—stiffly, with more than a trace of a limp. The discomfort did not seem to be a deterrent to movement, however.

"Done is done—as we say in the Borderlands. And your motive for revealing what Kieron . . . is . . . that's of no moment, except to me. It alters nothing in this situation."

Crocken waited, silent as his shadow.

"I could banish you. Revoke your credentials."

Still Crocken stood, as Rhisiart limped to the tall window and back again, passing before him, stopping a pace away.

"You do not protest this?"

Crocken shook his head. Expect it, aye—but not protest. "I have seen my lord dispense justice. I have never yet seen cause for contesting it."

"Is it not poor payment for your service to me?" Rhisiart seemed determined to argue both sides of the case.

He'd prefer to damn himself rather than have another do it, the shadow suggested.

"My lord, you have protected me like a kinsman and treated me as a friend," Crocken said, closing his mind to the shadow as best he could. "Allow me to commit the worst blasphemy a merchant is capable of, and not speak of debts. What I did, I had no choice but to do. Not to make you king, or save your life, or to advance my own fortunes—but because I had no choice. If the result has been most of those things—you of all men must understand how suspect guessing motives can be."

If he could remember he's king, he'd have your ears for that.

"Motives aside, I understand that this land will be in turmoil!" Rhisiart slammed his fist down on the tabletop, making an ink bottle and Crocken jump. "I have no proof to show of what passed this night! The rumors will run like a wildfire." He leaned upon his arms, at the worktable, and said in anguish: "My brother's only son—"

"My lord, your brother *had* no son," Crocken corrected urgently. "What need for the sorcery the queen wrought, if she'd been able to produce a true-born son?"

Rhisiart considered that. "That would ease my heart a measure, could I but remember it. 'Tis much to accustom myself to." His eyes opened wide, on another thought. "The princesses. Are they . . . as Kieron is?"

Crocken wanted, despite the pain on Rhisiart's face, to smile. He subdued the wish. "I would doubt that, my lord. What need? From what I have heard of your law, no royal-born girl could give the queen a tenth the power a son did. Ivy said the spell would have worked only upon a seventh daughter. Surely the first six are quite ordinary, and your brother's true-born daughters."

With only half their blood tainted.

Rhisiart scarcely looked comforted. His distress was a moving thing to witness—especially as Crocken could see how the steward-protector strove to stifle it. Had the man *no* safe place to turn, no friend he might trust? No one save a peddler—a stranger he *dared* not trust?

And it seemed Ivy had not mentioned her suspicions about the fate of Rhisiart's son—and his wife. Crocken knew there was no way he'd pass such tidings on to Rhisiart, who looked ill able to handle fresh revelations.

So does mercy damn us all, the shadow whispered darkly— but Crocken could not ask it what it meant. Assuming it had purpose beyond deviling him.

"Mistress Ivy wished to save her lady," Rhisiart said precisely, as if making a list. "And thus she acted. But dare I believe a man would risk what you did this night, only to do the right?"

Crocken wet his lips, but Rhisiart was not waiting for him to make answer. He still let the table support him.

"I must believe it. It happens, even in this cynical world . . ." The shadow leaned close, attending with sudden intensity.

"When my brothers fell out over Ruane's queen, Tierce was adjudged guilty of treason—he was not accorded much of a trial, but the king's word is the final law, at least if the king is king as Ruane was," Rhisiart said harshly. "The sentence was death, and as one of the offices my king had settled upon me was that of high constable, 'twas *my* duty to see it carried out."

On his own brother? Crocken was shocked.

"The night before, I went to the tower rooms where Tierce was kept confined. I had the keys to his jail by right, the authority to enter the guard tower unquestioned. It was very simple. I went to Tierce, and I set him free.''

Crocken sensed his shadow quivering, leaning close. A moment it held so. He expected some comment, but the hiss it made was too faint to be more than a breath released, and in fact the sigh might have come from Rhisiart.

"Then I went back to Ruane.''

For the mood of the tale, it should have been full night, but the sky was brightening steadily beyond the windows, and from outside there came the familiar sound of daytime activities. There were hoofbeats and footfalls. A scent of baking bread wafted from the bakehouse. Twice there came a discreet tapping upon the chamber door—which Rhisiart paid absolutely no attention to. The noise soon ceased.

"I confessed to my king what I had done and submitted myself to his judgment. I told Ruane, if he was minded to execute a brother it should as well be me—I at least would be guilty of the crime I was charged with.''

Rhisiart's thin face was pale as bone, and his eyes were empty, so utterly turned inward were his thoughts. Crocken wondered if he forgot that he spoke to another. Rhisiart looked more ill than he had the day previous, hard after escaping death by a handspan—and some dozen years older. He was pacing again, never more than three steps before changing direction, seeming unaware of walls or furniture, yet avoiding both.

"I had never seen Ruane so angered—not at anyone, certainly never at me. He was too furious, I think, even to punish me. I was sent back to the Borderlands, to keep the King's Peace there, and I heard never a word more—from my brother or from my king—until he named me steward-protector of his son and his kingdom, when he lay dying.''

The shadow rippled among the floor rushes, following Rhisiart, but it had no least crumb of Crocken's attention.

"I loved my brother,'' Rhisiart explained. "I knew he had at last forgiven me when he placed his only son in my charge. There was *nothing* that could make me betray his trust again— not friendship, not politics, not even my own family's safety. I held fast to the duty my king charged me with, I kept faith, and now it is a mockery—''

The word finished as a sob, but when Crocken took a step toward him, Rhisiart's head came up at last, and he got a look that nearly stopped his blood from flowing through his veins.

Rhisiart's red-rimmed eyes were dry as stones, above the smoky bruises beneath them.

"And Tierce died anyway," he whispered. "Though not by Ruane's hand." Then, straightening, abandoning the past, Rhisiart went to his worktable and seated himself calmly behind it, adjusting his beltran with care.

"In due course there will be ships leaving Armyn for ports beyond Sheir," the king said. "You have my leave to arrange your passage. If you have not prospered well enough here to afford the fare, my secretary will see to it." He picked up a quill and made to dip it into the ink bottle, not noticing that it had long since spilled, its contents run off to mingle with the floor rushes and Crocken's shadow.

Crocken, summarily dismissed, wanted to beg, to plead as he had not beforetime, to fall to his knees again—but he did not. He'd expected to feel angry, but guilt canceled out his self-righteous indignation. Nor did he rejoice, which utterly alarmed him. All he had desired, coming to Armyn, was to leave it behind him. Why could he not, now that the chance had been handed him, gladly seize it?

Chapter Twenty-eight

CROCKEN WENT BACK to his room, unescorted save by his shadow, which dragged behind him like a lady's train. No guard appeared outside his door. He checked on that oversight a dozen times before sun-high, but the passage was always deserted.

"I'm not arrested?" he asked his shadow, which splashed the wall, ignoring his pacing to and fro, since there was no one to observe either of them.

Of course not, it consented to make answer. *Officially, you are not even involved. Nor will Mistress Ivy be, save as the unnamed girl whose blood the witched prince chanced to taste. That wasn't a state inquiry—it was personal.*

"Personal?" Crocken halted in midpace. "But why—"

Is it not obvious? Rhisiart considered you his friend.

"His friend," Crocken echoed sickly. "And I—"

As he sees it, you betrayed him, having forced him to violate Ruane's trust.

Crocken sat down on his bed, which he had not otherwise touched in more hours than he could count. He felt ill with weariness and would not have been surprised to find his countenance as wan and lined as Rhisiart's—or worse.

A king couldn't afford friends, or trust. But Crocken's conscience was little eased by his insistence that Rhisiart should have known better. Instead, his thoughts drifted miserably back to a day when the steward-protector, spying him through an open casement, had invited him indoors to taste a favored beverage of the Borderlands, of a keg new-delivered that afternoon. Blood ale, they called it, for the color the red hill-grown barley lent it. Rhisiart had explained merrily how the common drink had given rise to tales that Borderers drank blood, and how the Borderlanders never denied such rumors, since the tales were worth an army when it came to dissuading invasion. Rhisiart hadn't been Borderlands born, but he plainly had been happy there, and might have gladly seized Crocken's visit as an excuse to return, had events permitted. He had wistfully said as much . . .

A king could trust no one—but could he stop wishing to trust? Where else could such a man seek friends but among those with no stake in old quarrels, folk new-come to the land? Himself. Mistress Ivy.

"He surely wouldn't . . . have ignored what Kieron was, if we'd just told him?" Crocken felt he'd been sure of that answer once, but he could no longer remember why.

He might have tried. Anything to atone for the wrong he thought he'd done to Ruane.

Crocken sympathized with that impulse—though he knew he'd never have had the strength of character to take it so far as Rhisiart had.

All that pain, all those years—and Tierce was by far the easiest man to hate that I have ever met, the shadow whispered.

"Loving Ruane, how could Rhisiart let him do something so wrong?" Crocken guessed, and saw the shadow flinch a bit. "Killing his own brother? He was saving *Ruane*, not Tierce."

Rhisiart has done worse.

Crocken lay back on his bed. It was no use—his spine felt taut as wire, and his sore eyes nonetheless refused to close. He couldn't see the shadow, as he spoke, and couldn't have said whether he addressed it or the air.

"I don't seem to keep friends long. People drift, in and out of the current, you know? A year or a day, but always gone, some morning. Family, that's the only connection that lasts, and I have none."

He did not see his shadow flinch yet again, almost shudder.

No kin at all?

"A sister, I was told once. She was grown already when I was born, and I doubt I ever saw her more than twice. I think she had red hair." He'd long since given up trying to give her a face—and now the only face he could recall framed by chestnut hair was Mirell's, not his sister Crewzel's. Even Litsa's was quite gone out of his recollection, if not some of his dreams.

"I was an orphan before I was old enough to be apprenticed. I slept in the streets and ran errands for half coppers till I was big enough to take on work that paid better. Not all that *much* better," he added on a bitter afterthought.

Resourceful, came the dark whisper.

"It was that or starve. Don't make it sound noble," Crocken snapped.

I merely observe your survival, against long odds. And I, too, have known loneliness.

Crocken supposed it had. He wondered how many years it had waited in the mountains, before he strayed along. Or did it hint at something else?

Loneliness, alas, is seldom strong enough to make an end to itself.

Crocken recalled a few times when he'd been miserable enough to long for death—and had lived on anyway. He nodded grudgingly. "All I wanted was a place to come back to at the end of the day—and someone who'd be glad I'd come back."

That cannot be bought, with gold or silver.

"No one else seems to have any trouble doing it!" Crocken retorted angrily.

A thing I also felt betimes, peddler.

Crocken scowled at the shadow, irritated. "How lucky we've got each other! We can go into exile together—" He paused. "Or can we? Whose orders do I follow now—Rhisiart's to leave or yours to stay?"

The shadow made no answer. Then the servant came in with wood for the fire and a ewer of water, and Crocken was too puzzled by the fact that he was still being looked after to wonder much about the shadow, or resume their conversation.

Chapter Twenty-nine

WORD OF THE change in kingship would be awhile reaching to the nethermost corners of the realm, but it had reached Rushgate at once, on a floodtide of Kieron's courtiers and Sulien's relations fleeing Rhisiart's presumed disfavor. Then there were the guardsmen, sent out from Axe-Edge in quest of some hint of Kieron's whereabouts. Their diligent searchings had spread the tale—and lurid variations upon it—into every quarter of the city within a day.

By the time Crocken went downriver, the first buzz of startling news had swept through, and he could not decide if the streets were quieter in fact or only in that he imagined they should be. There were still royal guards to be seen, distinguished by blood-scarlet beltrans, but folk did not walk in fear of them, unless they felt too close or public a tie to Kieron or his mother.

Crocken picked out a courtier or two, frantically pawning goods, raising hard coin needed for a journey. Were they fleeing to country estates, or farther? He had not heard that Rhisiart had banished anyone—himself excepted—for a closeness to Kieron. Andrayne was dead, Sulien still fast in the chapel she had chosen for sanctuary—the rest were minions, not worth troubling over. Evidently those who felt they ought to do so had been allowed to flee, as their guilt dictated. The population of Axe-Edge had thinned out considerably, with the princesses in sanctuary and Kieron's adherents decamping rapidly. Its halls had often been empty of a morning—now evenings found them deserted, as well.

Most of the mercers had reopened their shops—closed for a day or two in fear of rioting in the streets under the first surprise of the news—but there were few folk about. The need for fine

234

clothes or rich food was weighed against an uncertain future, and wanted a measure. Crocken had come in search of rumors. He was curious to discover against whom any bad feeling was directed, to judge what enthusiasm there was for the new reign— and how much lament for the loss of the old.

The mercers as a group were displeased. Some had extended credit that would likely never be repaid. Even those lucky enough to have stayed clear of such follies recognized a truth: There'd be less call for their best goods as Sulien's favorites went elsewhere, and they'd take heavy losses on goods laid in for Kieron's crowning. Rhisiart's coronation would not help them recoup— those most apt to spend real money were least apt to attend it.

Crocken heard a rumor that Rhisiart had poisoned his royal ward, and that all Mirell's purity and virtue had been insufficient to save the hapless lad. The shirt she had been so long a-stitching had failed in its duty to protect Kieron from his uncle's malice. The whole land wept with Mirell—for her, and for itself.

Crocken scoffed at that, as he'd seen little of weeping over anything save loss of coin in Rushgate—but the truth was hardly less unbelievable than the rumor, as even his ears heard when he tried to exchange them. That there were folk so ready to forget Rhisiart's decade of good government and chase so foul a rumor on flimsy proof appalled Crocken despite his own anger at the man. Then he was annoyed at his own censuring—was he not a practical man, quick to leap to the main chance when not shadow-directed or misled by big-eyed girls? Better he should apply himself to sorting out his own fortunes, and convert his goods to coins to carry away into his exile.

Along the street of the banner painters, nothing moved save Crocken, his silent shadow, and a thin cat bound on its own silent business at the fish market three streets over. Many a shutter had never been raised that morn—work was at a standstill. Banners with Kieron's devices were wasted labor, fit only to feed cookfires. Had the prince died rather than been disgraced, at least the banners would have been edged in black and exhibited for his funeral procession, Crocken thought sourly. As it was, the painters were beggared, without much hope of recovery when Rhisiart was given the crown formally in a much diminished ceremony.

Under an awning's shade, the old banner painter was at work, painstakingly applying a layer of gesso to a length of cloth that had borne Lord Stiles' snarling catamount badge. He looked up, staying his brushstrokes, and blinked as he recognized Crocken and remembered his last business there.

"Come for your banner, sir? The one with the steward-protector's boar on it?" The painter turned, laying a hand on a long roll of cloth. "I wasn't sure you'd be back for it, sir, or I'd have had it hanging, so the weight would pull it straight—'twill be wrinkled now, but that should pass away easily—"

Crocken paid twice the fee asked, his guilt mastering his thrift. Was what he and Ivy had wrought less evil than what Kieron *might* have done? He knew in his heart it was, but the fact was slippery, impossible to hold onto in the face of the city's turmoil and misery. He'd come to Rushgate hoping to convert his share-holdings into gold and instead spent most of the coin he had in hand, for a banner that he stuffed under his straw mattress the moment he reached Axe-Edge, lest any eyes discover it—even his own.

The Protectorate Council pressed Rhisiart urgently to take Armyn's crown at once—to which the steward-protector replied that he had no leisure at present for the frippery of a coronation. After much heated debate, he agreed to the same date fixed earlier for Kieron's crowning, that being under way. Likely he felt the wrangling wasted more time than the ceremony would.

Crocken overheard matters second and third hand—he was staying well clear of those very assemblies that might have brought him fresher tidings. He spent his days in mostly frustrated attempts to convert his complicated investments to coin—or at least some readily portable form—and tried to decide where he wished to go, should he actually be faced with a choice when he booked his passage.

Reasoning there might be worthy opportunities in Calandra, he took himself finally to Mistress Ivy, though with some trepidation. She and her lady were taking the afternoon air in the pleasure garths, deep in animated converse when he and his shadow drew near between the low hedges of lavender.

"Well, obviously now is not the time to tell him," Ivy was saying. "We'll just let it ride awhile longer—after all, the danger of the marriage is safely past now."

"But what if he sends us home?" Mirell asked softly.

"He won't," Ivy replied, with the certainty she attached to her dreams, then looked up and saw Crocken.

"Don't be too sure he won't," Crocken said, intruding upon what he'd obviously eavesdropped his way into.

"When do you go?" Ivy asked with sympathy.

"The moment there's a ship putting out from the port," Crocken answered bitterly, leaning against the low wall the ladies' bench nestled up to.

"You'll be here awhile, then." Ivy smiled.

"Another dream?" He wanted to hear no more such. It was time to come awake—time and past.

"No." Ivy indicated that Crocken might sit beside her upon the bench, and Mirell also stirred, making room. "You haven't heard?"

"All I've heard lately is that wool prices aren't what they were expected to be," Crocken said, slumping a trifle.

Mirell giggled, and Ivy shot her a look that was far from subservient, Crocken thought, but he had little inclination to wonder about it.

"There's rumor out of Sheir, that Kieron fled there and was welcomed at the Imperial Court," Ivy recited.

"Interesting what Sheirans have a taste for." Crocken shivered, imagining the thing Kieron was being presented to the Sheiran emperor and paraded before his court.

"Aye, and they're gullible," Ivy amended. "They appear to have swallowed the tale that Kieron's 'injuries' are the result of poisoned gloves, a gift from his wicked uncle."

Crocken felt a chill, as if his shadow had moved to block the sun. A hasty glance assured him it had not. "How much of this is true?"

"Known to be?" Ivy plucked a lavender sprig and twirled it swiftly, for all the bandages wrapping her right hand. "Just what I've told you. There are wilder rumors, and I would guess that those in Sheir would be more . . . colorful . . . still. If the Sheiran emperor believes enough of them, or disbelieves but finds meddling expedient and not too costly, he may choose to support Kieron's claim to the throne. That's why you won't be leaving us—at least by ship—for a good while. Rhisiart fears invasion, and he has every ship that calls Armyn home standing station to watch for a Sheiran fleet. Merchanters, too, with archers stationed on their decks."

Crocken made a quick reckoning of time and distance, frowning. "Sheir can't mobilize an invasion so quickly," he said confidently. He'd supplied goods to an army once, and was well acquainted with their methods—which he'd thought ponderous. "Even a standing army needs time to provision and gather ships. They can't do it."

Ivy shook her head most seriously. "Even assuming they don't just sweep out the jails and arm the dregs they have to hand, Sheir can muster a force faster than Rhisiart can, and they know it."

After all, she was a woman, fretful by nature. At the first alarm, she foresaw enemy soldiers breaking down her door. Her expertise in other matters had made Crocken forget that. "Mistress Ivy, Rhisiart has had his hand on Armyn's reins for how many years now? Surely—"

Ivy overrode his patronizing tone. "Until he's crowned, Rhisiart has naught but his authority as steward-protector. Of course he can muster his own retainers from the Borderlands, but the Borderlands are a far way off. The Council has granted him defensive powers, but lords who are honor-bound to supply forces may choose not to do so, with no king crowned to force them. What if they should choose to league with Kieron? Or wait upon war's outcome so that they may more surely choose the winning side? It could all be over with the first battle!"

"Aren't you a bit cynical, Mistress?"

She is not.

Ivy's eyes flashed. "I have made a study of this land, Master Crocken. This situation is none so different from the old civil wars come back again. There was plenty of turning coats then, so do not accuse me of being cynical! What happened once could well happen again. *Neither* Kieron nor Rhisiart is crowned. *Neither* has a clear right in all men's eyes. Yes, Rhisiart has allies—but can he rely upon all of them? Some lords are honor-bound to support him but know no honor. *I'd* not turn my back on them! Those he can best trust will have the farthest to journey, and word from him will take longer to reach their ears. The rest know Armyn's past better than I do, and they will follow the pattern and turn to whichever side they perceive to be winning—or mayhap to the losing side, if timely assistance can turn a victory and produce gratitude—"

"Isn't there a proverb about the gratitude of princes?" Crocken asked, interrupting the flow.

Ivy put a hand—the bandage-swaddled one—on his arm. "Crocken, I truly am sorry so much of his anger has fallen upon you. I did not expect that. I was prepared for myself, I thought he'd rage at me. If there had been more time to lay plans, or to ready Rhisiart for what we knew was coming . . . He's not himself. He looks so ill, it alarms me." Indeed, she was near to weeping.

"Sooner or later, he's going to accept that being alive and king is preferable to letting Kieron kill him," Crocken said, but his tone was hardly schooled to comfort. Ivy took her hand away.

"Sup with us tonight," Mirell begged. "Master Crocken, you have been too much alone."

If they but knew. He hadn't been *alone* for months. Yet Crocken accepted the offer politely, rather than distress the princess more than she already was. Small need now to concern himself over being seen too often with one faction or another— he was already banished anyway, therefore none of that mattered. But later, unobserved, he bespoke his shadow.

"Why so silent?" No answer. "I know you haven't gone, though you seem to have gained your objective," he persisted.

Did you ever know what that was? Shadows of tree branches interlaced across the path, dancing and obscuring the shadow.

"You wanted to know what Kieron was," Crocken said, with patience he in no wise felt. "When you knew, you made sure he was revealed—I *saw* you. Ivy's spell would never have worked, would it? But *you* knew what was needed, and you saw that it happened."

And now you reason that I should peacefully fade away?

"You have a way of extending my term of service," Crocken protested angrily.

Have I intruded? It managed to sound innocently amazed.

"No. That's why I inquire. I don't want a nasty surprise— like your forbidding me to take ship when I'm halfway up a gangplank. Are you content for me to leave? Do you expect me to ferry you back to Kôvelir? What if I want to go somewhere else, or have to?"

You have not gone anywhere as yet.

And no more would it say upon the matter. Crocken's head began to ache from frustration. He decided to spend as little time alone with his shadow as should prove possible.

The Princess Aveline came out of sanctuary, to take her rightful place in the court. It was rumored that most of her sisters would fain have joined her but were not brave enough. The fear was of their mother, not their uncle.

Aveline, the eldest, apparently feared the prison of the chapel and her mother's curdled fury more than the rumors about Rhisiart. Her gesture might be seen to support him, but was self-serving, too—the shadow pointed out that all of the princesses should have long since been wed. Their father had not lived to bestow them upon husbands, it whispered in Crocken's ear, so they had waited for their brother to come of age and do the office. Rhisiart would doubtless have been happy to stand a father's place and arrange marriages; plainly Sulien would never have permitted it. Aveline was making a bid for her freedom, possibly reckoning Rhisiart the lesser of two evils.

Crocken, having heard yet other rumors of the princess' behavior, reckoned that Aveline knew well her uncle would require a queen, and wanted to be available for the post. As Ruane's eldest daughter, she met two requirements—she was of high rank and of an age ideal for heir-getting.

The Princess Aveline's hopes, whatever they might have been, were forestalled. At the end of a fortnight's furious activity, Rhisiart departed Axe-Edge, taking such forces along as would not leave the citadel itself undefended. He aimed to position himself to more swiftly counter the invasion he anticipated—for a time he would lie at Crandell, while levies of men streamed to join the steward-protector's forces.

The Sheiran threat was felt to be real and present. There was Kieron, apparently at the emperor's court, demanding redress. And should he not survive the injuries Rhisiart was said to have committed upon him, Sheir might still take up his quarrel in right of one Harrick, an earl exiled from Armyn, dispossessed by the strife before Ruane ruled. Last sprig of the rival claimants to Armyn's throne, Harrick was now loudly vowing to wed Ruane's eldest daughter and rule with her in joint right. Rumors were rife. It was unknown which claim the Sheiran emperor would choose to trouble Armyn with, but it was never supposed that he might forgo the opportunity entirely. One quarrel or the other would be backed with force of arms.

More calumnies were heaped upon Rhisiart in his absence. He refused to acknowledge them by denouncing any of them and was evidently uneager to have even the true story of Kieron's transformation put about. Harrick's claim he might have discounted. The man was a joke—exiled since his very birth, living upon charity in foreign courts and often a hostage—tainted with bastardy to boot. Rhisiart might little heed Harrick's posturings, but *some* force would come, and the steward-protector had determined to face it in the field—never the sort of commander to wait while trouble came to him.

He was not yet crowned. That was a hindrance, limiting the support he might have commanded as king. Rhisiart recognized the difficulty and said publicly that, while he had laid down his protectorship of the prince's person, he had not relinquished his duty as Protector of Armyn. There was a threat to the land, and he would confront it. Time for pretty ceremonies afterward.

His enemies approved.

The final rattle of the last laden cart had died away an hour since. No clinking of harness disturbed the air—no carter's shout, no ringing of shod hooves upon cobbles—for the first time in two days. In the deepest reach of the night, Mistress Ivy lay upon her narrow pallet, dreaming.

She knew, without signpost, that the field she beheld was called Red Plain, for the reeds that grew all about its edges. Armies were arrayed there—the one, which had arrived earliest, upon what little high ground there was, its flanks guarded by the marshes. The slope upward from the plain was not so great as could be wished, but any charge uphill would hamper an armored foe. Above the ranked men, pennants and banners flaunted. The largest bore a silver boar, its tusks slashing angrily, savaging the wind.

High ground was ever the defense of choice, yet now it constricted the force upon it. There were many knights, but small space for them to maneuver, so most had been ordered to fight dismounted, with axe and sword and sundry weapons of destruction. Numbers were gained, but speed was traded away with the horses.

The tide of the young battle surged back and forth, up and down and across the face of the hill. The two forces were somewhat matched—those upon the hill were technically more numerous, but cramped together so, their full force could not be brought to bear. The day advanced, the sun's heat grew. Losses were heavy, and the defense was faltering.

Upon the hilltop, there was a tiny force of men yet mounted. One of them, a small man in bright armor, horsed on a white war-stallion, sat calm at the center of a flurry of activity, his messengers flying to and fro. Of a sudden he seemed to reach a decision. He spoke eagerly to the men around him, and the little body of horse went charging down the hill toward a position at the edge of the field, where a golden standard flew behind the lines. A quick way to put an end to the strife, for one commander to cut the head off the other.

Down the hill the horses galloped, the boar standard streaming with their pace, around the main strife and full into the ill-defended position. They were falling upon it, cutting down those few men left to guard the rear. Ivy dreamed Kieron's face among them, his mouth open to shout and only a serpent's hissing issuing forth.

Then the trap was sprung. From the cover of a little wood, knights and men-at-arms poured. The devices they bore were those of Armyn, not Sheir, but they fell upon the steward-protector's little force all the same, with no mistake about their dire intent. Men died, crying treason if they had time at all to know how they got their deaths.

Rhisiart was nearly through to Kieron, his ultimate foe, having hewn a bloody path to the very pole from which the golden standard fluttered. He closed with the Sheiran guards—then broke off as the commotion to his rear caught his attention. He recognized the forces killing his companions and knew his danger. He would need to retreat in the heartbeats that remained before the trap's jaws closed on him utterly.

The very ground conspired against the attempt—Rhisiart swung the white war-stallion about in the sucking mud, but its great hooves lost purchase and it stumbled. Stormraker made a valiant effort to win free nonetheless, but his way was blocked by another horse. He reared, but could not maneuver around it. Momentum lost in the attempt, he was suddenly and deeply mired, unable to turn swiftly, no longer able to move forward to drier ground.

Thus immobilized, neither horse nor rider could avoid the attack as it broke over them. A sword descended first. Rhisiart blocked the blow with his own blade, but the angle was ineffective. He was not hit, but he was thrown loose from his saddle, shoved from Stormraker's back to land amid the muddy melee along the course of the stream. Valiant Stormraker tried to defend his master as he had been taught, with hooves and teeth, but with Rhisiart afoot he was no more than a shield—and that but for a moment. One sword-blow he spared his master, before collapsing into the crimson mud.

No other aid was close enough to reach the steward-protector. A knight strove to make a rescue, shouting a warning, but a Sheiran pikeman sent his horse crashing abruptly into the mud, and the knight did not rise from the disaster.

Rhisiart fought afoot, staggering between far too many enemies. A blow cut the crest of his helm away, and there was bright blood on his face. Other attacks dented and rent his armor. Still he was a dangerous foe, as evidenced by the reluctance of his enemies to close with him. The alert flickering of the blood-spattered blade in the steward-protector's hand promised he'd take more than one man with him, and none of them much wanted to be first to that dubious honor. They'd hold—the man was doomed, with no escape route open, no chance of rescue, no aid within hope. Rhisiart could last only scant moments before he was overwhelmed, before some archer came up and saw his chance for glory. They had only to keep him there, and he could not prevent them.

At length, the notion of single, honorable combat began to bore them, and they closed the circle, their many to his one—

Mistress Ivy woke, screaming, and cared not that she woke Mirell, cared for naught and was incomprehensible for the next noisy hour. Mirell wisely sent the also-wakened and distraught ladies of her outer chamber away once more and held Ivy tenderly, listened to the few words she could make sense of. When the hour was more seemly, Master Crocken was sent for.

Chapter Thirty

"COME WITH ME," she'd said. "Or I will go alone."

And Crocken had known she would keep her word—there was not the slenderest shadow of a doubt for that in his heart. Mistress Ivy was not a maiden to be gainsaid.

Even Mirell did not attempt the feat, though Crocken thought 'twas surely her place to do so. The princess seemed as helpless before Ivy's insistence as Crocken was, for all her royal station. She had the use of her voice once more, but she mostly withheld it.

And so, against all sense and Crocken's better judgment—and against Rhisiart's express orders, for all they knew, if the steward-protector could have anticipated such folly—he and Ivy rode out of Axe-Edge on the track of the army.

Why had she moved him so? Crocken pondered that, as the horse he'd borrowed trotted along and jolted his teeth loose from his gums. There were other women in Axe-Edge as fair as Ivy, maidens who might have been warmer to him and asked less of him, women to whom he might readily have turned if he'd ever chosen to trust anything female again—which Crocken sternly assured himself was not the case.

But she'd begged him to go after Rhisiart, to carry the warning of her dream, and Crocken had agreed, which still amazed him. He'd been sober and in full possession of his wits—unless that blow the shadow had gifted him had done some permanent damage, which he told himself he could not quite rule out. He'd agreed to the madness and now found himself on yet another strange horse—though this one less mettlesome, all the better steeds having gone with the army in the first place—on an unfamiliar road, on the track of a man from whom he could look for no welcome.

He rode companioned, of course, by a shadow not his own, which mostly remembered to ape his movements when someone might be looking and which made his horse a wreck of nerves till it had finally got used to the idea during their first dozen miserable leagues together. And with them came a girl with such a set look to her white face that he feared more for her than for himself.

Crocken hoped Ivy had been accurate about Red Plain being the site of the battle to come, because that place was what they made for, upon the supposition that Rhisiart would have left his base of operations at Farle, whence he had gone after Crandell, long ere they could reach that castle. A pity, for the army's path had been plain, beaten out on both sides of the road it had overflowed. They'd had to leave that less direct way behind, striking out on smaller roads, going as the crows flew when Ivy so directed.

The weather was flawless, calm and hot and devoid of rain— if Sheir had possessed a sailing fleet, they might have felt less urgent, but galleys could serve well—better, in fact—when there was no wind and no storm-waves. Invasion might come at any moment, and Crocken did not have Rhisiart's spy network posted on the coastline to tell him when and where, if Red Plain was not indeed the place. At best, they must hope to intercept Rhisiart's forces before 'twas too late.

Surely, two folk ahorse could outdistance an army on the march. Particularly as Mistress Ivy would not hear of stopping beyond the rest the horses needed, and she gave the beasts precious little of that. Half an hour's grazing, then she would tighten the girths, remount, and kick her palfrey into a smart trot, and Crocken would need to make haste to follow her.

By the time the sun had slipped close to the horizon on the second day, the horses would maintain only a walk. Crocken was relieved—he doubted he could bear to sit a trot much longer. The road went up and down and around hills, and his horse followed it, or followed Ivy's mount—he was no longer much interested in directing it. Being pitched onto the roadside was beginning to seem an attractive alternative to going on, but the beast was too weary for nonsense.

The road was quite dusty—plumes rose up from each weary footfall, setting Crocken coughing. He steered his horse toward the nearer verge, but the grass there was thick-powdered till it was little better than the roadbed itself. It took Crocken a little while to realize what he was seeing.

"The army," he croaked in Ivy's direction. "We're on their track again."

"Yes," she said over her dust-shrouded shoulder.

There was no further conversation. The horses plodded onward, the twilight deepened, and Crocken, helpless to resist any longer, slipped into a doze.

It seemed to him that one instant he was awake, and struggling to remain so, lest he fall from the horse—the next, he was dreaming.

Could a rat shed tears, he would have wept—such a long and desperate way he had crawled, at the ragged end of his strength before he even began his creep—and now the airshaft's very end was barred with iron where the shaft reached the outer wall, with his freedom just on the other side of those rusted but implacable bars, in plain and heartbreaking view.

The disappointment was worse than the manacle he still bore about what was his wrist, when he was a man. *That* only made him lame, and fevered, and restricted him to simple forms such as rodents. He could drag the manacle if his will was strong, though he was sick with pain. But the bars—he dared not try to pass between them. The attempt would surely throw him back into human shape, and the airshaft was scarcely wide enough to accommodate a rat—human-size, he would be trapped till he died. The least wavering of his will or attention now, and he'd meet that fate anyway.

Disconsolate, he began the long descent back to his cell, hardly caring if he slipped and fell to his death.

Voices floated up the shaft, unencumbered by bodies, carried through myriad branchings, slipping through cracks and chinks in the stone, leaking in where mortar had fallen out. Mostly he ignored them, but suddenly recognition pricked his sharp rat ears.

"I thought you might wait for the morrow to serve out your office, Constable." The voice was pitched high with fear and outrage, slurred over with drink.

"Shut up." It was Rhisiart's voice, hoarse with emotion. "And try to sober up. Whatever you've done, it's not what they charged you with. I cannot allow Ruane to kill you. Not kill a brother, not like this. Get you gone, Tierce. This night's start is all I can give you—make the most of it."

The rat's tiny heart beat fast, its paws scurried frantically over

the stone. With all its shape-shifted being it held to one thought—
to be back at the cell when Rhisiart came to release *him* . . .

But Rhisiart never came.

Crocken sobbed, which hurt his dry throat, and opened his
eyes. His horse had stopped moving and hung its head in weariness. All about him there was darkness—greater darks that
were trees and bushes, a wider one where the sky arched above
his head. A world made all of shadows, or perchance being
inside a shadow.

Or like having a shadow inside him. Usually when he
dreamed, Crocken woke and then slept again, and the dreams
faded . . . but this one lingered, tasting as bitter as if he,
Crocken, had been the one betrayed where he least expected to
be. The betrayal the shadow had so often spoken of . . .

He could hear—though not see—a horse cropping grass. Mistress Ivy had dismounted and knelt in the long grass, her back
to him, her face invisible.

Crocken half fell out of his saddle and limped stiffly over to
her. Her eyes were tightly closed, but her lips parted when he
touched her shoulder.

"—a wind, blowing out of the Borderlands," she said, in
such a prophetic tone that Crocken felt chilled beyond the growing cool of the evening. He reminded himself that she was obviously sleeping, and he shook her gently.

"We were both asleep," he said apologetically, as Ivy blinked
at him in what he took for confusion. "Me still on the horse, if
you can imagine that! I think we'd better stop here—"

"I'll stay. You've got to go on. Get to Rhisiart," Ivy said,
more firmly than he'd anticipated.

"They won't fight at night, will they? And I won't leave you
here all alone."

Her brows lowered.

"I have work to do. There's a chance, just a chance, that I
can do something to help. Delay the battle, until—"

"I am *not* leaving you here," Crocken said flatly. "I'm done
consenting to crazy orders."

Her green eyes blazed at him. Her silver ring flashed like
lightning on her hand as she raised it. *"You will do as I say!"*

Crocken realized he had taken a step backward, closer to his
grazing horse. His legs wanted to take another, but he made
them stop. They trembled, almost failing to hold him up.

Ivy read the fear in his face. "Crocken—I'm sorry—" She

laid a gentle hand on his arm. The uncanny command was gone
from her voice, though she nonetheless pleaded with him. "You
have to warn him. What I'm trying to do will not be enough to
thwart the dream, not by itself. It only buys you time—"

He wasn't listening. His teeth wanted to chatter, and it was
hard to speak. "You . . . *are* a witch. Ivy, have a care! This
isn't Kôvelir, they may burn witches here—" He realized suddenly that his shadow was no longer with him but had made free
with the night. He didn't know when. Distracted, he lost the
thread of her explanation.

"—sorcery isn't forbidden in Armyn. It's only uncommon, or
Sulien could never have accomplished what she did. I'll be all
right here, Crocken. Will you go?"

He nodded, seeing that he was putting a foot into his stirrup
as he did so, wondering whose idea that was. Ivy had left off the
style of commanding that had frightened him, but that did not
mean she had left off getting her way by any means to hand.
"I'll come back here for you."

"No! Stay with Rhisiart. Guard him, in case this isn't
enough—"

"What do I expect 'this' to be?" he asked testily, settling into
the saddle, cinching his beltran tight against the cold. "So I'll
know it?"

Ivy laughed. "I'm not such a great witch as you suppose! I
am only going to craft a little fog, to buy us a few hours of
delay."

What purpose that could serve, Crocken could not guess. He
only hoped he could find the army before the mist settled in.
Though in unfamiliar territory, he could scarcely be *more* lost
than he was at the moment.

Ivy guessed his doubt. "Just go down the road. He will have
pickets out, but you ought to be able to slip past."

Yes.

Crocken started. The horse shied.

Did Ivy know? Crocken wondered. He felt certain she did,
and that 'twas the shadow she had spoke to. The horse danced,
then settled wearily.

*They expect no trouble from this direction, the way they came.
The sentries are few, and only on the road.*

Ivy drew off her ring and gave the silver circle a twist. Part of
it sprang free, Crocken was not surprised to see. "Put this on
him, if you can manage it. If not . . . I will not be sorry if I can
protect *you* tomorrow, my friend." She slid the ribbon of silver,

still warm from her hand, onto Crocken's little finger. The ring of beads remained on her own. "Good fortune."

Like to like, Ivy whispered to herself, repeating her father's words of instruction from a lesson long ago. She could never have witched fog from a desert, or in the merciless glare of sun-high—her gifts did not lie in that direction, and her skills were rudimentary, seldom practiced. But by night, in this damp spot . . . matters were otherwise. Failure was inconceivable. She heard the croaking of frogs and knew there was water close by, a pond or a slow-running stream.

As the sound of the frogs guided her to the water, Ivy gathered her weapons, readying her defense of Rhisiart's life. The seed-head of a dandelion, tenderly shielded. A huge white puffball mushroom, found hard by a rotting log. She wandered through plantains and long grasses by the streamside, looking for tools. How long had the night still to run?

She dared not begin the work too soon and risk her spell's faltering when it was most needed. Nor could she delay too long—if the charm did not work, she'd need time to begin it anew.

What of that wind from the Borderlands, in her waking dream? Troops did not march by night unless the need was dire—the Borderlanders could not know the urgency of Rhisiart's situation. They might guess it, but she could not rely upon that happenchance. She must assume they'd only take up their march again at dawn, and allow time accordingly.

Crocken arrived at the encampment after a further hour's ride, exhausted and sweaty, simply wanting by then to be done with the whole matter—not caring just at that moment how it resolved. He didn't need the shadow's help to get through the lines—the first of the pickets, come upon unexpectedly, recognized him and passed him through. The man did not order him escorted—a lapse for which Crocken suspected a commander such as Rhisiart should have flayed him.

His shadow, though it had stayed with him, had been a mostly silent companion—nearly as useless for conversation as his true shadow would have been. Braving rebuff—maybe to get into practice—Crocken bespoke it softly.

"Tell me, at least, how much time I have. Do you know where the Sheiran army is?"

Just down the hill.

"What?" That brought him fully awake.

Softly. The army rests, sleeps. They are not as yet in battle array. They will begin to move in at dawn.

"The battle's tomorrow?" He had not, somehow, believed Ivy about that; he had been unready to believe it.

That seems most likely. They came here to confront Rhisiart. He will not let them slip past. He will not parley, not with invaders. They are unlikely to choose retreat, their numbers nearly match Rhisiart's. The only outcome remaining is battle.

"But that means I'll have to get to him *tonight*, to warn him." Ivy's ring, on his finger, burned his flesh, or so it seemed in his imagination.

At least you have not long to dread the encounter.

Crocken made a little strangling sound. Rhisiart would be abed, getting whatever rest he could hope for. There was no way he'd be admitted at such an hour, even if he were still in the king's favor.

His tent will be the large one, with his standard in front of it.

"Well, do you recommend I just ride in, or should I lose the horse first?" Crocken was far past caring how the sarcasm would be received.

Ivy decided that the time had come. She scanned the clear, dark sky and felt the cool air of the night against her cheeks. She let herself feel the moisture trapped above the still-warm ground. She took the dandelion's head in one hand, the puffball in the other. Whispering, she slowly closed both hands, then rapidly opened them, snapping her fingers wide.

The seed-puff burst asunder, bits of down rising into the air. The mushroom released a cloud of powdery spores, which drifted up like smoke. Ivy blew her breath out softly, to mingle with both.

As the cloud drifted over the stream, mist rose from the dark water to join it. In the space of a dozen heartbeats the fog was thick as flannel and spreading outward, down the course of the streambed, lapping at the feet of the hills, following the lay of the valley to the marshy spot where two armies were encamped awaiting the dawn. Above, not a single star could be seen.

There was light inside the steward-protector's waxed-silk tent, but the toing and froing that Crocken had vainly hoped to encounter and lose himself within was long over with—the camp had settled for the short summer night. The pavilion's door flaps

were folded down, and two armed guards stood before them,
keeping watch lest any disturb the king. Crocken's heart misgave him. There was no way for him to simply slip in. The
immediate future looked more inevitable to him than Mistress
Ivy's dream—either Rhisiart would refuse to have him admitted,
or the guards would refuse to carry the message to Rhisiart that
he was there in the first place. He hesitated miserably, just outside the range of the torchlight before the tent. His tired legs,
glad a moment before to be off the horse, now wished to cease
carrying him.

There was a sigh from somewhere behind his left ear, where
the torches flung shadows, and his own drifted restlessly. *Just
walk in. I will disguise you in the guards' eyes.*

Almost Crocken was unable to move—that was how greatly
he disbelieved what the shadow proposed, despite all the dark
wonders he had seen it working.

You still trust your eyes, the shadow explained. *So—and far
more so—do Rhisiart's guards.*

A light breeze rippled the silk of the tent flaps and the torch
flames—as Crocken went past all of them: guards, flames, and
flaps. No outcry was made, and all was silence inside the scarlet
tent.

I have work to be about, the shadow said, and left him, when
'twas too late for Crocken to protest beyond opening his mouth
in silent outrage. So he shut his lips and took a deep breath and
a step forward. There was a silk panel hung, to provide an extra
bit of privacy. He held it aside and passed into the tent's inner
reach.

The floor was fresh grass, bruised and dusty from the many
feet that had trodden upon it. There was a small carpet unrolled
beside the sleeping couch, to keep the damp of the ground at
bay, and another beneath the small table where Rhisiart sat.

Crocken had hoped to find Rhisiart better rested, less devas-
tated by fate's buffets. It had been a good month since he'd seen
him close to—surely Rhisiart would have come to terms with his
situation . . .

Rhisiart's haggard face was a shock to him, therefore. The
king looked to have lived twice his years, and to be sick besides.
He had a pen in his hand, and a parchment before him. Was he
writing a letter? Likely not—those Rhisiart loved were all long
dead. Some final order to his commanders? His will?

Whatever he worked upon, the king's mind and heart were
leagues off from the tent where he worked upon it. Rhisiart

looked up, staring straight at Crocken for fully a dozen heartbeats before he seemed to comprehend what he saw.

"Did I not so desperately require every man in this camp for battle on the morrow, there would be ears nailed to my tent poles tonight," the king said dangerously. "How came you here, Master Merchant-Adventurer?"

"My lord, don't blame your guards." *Why not?* Crocken asked himself in wild alarm, hoping Rhisiart would not ask also. He cursed his shadow for deserting him.

"Indeed, no!" Rhisiart laughed bitterly. "Would that I might encourage Kieron to hire them on. They didn't even challenge you?"

Crocken took another deep breath, and what courage he could from the fact that the truant guards hadn't been sent for. "My lord Rhisiart, how I came is of small import, but *why* I came is vital to your safety! Mistress Ivy sent me. She has dreamed—"

The quill pen was snapped in twain. "I will hear no more of Mistress Ivy's dreams," Rhisiart said flatly. "Best she should forget them with the morn, as sensible folk do." He tossed the ruined pen into the grass. "And what can it matter? I know well that tomorrow will be a day of peril, without her to tell me." He shut his eyes, then went on.

"If she dreams true, as she claims, what good can her warning do me? What she has seen, will be. I am more interested to know—" He gestured for Crocken to come a little closer. "Why have *you* come with her word, and not some other? Why are you not off for Kôvelir?"

"You comandeered all the ships," Crocken answered angrily. He told himself he'd have been delighted to go and be spared such ingratitude.

Rhisiart stared at him a moment, then laughed until tears came to his eyes. He put a hand up in a vain effort to hide the fact. "So I did. I had forgotten." He rubbed at his eyes, the mirth leaving his face, much to its detriment. "Well, the invader has landed, the fleet that kept watch for him is released. You should be able to find some passage before word of tomorrow spreads to the coast. There will be captains eager to take their ships away from here for a space."

He considered, reached for a bit of parchment, then laid it aside again. "You look done-up, but if I give you a fresh horse, you could reach the coast while there's still time to do so safely. Make for a port city, not Axe-Edge, and you'll run into no trouble—"

"My lord, I would liefer stay."

Rhisiart looked at him, obviously baffled, no less confused than Crocken felt. His tongue seemed divorced from his brain, acting on its own agenda.

"There will be a battle here tomorrow," the king said.

As if he would not know. Mayhap Rhisiart thought him so stupid that he would not. "You did say you needed every man," Crocken answered, mad words again. He could almost have believed that the shadow directed them, had it been there to do so.

"What do you intend? To skewer the Sheirans with a tally stick?"

Crocken was offended. It surprised him. He had no knightly pride, to feel such pricks. "My lord, I grew up on Kôvelir's streets and have not forgotten its lessons. I may not be a horseman—small question of *that*—but I can fight afoot and give good account of myself."

"For perchance a quarter of an hour, or till you stray into some Sheiran bowman's line of sight," Rhisiart said dismissively.

"I had it in mind to stay by you."

"That's hardly safer!" Rhisiart snapped. A thought obviously struck him. "Is this madness more of Mistress Ivy's bidding?"

"No." Though the ring seemed to grow warm again, on his finger, refusing to allow him to forget his promise.

"No? Master Crocken, I have misjudged you. I took you for an opportunist, in over his head in a nasty game. Now I have no means to judge whether you simply *are* mad, or are perchance a spy in Sulien's pay."

"I doubt she'd pay well for the service I've rendered her," Crocken considered. "I would be most happy if I thought the lady was in ignorance of my name—and certainly my location." Crocken smiled, but not with mirth. "My lord, I'm no spy, not for anyone. And mad I may be, to want to stay. But . . ." He struggled to give words to the emotion that continually startled him. "You've been kind to me, and I have repaid you thoughtlessly. I didn't consider the outcome as I should have, before I helped Mistress Ivy. Still, it seems to me yet that there was great ill about to be done to you. You may not have *wanted* to know what Kieron was, but was the alternative better?"

He went on quickly, to forestall Rhisiart's angry rejoinder. "I'm sorry for your distress, and I'm sorry this situation has gone as it has. I didn't expect, coming in here, to want to make such amends, but I find I do—even if it means dying with the footsoldiers tomorrow. I'd prefer your leave, but I can manage whether you give it or no.''

He turned to leave. Rhisiart's command caught him just at the tent flap.

"Wait." It was not quite an order.

Crocken did as he was bidden but did not turn. He wasn't sure what he felt, what hope his face might show—or if he wanted it to be seen. He tried to curse himself for a fool. What had he to do with lost causes? Loneliness had warped his good sense, that he'd always been so proud of, and friendship completed the seduction.

"I did my king a great wrong," Rhisiart said slowly, "knowing it, and was yet forgiven; and I have felt . . . as you say you do, this need for amends. You did me no harm you could have known of, and great good as you could have seen it. Master Crocken, if you choose to stay here, I will not forbid you.''

"My lord—" Crocken turned eagerly, on the abused grass.

"It is not likely you will have cause to thank me for this," Rhisiart pointed out dryly.

Crocken bowed. "Then I won't presume to." He withdrew once more to the flaps.

Rhisiart was chuckling again. "Master Merchant-Adventurer, you have a knack for making me mirthful, and that is a great wonder. The night before a battle is difficult for all the reasons you might suppose and many I hope you know nothing of—and I have never felt so bereft of any good wish as I had this night before you came. I should reward you to the utmost of my power—which, at present, is to suggest that you sleep on one of my carpets rather than the cold dirt outside, then eat a bit of breakfast with me come dawn—assuming you are any better at swallowing down camp food than I generally am—and let my armorer see how he can equip you, to make that Sheiran archer's work a touch more difficult.''

"I have already submitted myself to my lord's command." Crocken smiled.

"You'll regret that, I'm certain. I am told I have become a restless sleeper, crying out continually at my foul dreams. I'll disturb you.''

"That's the Sheiran rumor, isn't it?" Crocken guessed, sifting through the tales he'd heard. "Your conscience is smiting you for your crimes?''

Rhisiart flinched a little, then saw the jest for what it was. "I *do* have difficulty sleeping," he admitted. "I'm seldom asleep long enough to *have* dreams, but 'tis true I do not rest well. Or quietly.''

Crocken shook his head slowly. "I fell asleep on my horse, riding here. Nothing short of an earth-shake is likely to disturb me once I bed down.''

Rhisiart moved restlessly, rising to fetch a wine flagon and a cup to match the one already on the table, striding from one silken wall to the other without remembering to pour for either of them. Desperate for company, he seemed uneasy once he had it, uncertain what to speak of.

Crocken glanced at the hour candle that burned steadily on its stand. "How much longer?" he asked, trying not to think about what they awaited. The candle might well be measuring out the hours left in his life.

"A few hours," Rhisiart answered. "The camp will be astir before first light, there's much to do before battle is joined. It takes awhile to arm.''

"Shouldn't you try to rest?" Rhisiart was still pacing, as much as the tent's confines would allow. At this rate he'd be unfit to walk by dawn, far less direct his army.

Perchance he doesn't want to sleep the rest of his life away.

Crocken jumped at the remark that heralded his shadow's return, but Rhisiart did not see, lost in the thoughts he spoke aloud.

"So many times I've passed nights such as this—not in years, but the trouble is not lack of practice. I never learned the way of it. Ruane always laughed about that. Said it was his fault I was so eager, because he started me at it so young, before I had learned patience. Just sixteen I was, the first time I waited for morning with an army.''

He was wearing a path in the grass, Crocken saw.

"I had so many brothers in those days. Full-fledged Falcons all, while I was just a sickly chick. Ruane, eldest, the one we all looked to. More, in every way, than any other man. Edmon, who died with my father—he was the second son, after Ruane. Tierce—doubtless you have heard tales of him, and most of them are all too true, alas. Proud, Tierce was, vain, and too fond of wine for anyone's good. He might have destroyed himself anyway—he had made a good start at it—but Sulien left him no chance of redemption." Years Rhisiart had kept an uneasy peace with Ruane's wife, Crocken knew, but he had not guessed what a feat that truce was, where hatred and blame ran so deep.

". . . and Miall," Rhisiart was wandering on.

"Miall who found Stormraker for you?" Crocken asked, remembering something he'd heard Rhisiart say, when the stallion came to Axe-Edge.

"Yes. Miall was always good with horses. He got that from his mother's people, I think. He said so." Rhisiart frowned at some memory. "He was always drifting back and forth, between her people in the hills and ours in the Borderlands. Of both places, and neither, and I think never at ease, wherever he was. He has not drifted this way in long years. I suppose he's dead, too."

Quite.

Crocken twitched once more, but mastered the reaction. "You're the only one I've heard speak his name." Though that was not quite true—he seemed to remember a dream . . .

"I am not surprised. Sulien had little liking for any of her husband's brothers, but Miall . . . well, Miall was my father's son—but not my mother's."

The misfortune of being born to the mistress rather than the wife.

"His mother having died, my father took Miall into our household, when we lived at Hearthover. Noble houses are full of children, and he was welcome, if never very happy." Rhisiart frowned again. "Tierce would never let him have a brother's right—not even a half brother's. But Ruane—if Miall had helped Ruane fight for his crown, Ruane would have given him anything he asked for. Lands, titles. He gave to the less deserving, certes, to Sulien's kin. But Miall wouldn't fight. I don't know why."

He frowned still more. "Even while my father lived—I can remember them quarreling over it, because Miall would not take up arms. That was when Miall first left us and went back to the hill folk. He wouldn't fight—but it was Miall who was my arms master, when I was small and only allowed wooden weapons. And Miall was good, *very* good—with them. There were things he taught me that spared my life a dozen times over, later. Miall had no need to fear battle, and I do not think he *did* fear it.

"So he had no place in Ruane's kingdom—not that he ever asked one of Ruane. Miall was almost of an age with Tierce—mayhap some of Tierce's disfavor rubbed off onto him, in Ruane's eyes. I have had no word of him in many years." Rhisiart rubbed at his eyes, which were surely burning with sleeplack. "How odd it feels, to have been smallest brother to so many and now to find myself alone. *I* was the one they all reckoned too sickly to live."

Heavy footsteps outside, the guard being changed.

"Would that Miall were here," Rhisiart said, almost inaudibly.

Liar!

Crocken almost lost hold of his senses, so loud the shadow's accusation rang in his brain. He fought to keep his balance and could scarcely believe Rhisiart had not heard the shout also. Then he was angry suddenly, furious that the shadow could watch Rhisiart's suffering and be unmoved. He refused to follow its lead any longer, to be party to the cruelty. What, after all, could it still threaten him with? He'd not likely live to see the next sun-fall. The depressing notion was somehow liberating.

Rhisiart had at some point abandoned both the flagon and the cups. Crocken captured both and poured wine, sniffing it appreciatively. Kings rated decent vintages, even in the middle of a marsh. He carried a cup to the king, a plan forming in his mind.

"Would my lord care to have the ins and outs of the wool trade explained, seeing as you intend to be wakeful? It's a fascinating subject, fit for an entertainment—"

In truth it was so, and would have undoubtedly held Rhisiart's interest, as he had leanings toward commerce anyway—but Crocken patterned his discourse after a caravaner he'd once known, a man who could cheerfully bore the grain out of wood. There was only the one chair, and Crocken took it, forcing the king to sit on the edge of his sleeping couch. They sipped the wine. Crocken droned on inventively, endlessly.

Rhisiart's head began to nod. He tried to shake himself awake, stifling a yawn. Crocken cleverly suggested another cup of wine, to ease his throat while they talked. Rhisiart kept him company, and little more was needful. A few moment's discussion of the grading and pricing of various and numerous types of fleeces, and Crocken was speaking for his own ears alone. Rhisiart was flat out on the bed, eyes closed, breathing slow and even. Crocken had one more sip of wine—his throat truly needed it by then—and let his own eyelids slide shut.

Crocken's dream was as clear as reality would have been—perhaps more so.

The boy in the bed woke abruptly when the older boy burst into his room. He watched the dim figure cross to the shuttered window, waited for its ragged breathing to quiet before he spoke.

"Miall?"

The intruder stiffened, then turned. "*Rhisiart?* I'm sorry—I forgot they'd moved you in here. Does the change of scene mean they think you're getting well?''

Rhisiart pushed himself up against his pillows. He'd been ill of a fever for over a month, ill with one thing and another for all of his six years, to his best recollection. He sometimes wished he could hurry the dying everyone expected him to be doing. "Miall, why is your nose bleeding?"

"I hit it on something."

Rhisiart digested that and required more answers. "What did you hit it on?"

"Tierce's fist."

Rhisiart felt a deep sympathy—and a morbid curiosity.

"Does it hurt?"

"Not as much as Tierce thinks it does."

"If you tell Hagga that Tierce hit you, he'd be punished." Rhisiart's sense of justice was strong for his years.

Miall laughed bitterly. "If Tierce hit *you*, maybe. For me he'd hardly get a cross word."

"Because I'm dying?"

"Who said that to you?" Miall asked, a different anger in his voice.

"Tierce," Rhisiart offered timidly. But Miall's anger was not directed at him, and he realized it.

"Ah. And Tierce knows all, of course?"

Rhisiart nodded solemnly, upon his pillows. Tierce was older, wiser than he, and never let him forget that fact.

"Then I'm sure he knew, yestereve, that someone had untied his hose points for him. He only paraded across the hall with his buttocks exposed for the fashion of it?"

Rhisiart laughed aloud, a rare and evidently unpracticed event. He nearly choked, then had to wait for breath to speak. "I wish *I* had seen that!"

"Get yourself well enough to sup in the hall with the rest of us, and I'll untie his points again, just for you."

"Promise?" the child asked, awed.

"Sworn. Blood to Blood." Miall sat on the bed's edge. "First, you get well."

Rhisiart frowned, unsure how to claim his reward, afraid he might not be able to. "I have tried. I don't know what to do."

And he was terrified. It showed plainly on his pinched face.

"I'll teach you something that will help," Miall offered. "A secret my mother showed me." He opened the shutter, to let light fall across the bed, splash the wall.

Rhisiart wriggled with anticipation. "Show me the rabbit again!"

Miall obliged him, twisting supple fingers together so that the requested shadow fell onto the wall. He did others: deer, horse, and hound. "Those are ordinary. I'm going to teach you some special shadows now—I'll show you how to do them for yourself, so you can have them whenever there's need. Pay close attention now.

"This is the Wolf. He will lend you courage, when you make the sign. You'll never need to be afraid again, little brother.

"This is the Raven, for wisdom.

"This is the Hawk, for swift dispatch of enemies . . ."

Crocken came awake in the darkness—the hour candle had burned itself out, or suffered from a draft. He heard steady, even breathing, which told him that Rhisiart still slept.

He knew whose memories he had, those not his own, those that leaked out into his dreams. He understood, with the clarity found between dream and waking, why the shadow both protected and reviled Rhisiart, for a betrayal committed all unwittingly.

But what did Miall's shadow intend? Was Kieron's disgrace enough, or did it plan to bring down the entire House of the Falcon, which had rejected it? Had it saved Rhisiart once, only that he might die later as Miall had, alone and betrayed? Would dying in the dark by an assassin's hand not have been enough to slake its thirst for revenge? Better for him to die desperate, despairing, knowing fully the fate that was overwhelming him?

What if the shadow interfered, when Crocken tried to thwart Ivy's prophecy?

"Can't you understand?" Crocken asked softly. In the dark, he couldn't tell where the shadow was—if it was there at all. "How could he rescue you? He didn't know you were there. He had no reason to think you were involved. He *didn't* betray you. He didn't even truly betray Ruane, yet he's lost everything he ever cared about because he *thinks* he did. Isn't that enough? Does he have to die, too, to satisfy you?"

The shadow had been Rhisiart's brother once—but it was not Miall any longer, merely a remnant of what the man had once been, a piece left behind. Inside the two dimensions of a shadow, there was scant room for the diverse qualities that make up a man. And if that little space was taken by hatred, by desire for revenge . . . was there room as well for mercy?

In the dark, there was no answer.

Chapter Thirty-one

CROCKEN WOKE WITH someone's toe poking his ribs and sat up, blinking at the seeming glare of a rushlight in a servant's hand. The man blinked back at him.

"Oh, it's the merchant, yes? Didn't know you'd come with us, sir. Didn't expect to find the ste—the king still asleep, either," the man said wonderingly, as he bent to touch Rhisiart's shoulder. "My lord? It's the last watch. Time to arm."

Rhisiart turned over and sat up, looking perplexed. "Truly? I cannot think how that can be. I did but rest my eyes—"

" 'Tis true, my lord. The camp's well astir."

Rhisiart frowned. "I must have slept. Did I miss any details of your discourse upon the wool trade, Master Crocken?"

Crocken was trying to ease a crick out of his shoulder, without success. "I hope not. It surprises me you didn't dream of sheep."

Rhisiart gave his shoulder a friendly squeeze as he strode past, heading for the tent flap and his preparations. "I believe I did. An interesting change."

There was a pattern to an army's readying itself for battle, as there was to a caravan's breaking of camp after a night's rest. Crocken saw similarities in the way each man had his assigned task and went about it—with varying degrees of success. There was bustle, and confusion, but things were for the most part orderly underneath it all.

He broke his fast with a crust of dry bread, ignoring the slabs of cold meat that appeared beside the loaf—and noticed that Rhisiart did likewise. If anything, the king ate even more sparingly. They both left the wine untouched, but took a mug of ale each, the brew thick enough to be almost a food itself.

Beyond the tent's outer flaps, the air was white and damp. The morning fog displeased the commanders, but Crocken was glad to behold it, even though he wasn't party to Ivy's plan for it. It meant she had succeeded and, if naught else, it would delay the start of the battle. And all shadows were nearly invisible, from which he also took comfort.

As Rhisiart picked at his meager meal within the tent's outer chamber, he was receiving reports from his commanders. His body squires busily buckled on his war harness, piece after piece until the king was totally accoutered save for his helm—which sat still upon the worktable in the inner chamber, its plume limp in the damp air. Crocken had expected the metal gear to be the gleaming silver the minstrels sang of, but the steel had all been blued to prolong its life, and so Rhisiart made a dark figure rather than a shining one.

Crocken needed no looking glass to know he made a comic figure himself, closer than anything to a scarecrow. Plate armor was crafted to a man's measure, so even had he had the funds for it, there was nothing in the camp to fit him—or to spare, for that matter. Rhisiart's armorer had grumblingly brought him a leather jack—a coat padded with thick layers of cloth within and studded by nailheads of brass without. It fitted well enough—save that its last owner had plainly been a taller and broader-shouldered man. The jack was less stained than the leather breeches that went with it—and none of those stains seemed to be blood, Crocken was relieved to note. Mayhap its last owner's luck would pass to him, along with the clothes. He draped his beltran carefully to conceal his garb's defects, ruefully recalling what a nuisance the garment had once seemed. He had grown accustomed to it and now welcomed it as a mark of his adoption into Rhisiart's company.

For weapons, Crocken had his own renowned knife, and a sword—which he doubted he could use with any skill—hanging at his hip. He ventured out into the flat white of the morning to practice swinging the blade. Knowing very little of swordplay, he needed to work out a few questions. Should he use both the blade *and* the knife, or keep both hands on the sword with his knife as a last resort? Did he cut, or thrust with the point? Or both?

Rhisiart stepped out through the limp silken panels of the tent flap, then hastily sidestepped again, out of harm's way. His attention distracted by the motion, Crocken lost control of the stroke, and the sword's point buried itself in the turf, almost wrenching the grip out of his hands. Rhisiart raised a brow, as he reached to take up his helm.

"Master Crocken, you may stay by me this day, if you are so determined, but I pray you, stay *well* behind me."

Crocken, flushing, rammed the sword home into its scabbard. He was no warrior—what was he thinking of, to insist upon playing one? At least he needn't pretend he felt no fear, he supposed. That should make the morning easier.

Rhisiart's gauntleted hand came to rest on his shoulder, offering comfort. "I will be glad to have someone at my back that I may trust," he said gravely. "The levies from the Borderlands were summoned, but have not had time to reach us. Now, come."

The sky and the fog blended together seamlessly. It was mere wisps, where Rhisiart's forces camped athwart the hill, but the lowland all about, the Red Plain and the marshlands, were totally obscured. The hill rose like an island out of a sea of milk. Crocken wished it could be as enchanted as it appeared, a haven for them all. But a fog is not a wall—it concealed but could not protect. And what was Ivy thinking of, to give their enemy cover behind which the Sheirans might be doing *anything*?

Horsemen appeared out of the fog—usually far-off and indistinctly seen, but Rhisiart sent a rider down to intercept one of the nearest. After a few moments the knight returned, reported to the king—and Rhisiart came striding back toward his tent, his face carefully composed to hide the anger plain in every other line of his body.

"I have offered single combat," he said evenly. "Myself against their champion. They have refused it. They insult my honor."

"They want to live," Crocken suggested practically. "*I* wouldn't want to face you, in an unjust cause."

Rhisiart gave him a measuring look. "Well said, and perchance there's some truth in it. But I would they had accepted—I like not the idea of armies striving in this fog. Sea-fret, some call it, but I have seldom seen any so thick, and we are far inland. Unnatural conditions are not good omens, and soldiers are a superstitious lot."

Crocken was glad the king had no means to know whence the fog had come. He recalled the ring Ivy had left in his charge and wondered how he might insinuate it onto Rhisiart's person. He had watched earlier for a chance, but seen none—Rhisiart had removed all of his own rings ere he armed for the battle.

The king had left his helm beside his shield, neither needed at present, since there would be no knightly single combat. Casually Crocken strolled over to the gear, glancing covertly about. He cursed himself for not having thought of the helm sooner, when he'd been alone with it inside the tent.

No one was paying him the slightest attention. The whole camp was loud with the sound of grindstones, as final touches were put onto edged weapons by the most finicky of the soldiers, those who had not trusted sharpening done by torchlight the night previous.

On its outside, the helm was smooth as water, so that blows would slide off rather than biting. Inside, the metal was padded with layers of soft quilting, however. Crocken shoved the silver circlet hastily under the fabric that lined the neckpiece, with a desperate wish that it would offer the protection Ivy had intended it to. He wished he could somehow have convinced Rhisiart to wear the ring openly, but there seemed little hope of that, and a refusal would have robbed Ivy's device of any hope.

The sun was rising. The silver disc of it showed like the moon through the fog. Minutes trickled by. Crocken tried not to tally the myriad ways death could find a man in battle. Minstrels' tales and his own active imagination would only do him a disservice. He tried to worry over whether Mistress Ivy was safe, but that was no use either. She was safer by far than he was, Crocken was certain, well able to care for herself.

He wished the battle would begin, if only so it could be over, and he'd need to dread it no more. Then, as if his wishes had a wizard's power, the fog began to burn off. Light flashed from metal plate, from keenly honed weapons. The sun beat down on the army. Crocken had a shadow again, howbeit a silent one.

A breeze swept the last of the mist from the hilltop, and the fog from the lowland rose and joined its ascension. In a matter of moments only, the Sheiran array was revealed.

It was apparently positioned much as Rhisiart had anticipated, for there was no nervous response to the first actual sight of the enemy. The king's army was ready. Companies were moving steadily into their places and would be in position ere battle was joined. Rhisiart conferred briefly with Garin of Idris, who had charge of the vanguard, and sent to Earl Meirion, commanding the reserves and the rearguard, to learn how matters went there. Meirion's answer was tardy coming, which annoyed

Rhisiart, Crocken could see. Indeed, the king had someone at his back that he might not trust, from all Crocken had heard.

The shape of the hill and the location of the marshes to either side dictated the form of the battle line. Indeed, 'twould be no line at all. Normally the forces would have been spread out—left, center, right. Instead they must needs be ranged one behind the other, and only one force would engage the enemy at a time. Crocken was relieved and a touch embarrassed to realize that he'd see no immediate fighting, staying under Rhisiart's command at the center.

The king, mounted now on Stormraker, rode hither and thither among his men, exhorting them, inspiring them—one hoped. Rhisiart was accounted a fine commander, but most of the men there gathered were not those men who'd fought under him so long in the Borderlands but strangers who had heard years of Sulien's lies. His task was not an enviable one.

In all, perhaps five hours had elapsed since they'd arisen and begun arming. Rhisiart came back to the crest of the hill and sat mounted under his boar standard, which hung limp in the warming air. Trumpets sounded distantly. The enemy forces were advancing. Armyn's own trumpets answered, and the vanguard moved a little way down the gentle slope, to close with the oncoming foe.

Crocken saw that maneuver repeated a good dozen times, as the lines of battle pushed this way and that. Ground was gained, ground was lost. The grass was trampled into dust, save where it was slick and red with blood. Crocken wondered if the losses he was seeing were considered heavy. They looked so to him, but he was no fit—or experienced—judge of such matters.

But when the commander of the vanguard went down—that he recognized as a disaster. Even Garin's standard vanished, amid a sea of Sheiran troops, and his men fell back raggedly upon the hilltop, their lines very nearly in retreat. Rhisiart swiftly sent a few score of his troops into the fray and shored up the faltering line, but only just. He did not send more men, and Crocken wondered why he chose not to—then remembered the threat there might be from their own rearguard, which Rhisiart could not be unwary of.

"Enough of this!" the king was raging. "Send to Meirion, bid him advance!"

"My lord, he says he may not," the messenger reported in only moments, white-faced from the heat, from fear, or perchance from indignation. "He says he must hold his position, lest the Sheirans flank the marsh and try to fall upon our rear."

"We can see them clearly, they cannot come at us unawares! Does he not appreciate the vantage this hill offers us?"

"So I told him, my lord Rhisiart. Yet Meirion will not budge."

Rhisiart was riding in tiny circles, his nerves and his temper infecting the white stallion, which rolled its eyes and fought the bit, spraying foam. He stood in his stirrups and peered down the hill.

"What's that? There, herald, can you make out that device?"

" 'Tis Kieron's," Crocken heard someone say. Afoot, he couldn't see what was being looked at.

"So I thought." Rhisiart chewed at his lip. "They will not allow him to fight. But will they fight on *without* him?" He stared hotly down the slope. "Guarded, but not well. A few decent horsemen could find their way around the edge of the battle, between the fray and the marshland . . . let us end this. Gentlemen, who will ride with me?"

And, too late, Crocken realized that Mistress Ivy's fore-dreaming was playing itself out in front of his very eyes. Rhisiart was already ahorse, and there *he* stood fifty feet away, with a dozen horsemen between, helpless to stop Rhisiart or even delay him. Crocken saw how fair Rhisiart's plan must seem, saw the whys of it—saw also the thick stand of trees from whence the trap would spring.

There were armed men in that wood, forces of Lord Esdrief—who'd claimed he could not bring his levies up in good time at his king's summons—waiting to be thrown into the battle on the very chance Rhisiart was now going to hand them. At the odds, there was only one possible outcome.

And Crocken was too far away to do anything to stop it. As his shadow had perhaps planned, leading him when he thought it followed.

Rhisiart dropped his visor into place, ready to begin a charge that could only end with his death. His standard bearer lifted his banner, dragging its pole free of the ground.

Crocken ran desperately toward the king—only to be shoved off his feet by the haunch of a hard-turned horse whose rider had not seen him. He went down before his brain registered the impact. *Damn you,* he thought at the shadow, which let him fall, to join it on the ground.

It was high summer. There'd been no rain for days, and despite the damp fog of the morning, the ground on the hilltop was hard as stones. Crocken lay dazed, his breath dashed from his lungs, so that he could not even shout a warning—far less scramble to his feet.

He could, however, watch his shadow stretching away from him, rapid as a crossbow bolt, flinging itself straight at Rhisiart.

Stormraker saw, also, and reared, screaming with alarm. The shadow flowed up his side, fast as a striking falcon.

No beltran to grasp hold of, and no need for it, with Stormraker still nearly vertical. The shadow simply laid hold of Rhisiart's dark armor, shoved him from his saddle, and took his place.

None of the horsemen paid heed to Rhisiart's fall. The white war-stallion, mounted by its dark rider, charged down the hillside toward Kieron the instant its forehooves touched earth, and the score of men already horsed rode after it, screaming war cries and cheering their leader's spectacular lead-off.

Crocken found his feet, staggered shadowless over to Rhisiart, and helped the king to stand—no easy feat after a fully harnessed knight had been most unexpectedly unhorsed. Rhisiart shoved his visor back so far as he could—it being somewhat bent, a difficult matter—and his eyes were wide and wild.

"That is not the first time that has happened," he whispered, his hand still on Crocken's arm. "I remember now—"

Others noticed their commander was still with them. Rhisiart abruptly pushed hands and questions away, and forced his way to the front of the hilltop, whence he could oversee the progress of the charge.

"What's happening? Who leads them?" Fragments of questions came out of the confused babble at his back.

"*Stormraker* leads them," one answered. "They follow a runaway."

"But he *leads* them," another quibbled. "How can he know the course?"

To Crocken, 'twas obvious, for he saw the shadow hugging Stormraker's broad back, urging the stallion on. What the others saw, he could not guess. Apparently some men saw a rider—and some did not.

"Do we ride after them?"

"Get me another horse," Rhisiart ordered urgently, and someone ran to obey. A knight offered his own mount to the king.

"*No!*" Crocken shouted. "Look!" He gestured wildly at the little wood, which the knights and Stormraker had just then passed. He had seen no movement yet from the troops within, but he dared not wait till Rhisiart was horsed once more and had a second chance to escape to his death.

And upon his word, armed men streamed from the wood. The charge had nearly reached Kieron's position, when it faltered and tried to turn back to meet the rearward threat. Crocken saw a white stallion rearing high, then vanishing.

"Aren't those Esdrief's men?"

"Aren't they supposed to be on *our* side?" The voices were shifting from consternation to outrage.

"A trap," someone whispered in shocked tones.

Crocken watched the swirl of combat about what had been Stormraker's rider. He turned away after a moment, dizzy. The sun stood above him, and he trod upon his own shadow once more—which moved only and exactly as he did.

"We might all have ridden into that—"

A sea-surge of shouts, of commands and reports, swirled around him. Crocken paid no heed—he could not. There was a great heaviness spreading through him, a grief he had never expected. It was all he could do to open his eyes.

Doing so at last, he beheld what no other was marking. The slaughter below was over, at the end of the charge. Those Sheirans who had been with Kieron, no doubt flown with their triumph, were beginning to stream in disorder toward the main battle, now uncommanded in their eyes.

Like ladies to the newest fashion in ribbons, Crocken thought dully.

The hilltop gave him an admirable vantage. He saw how the Sheiran movement exposed their rear to Rhisiart's still-commanded forces—and saw also that the Sheirans were crashing into the edge of the ambushing force. Some of those men struck back at the Sheirans, not much trusting their new-minted allies, fearing treachery. And were they not also trapping themselves against the marshland?

Even without the rearguard, Rhisiart surely had men enough to mount a counterattack. Crocken ran to the king, rudely grabbed his mail-clad arm, and pulled at it urgently until Rhisiart turned. Breathless, he simply pointed down the hill.

At first, Crocken saw only what he'd already seen, and waited for Rhisiart to realize its significance. Then he noticed that the scene had altered, while he struggled for Rhisiart's attention. There were more banners on the field, bearing devices he could not remember seeing ere this—wolves, bears, severed arms, and couped heads. The men under the flags were dark-clad and well disciplined in their fighting.

"The wind out of the Borderlands," Crocken whispered, repeating Ivy's foretelling. Her ensorcelled fog had granted them time enough after all. Unlike the Sheirans, Borderlanders were used to such weather and had not delayed their march for a bit of mist.

Rhisiart saw all Crocken had seen, saw it more clearly, perchance, from the vantage of his military experience. He watched for what seemed to Crocken a long moment, chewing absently at his lower lip whilst his companions babbled unheeded. When Rhisiart turned once more, he was smiling, and his eyes were saner than Crocken had seen them since Kieron was still king-to-be.

"Someone lend me a horse," the King of Armyn ordered.

Chapter Thirty-two

THEY STOOD WHERE the vain, valiant charge had ended—the bodies were thick on the soggy ground, men's and horses' both. A once-bright banner, stitched with a sunburst, lay at Rhisiart's feet, its shaft broken in two. By it lay his own boar banner, pocked with muddy hoofprints.

"Kieron wasn't here," the king said. "Only his standard, to bait the trap. He was never here, 'tis all shadows. *All* of it."

He looked down at dead Stormraker's white bulk, his face impassive. "He didn't run here blindly," Rhisiart went on evenly. "He was directed."

Crocken made no answer.

"Tell me," Rhisiart commanded, no less forcibly for the mildness of the tone he used.

Crocken began to tremble, feeling a chill despite the hot sun. He was unsure how to account for the weakness that swept over him—was it the still-aching wound on his left forearm, or more of the same giddiness he had felt the instant the shadow left him? When cold iron had severed it from him, he amended. He could not think how to begin an explanation, or whether he should. Whether he must.

"The thing that rode him was as insubstantial as a shadow," Rhisiart recalled. "I could see no face, no blazon. Naught but a man-shaped shadow where there was no man to cast it—" He bent to touch, with great tenderness, Stormraker's cold neck. "A shadow that stole my horse and spared my life from treachery."

Crocken's lips moved, but he could force no sound to pass them.

"I dreamed of my brother Miall last night," Rhisiart said. "I suppose because we spoke of him. I dreamed of a day when I

269

was young, and so sick I was like to die—Tierce had most cheerfully told me everyone expected I *would* die. Miall came, and
showed me how to make shadow pictures on the wall. A knack
he learned from the hill folk. For courage, he said. He saved
my life then, I think. And now a shadow has spared it again.''

Crocken remembered that dream, and all the others.

''Tell me—'' Rhisiart pleaded.

Crocken could hear men approaching, coming to lead the king
back to his army, back to his kingdom. Once they were within
hearing, Rhisiart could tax him no more with this matter, he felt
certain. The moment would be past. He'd be safe—if he wished
to be. He could deny it all. He could choose.

''I don't know *how*,'' he said quickly. ''I didn't understand
who he was, till nearly the end. Till you said his name last
night.'' *And I didn't know,* Crocken added silently, *whether he
intended to save you or execute you. I wonder if he did himself.*

''I was in the mountains, passing the spot where he . . . died.''
No need to tell Miall's brother how that death had taken place.
''His shadow—it hired me to help it get back to Armyn. It said
it had left a task unfinished.''

Rhisiart looked down once more at the body of his war-horse,
which had no rider lying by it. He lifted one hand, in the bright
sunlight, and moved his steel-gauntleted fingers slowly, stiffly
into the patterns long ago taught him. Just for an instant, the
Wolf-sign flashed across the bloody ground, then the Raven,
then the Deer.

''For courage,'' Miall's brother whispered, weeping. ''And
for farewell.''

The king's victorious army, Borderers and all, had ridden at
gentle pace back to Axe-Edge, sparing their wounded as best
they might. The journey had thus taken time, and so the air was
cool, and the sun washing through the pleasure garths of Axe-
Edge had more than a hint of autumn to it, though 'twas still
warm enough to be sat out in with a degree of comfort.

This was Crocken's activity, upon a bench hard by a wall of
herringbone-laid brick, which held the sun's warmth awhile,
then returned it gently. He sat moving his fingers to and fro in
the sunlight, watching his shadow ape the movements perfectly,
precisely, each and every time. Without a doubt, the shadow
was gone, but he kept testing for its return—and perversely
missing its company.

He was puzzled that its departure had given him no thrill of restored freedom. Rather than lifting, his sense of oppression deepened. Having his own true shade back was no comfort at all—it simply did whatever he and the sun ordered it to. No less. No more. If he bespoke it, it answered even less often than the other had—in fact, never.

Where had Miall's shadow gone, when it died in Rhisiart's place? What had it found—redemption or delayed damnation? It had, ultimately, done great good, whatever it intended. Did that count for anything? Crocken knew he had no hope of understanding the reckoning, and so he gave it up—but reluctantly.

No wonder it didn't help with Ivy's spell, he mused, recalling the categories of magic with which Kôvelir had left him familiar. *It wasn't a wizard.* Miall seemed to have been a shape-shifter in life, a talent not necessarily companioned by other magics. Crocken remembered the vague dreams he had been visited with in the Borderlands. There was no reason Rhisiart's fables of the hill folk could not be true, and Miall had been half one of them. Believing the fables, Tierce had set Miall a task he could not hope to accomplish until he had become that ultimate shifter of shapes—a shadow.

A shadow now vanished forever, under pitiless sun and magic-defeating cold iron weapons. The day went chill, despite the sun.

Crocken heard slippers rustling through the clipped grass of the lawn and watched without lifting his eyes as Mistress Ivy's shadow joined his own, the two dark figures merging seamlessly into one.

"How does it go?" he asked.

Ivy sighed, as she settled herself beside him. "You are fortunate indeed! Your wound grants you leave to quit the Hall whenever you choose to do so, Master Crocken. There are many who would gladly bear that wound in your place, for the like privilege. I have never sat through such hours of tedious speech in all my days."

"I suspect Rhisiart is sorry he called up the Great Council." Crocken rubbed at the bandage wound about his left forearm, where a sword-thrust he'd been fool enough to attempt countering with his dagger had sliced almost to the bone. He was lucky he'd kept the hand.

"It's a hard business now, but 'twill pass. It's the way he wants it—let every man have his say openly and be done with it. Rhisiart will still be king at the end of it, and have no regrets."

"I keep expecting that people will remember Rhisiart's been

running this kingdom for years anyway,'' Crocken said. ''I didn't expect so much fussing.'' His arm itched, and he tried vainly to soothe it, but the linen wrappings thwarted him.

Ivy pointedly lifted his fingers away, lest he disturb the bandages she had placed there with such care that very morning, redressing the wound with fresh herbs of healing.

''Armyn has lost a golden, glorious prince, with all his fair promise lying ahead of him,'' she explained. ''And gained, most unexpectedly, a small, plain-spoken man in his stead. A man who, nonetheless, fought against the enemies their prince leagued with and held back the disaster Sulien invited over the border. People can be shown that,'' Ivy went on. ''And shown it, they will care for Rhisiart as he has so faithfully cared for them, all these long years of the stewardship. These fickle, contentious folk are capable of loyalty, once they understand him— they just need time to come to it. And he *is* Ruane's brother. Rhisiart may doubt he can hold his people's love, or that he deserves it; that doesn't signify. He'll come round to it, too, in the end.''

''With you at his side?'' Crocken asked, in jest at her ever-quick defense.

Ivy did not return the merriment, but only looked at him rather sadly.

''Mistress Ivy, I am no Rhisiart, but I can still offer you a good life. And there's no Council can tell me I may not wed you.'' It was hardly the impassioned proposal a maiden hoped to hear, Crocken thought, but the words were out, if not as he had hoped to say them. He was after all a practical merchant, not a high-flown knight schooled in flowery courtesies.

Her expression if anything grew stranger, and Ivy responded with unaccustomed hesitation.

''Crocken, I'm flattered, but you're hardly making a wise choice. You don't even know me.''

''Ivy . . .'' There was, a dark corner of his mind insisted, a truth in what she said. He thought he ought to wed. There stood Ivy. Any other standing in her place—would any other not do as well? Crocken was unhappy to have his thoughts turned in such a direction and tried to steer them to a more cheerful path.

Ivy seemed disinclined to allow that. ''It isn't that I don't care for you, Crocken.'' She locked her gaze resolutely with his. ''We have been much together, and been *through* much in one another's company, and you are as dear to me as my own life. You are my friend.'' She bit her lip. ''It is Rhisiart I shall wed.''

"Mistress Ivy, he cannot—" Crocken could only shake his head, at hearing why she put him off. Part of the wrangling he had sat through in the Hall had concerned Mirell and what was to be done about her now that Kieron was vanished and deposed.

"Oh, *he* thinks not!" Ivy answered. "So, Rhisiart will not even speak of his feelings, lest he dishonor where he cannot offer lawful wedlock." Such restraint, so like Rhisiart, plainly gave Ivy difficulties and distress. "But I *will* wed him."

Crocken was so distracted by her illogic, he barely felt the sting of his suit being refused. Or perhaps he could not consider it refused, not for such faulty cause.

"While Rhisiart was steward-protector, you might have had some hope of that," he agreed. Crocken had never asked, but if Ivy had been chosen to companion a princess, her own family would not likely be low-born servants. Mayhap they were too grand for the likes of him—but he could surely claim something of Rhisiart now. Lands, if only those no other wanted. A title, if not a rich one. His station was not what it had been, and his prospects were good. "Ivy, I'm certain Rhisiart will marry again, but the bride will hardly be his to choose. These are matters of high policy. His Council, the lord barons—"

"When the time comes, Rhisiart will find his way smoothed," Ivy answered serenely.

You may be, Crocken told himself cynically, *trying to court a madwoman.* In which case, a prettily put proposal of troth-plighting would likely have been useless. He persisted.

"Isn't it most likely he'll just take Mirell to wife? The marriage is an important link in the trade chains he wants to forge between Armyn and Calandra." A chain his own fortunes were solidly attached to, he recalled.

"There is a perfectly valid marriage contract, pledging the Princess of Calandra to the King of Armyn," Ivy said. "It's still in force." She began to play with her ring, twisting it back and forth, a mannerism she and Rhisiart shared. She had, Crocken noticed, the whole of the ring back. He wondered whether Rhisiart had discovered it in his helm—and, if so, what he had thought. Or had Ivy recovered it secretly?

"On our voyage from Calandra, Rhisiart's ambassador took a sea fever and died," Ivy went on. "None else had ever seen us close or clearly, and I'd seen the portrait that was sent for Kieron to view—'twas so formal, it could have been *any* girl in a fancy gown, either of us, or neither. I was in great dread of what would be waiting for us after we reached Armyn—

true-dream after true-dream I had while on the sea, of the marriage that had been arranged—but I was coming to know that 'twas not Kieron I dreamed of.''

Crocken listened to the tale patiently, as he imagined Mirell must have likewise done, aboard the tiny, tossing ship.

"When we were small girls at Crogen, we had often heard stories of our mothers' girlhood, how they had switched places one with the other, to confuse a deadly enemy," Ivy explained. "It seemed a prudent course for us to choose, landing in Armyn. No one knew which of us was which—they had never seen the princess they'd bargained for. The one man who had seen us was dead. In light of my dreams, we felt it was safest if we . . . kept something in reserve. We concocted Mirell's vow, so she wouldn't need to deal overmuch with Kieron, and . . . we switched places."

The odd thing was, he believed her instantly. Crocken decided it was simpler if *he* was the one gone mad. It was the only way things could continue to make any sort of sense to him. He nodded as the Princess of Calandra went on speaking.

"Airie—that's Mirell—was happy to come here with me. There was no one left at home for her to marry, except my brothers. Two of them are already wed to two of her sisters, and one of *her* brothers had his eye on *my* eldest sister. There's only so much of that a family can bear." She smiled, without humor. "Airie thought she'd do better marrying here—a princess' lady meets many folk. She's been very brave through all this—we never guessed how bad things might be for her."

"It was Rhisiart you dreamed of." Crocken ignored the family history, trying to cut to the heart of her message, while Ivy's words and their implications sliced deep into his hopes.

"Yes. Crocken, he's the reason I followed the dreams here. Rhisiart's fate and mine are interwoven." Ivy laced her fingers together, unconsciously demonstrating.

Crocken took her left hand, separating it from the right, pointedly. This time, he resolved, he would not simply walk away, whichever of them might be mad. "And *ours*?"

"Tangled," Ivy admitted, full of distress. "But—I must ask you to accept—in quite a different way."

"Even though you've loved Rhisiart all the while?" Crocken exploded bitterly. He was such a *fool*, to think any sort of good fate would let him shelter by it. "Well, why not?" he asked. "It's hardly the first time—"

He encountered Ivy's eyes unexpectedly and felt that her

spring-green gaze reached to the bottom of his sore heart, with a tweak sharp enough to make him forget all other pain for one amazed instant.

"Oh," Ivy whispered, understanding what she read there. "*No*, my dear friend—but I see now why you must think so. It befell you once, and thus must ever happen so? You could guarantee that misery, trying to fit the present into the mold of the past. Smash the old prison instead, and let yourself be happy after."

She touched his temple, lightly, with two fingers as if to bless him. The scent of lavender surrounded him.

Eyes wide open to the autumn sunlight, Mistress Ivy dreamed, for the first time a foretelling coming in answer to her summons. Her powers were strengthening with use.

An expression of delight replaced the frown on Ivy's face. Her lips curved into a relieved and tender smile.

"That's even better than I'd hoped," she whispered to herself, and brushed her lips across Crocken's cheek.

Crocken blinked. He stood alone in the pleasure garth, beside the ivy-draped wall. A tendril of new growth was wrapped tightly about his first finger. Gently he unwound the vine and watched it spring back into its place.

Strolling away, he let his thoughts return to the trade mission to Calandra, which Rhisiart had asked him to captain. Why exactly had he hesitated over seizing his lifetime's chance? It seemed incredible to him that he'd ever been reluctant—far more so that he should have no least idea of the reason for his resistance. It might have had something to do with his proposal to Ivy—but had his heart been trying to tell him that he *should* wed her—or that he should not?

Whatever the true case, it was no longer a factor. Crocken bent his steps toward the hall where Armyn's king sat in council, and his shadow trailed after, copying his every movement.

A sheaf of parchments in his hand, their dangling wax seals yet warm, the memory of Rhisiart's pleasure at his acceptance of the trade captaincy yet warmer, Crocken made his way to his chamber. No more lodgings in the outer wall for him. He had a small suite in one of the dwelling halls, high up, with a quarter-dozen windows to let in the sunlight. There was a small carpet on the floor, washed scarlet in the sunset light, his shadow adding to the intricate pattern woven into it.

Crocken halted at the edge of the carpet. His shadow lay across it—cast *toward* the casement.

Crocken froze, not even drawing a breath.

I'm sorry, a voice whispered, fainter than a shadow subdued by heavy fog. *I had nowhere else to go.*

The sheaf of credentials fluttered to the floor, taking a long time about the journey. The seals clattered. Crocken finally managed a breath and spent it all on speech.

"You don't exist," he insisted breathlessly, not having gotten all that much air to work with. "You left me by day, you were out there in the full sun with nothing to cast you—"

The shadow shivered upon the carpet and came a little way up the wall, as if it leaned against it. It slid back suddenly, and Crocken dropped to his knees beside it as if to catch it.

I thought cold iron would kill me, if the light did not. They stabbed me through a dozen times, and I felt every thrust.

Crocken winced at the imagined pain.

The sun was so bright, and as you say, there was nothing to cast me, nowhere to hide. I faded away.

Crocken's throat hurt, remembering.

And then, when I thought my goal was grasped, when I thought no more but was oblivious—then suddenly I was hearing your voice and dragging at your heels again.

"I didn't—" Crocken protested, afraid he'd somehow inadvertently trapped it, foiled its suicide. He couldn't imagine how he might have, unknowing, unthinking.

I do not understand it, either. It should not be. I *should not* be.

Crocken stared at the shadow. It was darker than it had been, as if it recovered whatever sort of health it enjoyed, by virtue of being near him. It remained on the floor.

"So . . . what now?" he asked. He was disinclined to let it know how glad he was to see it, loath to confess his loneliness, which had very little to do with Ivy's rejection of his misplaced suit. He had never heard humility from the shadow before, but he suspected that pity might be a tool for it, good as any other. It would be very difficult at present for the shadow to offer him more promises—or threats. But it might beg.

"I'm leaving Armyn," he added, stooping to gather the spilled parchments together. "Rhisiart is sending me to Calandra with his ships."

Master Merchant-Adventurer?

Crocken didn't answer. A classic rule of bargaining: Never betray the depth of your interest.

I have long suspected that you have come to prefer the adventuring to the merchanting.

Crocken looked at the thing, startled by the truth of the observation.

Neither of us has what he expected, and the future is no easier to outguess than the wind. Would you consider taking a partner?

Crocken stuck out his right hand, for a clasp to seal the bargain. He could not feel the shadow-fingers meet his own, but his two eyes stood witness.

"Done," he said. And he laughed out loud.